BLOOD MONEY

DARK YORKSHIRE - BOOK 4

J M DALGLIESH

First published by Hamilton Press in 2018
This edition published 2020

Copyright © J M Dalgliesh, 2018

ISBN (Trade paperback) 978-1-80080-540-8
ISBN (Large Print) 978-1-80080-512-5
ISBN (Hardback) 978-1-80080-692-4

EXCLUSIVE OFFER

BLOOD MONEY

"We know nothing in reality; for truth lies in an abyss."

Democritus

CHAPTER ONE

THE AMERICANO WAS DRINKABLE NOW. Sitting in the café, having watched the world go by for the past thirty minutes, had given the liquid a chance to cool. Putting the last piece of his meatball panini into his mouth, he wiped his fingers, then his lips, with a paper napkin, before scrunching it into a ball and tossing it onto the empty plate. The mad rush of custom at this time of the day was easing off.

The establishment was still full. There were several families corralling their children in the narrow passages between tables. Presumably they were off school this week. Others, out for a dose of retail therapy, compared their purchases and discussed their next port-of-call. The general noise level meant voices were often raised to be heard above the sound of the coffee grinder and steam wands. He didn't care. His mind was a picture of calm, weeding out the unnecessary and focussing on the task at hand.

The day was overcast, the lack of direct sunlight meant the room was darker than usual. The entrance door opened as three people came in. The first held the door for the others, allowing an unwelcome blast of cold air. Some glanced in the direction of the newcomers, conveying unspoken displeasure at the draught. The street beyond the full-height window he was sitting next to was remarkably busy for a week day.

The sound of a beating drum turned his head. A throng of people were approaching from the east .

They stood out as they navigated York's pedestrianised zone. Whistles blew and those seated around him also looked out. Men and women of all ages and colours marched past. Those at the head of the column were clutching a banner. The ones who followed, brandished placards or blew into whistles with fervour.

His phone on the table vibrated. Glancing down as the text message flashed up, he shot a brief look across the street beyond the demonstrators and towards the figure directly opposite him, standing in the recess of a shop entrance. They made eye contact and he nodded, almost imperceptibly. The movement was acknowledged and the man casually set off. The attention span of those within the café was limited. The notion came to him that these people cared little for the demonstration passing by outside. They had better things to be doing: shopping, eating and chatting. *If only they knew,* he thought to himself, standing. Their lives were so simple, so superficial... so boring.

Leaving the half-cup of coffee on the table, he slipped his phone into his pocket and picked his way through the people seated around him. Wrapping his scarf around his neck, he buttoned up his overcoat in preparation for the temperature drop as he went outside. Brushing against one woman, he uttered an apology but she didn't hear it nor did she flinch, too engrossed in her conversation.

Stepping out into the street, he thrust his hands into his coat pockets. The weather had taken a turn for the worse. The brief spell of clement weather, the incredibly delayed Indian summer, someone he'd overheard call it, was now a distant memory. More rain threatened. This reminded him of home, although it was still warmer. At least *that* was his recollection.

Two police officers strolled past, accompanying the stragglers waving their placards in the air, their breath sending clouds of vapour around them as they walked. No doubt, the higher concentration of resources would be found at the counter protest, that engineered by the nationalists across the city. He admired the provocative nature of launching an anti-immigrant rally in a city with few migrants along with a high concentration of students. It was sure to draw attention which, of course, was the intention.

Setting off in the opposite direction, he felt his phone vibrate again. Taking it out of his pocket he registered the text and increased his pace. The last time he had walked the route it took him twelve minutes but today he had some ground to make up so would be quicker. Central York had an abundance of cut-throughs and passages that could assist in traversing the city, if you knew where they led and how to find them. Another message came through. This one brought a smile to his face. They had stopped briefly, either distracted or their presence had been noted. No matter. Everything was well in hand.

Leaving the hub of the merchant's quarter behind, he had to step from the narrow pavement into oncoming traffic to navigate a gaggle of window shoppers. Eyeing a break, he sprinted across the road, raising a hand in thanks to the nearest driver.

Taking a right onto Fossgate, he headed further out of the centre. The crowds rapidly thinned, as popular shops were replaced with niche establishments once he crossed the river. Fossgate became Walmgate and business premises intermingled with small, modern residential blocks.

Upon reaching his destination, he stopped, eyeing the communal entrances to each block. No one was coming or going, so the opportunity to slip through was unavailable. Knowing the security doors were not fit for purpose for someone of his skill set, he acknowledged they were merely time consuming. Of an evening, it would certainly be workable to enter that way but in broad daylight, a little too brazen even for him.

Further along were the gated entrances, giving access to the gardens at the rear. He found them to be locked. They were of metal construction, six feet high, and cast with spikes at the top.

Decorative but not effective against anything but an opportunist. A quick glance around to ensure he would pass unnoticed, and within seconds he had scaled the railings, hoisted himself over the top and dropped unobserved to the other side. Casually walking to the rear, he cut to his left and found himself in a grassed court-yard area overlooked only by the residential flats of the block. Nothing stirred. The uniform small, square windows of every flat had net curtains or dropped blinds. People here valued their privacy, even if it came at the cost of natural light. Moving with purpose, he walked to the fourth window along on the ground floor.

One last look around and he withdrew a metal strip, concealed within his coat. An inch wide, smooth and incredibly slim, he slipped it between window and frame, jockeying it into position. Once happy, he thrust it upwards and felt the reassuring sensation of the latch moving away. The window cracked open and he eased it out towards him. Putting his tool away, he brushed aside the curtain and clambered in, pulling the window closed behind him. The process had taken only the briefest of moments.

The room was as he had found previously, spartanly furnished and stale, desperately in need of some fresh air. Inspecting the dining table, he scanned a magazine that had been left open upon it, this month's *National Geographic*. Alongside that was a book on the fundamentals of economics.

A clock ticked on the wall in the narrow kitchen. A cat stretched out on the sofa, eyeing him suspiciously. He ignored it and walked towards the hallway.

Off to the left was the bathroom and another door to the one and only bedroom. To the right, three metres away, was the front door, accessed from the communal entrance. Glancing at his watch, he knew there wouldn't be long to wait.

As if on cue, a key was inserted into the lock, apparently in somewhat of a rush as the bearer struggled to get it into place. A vision of a flustered man came to mind as the latch disengaged and the door flew open. Taking a step back from view, he held his breath so as not to make his presence known, becoming one with the wall. He was a picture of measured calm, despite the adrenalin rush. The sound of someone entering and swiftly closing the door behind, dropping the latch and hastily attaching the security chain assured him that their quarry was aware of his presence.

Reaching into his coat, he withdrew the weapon, no more than six inches in length and easy to conceal. Depressing the power button, he allowed it a moment to activate. Stepping back into the hall, the resident was startled to find a man standing before him, gun raised. The red laser, levelled a dot directly to the centre of his midriff. He raised a hand in supplication.

"No, wait—"

The request was never completed. The barbed probes were deployed, punching through his heavy winter clothing and delivering their burst of energy. Both sensory and motor nervous systems were overwhelmed and the target dropped to his knees with a barely audible grunt, wide-eyed and straining every visible muscle. Covering the distance between them with speed, he pressed the Taser against the bare skin of the man's neck. Deploying the second charge incapacitated him yet further. The target slumped sideways to the floor, losing consciousness.

With a large stride, he stepped across the fallen man and over to the door. Activating the button to override the security lock to the communal entrance, he heard the outer door click open via the intercom. Next came the sound of the others moving through. Leaving the door to the flat ajar, he returned his focus to the man lying prostrate at his feet. Grasping him unceremoniously by the collar at the back of the neck, he dragged him down the hallway and into the living room.

The door to the flat was pushed open. A group passed, their footsteps echoing from the polished floor of the communal passageway. He closed the door to the flat behind them. It was time to get to work.

CHAPTER TWO

THE DOOR to the courtroom closed behind him and Caslin breathed a sigh of relief. Confident he'd conveyed his evidence in as an efficient and devastating manner as he could, he allowed himself the slightest of smiles, eyeing those standing a little way off along the corridor. For their part, they shot daggers in his direction. The three of them stood watching him as he made his way towards the washrooms. Caslin's throat was dry. Two hours on the stand had taken its toll but the end result would be worth it. Up next was their star witness. The clerk of the court called the name, as Caslin sidled past the three goons who, he was certain, would love nothing more than to wade in on him. Caslin chanced a wink in their direction. One bristled, only for another to place a calm, restraining hand on his forearm.

"Not here," he said softly.

"As you were, gentlemen," Caslin said, with a grin, turning his attention away from them. His feet suddenly felt that bit lighter. People stood in small groups, others sat alone waiting to be called in to give their evidence.

Courts were strange places, alien to most. The mix of fussy tradition, staid protocols and anxiety-inducing waiting periods all contributed to an air of suspense and trepidation. To Caslin, this week was a culmination of hard graft, months of stress and hopefully, a successful conclusion.

Pushing open the door into the gents, he held it for a young man leaving. He was barely eighteen years of age and ashenfaced, sporting a flattened hair-style and an ill-fitting off-the-peg suit. Either he had delivered his testimony or was about to. Caslin felt for him. Years in the job gave him trust in his instincts to spot a scumbag and that lad wasn't one.

No one else was present and Caslin took in his own appearance in the mirror. Despite the sunken eyes, having not slept particularly well, as was usual when due in court the following morning, he felt he looked in rude health. Having made a real effort in recent months with both his diet and exercise regime, his physical shape was improving. Running the warm tap, he cupped his hands underneath and gently placed his face into his palms, ensuring he didn't dampen his clothes. Daily, he wore a suit he wouldn't be too bothered if a drunk happened to spew on, but in court credibility was everything and appearance counted.

The entrance door flew open and Caslin jumped, instantly alert to the threat. DC Terry Holt burst in, a look of panic in his eyes.

"Sir. You better get back in there," Holt stated unequivocally. Caslin felt water running down his face and brushed it away with the back of his hand as it threatened to drip down onto his pristine, pressed shirt.

"What's up, Terry? What's going on?"

"Your man, Marquis. He's blown it!" Holt said.

"What do you mean, *blown it*?"

"Recanted his entire statement on the stand."

"What?"

"The confession, implicating the others… his entire bloody testimony… he's thrown us under the bus!"

Caslin pushed past Holt, who was too slow to get out of the way but resisted the urge to break into a run as he made his way back to Court Number Two. The men he had casually provoked, watched his approach only this time they bore the smug expressions. Caslin held his demeanour in check. They already knew. They knew in advance this was going to happen. Caslin felt sick as he took the stairs up to the viewing gallery, Holt only a step behind.

Easing the door open, they slipped back into the courtroom. The atmosphere was heavy. The assembled journalists, voyeurs and associated parties watched on intently as the judge intervened, asking direct questions of the witness.

"I wish the record of this court to be very clear. Are you indicating, Mr Marquis, that there has been police collusion in your appearance here today?"

"I am, Your Honour, yes," was the reply. Caslin stared down at the woman standing in the dock. Her expression was one of profound confidence, in stark contrast to the cold, stern look she had aimed at him whilst he was on the stand. Whatever had been said already, she knew she was walking out of court this morning. Caslin felt a knot of anger tighten in his chest. Turning his focus to the witness stand, he took in Anthony Marquis. It had taken Caslin months to turn him from an integral administrator into a mine of information. Only when he was sure the Crown Prosecution Service would have enough to convict, had he acted. Now, the case was unravelling right before his eyes.

"And to clarify, you are accusing officers of encouraging you to fabricate incriminating documentation against the defendant. Along with willfully coercing your testimony here today?" Judge Barker-Riley said.

"One officer in particular, My Lord," Marquis said.

"That officer would be?" the judge asked. Caslin knew what was coming, he muttered under his breath.

"You little shit." The words were heard by those near to him, causing several to glance in his direction but didn't carry to the chamber below.

"Detective Inspector Caslin, My Lord," Marquis said. There was a muted intake of breath from many within the courtroom, sparking conversations between those seated in the gallery. The judge called for calm.

"This is a very serious allegation, Mr Marquis. Do you stand by it?" Marquis glanced towards the dock before looking the judge square in the eye.

"Absolutely. DI Caslin has manipulated me, threatened both myself and members of my family with arrest and incarceration, unless I helped him bring evidence against the accused. I admit, I should have been stronger and not gone along with it but... Mr Caslin is an imposing figure with a lot of power in this city. His reputation speaks for itself."

"My Lord," the prosecution QC stood, his intonation showing how rattled he was, "hearsay regarding a serving police officer's reputation, one whom I am obliged to convey has an impeccable record of service—"

"You are correct," the judge said, cutting him off with a raised hand. "However, despite this not being the first occasion where a defendant uses police coercion as a defence, it is not often that the primary witness alleges the same with equal passion. I find this illuminating and... startling, to say the least."

"I also... see the issues with progressing in this case, My Lord—"

"As do I," the defence barrister cut in. "I must state that to see a successful conclusion to this case in favour of the Crown, based on the testimony we've heard today, will be challenging."

"I am inclined to agree," the judge replied.

Caslin looked to the prosecution QC who was preparing to respond, more in vain hope rather than expectation.

"Perhaps, we might seek an adjournment in order to assess what we have heard..." he stammered. He was attempting to buy them breathing space to try and regroup. Caslin found himself repeating the words *come on, come on,* over and over in his head.

"I might suggest that this trial cannot continue without sufficient evidence against the defendant, My Lord," the defence barrister offered.

Judge Baker-Riley sat back, mulling over his next course of action. The courtroom fell entirely silent. All eyes were on the judge and many, including Caslin, held their breath.

"I am inclined to agree with the defence counsel," he said, following a period of silence that seemed to hang for an eternity. "Unless I can be met with an argument to countermand that conclusion." All eyes fell on the Queens Counsel, representing the Crown Prosecution Service. He looked crestfallen at best, mortified at worst. He could find no words in response. Caslin let out his breath. It was over.

"They can't throw it out, can they?" Holt asked, unable to take his eyes from proceedings.

"He's about to," Caslin muttered in reply, glancing across at Danika Durakovic's associates, seated at the other end of the gallery. Several were looking at him, a few with broad smiles, others with menace. "She's going to walk."

"No way," Holt said, meeting Caslin's eye. As if on cue, the judge's voice carried over them.

"I see no alternative but to dismiss the jury in this case. I will also confer my wish that this case is reviewed with an immediate and far-reaching investigation," he said, with authority. There were audible gasps within the courtroom. "How we managed to reach this point in a High-Court Trial without this situation coming to light, I will never understand. I shall be writing to the Chief Constable of North Yorkshire Constabulary and initiating an investigation into policing standards under her command."

"And it gets worse," Caslin said quietly, to himself.

"What's that, sir?" Holt said.

"A storm's coming, Terry," Caslin replied, as if that answered everything. "Come on. We've seen enough."

Holt turned to head out of the viewing gallery. Caslin glanced down to the dock, only to see the accused looking directly at him. It was unusual for him to see Danika Durakovic without her trademark, large sunglasses. Her complexion was as pale as usual, even in the height of summer, she maintained the same look. Only now, he could read her gaze. The half-smile set upon her face belied the malevolence that her eyes cast towards him. He was back in her sights and he knew it. They remained locked together for a further few moments as neither wanted to be first to break off.

"Sir?" Holt called to him. Regrettably, Caslin broke eye contact and turned towards Holt, holding the door open for him.

"Yes, Terry. What is it?"

"It's the DCI, sir."

"Is she on the phone, already?" he asked, making his way up the steps to the door.

"No, sir. She's waiting in the QC's chambers downstairs."

Caslin shook his head. This day had started positively but was now rapidly descending into his worst in recent memory, and he had many recollections to choose from.

Caslin allowed Holt to lead the way and upon reaching the end of the passageway, he recognised a court assistant standing by the access to the barristers' chambers. As they approached, he opened the door ushering them through. Entering the room, Caslin found it furnished similar to a gentleman's club lounge with leather Chesterfield seating. A polished-hardwood desk was positioned to his right and matching panelling lined the walls. He caught sight of DCI Angela Matheson across the room, standing with her back to him. She was looking out of one of several windows overlooking the court entrance but at what, he didn't know.

"Ma'am," he said in greeting, one that Terry Holt repeated as she turned to face them. From the expression on her face, she was seething.

"Care to explain, Inspector?" she said with no attempt to mask her aggression, not that she ever did.

"They got to him," Caslin said. "They got to him and we didn't see it. It's the only explanation."

"Well, not the only explanation – from what Marquis has just said on the stand," Matheson said.

"Oh, come on. You're not buying into his conspiracy bullshit, surely?"

"No. Of course I don't, Nathaniel," she replied, tempering the outburst that was brewing. "But I told you, when you first brought this to me a year ago that you had to be absolutely bang on if you were going up against her organisation. No one has been able to get near her operation until now and this experience will probably ensure no one else gets to her any time soon."

Caslin looked away. Danika Durakovic had managed to inherit her late husband's contacts, allowing her to sidestep prosecutions as easily as he had managed to. Caslin knew why.

Their organisation was in bed with the intelligence services. A fact he had found out at great personal cost, not that he could voice the knowledge. Bringing Danika down was a challenge, one he'd relished and thought he was about to fulfil.

"I'm not done yet," Caslin said with steel resolve. The door to the chamber flew open and the prosecuting counsel marched in. Without greeting, he hurled his folders onto the desk before him. They scattered, some of the contents falling to the floor but he didn't care, such was his fury. Pulling off his wig, that also joined the paperwork. He turned on Caslin.

"You assured me that he was sound, Inspector," he said accusingly.

"He is... was," Caslin replied, "we can have him on perjury charges."

"I don't doubt that, Inspector, but please, do advise me of when he was lying, then or now?"

"You're out of line!" Caslin said. "They got to him. We can go again."

"A retrial?" the QC said. Caslin nodded. "Our star witness has just testified that he fabricated all the paperwork that we are using to gain a conviction. Not only that, if we get him to recant what he has just said, how on earth is he going to be credible to a jury in any future trial? Explain that to me, would you?"

Caslin drew a deep breath, "We can't just drop it. Danika will never allow such weakness again. Her guard will be up. We'll not get an opportunity such as this—"

"It is over, Inspector. I know you want this one but please accept it, this case is done. You're going to have enough on your plate in the coming months as it is."

"What do you mean by that?" Caslin asked, knowing exactly what he was insinuating.

"People will want answers as to how we spent what we have over the last six months, only to have it burn down, before our very eyes?"

"Setbacks happen—"

"Setbacks!" the QC cut in. "You'll need more than that when you're called in, Nathaniel."

"My conscience is clear," Caslin said.

"As is mine but where the public purse is concerned someone has to shoulder the responsibility and I assure you, it will not be me."

"Charming," Caslin muttered, drawing a stifled laugh from Terry Holt.

"You won't be laughing when you're back in uniform, walking the city centre in the early hours of a Friday night, Terry," Matheson said, putting Holt back in his place. The latter nodded an apology and remained tight-lipped. "Really, Nathaniel, what with the Neo-Nazis being in town just itching for a fight with the counter protestors, we also have journalists from across Yorkshire camped within the city to cover it. They'll be all over this like a rash. You pick your moments, you really do."

"Me? How is all that my responsibility?" Caslin said.

The conversation was interrupted by Matheson's phone ringing. She stepped away from the others to the far side of the room to take the call. The conversation was largely one-sided, therefore Caslin assumed it wasn't a subordinate she was conversing with. Seldom did Matheson allow anyone else to dominate the conversation.

Caslin turned his thoughts to today's events. He could understand the reaction. Six months of diligent case preparation and resources had just been thrown to the wind. Beyond that, the level of personal and professional humiliation before the media and your peers would be galling. Caslin understood that. His humiliation was yet to come.

"Right. Nathaniel, you get a reprieve," Matheson said, hanging up on her caller and walking back over to where they waited.

"Ma'am?" Caslin asked.

"DS Hunter's at the scene of a suicide but I want you to get yourself over there and check it out."

"Why? What's going on?"

"She can fill you in on the details. It'll get you out of the way while I try and contain the fallout from all of this," she said, waving her hands in the air in a circular motion. "I'm already getting enquiries from the chief superintendent which has probably spread from further up the chain. The press will be all over this... and you."

Caslin put the flat of his hand against his chest in a mocking fashion, silently mouthing the word "Me?"

Matheson ignored the gesture, "I want you out of the way. That means no comments to the media or anyone else for that matter. You'd better be the grey man for the next few days until we can figure this out."

"So, you won't let me go and nick Marquis for lying his arse off then?"

"No, I bloody won't," Matheson said forcefully. "Stay away from him and stay away from Durakovic. Is that clear?"

Caslin nodded although he was none-too-pleased with the agreement. He excused himself. The CPS counsel didn't acknowledge his farewell and the cynic inside Caslin assumed he was already being prepped as the one for the slaughter.

Leaving the chamber, he took a deep breath and let it out loudly as he walked. People were milling about him as he went, and taking out his phone, he looked up Hunter's mobile number and went to press call. Paying no attention to what was in front of him, he became aware of a physical presence and stopped abruptly. Glancing up, he found himself face to face with Danika Durakovic. Lowering his phone to his side, Caslin forced a smile as convincing as he could make it.

"Danika," he said.

"Inspector Caslin." Her expression stoic.

"What can I do for you?" he asked, glancing behind her at the half-dozen bodies who appeared to accompany her everywhere.

"I wanted to offer you my commiserations."

"Oh, I doubt that very much."

"Sadly, I fear we won't be seeing much of each other in the coming days."

"Why are you so sure? This is just the first round."

"Come now, Inspector. I fully intend to launch litigation proceedings against you and your colleagues for harassment, perjury, pretty much anything my legal team can come up with and, trust me, I pay them enough to be creative."

"I look forward to it. Perhaps they'll be able to keep you up to speed on visiting days but I doubt it."

"I won't see any jail time, Inspector. Your case has fallen apart and your witness is no longer cooperating—"

"Yes, however did you manage that?" Caslin asked, through a forced grin.

"Good people allow their moral compass to guide them. He followed his."

"I wouldn't bet on him sticking to his story. I can vouch for that."

"He's of no further use to you, Inspector," Danika said as a matter of fact. "He is, how does the saying go… a busted flush?"

"I'll be seeing you, Danika. Never doubt it," Caslin said, fixing her with a stare as he stepped to the side and made to move past her.

"Don't leave it too long, Inspector Caslin," she called after him.

Caslin ignored the group of her associates having lost the stomach for responding to their arrogance. *Their arrogance*. He couldn't help but see his own hubris in this day's events. Cursing himself under his breath, he scanned for Hunter's telephone number once again and left the courthouse.

CHAPTER THREE

ONCE CASLIN HAD RETRIEVED his car from Fulford Road, he took the A64 out of the city for the journey north towards Hildenley.

Set within the conservation area that made up the sprawling beauty of the Howardian Hills, his destination was nestled between Castle Howard to the west and the nearby town of Malton, off to the east. Before reaching the latter, Caslin took the turn onto Braygate Street and slowed, keeping his eyes open for his target. He had spoken to Hunter and knew to keep a look out for recessed gates leading to a private driveway.

He needn't have worried. Parked up before the gated entrance was a liveried police car. Pulling up, he acknowledged the officer standing alongside the vehicle. Lowering his window, he brandished his warrant card for he wasn't familiar with the constable who took several moments to confirm Caslin's identity.

"If you head up the driveway to the house, sir, keep to the left as you approach. The CSI team are setting up and you might get boxed in. You'll find DS Hunter down at the boathouse on the south side of the lake," he said, indicating to his right with a gloved hand.

Caslin thanked the constable and resumed his journey up the gravelled drive. On both sides were a line of trees, planted in a uniform manner. Despite their current, barren appearance it was clear they were immaculately maintained. As were the grounds, set further back from the road. Manicured hedgerows, dedicated beds that were already primed to offer colour from the onset of spring. A glance at the temperature gauge on his dashboard, reading only two degrees, reminded him that spring was still some way off. The recent dive in temperatures following on from an unusually mild December was winter's latest grab for attention.

The driveway curved up on an incline around to the left and the building honed into view, through the trees. A mansion was an apt description, stone-built with an imposing style and grandeur that didn't fail to impress. Caslin knew it to be a building that was centuries old. He guessed it was of late-Tudor or early Jacobean construction. The façade was broad with two imposing bay windows either side of the huge entrance doors. One was easily three metres in height. The stone mullions in that bay alone would have been sufficient for a structural support in most forms of modern buildings. Caslin caught sight of Iain Robertson, the head of North Yorkshire's forensic investigators. He greeted Caslin with a wave as he parked up.

"I was under the impression this was a suicide?" Caslin said, referring to the number of vehicles nearby. Apparently, Robertson had most of his team present.

"Jumping to conclusions without assessing the scene?" Robertson chided him playfully.

"Fair comment," Caslin replied.

"Anyway, I thought you were in court all day today?"

Caslin shook his head, his expression spoke volumes, "Don't go there, I beg of you."

"That bad?"

"Worse," Caslin said, offering little. He caught sight of DS Hunter appearing at the crest of an exterior staircase on the east side of the mansion.

"Hello, sir," she called down to him. Caslin nodded to

Robertson leaving him to assemble his equipment and hand out assignments to his team members. Heading in her direction, Caslin met Hunter at the halfway point between them.

"What do we have?" he asked.

"A deceased male, in his late fifties. We believe it's the owner, sir. He was found hanged, by members of his security this morning around half-past eight. They called the paramedics who then called us upon arrival."

"Suspicious?"

Hunter shrugged, "At first glance, am I ever not?"

"Good point."

"He went out for his usual morning run. When he failed to return, shortly after eight, they went looking for him. He was found in the boatshed. I'll lead you down," Hunter said. They turned and made their way back to the steps, Hunter had come from. A whistle came from behind, grabbing their attention. Caslin stopped and glanced back over his shoulder.

"Don't make a mess of my crime scene!" Robertson barked at him.

"Now who's jumping to conclusions," Caslin said with a half-smile, turning and trotting to catch up with Hunter. He scoped the number of security cameras mounted on the exterior, eyeing the grounds as well as himself. They descended the steps, framed on either side by crafted balustrades of stone, and onto a lawned area stretching some distance in front of them down to the lakeside. Circumventing the house, Caslin eyed more cameras. He was intrigued for it seemed over and above what he would expect.

"How come you're out of court so early?" Hunter asked him as they walked.

"Later, Sarah. Much... later," he replied, killing her inquiry dead. Hunter knew not to push it.

There was a breeze carrying across the lake drawing the cold of the water straight at them. Caslin shivered. Approaching the water's edge, Hunter guided them off to the right along a path leading to the boathouse. Clearly a later addition to the estate of the main house, it was a narrow, two-storey building, also of stone construction. Set back and nestling into the trees in what was a natural cove by the side of the lake, it blended well with the surroundings. There was a pitched slate-roof, covered in moss and a small balcony to the front accessed from the upper floor. A pier ran out into the water on one side, while on the other was a ramp to aid extracting boats from the water. A set of arched double doors opening straight onto the lake were currently closed.

Hunter took them to the rear of the building where they located the pedestrian entrance. They both donned boot covers and latex gloves in order to preserve the integrity of the scene. Until they determined otherwise, they'd consider it to be a crime scene. Stepping into the gloomy interior, Caslin immediately spotted the deceased. He was laid out flat off to the left. In front of them, tied up, was a small speedboat. There would easily be room for at least two more mid-size crafts but presently, that was the only one present. A brief inspection showed it to be covered and Caslin touched the casing of the outboard motor finding it cold.

Joining Hunter alongside the dead man, he briefly assessed the body. He was in his fifties with greying hair that would once have been of the darkest black. He was dressed in a red tracksuit and sported running shoes which, by the assembled detritus in the treads, indicated he had recently been moving through the grounds and most likely, the surrounding woodland. Nearby, Caslin noted a noose, fashioned from a thick rope the likes of which were commonly used by traditional fisherman. He'd seen similar attached to lobster pots in the coastal villages frequented during his childhood holidays. Casting his eyes around, Hunter noticed and appeared to read his thoughts.

"The emergency responders untied him from there," she said, pointing to one of the roof trusses above them spanning the width of the building. Caslin turned his focus to where the rope could have been secured once looped over the beam. He found several rusting, metal cleats attached to the outer wall. Any of them, he deemed, would've been sufficient for the cause. "He used the difference in height between the jetty and the water for the required drop."

"His staff didn't bring him down?" Caslin asked, surprised. Hunter shook her head.

"Apparently not, no."

"Was he alive when the paramedics got here?" Caslin asked.

"No, they were on scene eight minutes after the call."

"That was fast."

"They were attending an RTA not far from here but weren't required. They received the call on their way back to the ambulance station. When they brought him down there was no sign of a pulse but they attempted a resuscitation anyway. He remained unresponsive."

"Right," Caslin said aloud, processing what he was seeing before him. Turning his attention back to the body, he noted the man looked familiar. "I know him, don't I?"

"You'd have to have been living under a rock for the past few years not to, I reckon," Hunter said. "Nestor Kuz—"

"Kuznetsov," Caslin finished for her, "of course. Wasn't he in court for something last week?"

"Yeah, contesting a business arrangement. Suing one of his former partners as I understand it," Hunter confirmed.

"It wasn't going well, I recall," Caslin said, scanning the man's heavily-lined features. He knew of the Russian Oligarch's reputation, both as a ferocious businessman and a vocal critic of the regime back in his homeland. He was a controversial figure, popular in the columns of the print media but not one that Caslin often paid particular attention to. "I see why Matheson isn't taking any chances with this one."

"Sir?"

"Any suicide note?"

"Not that we've found so far. The door was apparently locked from the inside." Caslin stood and looked back towards the door. Scanning for other potential entry and exit points, he eyed several. There were windows set into the opposing walls. Each were single-glazed and opened onto land, running adjacent to the building. There were the double doors, used to take the boats out onto the lake and, turning his eye to the stairs in the far corner, there was also the access to the balcony he'd noted on their approach.

"I wouldn't put a lot of stock in that," Caslin said aloud, returning to the body. "Strange."

"What's that?" Hunter asked.

"In my experience, suicidal people aren't usually focussed on their personal fitness prior to killing themselves. Not beyond the realm of possibility I guess," he mused. "Also, his face is a little too purple under the circumstances. Do you know what I mean?"

Hunter nodded her agreement, "First responders said similar. They expected the face to be paler in a self-induced hanging. Much of the colour has already drained since they brought him down."

"Make sure Robertson is aware, would you?"

"I will."

"Terry Holt should be back at Fulford Road by now. Get him to do a work-up on this guy. We'll go through it later when we get back."

Caslin knelt down again, leaning over to enable a closer inspection of the deceased's neck, attempting to assess the markings left by the ligature. Without wishing to disturb the body further, Caslin viewed as best he could what looked like a V-shape, imprinted in the folds of skin where the rope had wrapped around the throat. Beneath the inch-wide groove were scratch marks, superficial and random. Hunter saw him checking them out.

"I'd imagine he was clawing at the rope as he was dying. An indication of foul play?" she asked.

"Or that he had a change of heart," Caslin countered. Hunter nodded briefly. Flicking his eyes around, Caslin looked for any indication of a struggle. Nothing apparently disturbed. Although he conceded there was very little present in the boathouse that could have been. In one corner, a number of containers were visible, probably with fuel or oil for the boats.

Similarly, to the rear, were built-in shelving that housed spare parts, buoyancy aids and associated equipment. None of which appeared to have been moved in quite some time. Probably not since the previous summer judging by the levels of dust.

Returning to the deceased, Caslin checked the back of his hands looking for damage to his knuckles, abrasions, cuts, or even evidence of soil to indicate he had been knocked to the ground in an altercation or dragged to his place of death. He found nothing. Caslin was hopeful that the pathologist, Dr Alison Taylor, would be able to find something if they'd missed it.

Rising, he crossed to the windows. Noting the simple latch and no further security, he also found one that had a corner of the pane missing. A cursory examination of the floor saw no signs of broken glass. Studying the glass further, he assessed the damage to be historic and therefore unlikely to be linked. The frames of both windows were wooden and in dire need of maintenance. In one case the entire frame was movable, with the minimum of pressure from his bare hand, away from the main fabric of the boathouse such was its degradation. Opening the window closest to him, he carefully extended his arm. The window opened outwards in a vertical arc. Without someone else to hold it clear, a single adult would struggle to climb out without catching themselves on the rotten wood of the frame or the brass latch that secured it closed. It would not be an optimum exit route in order to flee the scene. Spying the beam, at least six inches thick, securing the arched access to the lake proper, Caslin knew that no one left via those doors.

Walking to the front of the building, he looked out across the lake through several gaps in the aging planks that made up the doors. The house and its associated estate were substantial with sprawling wilderness in every direction. There wasn't a boundary in sight. There was every possibility that someone could have accessed this location by boat, using the lake as an escape route and departed the scene under cover of the surrounding woodland. Someone would need to walk the perimeter of the lake to check for any sign of recent activity.

"Who did you say found him?" Caslin asked, glancing back to Hunter.

"A member of his security team."

That aroused Caslin's interest, "How strong is the detail?"

"Five," Hunter confirmed, "at least, those present today."

"And where are they now?"

"Back in the main house. I have them downstairs in the library. There are officers with them. So far, no one's saying much. They are Russian nationals, though. I'm giving them the benefit of the doubt in that, perhaps, their English isn't very good."

"Get a hold of Fulford Road and tell them to have an interpreter on standby just in case. Would it be harsh to imply they're not very proficient at their job?"

"Depends on whether or not you see this as suspicious?" Hunter said playfully.

"Like you, I see everything as suspicious," Caslin replied, coming alongside her, "it comes with the warrant card. Any family members?"

"He was divorced. His wife remained in Russia as far as I've managed to ascertain from the staff. The housekeeper appears to know the most or at least, she's more talkative than anyone else. She's visibly upset."

"His protection detail?"

"Not so as you'd notice but then again..." Hunter allowed the thought to tail off.

"What?" Caslin asked, making eye contact with genuine curiosity.

"I get the impression they aren't too keen on women. Not those in authority in any case. Unless, I'm just too sensitive?" she said with mock indignation.

"I got you. Next of kin?" Caslin asked.

"He only has one daughter. She studies at university, in

London. Someone is on their way to speak with her as of now. Presumably, she'll head up but I'm not sure if she'll do so under her own steam."

Noise from outside carried to them signifying the arrival of Iain Robertson and his team of technicians. Caslin stepped out to greet him as they set about their individual assignments.

"Ruined all my trace evidence?" Robertson said, with a grin, his blue coveralls rustling as he moved.

"There wasn't much for me to damage, if I'm honest," Caslin replied.

"Is that so?" Robertson replied in his characteristic, strong Glaswegian failing to mask his sarcasm. Not that he was trying, mind you. "I'll be the judge of that, if you don't mind? Don't tell me, DI Caslin has actually come across a crime scene where he believes there wasn't a crime committed?"

"Perhaps," Caslin agreed. "Although, it's a little too clean, for me. If you follow me?"

"Aye, I know you well enough. Don't fret. If there's something to find, I'll find it."

Caslin knew it to be the case. Iain Robertson was the most thorough crime-scene analyst he had ever worked with and he'd worked with the best.

"Sarah," Caslin said to Hunter, "I'm going to have a word with the security team. You coming?"

She shook her head, "I reckon you'll do better without me, judging from the reception they gave me earlier. I'll recap what we discussed with Iain and you can fill me in later."

"Fair enough. Library, wasn't it?" he asked. Hunter nodded.

Leaving them to crack on, Caslin headed back to the house. It certainly wasn't unusual for wealthy people to have an entourage. In many cases, they were as much a symbol of status as a Bentley or a holiday home in the Caymans. That in itself meant little but why a businessman required a personal protection detail of that number gave rise to many questions. Least not, who was he afraid of and why would that be?

Ascending another beautifully carved staircase to the rear of the house, Caslin approached a uniformed officer. He pointed out the entrance to the building as well as to the library, just inside and to the right.

Pleased to be indoors, away from the bitter breeze sweeping across the lake, Caslin undid his coat and entered the library. It was an impressive sight. A double-height room with a gallery that wrapped around three walls above him in a U-shape.

Natural light poured in through a bay window, also double height, with a superb view of the lake and the woodland beyond stretching into the distance. The collection on display was equal to those preserved in the many stately homes, Caslin had visited over the years. There must have been thousands of tomes, many of which were leather-bound in traditional style and Caslin couldn't help but scan a few of the titles as he passed by.

Unsurprisingly, many of those he eyed were written in the owner's native Russian and so meant little to him. Although, he was pleasantly surprised to recognise the odd name.

At the centre of the library, Caslin found the men he sought, seated upon casual sofas, set out before a grand fireplace. The warmth radiating from the logs, burning in the grate, was welcome. One of the men stood off to the left, sipping at a mug which Caslin assumed contained tea or coffee, judging from the rising steam. He was immediately envious. The remaining four were spread over the seating, under the watchful eye of another uniformed constable. The latter acknowledged Caslin as he approached.

Caslin scanned the men, without saying a word. Clearly, they were all of a strong physique. Not necessarily heavy-set or full of muscle but evidently athletic in build. Those seated were all dressed in suits, quality materials, nothing off the rack. Caslin could tell the difference. The other wore suit trousers but with only a tight-fitting, white V-necked T-shirt above.

Caslin noted the jackets of the four men seated, appeared to be oversized or badly cut in stark contrast to the quality of the fabric and associated tailoring. He also knew that to be merely the response of the ill-informed. These men were professionals and their suits were tailored to factor in shoulder holsters for their personal weaponry. However, Caslin would put money on it that they wouldn't find a single firearm that wasn't currently licensed or under lock and key, as per their legal obligation.

Those four men paid Caslin little heed. They didn't flinch at his arrival nor did they appear remotely interested in addressing his requirements. The solitary figure, standing beside the fireplace, was a different case altogether. His eyes had not left Caslin from the moment he entered. For his part, Caslin had pretended not to notice, preferring to carry out his own examination. Now he turned his attention towards him. The man radiated gravitas. He was the leader of this group that was certain. Caslin took note of his heavily tattooed upper torso and forearms. A brief look at the others showed that they too, were adorned in a similar fashion. Their clothing however, masked any close inspection.

"You are the senior investigating officer here?" the standing man asked, in heavily-accented but otherwise perfect English.

"I am. Detective Inspector Caslin," he offered, "and you are?"

"Grigory Vitsin," he replied but offered nothing more.

"Which of you found Mr Kuznetsov?" Caslin asked.

"That was me," Vitsin stated.

Caslin nodded, "You have worked for Mr Kuznetsov for a long time?"

"Many years, yes."

"Can you think of any reason for Mr Kuznetsov to have taken his own life?" Caslin asked, scanning the faces of all those assembled as he spoke. No one appeared to be remotely considering the question, let alone listening to him, much to his irritation. Caslin chose to conceal the feeling for now.

"You must forgive them, Inspector Caslin. They speak very little of your language," Vitsin stated, almost apologetically.

"They might find it easier going about their day in this country, if they did."

Vitsin smiled, "Within Mr Kuznetsov's world there was little need. With our native language there are more than enough Russian speakers living here, within the UK."

"Can you tell me why your employer might take his own life?" Caslin asked again.

Vitsin shrugged, "He was a strong man. A proud man. Sometimes, men like this cannot live without both."

"Meaning?"

"I know little of these things but it is clear to see that his life was spiralling beyond his control," Vitsin shrugged. "A man can only fall so far." Caslin thought on that for a moment, pacing slowly around the room before coming to stand alongside Vitsin. He cast his eyes over the man's body art. The patterns across his chest weren't clear to see but Caslin could make out the image of a dagger, passing through the neck. The hilt was depicted on one side and the point appeared out of the other. In passing, he counted at least four drops of blood dripping from the tip of the blade onto what looked like a flaming star.

"Interesting work," Caslin said, inclining his head towards Vitsin's chest.

"You admire body art?" he asked.

"Not my thing, if I'm honest." Caslin casually cast an eye over the Russian's forearms. The right arm had what looked like a woman sitting with a fishing line seemingly caught on her dress. It struck him as an odd motif for such an evidently alpha-male to bear. "But I'm aware the detail is often symbolic of a deeper story. Is that fair?"

Vitsin inclined his own head, in response, "Sometimes."

Caslin returned to the subject of Kuznetsov, "Have you any knowledge of threats to Mr Kuznetsov? Anyone who would wish him harm?"

"Why do you ask? He killed himself."

"Did he?" Caslin asked. The four men seated appeared to understand that comment as a couple of them, almost imperceptibly, glanced furtively at each other.

"Of course, he did," Vitsin said flatly, unfazed by the question. "No one could have got to him without us seeing." Caslin turned to look out of the window towards the lake and the boathouse, although, the boathouse wasn't visible from here.

"He runs alone, your boss?" Caslin asked, locking eyes and trying to read the man standing before him. Caslin assessed this guy must be one hell of a poker player for he could determine nothing from his lack of a reaction. Vitsin merely went back to drinking his coffee. The smell of which carried to Caslin, only making him want it more.

"Every day," he confirmed. "Thirty minutes. The same route, around the estate."

Caslin did a quick bit of mental arithmetic, "That's probably around three miles?"

Vitsin shrugged, "Give or take?"

"That's quite a period of time to be out of your sight and away from your protection," Caslin said, casting a sideways glance towards the bay window.

"It was his choice."

"Did you object?" Caslin asked. Vitsin shrugged. "Humour me. Anyone you know that may have wished him harm?" Caslin repeated.

Vitsin shook his head, "Like I said. He was a tough man. In business. In life. Many people did not like him."

"So, he has enemies?"

"Quite probably, yes."

"And you? What is your role, here?"

The Russian didn't respond, breaking eye contact and moving to a single armchair and seating himself. "Grigory?"

"I have nothing more to say. You should get on with your job."

Caslin smiled, "Thank you for your time. I'm sure I will have further questions for you. I trust you'll make yourself available."

Vitsin nodded.

Caslin eyed the others one last time. Three of them refused to make any eye contact at all but the fourth met his gaze. His eyes were cold, unforgiving. Caslin had the impression all of these men were no strangers to the law either in this country or another. As for Vitsin, Caslin could take his rebuttal one of two ways. As head of security his pride was dented due to dereliction of duty or, the more interesting and darker possibility, he knew far more about Kuznetsov's death than he was prepared to share. Either way, Caslin intended to get more acquainted with him.

CHAPTER FOUR

TAKING the turn off of Fulford Road into the police station, Caslin couldn't fail to see the media scrum waiting on the steps up to the front doors. Picking his way through, he circumvented the outside-broadcast trucks arranged in a haphazard manner along the length of the road and on into the parking area. It was early afternoon and by now the opportunity to find space inside the secure yard to the rear, would no longer be possible. That degree of anonymity wouldn't be afforded to him. Finding one of the last available parking spaces, he reversed the car in and turned off the engine whilst considering his options. Getting through the waiting journalists was unappealing. Entering through the rear gates would be more agreeable and indeed preferable. He opted for that.

Getting out of the car, he locked it and headed for the eight-foot high security gates. He'd only covered half the distance before he caught sight of movement in his peripheral vision. Someone had seen him and he was high profile enough to be recognised. The death of Kuznetsov would already be trending, leading the news headlines and most likely the lead story on the next edition's front pages. His untimely death had lit the touch paper. Caslin increased his pace, pretending to be unaware of those moving towards him. Barely seconds later, the mass of assembled press also saw him, assuming the others knew something they didn't and the chase was on. Within moments, Caslin was where he hadn't wanted to be, besieged by journalists and nowhere near the solitude of the station.

"Inspector, are you investigating?" someone shouted, thrusting a microphone before him. Caslin pressed on as politely as he could. He had to keep moving.

"Was he murdered? Any suspects?"

"There will be a statement issued in due course," Caslin offered, the swarm seeming to increase with every step that he took.

"Does that mean it's suspicious?" another asked. Caslin ignored him as well as any further questions, his frustration beginning to mount. After what seemed like an age, he reached the relative sanctuary of the security entrance. Respectfully, the crowds parted allowing him to swipe his key card and pass through the outer door. Once inside, he found the custody suite to be a sea of calm in stark contrast to the barely organised chaos he'd left behind.

Acknowledging the custody sergeant as he passed by, Caslin made it to the stairs and headed for CID. The fact that he was now at the centre of the two biggest cases to break in recent months in York, failed to escape him. In reality, he was silently hopeful that Kuznetsov did indeed take his own life. Otherwise, the coming storm he'd predicted earlier was likely to be more intense than he'd initially envisaged. Entering the CID squad room, Caslin saw Holt deep in conversation with DC Kim Hardy. As he approached, both constables greeted him.

"Terry, tell me about Nestor Kuznetsov," Caslin said, continuing past and heading directly for his office. Holt fell into step behind him. Caslin took a seat behind his desk and Holt pulled up a chair. DS Hunter joined them having been momentarily behind Caslin on their return to the station. She closed the door and remained standing.

"Iain Robertson will give us a preliminary report on his findings by close of play," she said.

Caslin nodded his approval, "Terry?"

"Nestor Kuznetsov, sir," Holt began. "A Russian national. He's been resident in the UK since 2003. Owner of multiple businesses. He made his fortune in the post-Soviet era investing in former state-owned utilities and mining interests. He set up a television station and a mobile phone network. Both of which proved successful.

In recent years, his firms have fallen foul of multiple corruption scandals relating to the flouting of regulations, tax evasion and several investigations centering on accusations of embezzlement. Many of his assets, valued in excess of $17 billion dollars, have been frozen or seized over the past decade in Russia and other European countries with executives facing trial back home. Add to that the winding-up order brought by HMRC that is currently going through the courts at the same time, he owed a lot of money.

The estate where you've just come from, his apartment in the city centre and several properties in Kensington, were all about to be seized. He was in real trouble, financially speaking."

"That was my understanding too. Hence why he was attempting to claw back funds from one of his former business partners," Caslin said. "The case ended last week. I read about it in the *Financial Times*. Kuznetsov lost."

"That's right, sir," Holt agreed, looking at his notes. "He was trying to obtain £2.5 billion in damages. Money that he believes he was owed from another UK resident, Russian Oligarch. However, the judge said, in his summing up that he was an uninspiring witness and I quote, *a man who treats the truth as a transitory, flexible concept… that he is willing to mould in order to suit whatever story he desires to concoct*."

"Ouch," Hunter said. "That's pretty damning."

"Yeah. The British judicial system must come as something of a shock when you've been used to theirs back home," Caslin said.

"How so, sir?"

"I worked a few cases involving Russian mafia gangs during my time at the Yard. Territorial expansion sparked some tit-for-tat shootings. It was an eye-opening crash course in Russian Organised Crime to say the least. The Russian judicial system has over a ninety-eight percent conviction rate once a case comes to trial."

"Seriously?" Hunter asked.

"Absolutely. The rich and shameless may well get their own way and never reach a court but the problems arise when they come up against someone with a far greater reach. Then, they're screwed. Not that I'm passing comment on Mr Kuznetsov directly. I'm certain most of these Russian billionaires are good value for hard work and ethics," he said with sarcasm. "What brought him to the UK?" Caslin asked, indicating for Holt to continue his summation.

"Necessity," Holt stated. "Although, he officially moved here in the spring of 2003, when he was granted political asylum. He actually arrived in 2000. In the nineties, he was a wealthy businessman and philanthropist. He co-founded a political party, *New Democracy*. With this as a platform, backed by a media boost from his own television station, he was elected to the Russian Duma in '98."

"If he came to us in 2000, it couldn't have been a very successful stint for him," Caslin mused.

Holt shook his head, "Quite right. I'm not up to speed with all the details yet. That period of Russian politics didn't lend itself well to detail and scrutiny. It was a bit like the wild west, no rules, no boundaries. A smash and grab for whatever you could get and then hold. Fortunes were made and then some lost, in the years following the collapse of the Soviet Empire."

"Yes, except the Russian Empire remained largely intact with a lot of ruthless bastards set on exploiting the situation," Caslin added.

"I'd put Kuznetsov as one of those, sir," Holt stated. "He came from relative obscurity to be closely allied with established politicians and rubbing shoulders with the richest men in the country."

"So, he had powerful friends?"

"And powerful enemies," Holt continued. "We have three reports, filed by Kuznetsov, alleging that his life was under threat. The most recent being in October of last year."

"And where did he allege the threats originated?" Hunter asked.

"Each report had its own name attached to it. The latest one implied it was the Russian State apparatus who were targeting him."

"Nice and easy, then. We'll stop by the Kremlin for a chat," Caslin said with mock authority, drawing smiles from his colleagues. "Any credibility given to the allegations?"

Holt shook his head, "It doesn't appear so, sir. As with his recent court action, Kuznetsov appears to be light on detail, or indeed, evidence."

Caslin sat back in his chair, digesting Holt's analysis of the deceased. As always, he resisted the temptation to form an early judgement. Too often, he had been presented with overwhelming evidence at breakfast which was devastatingly rebuked by mid-afternoon. No matter what this looked like, there was still much work to do.

"What do you want us to do, sir?" Hunter asked. Caslin sat forward, resting his elbows onto his desk and forming a tent with his fingers.

"On the face of it we have a slam-dunk suicide. A wealthy, powerful man, set to lose everything ends it all to avoid the humiliation. Nice and neat. That may prove to be the case but let's humour my curiosity for a little while. At least until we get the Scenes of Crime report and Dr Taylor's had a chance to carry out an autopsy. Terry," he pointed a finger at him, "get a hold of everything that you can on these threats to his life. I want to know if there are any legs in them. I know they've already been looked at but the man is dead now and that changes our angle of focus. Who did he point the finger at, where were they and is there any substance to it that you can find? Judging by him being granted political asylum, I presume it's safe to say his list of enemies far outstrips that of his friends. So, get me a list of those as well. They might be able to shed some light on his life."

"Do you think they'll be willing to?" Hunter asked. "As you found with his staff, people in his circle tend not to hold a high tolerance for scrutiny."

"Not being forthcoming could be equally telling."

"What about me, sir?" Hunter said, as Holt scribbled down Caslin's instructions.

"Speaking of his employees. That security detail. I want you to find out everything you can on them. They may well have been his bodyguards but the leader has definitely done time. Those tattoos he's sporting are badges of honour for the Russian mafia. I've seen the type before with Eastern Bloc, ex-cons. Maybe none of them have been imprisoned here but I'll bet they've done real time back home. I want to know what for, their backgrounds, everything?"

"If it turns out not to be a suicide, you think they're involved?"

"I wouldn't rule it out. As much as the Russian mafia have their own codes of conduct, I doubt these guys wouldn't turn on their own mother if the price was right. Start with Grigory Vitsin. He seems like an odd choice for a paranoid billionaire, more used to the finer things in life."

"Sir?"

"If you could afford Spetnaz, why would you hire gangsters? They're a lower level of expertise. Tough, ruthless, certainly but far from predictable or, for that matter, stable. Unless of course—"

"They're more your kind of people?" Hunter finished for him.

"Exactly. Get to work."

Both detectives made to leave but Caslin indicated for Hunter to remain behind for a moment. Holt closed the door on his way out while Hunter took the seat that he'd vacated.

"What's up, sir?" she asked. Caslin met her eye before looking off to his left at nothing in particular.

"I just thought we could have a chat."

"Regarding?" she replied, flatly.

"What with the impending culmination of the case against Durakovic, I haven't had a chance to sit down with you. I figured I'd give it a few days and once things quietened down but, as it stands, I don't see it slowing down around here—"

"There's really no need," Hunter said.

"Sarah, please," Caslin said softly. He returned his gaze to her but she looked down. No matter what she said, he knew her confidence was at a low ebb. "I know you've really been through it, what with the time off and not taking the promotion. I'm trying to—"

"I know what you're trying to do, Nate," she looked up and met his eye. "But what do you want me to say? That I struggle to sleep at night. That Steve is sick to the back teeth of being married to a moody bitch? That I'm pissed off that I had to pass up the move to Thames Valley? Well, all of those," she snapped, "and then some!"

Caslin felt he'd picked his time wrong, not that there was a good one, "This might not be the easiest of cases to break you in on."

"It's hardly my first case, is it? I'll manage."

"Look, if you need some time to settle in, I can take the weight off of you."

"No, you can't," she said defiantly. "I'm your detective sergeant and I'll bloody well manage. The same as everyone else. Okay?" The last was said accusatorily. Caslin merely nodded. Hunter got up and made to leave.

"Sarah," he called after her. Having reached the doorway, she turned back to face him. "You're a damn fine police officer and when you're ready, you'll be a damn good, inspector." She smiled and departed. He felt some of the weight lift from his conscience. Whether she was ready to be back or not, he wasn't sure but

Hunter had passed her evaluations and it was out of his hands. Not that he would ever voice the concern but he suspected something had changed within her. Only time would tell how that change might manifest itself. Besides, Caslin knew he was the last person in the world who could claim that traumatic experiences hindered your ability to do the job, at the required level. Were that definitive, he would've been out of work, years ago.

Even so, Caslin felt a degree of responsibility for her suffering. Her trauma was caused in part by decisions he'd taken in that case. Hunter could have been killed. The resulting trauma had seen her walk a long road back.

Opening up his laptop, Caslin fired it into life. Moments later, he brought up a search page and tapped away at the keys. Within a few minutes his request for information on Russian mafia tattoos proved fruitful. Such was the level of folklore surrounding the practice of decorating themselves, he found a wealth of resource with ease. Scrolling through photographs, the majority taken of prison inmates over the course of the previous fifty years or so, Caslin searched for those he had seen on Vitsin.

It didn't take long for him to come across a variation of the flaming star alongside a substantial array of religious iconography, crosses, angels and demons among them. The significance of the star was such that it denoted authority within the mafia. Vitsin was high up the food chain or had been at one time. The dagger through his neck advertised he'd committed murders in prison with each drop of blood signifying a kill. The tattoo was borne as a mark to indicate the killer was available to take on contracts.

Caslin passed over detailed shots of inmates identifying as homosexual or marking their criminal heritage as well as others sporting inked versions of pre-Soviet medals. The latter, highlighting their proud status as enemies of the state. Eventually, he came across the image depicted on Vitsin's forearm. It wasn't an exact match but undeniably similar. A woman catching her dress on a fishing line. The image related to rape and marked the man who bore it, in this case Vitsin, as a serial rapist. Sitting back in his chair, Caslin figured it wasn't too much of a stretch to imagine Kuznetsov's entire security apparatus was recruited from the ranks of the Russian mafia.

A knock at the door brought him back from the immersive darkness of Russian Organised Criminals. DC Kim Hardy was waiting patiently for him to notice her. He didn't know how long she'd been standing there. He beckoned her in.

"Sorry to interrupt, sir," she said.

"That's okay, Kim. What can I do for you?"

"DCI Matheson wants to see you."

"Tell her I'll see her in her office in about five minutes."

"She wants you upstairs with the chief superintendent."

Caslin exhaled heavily, blowing out his cheeks, "I guess I should've anticipated that."

"There's more. I've just seen ACC Sinclair heading up as well," Hardy said, almost apologetically. Caslin sank back further in his chair, raising his gaze to the ceiling.

"Okay. I definitely didn't see that coming. Thanks, Kim." She smiled weakly and with a bob of the head, turned and left. It didn't matter what explanation he could come up with, regarding that morning's debacle in court, Caslin knew he wasn't going to come out of it without something of a kicking. The presence of the assistant chief constable told him that in all likelihood, he'd be getting a real pasting. Reaching out, he closed down the lid of the computer. Taking a deep breath, he stood up and braced himself before heading upstairs.

CHAPTER FIVE

CASLIN MADE his way up to the next floor. The events surrounding the apparent collapse of the Durakovic trial turning over in his mind. Should he have seen the manipulation of their chief witness coming? Undoubtedly. Since the death of her husband, Danika had proven more than adept at running his affairs. Having seen off a challenge to her authority from the organisation's head of security, she now commanded a fearsome reputation of her own. Caslin cursed himself for failing to get this one over the line.

Approaching the office of Detective Chief Superintendent Mark Sutherland, Caslin paused, acknowledging the welcome of his secretary. She reached for the phone but Caslin indicated for her to hold off on notifying the occupants of his arrival. She appeared slightly perplexed but smiled warmly as he took a deep breath, composing himself. With a brief nod, he returned her smile and she made the call. Moments later, he opened the door and passed through. Sutherland rose from behind his desk and greeted him.

"Nathaniel," he said stiffly, "thank you for joining us."

"Not at all, sir," Caslin replied, taking a measure of those present. Angela Matheson nodded in his direction and even ACC Sinclair cracked the briefest of smiles in his direction.

Another man sat alongside the assistant chief constable but Caslin hadn't come across him before. He was in his late fifties, immaculately attired and, evidently, not interested in conversing. He barely looked up from the paperwork he held before him in his lap. The notion that the latter represented the Crown Prosecution Service came to mind.

"We need to have the conversation about this morning," Sutherland said.

"I have my thoughts, sir," Caslin began. "I would argue that it's a little early to form any conclusions. Once I've been—"

"Forgive me, for interrupting, Nathaniel," DCI Matheson cut in. "I think we're at cross purposes. We've called you in to speak about Nestor Kuznetsov."

"Oh… I see," Caslin said, glancing around. ACC Sinclair was paying him no attention, scanning through some documentation. The man he didn't know, now sat, watching him intently, casually chewing on the arm of his spectacles. Caslin found his curiosity piqued. He splayed his hands wide before him. "To what end, sir?" Sutherland stood from behind his desk and crossed to the window. From here, he could view the front entrance to the building, besieged with journalists who showed little sign of leaving.

"You see that lot, down there?" he asked, rhetorically. "They came to our city because they can smell blood. There's a curious situation arising in our society at present. The desire to suppress the voices of certain groups of people and then scream loudly at their lack of a platform. Thereby, creating a problem where there shouldn't be one."

"I'm sorry, sir," Caslin said, "but I don't follow."

"What your superintendent is saying, Inspector," ACC Sinclair said, looking up from whatever he was reading, "is that our illustrious university, in what I believe to be a well-meaning policy of not allowing a voice for extremists, has sparked something of a backlash. The media have fuelled it and come here in their droves. After all, this isn't Bradford or Oldham. Race relations here have always been somewhat harmonious."

"We're not known for our large immigrant population, sir," Caslin attested. "Largely because we don't have any."

"And so, for this little enterprise, they've been shipping them in," Sinclair added.

Caslin was definitely confused, "Immigrants?"

"No, Inspector. The extremists," Sinclair stated.

"The far-right campaigners," Matheson offered. "Martin James, who I'm sure you'll remember was due to be speaking at an event at the university this week has come anyway despite having his invitation withdrawn.

It would appear, he has brought as many of his membership as he could muster along with him. They've descended on the city, several hundred strong and we're led to understand that more are coming. James has tapped into the mood of the day, rebranding himself as something of a free-speech advocate. People are flocking to him as if he's some kind of saviour to our democratic freedoms.

Intelligence anticipates an increase in the arrival of counter protestors which will coincide over the course of the weekend, with them expected to number in their thousands. They've picked York as their battle ground and we're stretched."

"Nothing that we can't handle, sir," Caslin said confidently.

"I don't doubt that for a second, Nathaniel," Sutherland said. "We've cancelled all uniform rest days for the remainder of the week and South Yorkshire and Humberside have offered us support, should we require it. No, the problem is the number of journalists present. They've stoked what was a decision made by the ruling body of the Students' Union and turned it into a national conversation on free speech. As usual, they're looking to amplify the story."

"Sir?" Caslin inquired, still none the wiser as to why he was standing there. "What's this got to do with Kuznetsov?"

"Nestor Kuznetsov was a champion of free speech," Sutherland said.

"He was?" Caslin was genuinely trying to refrain from laughing. To his mind, Kuznetsov was better described as a victim of the game of thrones that Russian oligarchs appeared to revel in.

"At least, a self-proclaimed one," Sinclair chimed in. "I understand your thinly veiled scepticism, Inspector. He was vocal about the state apparatus attempting to silence him both before, when he was in politics and since he came over to us. His death segues nicely into the media consciousness of the day."

"Are you aware of something that I'm not?" Caslin asked.

Sutherland shook his head, "His suicide is far from welcome, particularly today."

"If indeed, it was a suicide, sir?" Caslin said.

"And that is what you are being tasked to find out, Inspector," Sinclair said.

"Do what you do, Nathaniel. Only do it fast," Sutherland added. Caslin attempted to read the expression of his chief superintendent. New to his current role, Caslin was yet to figure him out. His predecessor had been difficult, often self-serving and led to them having something of a strained relationship but Caslin knew where he stood most of the time. DCS Sutherland, on the other hand, was an entirely different character. One whom, Caslin hadn't warmed to as of yet. Although nothing was ever said, the feeling appeared mutual. The present affability therefore, was unsettling. "We don't want the speculation surrounding this case to gather pace. Once it's rolling, an avalanche is unstoppable. Do you understand?"

"It's very clear, sir," Caslin said.

"Thank you, Inspector. DCI Matheson will require daily briefings which she will then bring to me," Sutherland said before dismissing him. Caslin bid him farewell, doing the same to Sinclair and the other man who hadn't made a sound throughout the entire meeting and made no attempt to rectify that.

Leaving the office, Matheson fell into step alongside him. She didn't speak until they were through the fire doors and into the stairwell, heading down towards CID.

"Don't let the pleasantries fool you, Nate," she said, in a

hushed tone, placing a restraining hand on his forearm. Caslin stopped on the stairs. Matheson glanced down, seeing they were alone. "They want this squared away, as soon as possible."

Caslin smiled but without genuine humour, "This isn't my first rodeo."

"Take it seriously, Nate. They'll be watching and this better not go the way—"

"The way of what?" Caslin said, with more edge to his tone than he'd intended.

Matheson took a deep breath, casting another eye around them to ensure they wouldn't be overheard, "On another day, they'd be tearing strips off of you for what happened this morning in court."

"Meaning?"

"Meaning?" she repeated, "Meaning something else has come over the horizon to eclipse your debacle in court this morning."

"Difference of opinion," Caslin countered.

"And the weight of opinion is determined by your rank," she replied, curtly. "Make no mistake, they'll happily hang it around your neck and let you hang yourself should the need arise."

"There's a thought," Caslin replied. "Makes you wonder why they didn't?"

"Unwittingly or not, you trade on your past successes, Nathaniel. At the end of the day, they won't protect you. Not without someone in your corner," she lowered her voice further, taking on a calmer tone. "It doesn't matter how good you are or what results you get."

"Who's in my corner? You?" Caslin asked.

Matheson locked eyes with him, "Yes. Until such time as I can't be."

Caslin flicked his eyebrows. At least, she was being honest. Any other answer would've been a lie, "What's with the hurry?"

"Like it or not," Matheson said, glancing over her shoulder to double check she wouldn't be overheard, "some cases come with a higher profile than we would like or than they might deserve. Just do your job efficiently and with minimal fuss."

"I won't compromise the investigation."

"I know that. Nor am I asking you to."

"Then what are you asking of me?"

"Just watch where you tread, Nathaniel. Ice can break, sometimes when you least expect it."

Footfalls on the polished stairs came to their ears and Caslin noted the approach of DS Hunter from below. They both fell silent as she made the final turn on the staircase, surprised to find her senior officers standing before her.

"Sorry, Ma'am," Hunter said, appearing awkward. "I didn't mean to interrupt."

"Don't worry, Sergeant. We're done here," she said, making to head back through the doors, towards her own office.

Caslin took a couple of steps back up to the landing, calling after her, "Who was that, in the super's office? You know, silent Stan, sitting on his own?"

Matheson stopped, holding the door open with one hand and looking over her shoulder at him, inclining her head slightly, "Watch your footing, Inspector."

He nodded, "I always do." With that, Matheson walked through, allowing the door to swing closed behind her. Caslin sucked air through his teeth, eyeing the departing figure of his DCI through the glass window of the door. Further down the corridor, he saw her meet up with the senior officers as they left Sutherland's office. Caslin took out his phone. Holding it up to the glass, he used his camera to zoom in and snap a shot of the group whilst they said their farewells in the narrow corridor.

"What was all that about?" Hunter asked.

"Not sure," he replied, not wishing to elaborate further and putting his phone away. Turning to face her, he asked, "What did you want me for?"

"Raisa Kuznetsova is downstairs, sir."

"The daughter?"

"Yes, sir. She's driven up from London."

"Has Iain Robertson removed her father's body, from the scene?"

Hunter nodded, "We just need the identification to take place and then Dr Taylor can begin the autopsy."

"You've spoken to Alison?"

"She called me, sir, to see if I knew when the next of kin would arrive. From what I can gather, she's been asked to fast-track it."

"That's becoming a recurring theme, today."

"Sir?" Hunter asked. He shook his head, indicating for them to head downstairs.

THIS WAS one of his least favourite aspects of the job. Caslin took a step back as Dr Taylor pulled the sheet back to reveal the face of Nestor Kuznetsov to his daughter, Raisa. In one movement, she expertly folded the sheet back beneath the chin, thereby masking the marks left by the ligature, on his throat.

Raisa gasped almost inaudibly. That was the first time where she had offered any reaction to the events of the day, having barely spoken a word since they met back at Fulford Road. Up to this point, Raisa Kuznetsova had maintained an impassive stance. This left Caslin to consider whether she was either in shock or managing her composure with a personal strength far in excess of most bereaved relatives, in his experience.

Raisa nodded almost imperceptibly, unable to take her eyes away from her father. At that moment, her eyes welled up and a solitary tear escaped to run the length of her cheek. Her face cracking, she stepped forward and reached out to touch her father's face only for Caslin to step forward and place a reassuring hand on hers.

"I am sorry, Miss," Caslin said softly, as she turned her anguished expression towards him. "I'm sorry."

She understood, or at least drew back her hand, accepting she wasn't able to make contact. Until certain there had been no foul play, they couldn't allow any potential contamination of the evidence. It was cold but necessary. Guiding her away from the mortuary table, Alison Taylor recovered the body while Caslin led Raisa back out of the room. No matter who had died, even when the deceased was someone Caslin figured society could do without, he always felt for the relatives. Everyone was someone's parent, child or loved one.

Hunter closed the door behind them once they reached the corridor. Caslin offered Raisa one of the chairs off to their left. She declined. Withdrawing a tissue from her handbag, she wiped away the tears gathered in her eyes and attempted to correct the run of mascara she figured had now smudged. Despite her best efforts, she failed. Caslin was impressed. He judged her to be in her early twenties but carried herself as he would expect someone of greater years. Nor did she dress as he expected, being clothed in high-quality garments more befitting of an executive rather than a student. She met his eye and Caslin had the notion that she was assessing him just as much as he was her.

"Who did this to my father?" she asked, in only slightly accented but otherwise perfect English. Caslin was momentarily taken aback.

"We are keeping an open mind," he replied, "but... we have to concede the possibility that he took his own life."

"No," she retorted. "Not my father."

"You seem certain," Hunter said.

"I am," she replied, glancing at Hunter. "If you knew my father, you would also understand that what you suggest is not possible."

"Were you close? With your father, I mean," Caslin asked. She inclined her head in his direction.

"Not particularly," she said. "He was... a difficult man. Driven, opinionated and decidedly arrogant. These characteristics made him a hard man to spend time with but I loved him, all the same."

"And yet, you're certain he wouldn't have taken his own life?" In most cases, he would give relatives space with which to find their feet following the death of a loved one. However, this time, Raisa seemed willing to talk.

"Not him."

"When did you speak with him, last?" Hunter asked, taking out her pocketbook.

She thought on it for a moment before answering, "Perhaps, three days ago."

"Was he concerned about anything?" Caslin asked, "Did he seem himself or depressed, anxious maybe?"

"No!" she snapped. "I told you. This is not a path he would ever have chosen."

"He had a recent court case. Were you aware of that?" Caslin asked.

Raisa nodded, "Yes, against that..." She left the thought unfinished. Locking eyes with Caslin, her expression changed to one of calm menace. He was startled but hid it well. "He was far from a perfect man, or father, and in business... well, he could play games as well as the next but he valued two things ahead of all else. His family and his country."

"Does he have any other family members?"

She shook her head, "Not here but back home in Russia, we have many."

"He must have missed them, judging by what you say," Hunter offered.

"I know what you are suggesting but you are wrong," Raisa countered. "My father has recently professed to a willingness for him to return home."

Caslin was surprised, "Was that even possible under the circumstances?"

"He has been conversing with the Kremlin through intermediaries for some months now. My father knew it would be difficult but spoke positively about it with me. As much as your country welcomed him, it is not Russia. It is not home."

"How advanced were these discussions?" Caslin asked.

"There are many who would rather he never returned or at least, only returned to be imprisoned," Raisa said with venom. "Perhaps, some of those got their wish."

"Can you give us any names, who you might con—" Hunter began but Raisa's attention was drawn away, looking over her shoulder as the doors at the end of the corridor opened. Two men came through. All present recognised them as they approached. Grigory Vitsin smiled as he came to stand before them, acknowledging Caslin. Both officers returned a polite greeting but Raisa merely fixed him with a gaze that Caslin found hard to read.

"Raisa," Vitsin began, speaking to her in their native tongue.

"You should speak English, Grigory," she instructed him. Vitsin's smile faded but his eyes didn't leave her.

"You should have called," he began again. "We would have met you and brought you here. There was no need for you to go through this alone."

"I wasn't alone," she countered, flatly, indicating Caslin.

"All the same," Vitsin said, "you should have called. We will escort you now. Make sure you are safe."

"Like you did my father?" she asked with a measured belligerence. Vitsin seemed unfazed by her tone. The smile returned. Caslin didn't like it.

"We would be happy to take you wherever you wish to go, Miss Kuznetsova," Caslin said, flicking his eyes towards Vitsin. She turned to him.

"There's no need, Inspector, but thank you for the offer," she said politely, glancing in his direction. Caslin took one of his contact cards, from his wallet.

"We have your details but, in the meantime, should you have the need, you can reach me on this number at any time," he said. She took the offered card. "If you ever want to talk." Taking the card and placing it in her pocket, she smiled in appreciation.

"Come, Grigory," she said, pointing towards a large suitcase resting against the wall. "My bag is over there." Before he could respond, she set off along the corridor. Caslin stifled a grin as Vitsin appeared to bristle. The latter turned to the other man he'd arrived with, gesturing towards the case. He scurried over and collected it. For his part, Vitsin was away, attempting to catch up with the departing Raisa without another word. They watched the three Russians leave in silence. Caslin exhaled a deep breath.

"Now that's a dysfunctional relationship if ever I saw one," Hunter said.

"Not a lot of love lost there," Caslin agreed. "I wonder why?"

"Let's find out," Hunter replied.

CHAPTER SIX

CASLIN ENTERED the pathology lab finding Dr Alison Taylor leant over her desk reading through some paperwork by artificial light.

"Things must be important to have you working over the weekend?" he said, playfully.

"Good morning, Nate. You're right. There does seem to be a little tension surrounding this one doesn't there?" she replied, standing and removing her glasses. Indicating to the body, lying on the mortuary slab, she crossed the short distance to it with Caslin coming alongside. "The cause of death was a combination of asphyxia and venous congestion. The deceased's body was more than adequate to apply the fifteen-kilo weight required to act as the constricting force. The ligature compressed the laryngeal and tracheal lumina which in turn pressed the root of the tongue against the posterior wall of the pharynx. Ultimately, this led to a blockage of the airway. The rapid rise in venous pressure within the head was caused by the tension exerted onto the jugular veins. Only two-kilos of weight would be sufficient."

Caslin leaned forward inspecting Kuznetsov's still form, "Well, I'll take your word for it, Alison. The marks around the neck are distinctive?" Caslin asked, indicating a wide, yellowish area a little over an inch wide.

"A few hours after death, the area of tissue affected by the ligature can assume the discolouration along with a texture of aging parchment," Dr Taylor explained. "The depression in the skin is narrower than the ligature itself, encircling the entirety of the neck apart from where the knot was located. You'll note the thin line of congestion, the haemorrhage, above and below the groove at various points on the neck?"

Caslin observed where she was indicating, "That tells us what?"

"Whether there's a suggestion of post-mortem hanging or not."

He cast her a sideways glance, seeking clarification, "Is that a possibility here?"

"I'll get to that," she inclined her head. "First off, let me tell you what I can say with certainty."

"Go ahead," Caslin said.

"The paramedics brought him down when they arrived, removing the noose. Therefore, I've had to make some assumptions regarding how the knot was tied, the rope attached and so on. I have had a conversation with Iain, at the scene, to limit the number of those assumptions. Now, the course of the groove, defined by the noose, tells me the knot was tight to the skin of the neck on the left side of the head. The impression left by the rope is at its deepest and nearly horizontal, on the side of the neck opposite to the knot. As the ligature approaches the knot the mark turns upwards towards it. This produces an inverted 'V'. The apex of which corresponds with the site of the knot. The ecchymosis... the bleeding under the skin, coupled with the abrasions on the surrounding tissue, are suggestive of suspension taking place while he was alive. I've sent a sample of the underlying tissue to the lab for a microscopic analysis, in order to test for any reaction within the tissue," she explained.

"That will confirm it, either way?" Caslin said.

"Patience, Nathaniel."

He smiled, mouthing a silent apology. "I have an issue

surrounding a lack of rope fibres present on the victim's hands. I would expect to find them in the case of a suicidal hanging, although never in a post-mortem hanging. You should press Ian Robertson for an analysis of the rope and its relationship to the beam."

"Relationship?"

"The beam will show evidence of whether the rope was moved up, as in when the body was elevated after death as opposed to the rope moving downwards from above, as the body drops. The latter is obviously what you'd expect to see in the event of a suicide."

"What about defensive wounds or signs of a struggle?"

"There are scratches around the neck, indicative of clawing at the ligature as one might expect to find. There's no indication these were injuries more conducive to having resulted from an assailant perpetrating the act, than from a suicidal person having a change of heart. I did, however, find significant levels of saliva at the angle of the mouth. This pairs well with death by hanging. The glands would have been stimulated by the ligature, leading to increased salivation. I've found no other significant injuries that might extend to defensive wounds."

"How about insignificant ones?" Caslin asked.

Dr Taylor smiled, "I found grazes on his right elbow and the corresponding shoulder blade. They were recent. Soil samples, taken from the outer layer of his running kit, imply he took a tumble at some point earlier in the day. Even with the frozen ground, if the area was shrouded by trees or vegetation it would still have been soft enough to mark."

"Apparently, he was out for his morning run around the estate."

"He may well have slipped. They are not severe injuries but worth investigation in my view."

"We'll walk the route and see if there's a tie in," Caslin said, thinking aloud. "Anything else?"

"Nothing to suggest foul play, no," she replied.

"So, where are you taking this if suicide is the likeliest outcome?" Caslin asked.

"I never said that," Dr Taylor smiled, crossing back over to her desk and returning with a file. Opening it, she moved to her wall-mounted light box. She pressed the power switch and Caslin came alongside as the neon-tubes flickered into life. Arranging three X-ray scans next to one another, Dr Taylor pointed to the first. "I take these routinely, looking for any obvious signs of violence. In a case of hanging, victims over the age of forty are prone to the fracturing of the larynx. Less so, if they're younger."

"So, if you're over forty, you're past it?" Caslin joked. "Terrific."

"Only in matters of being hanged, until dead," Dr Taylor replied, with a grin of her own. Caslin smiled. It had been some time since they had been able to share anything but a professional conversation. Internally, Caslin hoped she had forgiven him for his pathetic attempts at maintaining their now defunct relationship.

"Silver linings."

"The X-rays," she said, indicating them with her index finger. Caslin refocussed his attention. "I found no fractures, either to the larynx or any other part of the body to suggest a violent strangulation and let's face it, who willingly allows themselves to be asphyxiated?"

"Unless of course, they are unconscious," Caslin said.

"True," Dr Taylor agreed. "Although, a deadweight is far harder to suspend in an atypical hanging, where the body is fully elevated. Particularly, if disguising a homicide as a suicide." Caslin cast his eyes over the remaining two images. Both were X-rays of the upper body.

"Now, having led me all this way, you're going to tell me you found something that blows all of this ambiguity out of the water, aren't you?"

Dr Taylor laughed, "Take a look at the next two. This one," she pointed to the third image along, "is a close-up of the second."

Caslin looked and although he could see they didn't appear correct, he couldn't say why. Dr Taylor interpreted his expression and elaborated. "Look at the vertebrae, at the top of the spine but the base of the neck."

To Caslin, the area looked like a mass of white and he couldn't make out any breaks or artificial objects present, "Help me out. What am I looking for?"

"Ankylosing Spondylitis," she confirmed. Caslin looked to her, raising an eyebrow in an unspoken query.

"I think I've heard of that," he said, narrowing his eyes. "It's something to do with inflammation of the joints, isn't it?"

Dr Taylor nodded, "Very good, Nathaniel. Yes. It causes the vertebrae and lumbosacral joint to ossify due to inflammation. As the disease progresses, it can lead to the vertebra fusing together. It's often painful, particularly as it develops and can affect seemingly unrelated areas of the body. The legs, hips, and in forty percent of cases, the anterior chamber of the eye. Mr Kuznetsov had quite an advanced condition, judging by the medication I found in his toxicity-screen along with what Iain Robertson confirmed was back at the house."

"His medication?" Caslin questioned, for clarity.

She nodded a confirmation, "The main symptom for us to consider in this scenario is the restriction of his movement."

"It was significant?" Caslin asked.

"Iain confirmed the knot used was a reef. For him to tighten that knot so close to the skin, at the rear of his neck, would be something of a challenge. Not least because he is right-handed and the knot was tightened—"

"On the left side," Caslin finished for her.

"Exactly. There is the possibility that the knot moved as the slack of the rope was taken up but I see no evidence to confirm that."

"Are you saying he couldn't have done it?"

Dr Taylor held up a hand, "I'm afraid I can't be so definitive, Nate. However, I'm confident enough to say that in my opinion, he would have found it very difficult and to envisage him doing so is problematic at best."

Caslin considered everything Dr Taylor had told him, churning the key points over in is head. Her findings caused concern.

"You throw up something of a dilemma for me, Alison," he said. "You're not doubting the cause of death but whether he was capable of actually carrying it out. Could his medication have given him enough respite from the pain in order for him to manage it?"

"Absence of pain doesn't negate the fusing of the vertebrae though," she said, shaking her head. "I'm not convinced he would be able to raise his hands across and behind him, to sufficiently tighten the knot. It isn't a case of pain. It's more a physical impossibility."

"Which brings us back to why someone would not fight to survive. Basic human instinct dictates you'd react, wouldn't you?"

Dr Taylor nodded emphatically, "One of the first symptoms would have been a loss of power and subjective sensations such as flashes of light and ringing or hissing in the ears. At that point the survival instinct would override everything else and a conscious person would react. If the pressure continues however, intense mental confusion soon follows and all power of logical thought disappears. By then, he would've been unable to help himself even if the notion occurred. There follows a loss of consciousness."

"Any sign of a sedative in the tox-screen?"

She shook her head, "I found nothing that leads me to believe he wasn't conscious during the asphyxiation."

"How long would it have taken?" Caslin asked, walking back over to the body and looking intently at the ligature markings as if hoping to see something they'd missed.

"Had we found a fracture in the cervical vertebrae death would have been instantaneous but even in this case, it still would have been rapid. Perhaps three to five minutes."

Caslin thought on it, "That's a long time for a conscious man to be subdued without a struggle, especially without leaving an indication of having done so. Could we be looking at a professional?"

"If it's a murder, then I would expect nothing less," she said, thinking aloud. "They barely left a sign they were ever there. In this scenario, I would add that circumstantial evidence becomes of paramount importance."

"Sadly, that doesn't bring a case to trial," Caslin said despondently, "and rarely a suspect to the interview room."

"Unfortunately, you're not going to be able to prosecute anyone off the back of my report. With that said, I would doubt very much if a coroner would rule anything but an open verdict, on this one. Of course, we must consider the possibility that he didn't fight because he chose not to."

Caslin glanced at her, "That this was an assisted suicide?"

Alison nodded, "If he couldn't do it himself but wanted to. It's possible. He wouldn't be the first."

"Thanks, Alison," Caslin said. "You've given me a headache that I don't see an easy cure for."

"You're welcome, Nate," she replied. "It's good to see you. It's been a while." Caslin smiled. She was right. He had been keeping his distance to avoid any chance of an awkward meeting. Alison, on the other hand, hadn't exhibited any similar concerns and now he felt foolish. That wasn't a sensation he either cared for or wanted to experience.

"I know," he began, "I guess… you know how it is, right?"

Alison smiled warmly, "Don't worry, Nate. Besides, sometimes things happen for the best. There's no need for you to avoid me."

He nodded in a relaxed manner as if he was surprised she felt the need to bring it up. He wasn't convincing. Having mumbled a brief request about her sending him a copy of her finalised report, Caslin left pathology and headed out to his car.

There was something about Alison's demeanour that struck him as odd. Not out of character as such but not in keeping with how she usually came across with him. Resolving to give it more thought later, should the opportunity arise, he pushed it from his mind. Reaching the steps to the building, Caslin trotted down them and into the car park. The wind had dropped, ensuring the morning was far warmer than it had been in recent weeks.

Turning his thoughts to the demonstration of the previous day, he realised it was merely a warm-up to the main event of the coming weekend. The next march was scheduled for that very afternoon, with the anti-fascists lining up at midday in the shadow of York Minster. The emotionally charged warriors representing either side had to wait until they'd finished the working week before they could make their feelings known.

The plans of the far-right, those expected to cause any potential unrest were not yet known. Since arriving in the city, they had broken up into smaller groups, presumably to confuse the police and make tracking them more difficult. So far, they were being proved right. Taking out his phone, he called Hunter. She picked up within three rings.

"Sarah, where are we with Kuznetsov's security?"

"Not very far, sir," Hunter replied. "I've been onto the Russian Ministry of Internal Affairs but they've not been forthcoming. I was passed around several departments before I got through to anyone even remotely interested."

"And what did they give us?"

"Still waiting on a call back, sir."

Caslin sighed, "I suppose that was to be expected. All right, get onto Europol and see if any of the names are tagged."

"Way ahead of you, sir," she said triumphantly. "We got a hit on three of them. Two are low-level *Brodyag* or—"

"Foot soldiers," Caslin interrupted, "each with a speciality that they bring to the team."

"You've come across these types before then?"

"Yes. Go on."

"Those two have records detailing their arrest in an alleged protection racket in the south of France. Although no charges were brought against them. They were subsequently deported, three years ago."

"And the other?" Caslin asked.

"Your friend, Vitsin."

"Tell me about him."

"He's also popped up on the radar of the Gendarmerie. He was an *Avtotitet*, a captain or brigade commander, aligned with the *Mikhailov Bratva*, based in Rostov-on-Don, Southern Russia. Intelligence had him at a more senior level running a *Sovietnik* or support group. There was some kind of investigation surrounding bribery of state officials and he went to ground."

"I would've thought that was par for the course when it comes to Russia," Caslin said, reaching his car and unlocking it.

"Most likely the bribe was not enough or there was some kind of internal power struggle with Vitsin coming off worse. Either way, he reappears six months later in Montpellier, France. The French came across him and he was visible enough for them to document his comings and goings for a while at least, before he again, disappears from view."

"Until now," Caslin said, putting his key in the ignition and firing the engine into life. "Keep digging, Sarah. I'm on my way back to Fulford Road. I reckon this isn't going to be as cut and dried as some people might have hoped."

"I will, sir, but before you go there are a couple of things."

"Okay, go on," Caslin said, sitting back in his seat and leaving the car ticking over in neutral.

"Firstly, we're a bit thin on the ground today. The DCI has had to allocate a lot of the team to today's protests. Management are worried it's all going to kick off."

"Might do," Caslin said. "What's the second thing?" Hunter didn't speak. Caslin checked his phone to make sure the call was still connected. It was. "Sarah?" he asked again, hearing her breathing at the other end of the line.

"There's no easy way to tell you this, sir."

Caslin eyes were drawn to a young family passing by.

Focussing his attention squarely on the call, he asked, "What is it, Sarah?"

"It's Sean, sir. Your son."

"What about him?"

"He's in detention. Here, at Fulford Road."

"Don't be daft."

"Sorry, sir. He was picked up in a raid last night, carried out by the Drug Squad."

"Last night?"

"Yeah. Apparently, he didn't have any ID on him and lied about his name, age, everything. Understandable I guess, seeing as who his father is. They've only just found out downstairs."

Caslin's head dropped and he rubbed fiercely at his forehead with his one free hand. "Oh, for fu—"

"I'm sorry, sir. Should I let Karen know?" Hunter asked carefully, referring to Caslin's ex-wife. Caslin took a deep breath and took a moment in an attempt to gather his thoughts, exhaling heavily before answering.

"No, don't do that. I'm heading back now. I'll take care of it," he said, hanging up. A momentary pulse of irritation passed over him. Karen hadn't let him know that Sean had failed to come home. Although, the boy was fifteen and as such had some leeway regarding what he did with his time. Maybe he had permission. Even so, he was still only fifteen. Pressing the mobile to his lips, he thought on what he should do, but all that dominated his mind was a growing sense of frustration. With a resigned shake of the head, he tossed his phone onto the passenger seat. Fastening his seatbelt, he engaged the car in gear and set off out of the car park, pulling onto the ring road and heading for Fulford.

CHAPTER SEVEN

TAKING the turn into the car park of the police station, Caslin was relieved to see the assembled journalists had decamped for the day. Most likely they were in the town centre covering the protest marches; to witness the anticipated confrontation. Getting out and locking the car, he made his way to the rear entrance and the custody suite. Even as he entered his pass code into the security pad, he was still unsure of how he would respond to his son's arrest. The initial anger had subsided. Neither of the children had given him much of a headache over the years. Certainly, Sean had felt the brunt of the negativity since the break-up of the family. Shifting schools, looking out for his mother and being a stable influence on his younger sister had taken their toll. Then there was last year. Caslin felt immensely guilty for that, regardless of whether he could've prevented it or not didn't matter.

The door buzzed as he opened it and walked through into the reception area. The custody sergeant glanced up from behind his desk.

"Hello, sir," he said, trying to be casual. Caslin approached. Two constables were nearby and both acknowledged him but quickly made themselves scarce. Perhaps they were on the move anyway but to him it felt like they were getting out of his way. No doubt, the news would be across the station by now.

"Hello, Mike," Caslin said as he greeted Mike Edwards, the custody sergeant, an ascetic-looking man with a narrow, well-lined face. "Where do you have him?"

The sergeant indicated towards the interview rooms, "He's in number five. Once he told us who he was and his age we got him out of the cell."

Caslin raised a hand, in supplication, "Don't worry. I know how it is. What's the story?" he asked, with an air of resignation.

"He was present at an address on the south side of the city, when it was raided last night. It was a planned op, shaking down a number of low-level dealers."

"Yeah. I know they've been getting a bit cocky of late," Caslin said. He glanced around. No one was within earshot. "What did they find him with?"

"A bag of weed. Nothing too serious."

"Thank God for that," Caslin said, relieved.

"Well, that's the good news."

"What's the bad?"

"He was also carrying a little over four-hundred in cash." Caslin was open-mouthed.

"Where the hell did he get that kind of money from?" he said, before formulating his own answer. Edwards met his eye. Clearly, the sergeant was thinking the same thing. Caslin felt fatigued all of a sudden. He shook his head in disbelief. "What was it, five?" he asked, pointing towards the double doors. Edwards nodded and Caslin set off to find his son.

Coming before Interview Room Five, Caslin paused, closing his eyes. He took a deep breath and let it out slowly. The doors adjoining the custody suite opened and an officer came through. She hesitated upon seeing him, slowing her walk ever so slightly. Caslin glanced to his right.

"Sir," she said, rigidly, nodding in his direction as she passed by. Caslin returned the greeting with a bob of the head but he didn't speak. Muttering quietly under his breath, he knocked on the door and entered without waiting for a response.

Sean was sitting on a chair, opposite him and behind a table. His head was down, face resting in the palms of his hands. Upon hearing someone enter, he glanced up. Seeing his father standing before him all colour appeared to drain from his face. Not wanting to meet his eye, Sean returned his gaze to the table before him.

Caslin didn't speak, merely chewing on his lower lip as he turned his attention to the constable standing off to the left. With a flick of the head, Caslin indicated for the officer to leave and he did so. The two of them were alone. Caslin closed the door behind the departing chaperone. The latch clicked and he remained with a steadfast hold on the handle, not wanting to turn to face his son. Another flash of anger bubbled beneath the surface and the urge to tear strips off Sean was tempting.

"Dad, I'm sorry," Sean said, before Caslin had a chance to speak.

"What are you sorry for exactly?" Caslin asked in a far more accusatory manner than he'd intended, turning around and leaning his back against the door. Sean visibly appeared to crumble. His head dropped and within moments, he was shaking as tears came unbidden to his eyes. Caslin felt his anger subside almost immediately. The guilt returning with a vengeance. He gritted his teeth. Somehow, they'd reached this point. He didn't know how but Caslin felt like he was to blame. Less than twelve months ago, he had almost lost his son at the hands of a professional mercenary. A teenager, swept up in something totally beyond his control or understanding. That day, Caslin saw the face of evil, up close and personal and nearly lost something precious to him.

Crossing the room, he perched himself on the edge of the table, placing a reassuring hand on his son's shoulder. Sean lifted his head. His eyes were brimming with tears, red and swollen.

"I'm so... sorry, Dad. I never meant to..." Sean stammered.

Caslin pulled him in close and hugged him with both arms, as tight as he dared, looking to the ceiling as he did so.

"We'll sort it out, son," he said. "We'll sort it, don't worry. Wait here. I'll be back."

Caslin disengaged from his son, stood up and made his way out of the room. In the corridor outside, he found the constable waiting for him. They exchanged places in the room and Caslin headed back to the custody suite. When he arrived, he found two officers booking in a man who had failed to appear at court the previous day and had been picked up as a result.

"I'd have thought you'd have to leave that sort of thing, today?" Caslin said as the man was frog-marched down to the detention cells. Sergeant Edwards grinned.

"The magistrates wait for no man," he said. "But you're right. We'll have to put him up over the weekend and drag him back to court first thing Monday."

"Fair enough," Caslin replied. "So, what am I looking at with Sean?"

Edwards glanced around, lowering his voice. "The arresting officer is probably looking at a caution for possession. The quantity he was holding was minimal. Personal use only. After all, the dealer was the target. But," he paused, selecting his words carefully, "there is a sticking point. This guy deals more in heroin and spice than anything else. He's a proper low-life and Sean was carrying a lot of cash. If our team had gone through the door ten minutes later…"

"I know what it looks like," Caslin said. Edwards relaxed a little. He didn't want to spell it out and with Caslin, he didn't need to. "Where do we go from here?"

"Sean's currently the little fish in a big pond. For now, he's free to go but he'll need to be interviewed with an appropriate adult present in a day or so. Whether that's you or not, I'd advise—"

"Yeah, don't worry. I'm sure his mum will come in," Caslin said, already dreading the conversation he was going to have with Karen. He thanked the sergeant and returned to fetch Sean.

Minutes later, they were back in custody collecting Sean's posses-
sions. Just as they were signing off the paperwork, DCI Matheson
appeared. She caught Caslin's reluctant eye, beckoning him over.
He directed Sean to take a seat on a bench to wait for him and
crossed the short distance to where she stood.

"Ma'am," he said, meeting her stern expression with one of
her own.

"Nathaniel. I suspect I don't need to tell you how bad this
looks?"

"Not really," he replied, casting an eye back to his son.

"There won't be any special favours regarding this," she said
flatly. Caslin was annoyed by that.

"I wouldn't expect any."

"Good. I trust this won't become a distraction?"

"Not at all, Ma'am," Caslin said. "I'll run him home, speak to
his mother and be right back. Provided, that is, that's all right
with you?"

Matheson turned to face him, "This is not a good look for you
and reflects on the team."

"I don't see that," he countered. "He's a kid. They have lapses
in judgement, do stupid things. It happens all the time. It has sod
all to do with the team or my ability to do my job."

"We can agree on one thing. He is a child," she said, fixing her
attention on the waiting teenager, looking very much the lost
little-boy. "And I'm a firm believer that the behaviour of the child
reflects their parenting. I suggest you sort your family out, Inspector. I think you've taken enough hits to your reputation already
this week."

Caslin made no further comment as Matheson made to leave.
He indicated in the direction of the exit and beckoned for Sean to
join him.

"Who was that?" Sean asked, approaching.

"My boss," Caslin replied.

"She didn't look very happy with you."

"Very astute, Sean," Caslin said, pressing the door release to the outer chamber, unlocking it. They stepped out into the caged air lock which in turn, gave them access to the car park.

"Is that my fault?" Sean asked, as they walked. Caslin put an arm around his shoulder.

"No. She always looks like that," Caslin said, faking a warm smile. It didn't fool anyone. They were barely ten yards from the building before a shout came, from behind.

"Sir!"

Caslin turned to see Terry Holt coming across from the direction of the main entrance. He was red-faced and out of breath, by the time he came before them.

"What's up, Terry?" Caslin asked. Holt glanced at Sean, not wishing to speak. Caslin passed his son the car keys and pointed to where he was parked. Sean said nothing but walked over, unlocked the car and got into the passenger seat.

"Uniform were asked to carry out a welfare check on a guy in town. They think it's something we should definitely take a look at." Caslin glanced towards the car. Sean was already busy, tapping away on his mobile phone. "I could check it out with Hunter if… well, you're busy or something?"

"No, it's all right, Terry. Give me the address," he said, turning back to face Holt. "You head over and I'll meet you there in a bit. I'll have to drop him off first," he said, indicating Sean, "but I won't be long."

"Right, sir," Holt said. "I'll text you the address."

Caslin walked over to the car and got in. Sean passed him the key fob and he inserted it into the slot before pressing the start button. Firing the engine into life, Caslin fastened his seatbelt. Sean did the same. The windscreen of the car was misting over even in the short time, Sean had been waiting. Caslin pressed the button to initiate the heated windscreen and set the blowers to maximum. The two sat without conversation, accompanied by the noise of the fans until Caslin judged his visibility was good enough. They left the car park and Caslin turned out onto Fulford Road and accelerated, leaving the city behind them. Karen's house was only a fifteen-minute drive away, into the suburbs. They drove in silence for a while but as their destination neared, Sean became more agitated.

"What did she say?" he asked, staring out of the window at the passing trees.

"Who? Your mum?" Sean nodded. Caslin noticed in the corner of his eye. "I've not spoken to her, yet."

"Right," Sean replied, turning to him. "What *are* you going to say?"

Caslin shook his head, "I've no idea. I'm a bit pis..." he stopped himself, "a bit annoyed with her to be honest. She didn't call to say you hadn't come home. I'd have expected her to."

"She was out," Sean said, "and I can take care of myself."

"Maybe you can but what of your sister?"

"Lizzie spent the night at a friend's," Sean offered, returning his attention to the passing landscape.

"And your mum went out?" Caslin asked. Sean nodded.

"It's a regular thing."

They arrived at the house soon after. Karen's car wasn't in the driveway. Checking the time on the dashboard clock, it was lunchtime. He wondered whether she had come home and gone out again or hadn't come home at all. Quite frankly, it was none of his business.

"What time does your mum usually get home? If she's out, I mean?"

Sean shrugged, "It depends on what time she has to pick Lizzie up, I guess."

"Well, she's with me almost every other weekend. Does she go out a lot?" Caslin replied, drawing another shrug of the shoulders. Caslin thought about it. He should have called her from the station but it was too late now. "All right, look, you need to take a shower and get your head down, for a bit. I'll call your mum later."

"All right," Sean said, pulling on the door handle. Caslin

reached across and stopped him from getting out. Sean met his eye.

"We still have a lot to talk about," he said sternly. "Not least what you were doing there."

Sean sighed, "Dad, I was scoring some weed."

"And where did you get four-hundred quid from?" Sean slumped back in his seat but offered nothing in explanation. "You'll need to say something, Son. It's not going away. You were carrying money to buy enough that'd qualify you as a dealer. If you'd already made the buy..."

"Dad..."

"Don't palm it off." Caslin turned his attention to a far-off point somewhere in the distance. He adopted a more conciliatory tone, "I know how it works. Everyone knows someone and whoever's in stock determines who makes the purchase. You were scoring for your mates as well, weren't you?" Sean remained silent, staring straight ahead. "You've put me in one hell of a position, you know that?"

"Yeah, that's right, Dad. It's all about *you*. It's *always about you*!"

Sean got out of the car at speed, slamming the door shut before Caslin had a chance to respond. He stalked off up the driveway. Caslin watched as he dug out his house keys from his pocket and unlocked the front door, stepping inside. The door closed without him casting even a cursory glance in his direction. Not that Caslin expected him to.

That feeling of guilt returned. Sean spent months in counselling the previous year. Sleeping pills helped to subvert the night terrors but there was always the sense that they were only battling the symptoms and never getting to grips with the cause. Caslin had hoped they were making headway. Sean's need for the medication had dipped and his school reports were improving. He sighed. Maybe this was little more than the usual teenage response to life. Another stage in the transition from adolescence to adult-life that needed to be experienced. With a heavy heart, he pushed it from his mind, resolving to give Karen a call before she would return home, not that he knew when that would be. In the meantime, he looked up the address, Terry Holt had sent through. Slipping the car into reverse, he turned around and set off back into the city.

Leaving Heslington behind, the build-up of traffic was steadily increasing on the approaches to the centre. Caslin skirted the university campus, bringing him into York from the south-east. Even this route started to slow as he reached the Old St. Lawrence Church, just short of the ring road. Here the cars were inching forward at a frustrating pace and it took a further ten minutes before Caslin was able to take the turn onto Walmgate and pass through the ancient, fortress walls of the city.

The police cordon was easy to spot and an officer directed him to park up on the pavement, such was the limited space available. Traffic was still moving out of the city, this being one of the main thoroughfares but passage was cut to one lane due to the police presence and tempers were fraying on a Saturday afternoon.

The communal entrance was taped off and a uniformed constable stood guard with others marshalling the bystanders. One officer lifted the cordon to allow him to duck beneath it. A number of locals were gathering behind the tape, peering through the open door and trying to make out what was going on beyond. Their curiosity was similar to those passing an accident on the motorway, a ghoulish voyeurism. Caslin was met by DC Holt at the open door to a ground-floor flat.

"Hello, sir," Holt said with a pale, grim expression. That piqued Caslin's curiosity because it took a lot to unsettle the experienced detective constable.

"What do we have, Terry?"

"Uniform understated it, sir," he offered. "I've never seen anything like it... it's... bloody awful in there."

CHAPTER EIGHT

HOLT STEPPED ASIDE ALLOWING Caslin to take the lead. When he entered the smell hit him first. The best he could figure it to be was a mixture of cigarette smoke, sweat and faeces. The air was stale and the atmosphere oppressive. The hall was nondescript with four doors leading off it. Glancing over his shoulder, Holt indicated for him to walk to the end. The first door, set to his right, was closed.

"Bedroom," Holt told him. The next two doors were almost opposite each other, staggered on either side. This time, he needed no guidance. The door to the left was open and Caslin could tell that this was the focal point of what was undoubtedly a crime scene.

Caslin held his breath as he stepped into the room, exercising great caution not to disturb any evidence as he went. Little more than four feet away, a man was kneeling on the floor with his back to Caslin. The curtains were drawn restricting natural light to a bare minimum that crept through the narrow crack between them. Further light came via the arched access to the kitchen but even this was subtle and did little to illuminate the room. Artificial light was provided by two lamps, one wall hung to Caslin's right and a further reading lamp, set upon a table in the far corner. The gentle hum of the passing traffic in the background was accompanied by the ticking of a wall-mounted clock.

Walking forward, Caslin was joined by Terry Holt.

"I've requested CSI," he said quietly. "They'll be here within the hour."

Caslin nodded slowly, his eyes scanning the room. "They'll be busy," he said, without looking at Holt. Approaching the kneeling figure to within a couple of steps, mindful not to threaten the integrity of the forensic evidence, he dropped to his haunches to assess the victim. The man was perhaps in his early fifties although in this light it was difficult to tell. He appeared to be of Asian or of middle-eastern origin, stripped naked and kneeling on what Caslin guessed to be a prayer mat, judging by the size and pattern. His hands were clasped into his lap before him and his head was bowed as he was slumped slightly forward. Evidently, someone had worked him over. The man's body, his back in particular, exhibited early signs of bruising and multiple lacerations. The wounds stretched from one shoulder across the full width of the body to the other. Matching injuries were visible to the ribcage at the front and sides.

The face was swollen, consistent with a severe beating. Crouching further, Caslin positioned himself to see the man's face from below. He recoiled.

"What is it?" Holt asked. Caslin flicked his eyes up for a second before returning to inspect the dead man.

"His eyes have been removed," he said softly.

"Why would someone do that?" Holt asked, fear edging into his tone. Caslin didn't answer. The cheeks were swollen and split in places. As were the victim's lips although they were set apart due to something being wedged into the mouth. Caslin couldn't make out what it was. Blood had now ceased flowing. Most of the injuries, Caslin could see were superficial and not life threatening. Painful, certainly but wouldn't have led him to bleed out. However, in contrast, it was clear his throat had been cut. A wound four inches long, as well as substantially deep, stretched across the neck just below the larynx. As a result, the torso, waist and legs were all soaked in blood. The blood on the body was dry. Much of it had flowed down seeping into the prayer mat and carpet, pooling into a deep shade of crimson. This had saturated the floor and still appeared sodden such was the volume. The smell of excrement was intense. Caslin figured the deceased's bowels must have relaxed upon death.

"Take a look around for the eyes, would you?" Caslin said.

"Where?" Holt asked.

Caslin shot him a look of consternation, "I don't know. Just use yours, yeah?" Holt nodded and set off.

Turning his attention away from the body, Caslin surveyed the remainder of the scene. There was blood spatter across three of the walls as well as areas of the ceiling. In several places, they took the form of curves or arcs. No doubt, Robertson would confirm but having attended enough violent homicides in the past, Caslin knew this to be cast-offs. The blood was thrown from a weapon as it decelerated before and after each swing or blow. Looking around, Caslin noted a small dining table and two chairs. One of the chairs had been pulled out and it too, was covered in blood. Gaffer tape was visible on the arms and at the base of the legs. Apparently, it had been sliced through with a sharp blade. Checking the victim's wrist, hair was missing. Standing up, Caslin crossed to the chair and took a closer look at the remnants of the tape. Hair was visible, embedded in the adhesive. The victim had been forcibly removed at speed. Turning, he glanced at the wall directly in front of the kneeling man. Caslin held his breath. Roughly five-feet high and three wide a white cross had been crudely spray-painted onto it with the words *vermin out* scrawled alongside. Caslin let his breath out slowly.

The silence was interrupted by a stifled scream. Caslin jumped momentarily before running into the hall, calling out, "Terry?" He found Holt in the bedroom.

"Sorry, sir," Holt said, looking sheepish. "It startled me."

"What did?" Caslin asked, glancing in the direction of the bed where Holt was pointing. Caslin dropped to one knee and lifted the overhanging duvet so he could see under the bed. A pair of eyes were staring at him, narrow and frightened. "Terry, it's a bloody cat."

Holt nodded, "I know. Sorry. I didn't see it and it hissed at—"

"All right," Caslin said, interrupting him. Spotting a carrier atop the wardrobe, Caslin crossed the room and brought it down.

Indicating for Holt to block one side of the bed to deter the animal from escaping that way. Caslin went to the other. Reluctant to be clawed, he put the carrier close to where the cat waited before attempting to flush it out. He needn't have worried. The safe haven of the carrier was appealing and the animal darted in. Caslin swiftly closed the door and dropped the latch.

Holt shook his head. "I don't like cats, sir. Horrible creatures."

"We can leave it here, for now," Caslin said, standing and heading back into the living room. Holt went with him.

"I've checked the bathroom and the kitchen. I couldn't find the eyes unless they've been well-stashed. Do you think he took them?"

"Who?"

"The killer?" Holt asked.

"Or killers," Caslin mused, scanning the room. "You know what, Terry? This took a lot of time and patience. Despite what we see we're not looking at an act of uncontrolled fury here." Caslin swirled his hand in the air and indicated the scene before them. "There was method applied to this. The eyes were probably cut out for a reason."

"What reason?"

"A message, perhaps? I don't know. That's what we're going to have to figure out," Caslin replied. He walked across the room and casually inspected the spartan contents of a bookcase. There were two books on philosophy, several on economics and another on the history of finance. He couldn't see any items of sentiment. There were no picture frames, family photographs or belongings to signify a personal association. Looking around, Caslin noted there was no television nor a place set aside for one. Nothing appeared to have been disturbed or ransacked, putting a doubt in his mind as to robbery being a motive. "What's his name?"

Holt consulted his notebook, "According to the neighbours this flat is rented to a Farzaad Amin."

"Who called in the request for a welfare check? The same neighbours?"

Holt shook his head, "No, sir. By all accounts, the neighbours only found out when uniform tried to gain entry this morning."

"They didn't hear anything?" Caslin asked, surprised.

"Apparently not, no," Holt said. "But I'll follow up on what uniform heard when I go door-to-door, once CSI get to work."

"Good," Caslin said. "This would have made quite a bit of a commotion. Someone had to have heard something. What do we know about Mr Amin?"

"Not known to us, sir. No priors, nothing."

"All right. Find out what you can from the neighbours and we'll see where we go from there."

"Do you think he was killed during prayer time, sir?"

Caslin glanced across at the deceased and then towards the window as if looking at something in the distance, "I doubt it. I'm pretty sure this is staged."

Holt seemed perplexed. Looking around, he tried to assess what Caslin saw in order to reach that conclusion, "You seem confident. Why do you think so?"

Caslin fixed him with a stare, "He's facing north."

Holt raised a questioning eyebrow, "So?"

"You've not spent a lot of time around Muslims, have you?" Caslin replied. "If he was praying, he'd be facing east."

Hunter's voice carried to them, from the front door. By the accompanying noise level, she was not alone. Caslin judged CSI had arrived at the same time. He called back in response. Moments later, DS Hunter appeared from around the corner. Her first reaction was arguably the same as theirs. One of abject horror.

"Good Lord," she said quietly, furtively looking around. Iain Robertson came to stand behind her. He also took a sharp intake of breath.

"Right. Everybody out of my crime scene, if you don't mind?" he said, in his gruff Glaswegian. Caslin knew not to argue and the team had a lot to process. They would be there for some time.

"Terry, you and Sarah start by canvassing the neighbours," he instructed. Holt nodded but Hunter appeared lost in thought. "Sarah!" Caslin said, forcefully getting her attention.

"Yes, sir. Sorry, what did you say?"

"Go with Terry. Find out what you can about this guy. If he had many friends, how did he live, what he got up to?"

"Will do," she said, seeming glad to be leaving the room. She turned and Terry Holt followed her out. Caslin stepped across to speak with Robertson.

"There's a cat in the bedroom," he said. "I've got it crated. Presumably, you'll be quite happy for me to shift it?"

"Is it a suspect?" Robertson asked, jovially. Caslin cast an eye around the room. Robertson wasn't deterred, "You have to laugh at death as much as life, Nate. Without it, you're as good as lost."

Caslin nodded, "The cat?"

"Aye. As long as it doesn't have any blood on it. Does it?"

"Not as far as I could tell."

"In that case," Robertson said, "be my guest. I don't want it running around contaminating the forensics. What'll you do with it?"

Caslin shrugged, "Get one of the neighbours to take it or something."

Leaving Robertson to get himself set up, Caslin went to the bedroom and retrieved the carrier. Making his way out of the flat, he could hear conversations already happening as his officers canvassed the neighbours.

Emerging into the bright sunshine, Caslin blinked and shielded his eyes with his one free hand. The sun was sitting low in a crystal-clear, blue sky. A larger crowd was gathering now.

Word must have spread. Unlocking his car, he put the carrier on the back seat before relocking it and heading back towards the building.

Parked on the other side of the street, he noted a black limousine. The metallic paint sparkled into the afternoon sunshine. Unsure of the model, Caslin thought it could be a Maybach. It wasn't every day that you saw one of those kicking about. A uniformed chauffeur sat in the driver's seat, bearing a cap and gloves. Shielding his eyes against the sun, Caslin tried to make out the figure sitting in the rear but couldn't. Clearly, they were drawing a higher status of voyeur these days.

A few voices carried from the crowd seeking answers to questions about what was going on. Caslin turned his attention to them and scanned the assembled. The thought occurred as to their motivations. Many were merely curious, others, so bored that this was the most excitement they'd experienced in years. Family or friends could arrive seeking knowledge about their loved ones. Occasionally though, there were the others. Those who took pleasure in seeing the response to their efforts. A killer might return to observe the goings on, revelling in the chaos they had created.

Caslin stood and watched them for a few moments trying to spot anyone who stood out. A lone figure, standing in silence. Someone taking photographs or filming the incident on a mobile phone. Anyone who looked like they didn't belong. Satisfied that no one fitted his criteria, he returned inside.

Farzaad Amin's flat was one of two on the ground floor. Caslin saw Hunter at the top of the stairwell. He trotted up the polished stairs, his shoes echoing as he went. She waited for him. When he reached her, he noted her odd expression.

"Are you okay?" Looking beyond her, over her shoulder, he registered Holt casting a sideways glance in their direction.

"Yes. Of course," Hunter replied, almost defensive in her tone. "Why wouldn't I be?"

Caslin shrugged, "No matter. What have you got?"

Hunter consulted her notes, "There was no answer when we

called at the other flat on the ground floor. The neighbours say it's currently vacant. The inhabitant went into a care home and the housing association haven't reallocated it yet. We've had more luck up here. Neither of the incumbents on this floor knew him very well. They say he's quiet, keeps himself to himself. They've never seen him receive any visitors. Although, he was always amiable whenever they crossed paths."

"What do they know about him?"

"They believe he's from Afghanistan. Whether he has refugee status or is an asylum seeker, neither were sure."

"How long has he lived here?" Caslin asked, watching Holt say goodbye to an elderly gentleman and come across the landing to join them.

"Several years by all accounts."

"When you get back to Fulford Road, give the Home Office a call and try and to ascertain his status. It might be relevant."

"We've got something of a hate-crime, sir," Holt said, coming alongside. He glanced at Hunter, "You all right?"

"Yes, Terry. I'm fine," she snapped.

"The thought had occurred, Terry but why? What do you have?" Caslin asked him.

"The above neighbours," he paused to check his notes. "The Sahni family reckon Amin's been getting some serious grief from the locals. As have they, on occasion."

"Which locals?" Caslin said, glancing out of the window over-looking the street beyond. The crowd appeared to be increasing by the minute.

"Kids, mainly," Holt said.

"Come off it, Terry," Caslin said. "That, downstairs, wasn't done by kids picking on the neighbourhood brown guy."

Holt shook his head, "No, no, but there's been talk about him interfering with them. The kids, I mean. Some are alleging he's a nonce."

"Well if he is, it's the first we are hearing of it," Caslin said. "Try to get some more details, would you? We'll have to consider every possibility but let's face it, this wouldn't be the first time a bit of a loner has that accusation thrown at him. Particularly, if he's a foreigner."

"Yes, sir," Holt said, turning and heading off up to the next floor.

"Any weight in that, do you reckon?" Hunter asked.

Caslin thought about it, "Kiddie-fiddlers are usually on our radar in some capacity or another and he wasn't. I guess that's not conclusive, though. What was done to him looked personal to me. Not kids, not a burglar. Much more than that."

"A relative?" she suggested. "A father of a victim?"

Caslin thought on it, "It'd take a special kind of someone to have the stomach to do what was done downstairs."

"True. That's not to say we don't have them here in York. What do you make of the religious overtones?" Hunter asked.

"Best to keep that quiet for as long as possible," Caslin said, lowering his voice. "That's the last thing we need this weekend. You crack on with Terry. I'm going to head back to Fulford and see if there is anything in the database similar to this. I have the feeling this wasn't the first time our guy did something like this."

CHAPTER NINE

DESCENDING THE STAIRS, Caslin sensed the situation outside was escalating. Raised voices carried into the foyer of the communal entrance, punctuated by the occasional shout. Picking up the pace, he took the last few steps at a canter, emerging into the daylight and a fractious scene. The crowd of onlookers appeared to have swollen within the past few minutes and the number of placards visible above the throng indicated trouble was brewing. A situation of interest to the local residents was now turning into something deeper.

The four officers, tasked with maintaining the security of the cordon were currently standing between two distinct groups, numbering approximately thirty in total. The crowd were spreading out into the road and blocking the remaining lane. No traffic was flowing. Beyond, more people appeared to be heading their way. One man had taken to a dwarf wall, elevating himself above the others in order to address those assembled. He was in his forties, sporting closely-cropped hair and smartly dressed in a suit and tie. Reaching down, someone handed him something and he raised it to his mouth. It was a microphone, attached to a portable megaphone held by another.

"Who wants to be free?" he called into the microphone. Imme-

diately, a raucous cheer went up alongside several denounce-
ments from others. "Mass migration is eroding Europe's Christian
culture to the point that we, the indigenous population, no longer
have a place to call home."

The crowd began to chant, "Yes! Yes!" Sensing the situation
was about to deteriorate further, Caslin took out his mobile and
dialled the station. With officers spread out across the city, he
knew that they needed to be here.

"Open immigration has brought them to us, with no affinity or
allegiance to the country they've ended up in. This is *our fault*
because we don't demand it changes!" the speaker shouted.

"England for the English!" someone shouted, only for others
to begin repeating it along with accompanying applause. The
opposing sides were advancing on each other, jostling for position. More officers arrived having escorted protestors from the
town centre. Caslin was incensed at how the policing plan had
apparently fallen apart in such a spectacular fashion. The sides
were never supposed to meet.

Tempers frayed as accusations were traded. So far, bravado
was all that was on display but it wouldn't take much for that to
change. Caslin's call was answered and he requested immediate
support as he assessed the developing melee. DC Holt came
alongside, appearing flustered.

"What's all this?" he said. Caslin didn't have time to answer.

"Family. Church. Nation," the speaker stated to rapturous
applause. "We need to rebuild our country based on our tradi-
tions, our culture and our beliefs. Our sense of self is ebbing away
because of a cancer gnawing away at the heart of our democracy.
Our system, the police," he said, pointing towards the thin line of
high-vis jackets, struggling to keep the conflicting groups apart,
"defend rapists, criminals and paedophiles."

The volume of opposing chants escalated, "Racists out! Racists
out!"

A missile was thrown towards the speaker, narrowly missing
him as he flinched, ducking to avoid it. Both Caslin and Holt

stepped forward, vainly trying to support their fellow officers in pushing the sides apart. A man screamed for Caslin to step aside, he was flushed with rage and cut a physically imposing figure. Caslin bellowed at him to step back. An arm brushed past his face from behind, striking out at the man, Caslin was trying to control. Instinctively, Caslin turned, reaching out to grip the jacket of the man throwing the punch. Something struck the back of his head, he didn't know what. Almost all perception of the big picture was lost as the small contingent of police threatened to lose what little control they'd had up until now.

Glancing up, Caslin saw one of the placards launched over their heads, coming down into the nationalist ranks. A roar of anger followed and the crowd surged forward. Pushed off balance, he stumbled backwards losing his grip on his charge as well as his footing. A gap opened up between himself and the uniformed constable alongside, as the group pressed onto them. A fearful shout went up nearby but from whom, he didn't know. Feeling a kick to his back, Caslin grimaced. That was followed by something striking the side of his face. Whatever it was, fist or missile, it stung and brought tears to his eye. Trying to re-establish contact with his colleagues and maintain the line, Caslin reached out. The nearest officer attempted to link arms. Another surge came. This time from the rear and the link was broken. Caslin tripped on an unseen kerb and fell forward. He hit the ground harder than anticipated, the force of the swell pushing him down at speed. The instinctive reaction was to panic, fear flashing through his mind but he fought against it.

Caslin tried to stand, only for the movement of those around him to knock him back. Someone took a firm grip of his jacket and he was hauled back onto his feet. Relieved to see Terry Holt pulling him upright, he conveyed his gratitude with a nod. Sirens greeted them, arriving from beyond the city gates. The blue lights of two vans and several patrol cars approaching were a welcome sight. Managing to regain their composure, the two officers returned to the fray. Scuffles were breaking out as the illusion of control was given over to unfolding chaos. The crowd became a blur of angry faces. Some were masked with only their visible fury highlighted in their eyes.

The newly-arrived reinforcements formed up and drove forward into the crowd. The spearhead moved to draw Caslin and the other isolated colleagues back into the relative security of the ranks. Almost as swiftly as the situation had deteriorated, a semblance of order was restored with the scuffles breaking up.

Caslin retreated from the line, spotting the duty commander arriving to take charge and marshalling the increasing uniformed presence. He was relieved to be clear. Looking around, the speaker who'd incited the crowd was nowhere to be seen. The anger and aggression from each side was still vocal but further violence was deterred by the volume of the police presence. Several key antagonists from both sides were targeted and pulled away from their associates. Most were dragged kicking and screaming into custody.

"Are you okay, sir?" Holt asked, pointing to the side of Caslin's face. He reached up and felt something wet. Inspecting his fingers, he found blood but figured it to be superficial. Holt passed him a tissue and Caslin pressed it against the side of his head, near to the temple. His ears were ringing and he felt a little dizzy. "Pity some of us didn't care to get involved," Holt added with an edge to his tone.

Caslin looked back in the direction of the building. DS Hunter stood in the doorway. Seeing both of them watching her, she turned away and dropped out of sight. Caslin removed the tissue. It was saturated with blood, failing to stem the flow.

"Well, we're all a bit out of practice when it comes to crowd control," Caslin replied, brushing away the comment. Looking around, he was confident that everything was back under control. Across the street, the Maybach was still there. That piqued his curiosity and Caslin walked towards it. Reaching for his pocket-book, he was intent on noting the vehicle's registration. The action proved difficult with only one hand. The engine started and before he could get into position to view it, the car moved off. Not at speed but with gradual acceleration. Coming past where he stood, Caslin eyed the passenger seated in the rear who remained impassive, focussed on the road ahead with not even a glance in his direction.

"Anything interesting?" Holt said, coming to stand alongside and reading Caslin's expression.

Caslin shrugged, making a mental note of the licence plate. "It's been an interesting day, Terry."

"Too right," Holt replied. "You ought to get your face looked at."

"I will, later. Why don't you finish up inside," Caslin replied, pointing back towards the flats and putting his pocketbook away. A wave of dizziness washed over him and he felt unsteady on his feet.

"I think I'll run you to the hospital first. Just in case," Holt said. Caslin was about to object but feeling a trickle of blood run down the side of his face, dripping off onto his arm, encouraged him to change his mind.

"All right," he agreed.

IT WAS ALREADY PUSHING 9 pm by the time he pulled the door to his apartment, in Kleiser's Court, closed behind him. Flicking the light switch with his elbow, illuminated the hallway. His face felt tender and he tentatively lowered himself to his haunches and emptied his arms of everything he was carrying. Walking to the bathroom, he pulled the cord and went to inspect himself in the mirror.

Turning sideways to get a better look, he was dismayed. What he'd initially thought to be a minor wound now sported seven stitches and a deepening colour that would soon be a mixture of black, purple and yellow, as the bruising manifested. The cut ran forward, for an inch, across from the base of his temple and narrowly missed the corner of his eye. Being a Saturday afternoon and considered a low priority by the triage nurse, Caslin spent four hours waiting to be seen at the hospital. There followed a trip to the X-ray department, an inordinate wait for the results and the application of the sutures themselves.

At least the wound was sealed and provided he kept it clean, no infection should follow. Opening the cabinet in front of him, he took out a blister-strip of paracetamol.

Leaving the bathroom, he went into the kitchen and rooted through the cupboards. Not finding anything suitable, he opened the fridge, locating a half-used pack of raw beef-mince at the rear. Taking it out, he tipped the contents into a bowl.

Returning to the hall, he knelt down and unhooked the latch to the front of the pet carrier. Opening the door, he coaxed out the cat with the promise of food. It gradually emerged. Having spent a lot of time in the safety of the confines of the crate and indeed, Caslin's car, the traumatised creature was now far calmer. He wasn't really a cat lover nor a fan of any pet if he was honest but it proved a bit late in the day to arrange any alternative. Holt flatly refused to take it, claiming allergies as an excuse, so what other choice did he have so late on a Saturday evening?

Picking up the pack of dressings and alcohol solution, the staff at the hospital had furnished him with, Caslin went into the living room. Tossing the package onto the sideboard, he threw his keys alongside it. Reaching for a glass, he took the stopper from a bottle of Macallan and poured a healthy measure. Crossing to his chair, he sank down. Popping a couple of tablets from the strip, he put them in his mouth and swallowed hard. Washing them down with some whisky, he closed his eyes.

The thudding pain behind his eyes was irritating but nothing he wasn't used to. He heard movement alongside him and opening his eyes was surprised as the cat leapt up onto his lap. His first thought was to brush it aside but as he reached forward, it nuzzled against his hand, purring in an almost hypnotic, repetitive chant. He smiled and instead began stroking it.

"If you insist," he said quietly.

The intercom buzzed. Caslin glanced at the clock. It was late for a personal call but not late enough for the weekend drunks to be messing with him. The cat was reluctant to move and so, Caslin slid it off to one side, depositing it onto the chair as he stood. Finishing his scotch, he placed the empty glass on the coffee table and headed to the front door. The movement caused the banging in his head to intensify once again.

"Hello," he said, activating the intercom.

"Hi Nate, it's me."

Caslin was momentarily thrown, hearing the voice of his ex-wife, "Erm… Karen. Yes, of course. Come on up." He released the exterior door and heard her pass through it before he disconnected the speaker. Chiding himself for not having called her earlier, as he'd planned to, he took a deep breath. Unlocking the front door, he quickly stepped back into the living room. Scanning the interior, he judged the standard acceptable for a visitor, even one as particular as Karen. Returning to the hall, he pulled the door open to see her out on the landing. She stood with her hands before her, nervously rubbing her palms together.

"Hi," she said quietly. Caslin looked at her, smiling. She returned the smile with one of her own, accompanied by an inquisitive flick of the eyebrows. "Can I come in? Or should we talk out here?"

Caslin snapped out of it, shaking his head, "Of course, please." He gestured for her to enter, stepping back to make room. She came past him and he ushered her into the living room. "I'm sorry. I meant to call you but…"

Closing the front door, he followed her in. She turned to face him, taking in his appearance. "My god, your face. Are you okay?" She reached towards his face with her hand. Caslin flinched.

"Oh, this," he replied, touching a hand to his cheek, "It's nothing, really. Looks worse than it is but that's why I didn't call. Who's got Lizzie?"

"She's staying over at a friend's this weekend," Karen replied, her eyes drawn to Caslin's left. She inclined her head slightly, indicating towards the armchair. "Since when have you had a cat?"

Caslin looked. The cat was sitting up, eyeing them expectantly. "That's... a long story."

"What's its name?" she asked.

"I... just call it... Cat," Caslin said.

"You have to give it a proper name. Is it male or female?"

"No idea," Caslin said.

"You haven't looked?"

"I respect its privacy," Caslin said with a smile. "Do you want a drink?"

Karen nodded, taking off her coat and placing it across the arm of the sofa, "I could do with a glass of wine. Red, if you have it?" Caslin walked through to the kitchen, returning with a half-decent Bordeaux he hadn't finished from a previous night. "Sean filled me in on what happened. How much trouble is he in?"

"With us? A hell of a lot," Caslin said, passing her a freshly poured glass. He should let it breathe but he knew his ex well enough to know she wasn't bothered. "With the police? I'll have to speak to the lead investigator tomorrow or Monday. We can take it from there."

"You can fix it?" Karen asked hopefully.

Caslin smiled, "Anything can be fixed." He tried to sound upbeat and positive. If the truth be known, on this occasion, his influence might not be enough.

"I read him the riot act. But, to be honest, my heart wasn't in it."

"I know. He's had a rough year," Caslin agreed, the guilt returning. "It feels pretty harsh to go in too hard on him but, at the same time, maybe laying off him has brought us here. Listen, I haven't eaten. Would you like to stay for dinner? I'm planning one of my specials."

"Indian or Chinese?"

"I figured Indian. They're closer," Caslin said with a smile.

"I'd like that," Karen said. "It's good to see you looking well, Nate. This is the best I've seen you in ages. Apart from your face being all smashed up. Mind you, most people would say it's an improvement." Caslin laughed. "I mean it, though. You look in good shape. You've stuck to your twelve steps… and you've even got a cat," she said, sipping at her wine and sitting down on the sofa. Caslin crossed to the sideboard and took out a leaflet for his preferred takeaway restaurant.

"It is a return to the good old days in many respects," Caslin offered, passing her the menu. She declined.

"Whatever you fancy is fine," she said. "I'm not fussy."

"You can't have been. You married me," Caslin joked. They both laughed.

"You see," she said. "That's more like the old Nathaniel. Whatever happened to him?"

"He married you for a start," Caslin countered. Karen nearly blew wine from her nostrils as she laughed. He turned away from her, crossing to the front window and looking down on the cobbled streets of York's Shambles.

The weekend festivities were getting underway as the onset of spring tentatively threatened to come upon them. Just for the moment at least, Caslin was able to put the horrific nature of his day to one side. Scrolling through his contacts, he dialled the restaurant, a smile on his face.

CHAPTER TEN

THE WHIR of the machine pumping boiling water through the filter head was a comforting sound, first thing in the morning. Sunlight streamed through the kitchen window giving the false impression of warmth outside. Once the cup was full, Caslin picked it up and placed it on the warming plate above. Removing the head, he knocked out the contents and refilled it from the grinder. Setting that back into position ready to make another, he was interrupted by the buzzer of the intercom. Leaving the kitchen, he walked down the narrow hall to the front door and lifted the receiver.

"Morning, sir," DS Hunter said. He buzzed her through the communal entrance into the lobby. Unlocking the front door, he left it ajar and returned to the kitchen. By the time she had ascended the stairs and entered the apartment, he was already filling the second cup of coffee. Hearing the machine, she came through to where he stood offering him a brown paper bag. Taking it from her, he glanced inside.

"Nice. Thanks," he said, admiring the selection of pastries. Taking a plate down from one of the cupboards, he tore open the bag and tipped them out. The cat appeared from nowhere, leaping onto the table and making a beeline for the plate. Hunter laughed and Caslin scooped it up, placing it back down on the floor. "Remind me to get some cat food later, would you?"

"I'd also suggest a litter tray," Karen added, stepping over to the kitchen window where the cat now waited expectantly. She opened it allowing the creature access to the fire escape.

"Good call," Caslin replied.

"I figured you'd want—" Hunter started before stopping as Karen appeared in the living room. Hunter was open-mouthed. "I'm sorry," she said, casting a sideways look towards Caslin. "I didn't realise you had company."

"That's okay," Karen replied. "How are you, Sarah?"

"Very well… Karen. Thanks," Hunter replied, looking and feeling a little awkward. "You?"

"Me, too," she replied, glancing down.

Caslin picked up one of the coffees and crossed the kitchen. Confident he was the only one not experiencing a level of discomfort, he made to pass the cup to Karen but noticed she had her coat across her forearm.

"I'd better be off, Nate. I know it's early but I've things I need to do."

"You don't have to," he said warmly.

"It's okay," she said. "Besides, you've clearly got work to do anyway."

He put the cup down on the kitchen table. "No problem. I'll see you out."

Karen held up a hand, "There's no need really. I know the way." He smiled, leaned in and kissed her on the cheek. "Thank you for last night," she said, with a nervous smile. Looking to Hunter, she offered a broader smile, "Nice to see you again, Sarah."

"You, too," Hunter replied, returning the smile and bobbing her head before looking away. Karen left via the living room. Caslin picked up the coffee he was intending to present to his ex and instead, passed it to Hunter.

"Coffee?" he said.

"Thank you. So…" Hunter said, holding the cup with both hands to warm her fingers, "you and Karen, eh?"

"Stop it," Caslin said, turning his back and reaching for his own cup. Internally, he was grinning. "So, what brings you to my door, this early, on a Sunday morning?" Hunter sipped at her drink but found it far too hot for her liking. Putting it down on the table, she fished out her notebook from an internal pocket of her coat.

"When I got back to the station yesterday, I ran the background on our victim, Farzaad Amin. The initial checks proved accurate. He has no priors, no convictions. According to the national database, he's not come up on the radar of any constabulary."

"No legs in the rumour of child abuse, then?"

Hunter shook her head, "I've also been to the National Crime Agency and they've no record in Child Exploitation and Online Protection either. If he's up to anything, we've nothing to substantiate it. I've asked Terry Holt to follow up and see if anyone can verify the allegations. Some of the neighbours have documented complaints about the locals, though. Anti-social behaviour in the main. Although, there were two incidences of bottles being thrown, along with racist abuse aimed at the ethnic minority residents of Amin's block."

"Kids?"

"It would appear so. Nothing came of it."

"Good work," Caslin said, leaning against the kitchen counter and blowing the steam from the top of his brew. "What did he do for a living, Farzaad Amin?"

Hunter returned to her notes, "That's where I'm struggling. The neighbours implied he arrived here from Afghanistan as an asylum seeker at the end of the mission. Or at least that's what they believed. If so, until his status was confirmed, he wouldn't be able to work."

"And?" Caslin asked, not seeing an issue.

"UK forces pulled out of combat operations back in 2014. Most of those who assisted our troops applied around then or before the withdrawal. Interpreters and the like – others who worked overtly with the occupying forces – were concerned about retaliation."

"From our former enemies, once our protection was removed. Yes, I know," Caslin said. "Did Amin work for ISAF?"

"That's just it, sir," Hunter continued. "I can find no record of him in the Home Office database. I can't tell you when he arrived in the country or what the details surrounding his asylum application were. Likewise, there's no confirmation of his status. No tax registration or national insurance number has been issued in his name."

"Have you been on to the department?"

"Yes but, what with it being a Saturday afternoon I was brushed off. Apparently, I'll need to speak to a case handler on Monday."

"Bank account or credit card?" Caslin queried, thinking hard. "He'll have to be paying his way somehow."

"I spoke to Iain Robertson this morning. He's finished cataloguing the contents of Amin's flat and is shipping everything back to Fulford Road as we speak. We'll be able to go through the paperwork there." Caslin picked up a cinnamon swirl to go with his coffee and took a bite. Speaking through a mouthful, he waved the pastry in Hunter's direction.

"While I think about it," he said, wiping his mouth with the back of the same hand, "get some names for those at the demo yesterday. Particularly that one stirring it with the megaphone. Add those nearest him to the top of the list as well. If it is a racially-motivated attack, then we have plenty of new faces floating about town to shake down."

"Will do, sir," Hunter said, making a note.

Caslin picked up his coffee and walked towards the living room, "I'll take a shower and then we can head in. Make yourself comfortable."

CASLIN SURVEYED THE BOXES, now stacked upon the desks in the CID squad room. Scanning through the nine-page inventory, he called out two box numbers. Indicating the first was for Terry Holt.

"Yours contains the financials, Terry. We're still none the wiser as to how this guy funds his existence," he said, re-reading the list. "I know, by all accounts, he led a simple life but where did he get his income from? If he has a job where is it? Who did he work for and with? Once you know that, I want you following up on his colleagues, clients, delivery personnel, everything. Has he fallen out with anyone? Is there a grudge being brought to bear? Likewise, is there anyone in his circle who has form for violence, racially motivated or otherwise?"

"What if he isn't working, sir?" Holt took the lid off of his assigned archive-box and removed several large, sealed, plastic bags, placing them on the desk in front of him.

"The man still had to eat, Terry. Find me who was picking up the tab," Caslin said, returning his attention to the inventory. Scanning down, through the subsections detailing the contents he paused, hovering his finger over the description of a charger for a mobile phone. Resuming his search, he flipped through the following pages until he came across a list of the deceased's reading matter. "No phone."

"What's that, sir?"

"No mobile phone."

"Not that was found at the scene, no," Hunter said.

"And yet, he had a charger stuck in the wall," Caslin said. "This guy liked reading. His books were focussed on economics, science and the like."

Hunter nodded, "That'd be fair to say. So?"

"That's pretty heavy reading matter. I didn't see anything else that he may have occupied his time with. No computer, stereo... he didn't even have a television."

"And yet, he had a mobile phone?" Caslin nodded. "Who doesn't these days? You can barely get by without one."

"True," Caslin said. "Still seems odd, mind you. At the very least, it's missing so let's find out as much as we can. Start chasing the providers and with a bit of luck it was a contract and we could get some joy with his call history. Something tells me this wasn't a burglary gone wrong."

"The racial motive is pretty strong, sir," Hunter said. "Judging by what we found at the scene."

Caslin nodded, "Undeniable. Particularly, bearing in mind the unrest we have in the city at the moment. Anybody else find it curious how the black shirts turned up when they did?"

"You mean, Martin James and his Free Templars?"

Caslin nodded, "Is that who it was?"

"Yes. Along with the Seventh Brigade of the Free Templars," Holt added. "Or at least, the five of them holding their flags with that printed in the corner."

"What is it with these fascists and their suits and uniforms?" Caslin asked.

"If you want to preach hate, you've got to do it in decent threads," Holt said with a cutting smile, "apparently."

"What do we know about them?"

Hunter flicked through her notes, "A substantial amount. Martin James, as he likes to be known these days, has also gone under the names Simon Brown and Gary Wilson. His real name is Peter James Osgood-Bellamy. Presumably, his birth name doesn't fit the *man of the people* persona that he wants to put across. Book sales to think about and all that."

"Strewth, he can write?" Caslin asked.

"Several books, sir. Although, you won't find them on the high street. I'm also certain they won't mention his two convictions for assault, one being a domestic attack on a former partner or his nine-month sentence for fraud, three years ago. He served six months in Pentonville for the last one."

"And the assaults?"

"He was given a year-long suspended for the first and spent another, tagged on licence, for the second. No subsequent arrests."

Caslin thought about it, "Motivations?"

Hunter shook her head, "Nothing racial if that's where you're going?" Caslin frowned, indicating for her to continue. "As for his lieutenants, they're a nasty bunch. Several of those present at the demo are well known to their local police. We've convictions ranging from ABH, possession of offensive weapons to burglary and incitement to commit racial violence. They're definitely worth a thorough look at in this case."

"Okay. Get a dossier together and we'll go one by one. See if we have intel on their movements prior to Saturday's altercation. If any of them were in the vicinity of Amin's place let's get them in. Seems odd, though…" he said, the thought tailing off.

"Sir?" Hunter asked.

"That they were so vocal under the circumstances."

"They were on the scene quickly, weren't they?" Hunter said. "Although, the word was out right enough and local gossip was rife about what was going on."

"Surprised you noticed," Holt said to Hunter, without making eye contact.

"Meaning?" Holt shook his head.

"Well, you know. What with beings indoors."

"And just what do you mean by that?"

"Enough. The pair of you. The thing about word spreading, though…" Caslin said, raising an eyebrow as he coaxed out the thought from his mind, "is that James and his nationalist idiots aren't local. Someone said we had a call about Amin's welfare."

"That's right," Holt said, glancing up from a loose collection of utility statements.

"Who called it in? Do we know yet?"

Holt shook his head, "It was anonymous, sir. I've got the recording from the log but they used a payphone."

"I'm amazed he found one that still worked. So, for all we know, it could've been the killer tipping us off?"

"I guess that's possible, but why do that? It just puts us onto him sooner."

"Or distracts us, pointing the investigation away from him and towards the demonstrators."

"I'll see if I can locate any CCTV from the area around the phone box," Holt said. "Maybe we'll get lucky."

"Good idea, Terry. In the meantime, Sarah," he indicated Hunter, "is there anyone local who might fit this particular bill? I'm thinking of anyone with a record of racially aggravated violence, affiliations to neo-Nazi groups or such? In the absence of anything direct, let's cover the obvious and take it from there." Caslin stood and picked up his coat.

"Where are you headed, sir?" Hunter asked.

"I'm off to see Dr Taylor to get the preliminaries from her. The detail will follow tomorrow but I'm hoping she can give us a steer. Robertson's promised his initial assessment of the crime scene in a couple of hours. I'll be back for that. What's the time in Kabul?"

"I've no idea, sir," Hunter said, sounding bemused. "Why?"

"They can't be much more than four or five hours ahead," Caslin offered. "If the Home Office is rubbish on a Sunday, perhaps their Interior Ministry may be more useful?"

Hunter smiled, "Can't hurt to ask."

Caslin left CID, turned to the right and headed for the stairs. The skeleton team staffing the station on a Sunday meant he didn't cross paths with anyone. Despite all scheduled rest days being cancelled, the majority of officers were out on patrol or beating the streets trying to ensure the demonstrators were kept apart from one another. His footfalls echoed in the corridor as he made his way to the front entrance. Passing out through the security door to the lobby, he noted the civilian staffer on the front desk. He didn't recognise her, assuming she was new. Casting a sideways glance, he smiled, one that she returned. Reaching the front door, the sound of voices came to his ear in far greater numbers than he'd anticipated.

Stepping out into the brilliant sunshine, Caslin shielded his eyes whilst they adjusted. At the bottom of the steps, barely six feet wide, he faced a bank of people perhaps twenty strong. They blocked his path. It didn't take him long to realise who they represented. On either side of the front line stood two men. Both were dressed in black with matching military-style berets, sporting white gloves that covered much of their forearms. They held Union Flags aloft embroidered at the edges with gold thread. Behind them were others, hoisting black flags, each with their own golden trim.

At the head of the group stood a man who Caslin recognised from the protests of the previous day. Martin James, self-styled advocate for free speech with his neatly-trimmed hair and pin-striped suit, was standing front and centre. Observing Caslin exiting the police station, he stepped forward.

"And here is one of those covering up for the paedophiles that our government insists on bringing into our country!" he called in as dramatic a fashion as he could.

Several of the group backed up the comment with muted appreciation. Caslin took a deep breath. The urge to return inside and slip out via the back was tempting. Only then, did he notice the assembled journalists off to his right-hand side. Looking beyond the crowd, Caslin judged his car was a minimum of fifty yards away. Steeling himself, he walked forward descending the steps.

"Anything to say in response to that accusation?" a voice came at him from the journalists. Caslin ignored it, pressing on. The crowd allowed him some space although not much.

"Defenders of paedos and rapists," James continued his verbal barrage as Caslin walked past him. "It makes me sick!" Caslin couldn't check himself in time. He turned to face his accuser, finding himself up close and far too confrontational in his stance.

"There is no cover up," he countered. Turning to the journalist who asked the question, he sneered, "What's being discussed is a blatant lie. No doubt fuelled by this idiot!"

"It's Rochdale all over again," James argued, referring to a high-profile case of sexual-grooming of vulnerable children that'd occurred in the city.

"There's no evidence for that, *none!* You and your lot are the problem here. We've got no issues with immigrants in this city," Caslin snapped, pointing an accusatory finger. Martin James smiled in return. "Any issue that's raised, any suggestion of impropriety and people like you descend on it with your dog-whistle rhetoric. We're investigating a murder. Nothing more."

"Free speech," James countered to much applause and cheering from those around him. "And you've all heard it. They're turning a blind eye... again!"

Caslin turned away, with a shake of the head and resumed his walk to the car. A microphone was pushed in front of him and he brushed it aside scowling at the man holding it.

"You lot aren't much better," Caslin stated, increasing his pace.

Photographers were taking pictures of him and Caslin regretted his part in the entire altercation. With hindsight, he should never have engaged at all. He knew better than to do so.

No one followed him to his car and he was relieved to reach the sanctity of the interior. Pulling the door closed, he started the engine and pulled away as quickly as he dared. Once out of the car park, he turned right onto Fulford Road and travelled barely a hundred yards before pulling into the kerb. Putting his hazard lights on, he sank back in his seat and tilted his face skywards. Pressing into his eyes with the heel of his palms, he sought to calm down. Martin James was one hell of a self-publicist who knew how to keep himself relevant. Of that, Caslin had no doubt. Something told him, he hadn't seen the last of him and his so-called Templars.

Glancing over his shoulder, he eyed a break in the traffic. Pulling out, he resumed his drive across the city to Alison Taylor's pathology lab.

CHAPTER ELEVEN

IF THE STATION was considerably quieter on the weekend, then pathology was a ghost town in comparison. Caslin waited at the entrance for what seemed like twenty minutes but in reality, was less than ten, for Alison to come up from her laboratory and let him through.

"If you could see your way clear to not delivering me a body for a couple of days, I'd appreciate it," she said, with a warm smile, pulling the door open. "A weekend off would be nice."

Caslin grinned, "I'm sorry. Death waits for no one." Dr Taylor returned the smile and they set off back into the building. Despite being indoors, Caslin drew his coat about him. "I know you have to keep it cool for the bodies but any chance the rest of the place can be a bit warmer?"

"The heating's on a timer," she explained. "It's Sunday. No one is supposed to be here. I pulled an all-nighter with your man. So, once we're through I won't be here either."

At that point, Caslin noticed the dark rings under her eyes. He should've picked up on that earlier. Within a couple of minutes, they arrived in the mortuary. Dr Taylor crossed to her workstation in order to retrieve her notes. Caslin looked around for the body.

"He's in D4, if you want to pull him out," she said, realising what he was thinking. Caslin scanned the numbering of the storage refrigerators where she indicated and located the unit. Pulling the handle, he swung the door open and pulled on the shelf. The metal tray slid out effortlessly on its runners. Farzaad Amin was enclosed in a black mortuary bag. Dr Taylor came alongside, passing him a small tub of nasal decongestant. Unscrewing the lid, he dabbed a little of the gel under his nostrils. The burning sensation began almost immediately, intensifying within seconds and bringing tears to his eyes. This was, however, far more agreeable than the smell of a decomposing body.

Caslin unzipped the bag, running it down to Amin's waistline. Paradoxically, the body seemed in a far better condition than when he had last seen it at the crime scene. Despite the extra incisions, caused during the autopsy process and subsequent stitching, the wounds appeared less violent now what with the excess blood having been cleaned away.

"You'll need to unzip it further," Alison said without looking up, familiarising herself with her notes.

"Really?"

"Yes. You'll see," she replied. Caslin did as instructed, running the zipper down. No further explanation was necessary as Caslin noted Amin's penis had been removed approximately halfway up the shaft. Even to his untrained eye, the process was executed somewhat roughly. Caslin winced at the barbarity of the action.

"Cause of death?" he asked.

"A massive haemorrhage following a single cut to a carotid artery, in the throat," Dr Taylor confirmed. Caslin moved to the victim's head and inclined his own in order to get a better view. He could see several wounds whereas previously, he'd only noted the one. "I would suggest that the victim didn't remain still to allow his throat to be cut. The wound itself, that caused the arterial rupture, is not large. As you can see, there are several other, shallow incisions above and below. That suggests the head was not sufficiently immobilised and there was a brief struggle."

"Why do you think it was brief?"

"The number of other cuts tell me there was resistance but they are not random enough to indicate he was moving significantly."

"Someone was holding him?"

"Probably," she confirmed.

"Two killers?" Caslin asked, casting a glance up to her.

"Possibly. However, the other injuries he sustained prior to that would've left him weakened and so, that would require speculation on my part. Interestingly though, most homicides of this nature, where a throat is cut, produce similar results.

The wound is usually located from just below the ear and then runs obliquely downward and medially across the throat, towards the other side. If the killer is right-handed, the cut is deeper on the victim's left side and tails off as the blade comes across to the right, ending slightly lower than the starting point. The opposite being true with a left-handed individual.

This is the norm if the killer is standing behind the victim and pulling back on the scalp in order to open up the target area. However, in this case, the killer was standing in front and towering over the victim."

Caslin assessed the wound. It was far less significant than what she was describing, as were the other, more superficial cuts, nearby.

"These are shorter and more angular," Caslin said, looking to her for reassurance of his assessment. She nodded.

"Indicative of the killer standing before him," she confirmed. "They are more like swipes or slashes, rather than a methodical cut."

"Frenzied?" Caslin asked.

She shook her head, "I would say not. They were still delivered with an element of precision."

"What of the other injuries?" Caslin asked, scanning the bruising to the face and abdomen.

"He was severely beaten. Probably with a blunt implement although I cannot tell you what it was. They could have been caused by a cosh or just as likely by a rounded chair leg. I didn't find any wood fibres present in any of the wounds so, I'd speculate that something specific was brought for the task.

Makeshift weapons, such as chair legs or ornaments will splinter or fracture upon impact, leaving forensic evidence in the wound. I've found none of that in this case. He has multiple fractures of the ribcage, both front and back. His fingers are all broken. Several in more than one place and I'm sure you've not failed to notice the number of cuts elsewhere to the body?"

"You can't miss them," Caslin said flatly, his eyes running the length of the deceased's body. There were too many to count.

"Fifty-six individual knife wounds. None of which were severe enough to kill or incapacitate but accumulatively, very damaging. It looks more like torture to me. They appear random but, if you are a student of anatomy, as I am, you would be aware that in the most part these wounds are located in areas that would be extremely painful for the victim."

"Anything left forensically that could help identify who the killer is, skin samples, that kind of thing?"

"I'm sorry. As much as I'd love to make your life easier, I've been unable to locate any forensics that will assist you. There's no skin under the fingernails. No defensive wounds that might offer up indicators that the attacker could be injured. Perhaps Iain Robertson and his team may have something but sadly, I don't."

"To take that much of a beating in silence would be impressive," Caslin said, thinking aloud. "The neighbours reported hearing nothing untoward and this must've gone on for quite some time."

"Unsurprising," Dr Taylor said. "He had his tongue cut out." Caslin raised his eyebrows in shock.

"Then what's the point of the torture? If he can't speak, he can't tell you anything."

"It strikes me that you have a particular kind of sadist, on your hands," she replied. Caslin rolled his eyes heavenward.

"I noted something was wedged in his mouth."

"That would be the end of his penis," Dr Taylor confirmed. Caslin exhaled deeply. "I believe it was removed post-mortem, judging by the blood flow from the area. I trust that Iain Robertson will find the tongue because I have no sign of it here."

"What would be the point of that?"

She shook her head, "Symbolism, maybe? Perhaps he wanted to emasculate him for some reason, either driven by hatred or religious ideology. An attempt at humiliation or simply to send a message."

"To whom?"

"That escapes me," she shrugged, "but there will be a reason. There always is. Likewise, the removal of his eyes. They were gouged out with a smooth implement. Although, the trauma to the surrounding tissue is obviously severe, it was done with skill."

"See no evil, speak no evil…" Caslin mumbled under his breath. "Do you think the killer had experience of doing similar previously?"

"Quite likely, yes. Whether or not in a professional capacity, I couldn't say but this wasn't the first time."

"Anything else?" Caslin asked in a forlorn tone, thinking over what he had been told.

"There are two marks to the chest," she said, leaning over and indicating two small puncture marks on Amin's chest, barely an inch apart. "I nearly missed them at first what with the level of trauma to the upper body, in particular. But I got to thinking about the lack of defensive wounds, bearing in mind I couldn't see any injury that may have accounted for him being incapacitated. For example, a massive blow to the head."

Caslin eyed them, "A Taser?"

Dr Taylor nodded, "I believe so, yes. If you look at his wrists and ankles, you can make out skin abrasions where he was restrained. Probably to a chair. If he was resistant to that process, there would be some indication, a greater depth to the abrasions of the skin perhaps, but there isn't. The only deduction I can make is he either went willingly into a torturous death or he had no opportunity to resist." Caslin thought on that for a moment before passing comment.

"I felt the scene was staged, his kneeling as if in prayer. The cross painted on the wall in front of him. Would he have been dead before the staging took place, do you think?"

Dr Taylor looked down at her notes and cast a sideways glance over the body. With a shake of the head, she met his eye, "Impossible to say. If he expired prior to setting the scene, it becomes difficult to manhandle the deadweight into position."

"If you are doing so alone, yes," Caslin offered.

"Agreed. Judging from what Iain told me from the scene, the amount of blood loss would most likely suggest he bled out in situ, where you found him. That would mean he either died afterwards or shortly before because, as you know, the blood will flow for a time post-mortem."

"How long do you think it took him to bleed out from this type of injury?"

"It's quite possible his heart was still pumping for up to ten minutes, maybe more, but I'd doubt it."

"He would have been aware of what was happening?"

"Absolutely. Whether or not he had the strength or will to try and do anything about it, is another matter entirely."

Caslin zipped up the bag, pausing as he reached the neckline of the deceased. The speculative image of Amin's last moments in this life flashed through his mind. An image of abject horror. Whoever did this, someone so depraved they could stomach such an intense level of violence, he was sure it wasn't their first. It couldn't possibly be. Closing the bag, he took a step back and Alison pushed the tray back into the fridge, closing the metal door. The latch snapping into place echoed through the lab. Once again, he felt cold.

"Nate..." she said, trying to get his attention. "Did you hear me?"

He glanced across and met her eye, "Sorry. What did you say?"

"I was saying I'll write the report up tonight and get it over to you first thing. If that's okay?"

"Yes, yes. Of course," Caslin replied, rubbing at his face.

"Are you okay? I mean, we've not seen an awful lot of each other, aside from the last couple of days anyway."

He smiled, weakly, "I've just got a lot on my mind. And, I had a late one, last night."

"At A and E?" she asked, indicating the stitches on the side of his face whilst brazenly inspecting the handiwork. "I didn't want to mention it. Are you all right?"

Caslin shrugged off the question. He also had no intention of sharing with his ex-girlfriend the reason for his lack of sleep: spending the night with his ex-wife. Memories of which flooded his mind, pushing aside the last moments of the victim. They raised his spirits and he smiled to himself.

"I'm fine, it's just a scratch," he said. "You know what the emergency room is like on a Saturday. All drunks and sports injuries. It takes an age to get seen."

Alison Taylor agreed, "So, you're all right, generally speaking?"

"Yes, I'm fine," he replied. "Thanks for pulling this off, so quickly. You'll probably want to get your head down. I'll let you get off."

He turned and headed out of the lab. Dr Taylor returned to her workstation and he was aware of the sound of her notes landing on the desk. Caslin grasped the door handle and pulled it when she called after him.

"Yes, I'm fine too, Nathaniel. Thanks for asking." He paused in the doorway but didn't look back, somewhat aware of both the rhetorical nature of her comment as well as his personal failings. The realisation of the latter in itself demonstrated an improvement in his character but was, sadly, nowhere near enough to make up for the flaws in his social skills. Silently cursing himself, he left the lab allowing the door to swing closed behind him.

Passing out through the main entrance lobby, Caslin ensured the door locked back into place as he left the building. The wind was picking up and the chill that it brought, cut through his overcoat, causing him to shiver. Pulling his coat tightly about him, he picked up the pace and headed for his car. Once inside, he fired up the engine and set the demisters to maximum. The windscreen was already fogging over. Taking out his phone, he called Hunter.

"Sarah, is Iain ready for the briefing?"

"Yes. We're all set here, just waiting on you."

"I'll be back in about fifteen minutes," he said, glancing at the clock on his dashboard.

Hanging up, he put the phone back into his pocket and wiped the window next to him. Eyeing the skies, they threatened rain. The sun wasn't due to set for another couple of hours but with the dark, brooding clouds rolling in from the west it was hard to tell where the sun was. At least the rain would cancel out the frost. Judging the screen to be sufficiently clear, Caslin engaged first gear. As he did so, he caught sight of Alison Taylor leaving via the front door as he had only minutes earlier. She walked with a mobile clasped to her ear, laughing as she chatted, unaware of him watching her.

A pang of regret struck within, catching him off guard. He could honestly say he hadn't given her much thought since their relationship had run its course, so why now? She reached her Audi and the lights flashed as she unlocked it. He shook his head, telling himself it was probably due to revisiting the feelings he had for Karen, thereby stirring the emotions within that'd unsettled him. Regardless, he decided to not think about it anymore. Although, Alison's perceived happiness troubled him but he didn't know why.

"Stop living in the past, Nate," he told himself, looking away and moving off, attempting to cast aside any lingering thoughts about their chequered past.

CHAPTER TWELVE

DESPITE THE INCREASE in traffic due to people hitting the post-Christmas sales, the drive back to Fulford Road was uneventful. The demonstrators were still present at the front of the station and so he took a circuitous route around to the rear. At least now, they were being supervised by a uniformed presence. The security gates parted and he drove through. Finding a narrow space alongside a liveried van, he reversed the car in.

Entering through the custody suite, he acknowledged the duty sergeant and made his way to the stairs. Taking them two at a time, he entered CID moments later. The team were assembled and ready for the briefing. Offering an apology for keeping them waiting, Caslin pulled up a chair. Casting an eye across the two wipe boards, set up alongside the desks, Caslin scanned the new information. Iain Robertson had spent the morning updating the one relating to Farzaad Amin's death.

The crime-scene photographs brought back the stark memories that he'd managed to push aside, in the previous twenty-four hours. The brutality was equally shocking the second time around. Robertson cleared his throat, garnering the attention of the assembled detectives. Conversation ceased as people focussed on him.

Robertson's eyes flicked to the entrance doors and he nodded towards a latecomer. Caslin glanced over his shoulder, seeing DCI Matheson entering. She perched herself on the end of a desk towards the rear of the room, folding her arms.

"Okay, folks," Robertson began, "I've got an abbreviated copy here for all of you. Please take one and pass them on."

Hunter picked up half of the stack, piled on the nearest desk and handed it to Terry Holt who took the top one and moved them along. Hunter sent the remainder in the other direction. Caslin took a copy and began leafing through the pages.

"I'll give you the headlines," Robertson continued. "There were no clear indications of a forced entry but the security of the flat was insufficient. Slight abrasions on this window latch," he pointed to a photo up on the board, alongside another documenting a black mark, "and a boot scuff, on the corresponding window sill, indicate this is the point of entry. It took some finding. The window was closed, latch set in place. It's fair to assume the killer, or killers, left via the front door."

"Killers?" Caslin said.

"Two partial footprints, left in the victim's blood, have been identified. They have tread patterns on the soles that don't match any other footwear present in the flat. One was alongside the chair that the victim was strapped to. More on that later. The other was found alongside the prayer mat, Mr Amin was found kneeling on. They are both incomplete and neither measures up to more than a sixth of the available coverage. It does however, give us enough to confirm two other people were at the scene either at the time of Amin's death or very shortly after."

"Any fingerprints?" Hunter asked.

Robertson shook his head, "We swept the property twice and found only those belonging to Amin himself. I would go so far as to say the residence had been thoroughly cleaned. The prints we found were in the kitchen on cupboard doors, handles and utensils. No prints were found in the living room, the bathroom or the access hallway including the front door. We're not talking about a quick wipe down either. Whoever was there did a good job of masking their presence."

"Dr Taylor says the victim was tortured over a period of time," Caslin said, lifting his eyes from the paperwork he was reading through. "How long do you think they were on the scene?"

"That depends on how many were involved in the clean-up," Robertson said. "The victim sustained a prolonged assault. I've also discussed the injuries with Alison and we are agreed, in that we cannot ascertain what weapon, or weapons, were used.

Despite an extensive search, nothing was left at the scene that fits the bill. Likewise, none of the victim's knives were used. The knife block, in the kitchen, is full and no trace evidence was found on any of the blades. We can only presume that the weapons were taken away and therefore, it is reasonable to assume, were also brought with them to the scene."

"What about the paint on the wall?" Caslin said, eyeing the photograph on the board depicting the white cross alongside one of the graffiti.

"Acrylic based, deployed from an aerosol. The standard formula you will find for sale in auto-factors or DIY shops. For use on rigid metals, glass fibre or plastics. It's too common to narrow down to a purchase point. The choice of wording was interesting, though. The use of the word 'vermin' has connotations," Robertson said, talking to Caslin.

"Vermin is commonly used within far-right propaganda. Often in reference to those of Jewish descent but also ethnic minorities," Caslin said for the uninitiated.

"Are you approaching this as a racial hate-crime?" DCI Matheson asked, from the back of the room. Caslin stood, so she could see him better.

"Not at this stage, Ma'am," he replied. "With everything that's going on at the moment we'll keep it in the mix, but it's just as likely to be misdirection at this point."

"And you're basing that conclusion on what?"

"I prefer to follow the direction of travel the evidence sends us rather than the route set out by the perpetrators," he countered. She acknowledged his answer and didn't comment further. Caslin indicated for Robertson to continue.

"We have failed to locate the victim's eyes or tongue," Robertson said gravely. A few people exchanged concerned glances. "We've explored the building's drainage in case of disposal there, but found nothing. It is possible that they were flushed and any evidence sanitised before our arrival.

Alternatively, the more macabre conclusion is they could have been taken as trophies. The remaining details that I can offer relate to the blood spatter," he continued. "You'll find detailed illustrations within your individual reports. The victim was strapped to one of his dining chairs, secured at the wrists and ankles with duct tape.

There, he received the bulk of his ordeal. He was stripped naked and tortured. The arcs of blood on the surrounding walls and ceiling tell us this. The victim defecated in the chair before he was cut free and dragged the short distance to the prayer mat, where we believe he was positioned in the manner in which he was found."

A few brief questions were traded but nothing beyond clarification issues. Caslin stood as the briefing ended and the team returned to their assigned tasks. Taking Robertson by the forearm, Caslin led him aside.

"Nestor Kuznetsov," Caslin said. "Have you found any evidence to indicate anyone else was present in the boathouse?"

Robertson shook his head, "No, nothing to place anyone else at the scene."

"That's what I thought."

"Doesn't mean I think it was a suicide, mind you."

"No?" Caslin asked. "Can you tell me why?"

"Not really," he replied. Caslin was momentarily puzzled. Robertson noticed, elaborating, "Everything points to death by his own hand. The boathouse was apparently locked from the inside. There's no sign of a struggle nor any damage to the interior or contents of the building. Psychologically speaking, his life had taken such a battering it is easy to conclude why he'd have taken the decision to check out."

"Got to say it, Iain. You're not selling suspicious very well," Caslin said with a smile.

"Well, that's just it, isn't it," Robertson said. "It all points to suicide and yet, according to his medical records, there's a possibility that he couldn't have managed it."

"Exactly, Iain. A possibility. That's not evidence."

"I know that," he countered forcefully. "But sometimes... you just have a feeling about something, right? It's like you with your man, Farzaad. It's too clean. Too obvious."

Caslin nodded, thoughtfully, "Sometimes things are obvious, though. Maybe we're guilty of overcomplicating by looking too deeply."

"That's the job," Robertson replied quietly with a stern expression. "Ma'am," he said to the approaching DCI Matheson.

"Nathaniel. Can I have a word in your office?"

"Of course," Caslin replied, before saying goodbye to Robertson and thanking him for the speed of his report.

Following her into the office, he closed the door behind them. Something in her demeanour was a little off. They may not have the greatest working relationship over the course of her tenure as DCI but he could read her well enough.

"Where are you with the Kuznetsov suicide?" she asked, pulling out a chair.

"I'm still not convinced it was a suicide," Caslin replied, walking behind his desk. Matheson rolled her eyes and he sought to head off the direction the conversation was likely to take. "His daughter is adamant."

"His daughter, who he barely appears to spend any time with—"

"Who is still the closest person to him, barring his gangster security detail anyway," Caslin said.

"He was bankrupt, going from billionaire status to nothing," Matheson argued. "Men like him don't take failure well."

"Men like him never accept failure. They get what they want one way or another."

"And if all his options expired?" Caslin took a deep breath breaking the eye contact Matheson appeared to cherish during a confrontation.

He sighed, "Raisa, his daughter, claims he was negotiating a return to Russia. That he was homesick and looking to find a way back."

"Perhaps his request fell on deaf ears?" Matheson said. "Either way, I don't see an awful lot left for you to investigate. There are a few minor anomalies contained within the pathologist's report but aside from that, I fail to see why you're not deferring this one to the coroner and moving on."

"This is too high profile to pass off so quickly. We'll only fuel the conspiracy theories if we don't do a thorough investigation," Caslin said, pulling out his chair and sitting down.

"And if we spend too long on it, the end result will be the same. They'll claim we're hiding something."

"I'm not ready to tie it off just yet but," he added swiftly, "I do take on board your concerns."

"Don't patronise me, Nathaniel," Matheson chided him. "I'm not a junior detective. I'd also like to know why the chief constable has received a complaint about you?"

"Me?" Caslin asked, incredulous. "What have I done?"

"Accusing the press of fuelling racial hatred," Matheson said, stony-faced.

Caslin frowned, "When did I do that?"

"This morning. Outside the station during your verbal confrontation with the demonstrators," Matheson informed him.

Caslin sank back in his seat, pressing a thumb and forefinger to his eyes, "Oh, yeah. I remember." Matheson stood up and made to leave the office. She stopped as she reached the door, gripping the handle, poised to open it and looked back at him. She spoke in a softer tone.

"The chief constable was asked for an interview for this evening's television news," she said. Caslin's heart sank. "She declined, obviously. However, they will be running footage of the confrontation, so you ought to brace yourself."

"Local or national?"

"National," Matheson said.

"Great."

"You need a quick win, Nathaniel," Matheson said. "We both do."

With that, the DCI departed leaving the door to his office open. Caslin turned his attention to the window and his view of the infantry barracks in the nearby compound running adjacent to the grounds of the station. The light was fading and it was raining. He didn't hear Hunter enter.

"Sir?" she said, gaining his attention.

"Yes, Sarah. What do you have?"

"I contacted the Interior Ministry in Kabul."

"How did you get on?"

"Very well. They were extremely helpful, which was a pleasant surprise."

"What could they tell us about our victim?"

"Absolutely nothing, sir," Hunter said, enthusiastically. Acknowledging Caslin's disappointment, she continued, "But that's where it gets interesting. They have no record of a Farzaad Amin emigrating to the UK. The only mention they found of that name recorded in their files was of a civil servant working in a low-level administration role."

"Same guy?" Caslin asked. Hunter shook her head.

"No. He retired last year, shortly after his sixtieth birthday. Oh, and he still lives in Kabul." Caslin sat forward, resting his elbows on the desk in front of him, interlocking his fingers. Hunter met his eye. She found this as intriguing as he did, he could tell. Pushing his chair back, he stood and walked around the desk and out into the squad room. Hunter followed.

"Terry," he called. Holt scurried over from the other side of the room. "Where did you get to with Amin's financials?"

"No employer, as far as I could see from his bank statements, sir. There is a possibility he worked cash-in-hand but I don't see it. There's no evidence of him being the manual-labouring type. He does, however, have a payment going into his account twice a month. Equal amounts on the same days of each month. Regular as clockwork."

"How much?"

"A thousand pounds, sir," Holt stated. "But it doesn't say where the money comes from."

"Two grand a month. How is it paid?"

"Via BACS, sir," Holt said. "I've asked the bank for clarification of where the payments originate but they're unwilling to say. Not without a warrant anyway."

"They know this is a murder inquiry, right?"

"Yes, sir. I explained that."

"Get a hold of a magistrate. Obtain a warrant," Caslin said.

"It's Sunday afternoon, sir," Holt replied. Caslin fixed him with a stare. Holt didn't protest any further, merely nodded and returned to his desk. He'd already picked up his phone before Caslin turned back to Hunter.

"I want to know who Farzaad Amin is and I want to know now," he instructed her, heading back into his office and pushing the door closed.

"Yes, sir," Hunter said to herself. "Me, too."

Caslin cut a frustrated figure pacing his office. Up until now, all the available evidence indicated that Amin was the victim of a vicious, racially aggravated assault. That was, however, Caslin's biggest issue. So much of the evidence had been laid out for them and the real detail, the forensics they would expect to find, had been sanitised. To Caslin, this signified an understanding of police procedure or at the least, a knowledge of forensic methodology. A knock on the door snapped him out of his thought process. Holt entered with a smile on his face.

"I've got a magistrate who is willing to see me. It'll mean heading out to his golf club but we'll have the warrant for Amin's bank account by the close of play," Holt said with enthusiasm. "That means I can be on to the bank first thing."

"Good work," Caslin told him. The detective constable appeared to hover in the office doorway, almost as if considering whether or not to say what was on his mind. "What is it, Terry?" Holt stepped in, closing the door behind him. He appeared nervous but buoyed by Caslin's willingness to hear him out.

"I wanted to have a word, sir," he said, glancing over his shoulder in the direction of the squad room beyond. Caslin followed his line of sight, catching Hunter's eye for a fleeting moment.

"And?"

Holt cleared his throat. "I've been in the job for ten years now. CID for the last four," Holt said. "I know my performance hasn't always been... the most prolific in terms of results but... I've improved. I mean, I've made a real effort..."

"You want a leg-up?" Caslin said in conclusion.

Holt nodded, "I think I've earned it."

"Earned it?" Caslin said, furrowing his brow.

"Yeah," Holt stated. "With Hunter moving to Thames Valley, I thought I'd have a good shot at making DS but now, what with her staying put, I don't see it happening." Caslin sat back in his chair, putting his hands behind his head and interlocking his fingers. "I mean, she's a decent officer and all but do you think she's still up for it?"

"Are you saying she isn't?"

Holt shrugged, "Not exactly."

"Then what, *exactly*?"

"Well, you saw it yourself the other day. When it goes down, do you honestly think she'll have your back, or mine, when it comes down to it?" Caslin sat forward, placing his palms on the desk before him and drumming his fingers. In the corner of his eye, he saw Hunter watching them, doing her best to appear casual. He wondered whether she knew what they were discussing. Turning his gaze back to Holt, he fixed his gaze on the younger man.

"Let me make something very clear to you, Terry," Caslin said, his tone taking on a level of menace that most seldom witnessed. "DS Hunter is a far superior detective to you, in ways that you will never comprehend. Even working sub-par, she puts you in the shade and if I hear you questioning her competence or attitude in this way again, you and I will be having words. Bottom line, Terry, you go before she does. Is that clear enough for you?"

Holt visibly shrank before him. However he'd envisioned the conversation playing out, this wasn't it. Ashen-faced, he was at a loss for words, merely murmuring, "Yes, sir."

"As for your performance," Caslin went on, "when I first came to Fulford Road, you were underperforming in all aspects, other than studying the form at the bookies. It did not go unnoticed." Holt looked down, averting his eyes from Caslin's gaze. "With that said, you're right. You've improved. You'll walk through the exams but whether you'll make a decent sergeant remains to be seen. If you want me to back you, then really *earn it*, Terry. Prove to me you're capable but don't do it by stepping on your colleagues. One day, you might need them and we've all got long memories."

Holt raised his head and met the stare of his senior officer. He nodded an acknowledgement and stood up, leaving the office without another word. Caslin watched him go, annoyed by his comments but at the same time, admiring the renewed ambition that had always appeared to be so sorely lacking in the DC.

Glancing across to Hunter, Caslin noticed her gaze was tracking Terry Holt all the way back to his desk. He would never share the thought with Holt nor anyone else for that matter, but he'd be lying if he said he hadn't contemplated similar concerns about his detective sergeant. Hunter was different since she'd returned. A brush with death was traumatic and hers had severely impacted her personal life, not only her career. Time would tell whether or not she could find her way back.

In his mind at least, she deserved the shot. Scooping up his phone from the desk, Caslin scrolled down through his contacts until he found his target and dialled it. The call connected and was swiftly answered.

"Just the man," a voice said from the other end of the line. "I was hoping to pick your brains over something."

"Great minds think alike," Caslin replied. "The usual?"

"The usual," the voice responded and both men hung up.

Caslin stood up, crossed the room and pulled on his coat. Slipping the mobile into a pocket, he left his office. Passing Hunter in the squad room, he drew her attention.

"I'll be on the mobile if anyone needs me," he said without breaking step. Hunter fell into step alongside him. Once out of the squad room and the earshot of others, she stopped him.

"Can I ask what that was about before, with Terry? It looked pretty heated and he's been quiet ever since."

Caslin met her eye, "Nothing to be concerned about. Okay?" Hunter didn't break the eye contact, almost as if she was trying to read inference into Caslin's expression but failing to do so.

"Okay," she replied. Caslin set off, leaving her alone in the corridor. He sensed her watching him as he made his way to the stairs. No good would come from him enlightening her as to what Holt had said. If she was curious as to where he was heading, she didn't voice it.

CHAPTER THIRTEEN

THE PUB WAS DOING a brisk trade for early on a Sunday evening. It would appear that the darkening of the skies leant itself to being in an establishment found largely underground. The Cellars were equal to the needs of its patrons throughout the year. In the summer, they were blessed with a large walled beer-garden that could comfortably accommodate a hundred people or more. Whereas in the depths of winter, the vaulted brick ceilings and atmospheric lighting of the old cellars themselves proved to be quite a draw.

Caslin found Jimmy Sullivan in a booth in the lower tier. The next table had a small group of diners seated at it, enjoying an early meal. Caslin slid into his seat opposite his friend. A pint was pushed across the table which he gratefully accepted. Acknowledging Sullivan by way of taking a mouthful of beer, he wiped the froth from his mouth with the back of his hand.

"How's life treating you, Jimmy?"

"Better than if I was a billionaire," Sullivan replied with a cheeky wink.

"There is that," Caslin replied with a smile. "What can you tell me about him?"

"Kuznetsov?" Sullivan replied, Caslin nodded. "Atypical of

his kind. A real rags-to-riches story. If I wrote it as fiction, my editor would toss it aside as too far-fetched."

"He came from obscurity, didn't he?"

"Son of a coal miner from a provincial town. He made some acquaintances that served him well. As the Soviet Bloc collapsed, he found he was well placed to benefit. He had a knack for media, a natural talent you might say. The technological revolution that we all got swept up in back in the nineties, changed things."

"Some of us are still trying to catch up," Caslin stated, seeing off half his pint.

"As I understand it, he just understood the way things were changing and turned it to his advantage," Sullivan continued. "What with those old party allegiances that he'd fostered, he found himself in the unlikely position as something of a king-maker when it came to politics."

"Sounds like you know him pretty well?"

Sullivan smiled, "It's my job to know."

"So, what went wrong?"

"Ahh…" Sullivan said, drinking from his glass. "Arrogance, greed, alongside the old adage of becoming a victim of his own success."

"How so?"

"He rapidly made himself the *go to* man of the moment. You know what politics is like. The rewards are fantastic, whichever country you're running in. With that comes a lot of competition. Once you pick a side, you make enemies. And let's also not forget we're talking about a man who seemed to revel in poking the bear."

"With a landscape such as the one in Russia, even those on your side will come to fear you," Caslin added. Sullivan nodded, draining his glass. He pushed the empty across the table, in front of Caslin, who finished his own at the same time.

"Your round."

Caslin stood and made his way up to the next level, picking his way through the throng towards the bar. Putting the glasses on the counter, he thought about Sullivan's words. Had Kuznetsov overreached? If his enemies were powerful political figures, there may well be some mileage in the threats made against his life. That would place his investigation against formidable opponents. The barman took his order, two more pints and a couple of chasers to go along with them. Receiving the change from a twenty, he pocketed the money and picked up the tray bearing their drinks. Returning to the booth, Caslin negotiated the steps down and Sullivan picked his drinks up before he'd managed to set the tray down on the table.

"Cheers," he said, downing the scotch in one. Caslin followed.

"If you had to guess," Caslin asked, "hypothetically speaking, were he to have been killed, where would you target your focus? The politics or the business?"

Sullivan laughed but lowered his voice before answering, "He was a Russian billionaire. Do you really think you can separate the two?"

"Humour me." Sullivan sat back, pursing his lips as he considered the question. After a few moments he leant forward, placing one hand on the table and the other on his fresh pint.

"Much of his business interests have been seized in the past few years."

"Either in the east or, more recently, by European governments. I know."

"Those that they are aware of anyway," Sullivan said, his eyes flitting about the bar. Caslin sat forward in his chair.

"I understood he was facing a winding-up order and was practically broke?"

"So, they say," Sullivan said. "Personally, I don't buy it. Not that I doubt the competence of the HMRC, mind you. When it comes to money, they are surprisingly efficient if they choose to be."

"Meaning?"

Sullivan took a large swig from his drink, looking around to make sure those nearby weren't paying them any attention before continuing, "Guys like Nestor Kuznetsov, who made it big very quickly, came onto the international radar in quick succession. Some of them were *apparatchiks* –politicians who survived from the old communist regimes – others arose out of the ruins of the KGB. They were lesser-known faces. Some, such as Kuznetsov, were tied to these people and made fortunes off the back of them. Whoever they were, they didn't want their money staying in the Motherland but to move it was, and still is, not easy."

"Why did they need to move it?" Caslin asked.

"Not least because they'd acquired it in an underhand, if not illegal fashion. If they'd stolen it, either through purchasing state-owned assets at knockdown prices, bribery or a mixture of both, what was to stop others from stealing from them?"

"They had to get it out of the country where it would be safe," Caslin concluded.

"Exactly. Once into the international markets, the state apparatus was nullified," Sullivan said emphatically. "The problem is, state controls on the levels of financial movement restricted how much they could transfer. The regime didn't want an exodus of wealth so they sought to control it through ever tighter means. Factor in European money-laundering regulations and you have quite a problem with which to overcome."

"They can get around these problems, though?"

"Of course. You just need to be creative that's all."

"Sounds easy," Caslin mused with a hint of sarcasm.

"Far from it," Sullivan continued, "but once you have a network of foreign assets to call upon it is eminently doable."

"Assets?"

"Willing locals. A network of people with vested interests to help you. We're getting into offshore accounts, shell companies, trusts that administer philanthropic funds. All of which will be used to funnel money in and out of countries to fund investment projects, property deals, business acquisitions and the like."

"They still need to transfer money, though. Right?"

Sullivan rocked his head from side to side, scrunching up his nose as if to imply Caslin was on the right track, "Sort of," he said. "Look at it this way, for example. You have a deal that needs financing back in Moscow. Your asset, a UK national, agrees to buy a property you own in Belgravia," Sullivan referenced one of the most prestigious property locations in London, "to fund the purchase, he takes out a mortgage but instead of transferring the money to you, he invests it in your Moscow scheme. When the deal comes off, the profits from the development come in and only then does he pay you the purchase price."

Caslin thought on it, "So, what happens next?" Sullivan chuckled at his lack of comprehension, irritating him.

"What do you mean? That's it. It's done. You've raised money to pay for your investment without having to transfer anything out of Russia. The profits come back, paying you for the house in Belgravia, paying back the mortgage and none of it is in your name. The trail becomes hard to follow, particularly if your involvement is kept a secret."

"But you don't have the money."

Sullivan shook his head, "No but your trusted lieutenant does and it's untraceable to you. What's more, it's clean as a whistle."

"What happens to the money then?"

"Your associates will buy cars, property, whatever you like. You purchase them at stupid prices, sell them on, draw your money that way. Of course, often you never see or touch any of these assets. They are bought and sold in seconds, laundering millions in a few strokes."

"Sounds crooked," Caslin said, sipping at his pint.

"Oh, absolutely but, and this is the kicker, it washes the money to the point of being untraceable."

"And that was important for the likes of Kuznetsov?"

"With Kuznetsov, he is hardly popular in some parts of eastern Europe these days. As soon as his money is tagged somewhere, someone will go after it. It was in his interests to be as opaque as possible."

"Are you suggesting Kuznetsov had money that we are not aware of?"

"Without doubt."

"Where?"

Sullivan shook his head, grinning as he raised his pint to his lips.

"Now, if I knew that, so would the HMRC, wouldn't it? Besides, I'm a journalist. You're the detective!"

Caslin sank back in his chair, cursing himself for hoping that Sullivan was about to give him a massive heads-up. If he was right, however, analysing Kuznetsov's associates could provide a strong lead.

"Not a suicide then?" Sullivan asked.

"I never said that."

"You didn't have to. It's written all over your face."

"Is it that obvious?" Caslin asked. Sullivan grinned.

"What about the other one? The murder of the paedo?"

Caslin shook his head, "He's not a paedophile as far as I'm aware. Not having a great deal of joy with that one, though, if I'm honest. It's early days."

"Doesn't help to have Osgood-Bellamy in town either, does it?" Sullivan said. Caslin shook his head. "Nasty piece of work, he is," Sullivan added.

"Tapped into the mood of the public, though. Somehow, he's being touted as some kind of hero. Not too long ago, the likes of him wouldn't have gained any traction at all," Caslin said bitterly.

"Sign of the changing times."

"Hopefully, it's more of a blip than a sea change."

"Amen to that," Sullivan replied, standing. Indicating towards Caslin's drink with his own empty glass, he asked, "Same again?" Caslin checked the time, knowing that he probably shouldn't but nodded an affirmative anyway.

THE SOUND of the clapper striking *Great Peter*, York Minster's largest bell, carried from the North-West Tower across the city to signify the time had reached eleven o'clock.

Caslin stumbled on the uneven slabs beneath his feet. At least, that was his excuse. Although, he sought to mitigate the outcome of the impromptu drinking session by acknowledging it had been a while since he'd spent an entire evening with a friend, at his favourite haunt. Jimmy Sullivan was good company. Quick witted and, almost always, relaxed company.

The evening had passed swiftly. The journalist's knowledge of the darker elements of society never ceased to amaze Caslin. His own world was forever populated by shady individuals who most members of society only ever came across in works of fiction. They were both paid to wade through the cesspool, albeit for different reasons.

One day, Caslin thought he might find out what motivated his friend to do what he did. For himself, Caslin was driven to make a difference. As the years passed, the tiers of success became harder to measure. Feeling a little nauseous, Caslin reckoned it probably hadn't been the best idea to head back to Sullivan's apartment after leaving the Cellars. Hopefully, the walk back into the centre to his home in Kleiser's Court would revive him a little.

A shriek cut through the still air of the freezing night, startling him. Stopping in his tracks, Caslin looked around in an attempt to determine where it originated from. At this time on a Sunday night, most of the city was deserted without even the hum of traffic to break the silence. The clouds parted, revealing a bright, full moon in the sky above. The surrounding area was bathed in silver light, eerie and foreboding. Another scream. Caslin took off along the street, making a right turn at the next intersection. Within fifty feet of the turn, he saw a figure slumped on the steps at the entrance to a building.

Breaking into a sprint, he approached the woman, dropping to his haunches alongside her and reaching out he touched her shoulder. She looked up at him, fear and borderline panic in her eyes. Tears wet her face and she was shaking.

"What is it? What's happened?" Caslin asked. She couldn't speak, such was her emotional state but raising her right hand, she pointed into the building. Caslin looked at the entrance doors, now realising where he was. He was outside the Islamic Centre, the largest mosque in the city.

One of the double doors was open and Caslin could see a flickering light further inside. At first, he thought it was the electrics but within moments the light grew in size and intensity. The building was on fire.

"Is anyone inside?" he asked. The woman nodded. Rising, he rummaged through his coat pocket searching for his phone as he took the steps, two at a time. He was inside before he made the emergency call for assistance, requesting the attendance of all three emergency services.

The entrance lobby was empty, spartanly furnished with a noticeboard detailing upcoming events, prayer times and the like. A wide staircase was set off to his right, providing access to the upper floors and a corridor in front of him led further into the building, now lit by an orange glow. Caslin hesitated but only for the briefest of moments. He knew where he had to go, towards the flames.

Moving forward, the fire appeared to be confined to an interior room, he deduced to be roughly halfway into the bowels of the building and on the eastern side. Slowing as he approached the doorway, Caslin steeled himself.

Peering around into the room, he saw the fire was taking hold. The far side of the room was ablaze where the flames were at their most intense. They were climbing the curtains and the walls, running at pace across the ceiling, spreading throughout the room. Black smoke billowed out into the corridor where Caslin stood, fanned by the breeze of a broken window at the heart of the fire.

At that moment, the lights went out as the electrics shorted.

He ducked low, covering his mouth and nose to limit his intake of the acrid smoke. Beside a table, frighteningly close to the advancing flames, a man lay apparently unconscious. Keeping low, Caslin made his way towards him. The intensity of the blaze was such that he had to use his coat as a shield.

Coming alongside the stricken man, Caslin knelt. He was elderly, probably well into his seventies and dressed in a cream thobe that stretched from shoulder to foot. Seeing no sign of visible injury, Caslin knew he had to get them out and fast. He could feel the intensity of the heat against his skin and it was alarming. He unceremoniously took a hold of the older man, grasping him by the clothing of his chest and hauling him upright. Glancing back towards the door, their only exit, Caslin was dismayed to see the flames rolling down from the ceiling above and licking at the doorframe. He assessed they had but seconds to escape.

Finding the strength from within, Caslin hoisted the man up and across his shoulders. Despite his age, he was far from frail and his frame was significant. Caslin suddenly felt a surge of fear, borne from a realisation that he might not be able to manage. Brushing the feeling aside, he made for the door, almost stumbling at two points under the weight of his load. The polystyrene roof tiles of the suspended ceiling were falling all around them, some on fire, others raining down droplets of molten plastic. The flames were in the cavity and spreading with frightening speed. Caslin staggered towards the door, knowing they would have to pass through the fire itself. He did so at pace.

Reaching the sanctuary of the corridor beyond, he found it too was now filled with black smoke. Above him, the heat from the ceiling told him they were in serious trouble. Breathing heavily, he set off for the entrance but he could no longer see the streetlights beyond, such was the ferocity of the flame and the smoke. Every breath stung within his lungs and seemed to offer less air. Every step became more laboured and Caslin felt his panic rising. Trying to keep low, away from the smoke, proved to be impossible with his charge across his shoulders and Caslin stumbled. Both men crashed to the floor.

Knowing that to remain where they were, even for a few seconds, could be the difference between life and death, Caslin rolled back onto his front and pulled himself up onto his knees. Visibility was now such that he couldn't see his hand in front of his face. Scrabbling around in the dark, he located the unconscious man's upper body and looped his own arms under the armpits, interlocking his hands across the chest. Having completely lost his bearings, Caslin felt the heat from the fire was more intense before him. Therefore, he set off down the corridor in the opposite direction, confident that was the way out.

His eyes were stinging and water was running from them along with the sweat. Trying to hold his breath, fearful of the toxic cloud surrounding him, Caslin found the going tough. He knew the distance to safety, once in the corridor, was less than forty feet from the source of the fire but it seemed an interminable distance now. Why weren't they safe already? The thought flashed through his mind that he'd taken the wrong decision and was now leading them into the building and not out of it. Panic threatened to consume him but he kept going.

With each step his charge felt heavier as did his own body. Each movement was slower. From nowhere, he felt a surge of pressure come at them. Before he knew it, Caslin found himself flat on his back with a rush of colour passing over him in stark contrast to the black that'd encompassed them thus far. Darkness followed and Caslin lay there. The polished concrete floor was solid beneath him, unforgiving and yet comfortable. The will to move was lost on him as was any sense of urgency. Caslin closed his eyes only to sense movement alongside, bringing him back to reality. A small, dancing, white light flashed before him. Suddenly, he felt something take a firm hold of him and he was moving again. This time, he was being dragged along the corridor only at a far greater speed. Caslin could see movement around him but no detail, just a vague notion that he was no longer alone.

Within moments they were outside. Caslin coughed. A violent, hacking cough that racked his entire body. A hand placed a mask over his mouth and nose, the oxygen that flowed into his lungs from it was a relief. Rolling his head to the side, against the protestations of his medic, Caslin scanned the scene for the man he'd left behind only to see him being lifted onto a gurney with paramedics and firefighting personnel in attendance. Only then, could Caslin relax. As his senses stabilised, Caslin took note of the two appliances dispatched to tackle the blaze along with several ambulances. Police were also in attendance, cordoning off the area and assisting the firefighters in doing their job.

"Sir, is there anybody else left in the building?" a voice asked. Caslin looked over to see the station officer standing alongside, identifiable by his white helmet.

"I'm sorry. I've no idea," he replied honestly, removing his mask. The man left without another word and Caslin could hear him handing out instructions to his assembled team. There was no sign of the woman he had encountered outside the mosque when he'd first arrived. He assumed she was being taken care of. Now feeling no ill effects from the alcohol he'd consumed, the surge of adrenalin having successfully countered it, Caslin considered the fire. Tapping the forearm of the paramedic who was in the process of wrapping a blanket around him, to fend off the cold and any potential advance of shock, he sought the attention of the station officer. The paramedic brought the officer back. Caslin, feeling in better control of his faculties, sat up but kept the oxygen mask close to him. He spoke between deep draws.

"I'm not sure what happened but from the look of the room, where the fire started, I'd say there was an accelerant in play."

"How are you so sure?"

"The intensity of the blaze where it originated. It was too fast. There were no appliances, open fires or anything like that that would justify such a fire to start there," Caslin explained. "The window to the adjacent street was also smashed."

"Thanks, I'll tell the investigator as soon as he arrives," the officer said.

"The man. The one I tried to pull out."

"The Imam? It looks like he suffered a heart attack," the officer told him. "His wife was with him and claims something was thrown through the window at them. It all started from there. Probably the window you were talking about. By the sounds of it, the police will have another investigation on their hands."

"Like I'm not busy enough," Caslin said. Then it must've dawned on the officer that Caslin was a policeman. "Something knocked me over, before your team pulled me out."

"We think there was a flashover. It's a bit early to say but possibly that was caused by the fire reaching the kitchens."

"Right," Caslin said quietly. The officer nodded to him and excused himself. Caslin took another draw on the oxygen.

"We're going to take you to hospital and assess how much smoke you've inhaled, okay?" the paramedic told him. Caslin acknowledged him but offered no further comment as he watched the hoses of the brigade appliances being trained on the building. The fire had spread rapidly. If anyone else was inside, chances are it was already too late for them.

CHAPTER FOURTEEN

CASLIN CLIMBED out of the passenger seat onto the pavement on High Petergate, a stone's throw from York Minster. Handing the taxi-driver a ten pound note, he didn't wait for the change and set off for home. His apartment, located in the historic Shambles, was a mere two-minute walk away nestled amongst the artisan shops and cobbled streets.

During the day, the ability to negotiate the crowds at any time of the year was essential. However, nothing moved at this hour. Satisfied he'd suffered no major damage from his earlier exploits that evening, the medical staff discharged him. A chest that tightened each time he drew breath along with the occasionally hacking up of phlegm, the colour of coal dust, was considered normal under the circumstances. Discomforting, certainly but unworthy of an extended stay. A conclusion Caslin was more than happy with. He'd had enough of stays in hospital to last him for quite some time.

Rounding the corner onto Stonegate, he was a few steps from home. Glancing at his watch, it was a little before three in the morning and it felt like it. He unlocked the communal access door, entered the passageway and trotted up the steps to his apartment. The exertion brought on yet another coughing fit and he had to brace himself against the wall of the stairwell. Entering his apartment, he didn't bother to flick on the lights. Instead, he walked into his living room, illuminated with an orange glow by the lights hanging from the buildings in the street outside. He chose not to draw the curtains and ignored the fleeting notion to pour himself a scotch, instead, sinking into his armchair and resting his head. Any feeling that he'd had a drink earlier in the day had long since left him. The only urge he had left to fulfil was that of sleep. Closing his eyes, Caslin sought to clear his mind of the jumbled thoughts gnawing away at him.

The Kuznetsov case had more to it, his instinct told him so. More pressing though, was the spark of racial hatred threatening to set light to the city. His fear was such that the attack on the mosque was but the beginning and although on this occasion, no one had died, any further escalation could well change matters. Fortunately, it transpired no one else was in the building when the fire was lit and the Imam was now in a stable condition, at least, when Caslin had left the hospital. Had he not been passing, Caslin was well aware they'd have another murder case on their hands rather than an arsonist to chase down.

CASLIN AWOKE WITH A START. It took a moment to get his bearings. Still dark outside, he glanced at the clock on the wall. It was nearly four in the morning. He must've dozed off in the chair. There was a forceful knock on the door to his apartment. Figuring that was what had woken him, he dragged himself upright, ignoring the pain that screamed at him as a result of stiffened muscles. Crossing to the front windows overlooking the street, he cast a wary eye down onto Stonegate. Everything was still, without any movement in sight. There was another knock. Whoever was seeking his attention had already bypassed the security door to the communal entrance or had he left it open? He couldn't remember. Whoever was so keen to see him would, in all likelihood, wake his landlady in the next apartment if they didn't rein it in.

Making his way into the hallway, he approached the door and peered through the spy hole. Two men stood on the landing, one in front of the door while the other waited a few steps to the rear, facing down the stairwell. He didn't know them, of that he was sure but the first appeared somewhat familiar. Unhooking the latch, Caslin opened the door. The man standing before him was probably in his late fifties, smartly dressed in a well-tailored over-coat. His facial appearance was well manicured, clean-shaven and bearing frameless glasses. He smiled warmly, in greeting.

"Inspector Caslin, I believe?" he said in a tone matching his smile. Caslin bobbed his head in acknowledgement.

"You do know what time it is, don't you?"

"I apologise, Inspector. I'm still on Washington time," he said sincerely. Caslin did a quick calculation in his head.

"Still makes it late," he said, wondering whether he was right.

"Indeed, but some things just cannot wait," he agreed. "My name is Walsh, Cory Walsh. May I come inside?" he asked, removing his gloves and offering Caslin his hand. Caslin took it and inclined his head to invite him inside.

Caslin glanced beyond him as he stepped aside, allowing his visitor room to enter, towards the other man standing patiently in the background. As if aware of the attention, he glanced in Caslin's direction but only for a fleeting moment. He was younger, focussed. Caslin had seen the likes of him before, most likely ex-military, now working in the private sector. Walsh turned to see Caslin checking out his associate.

"My friend will wait outside, Inspector Caslin. We are quite sure I am safe with you."

"Any reason you wouldn't be safe anywhere else?" Caslin asked, pushing the door to and directing his guest into the living room.

"One can never be too careful," Walsh replied, eyeing the surroundings as he entered the room. Caslin followed, flicking on the nearest light. The lamp caused him to blink with it being far brighter than the light permeating the apartment from the street outside. Caslin offered a seat with an open hand, leaning his back against the wall and folding his arms before him.

"What brings you to my door in the middle of the night, Mr Walsh?"

"Forgive the clandestine approach, Mr Caslin. I know it appears a little cloak and dagger but I do have my reasons," Walsh said, putting his gloves together and placing them neatly on the dining table alongside him. "I saw you the other day at the demonstration on Walmgate. The one that got out of hand. You saw me too, didn't you?"

"I did," Caslin recalled. Walsh had been the passenger in the Maybach. He hadn't gotten around to following up on the licence plate. Presumably now, he no longer had the need. "Why were you there, Mr Walsh?"

"Please, you can call me Cory," Walsh replied.

Caslin shrugged. "If you like."

"I was in the city for a meeting. A rallying call so to speak. That's what I do these days, since I retired from my business activities."

"What kind of business did you do, Mr Walsh?"

"Investments, brokerage. I ran my own firm, quite successfully I should add, for several decades."

"Financial securities?"

Walsh nodded.

"And now?"

"I'm a lobbyist, you could say," Walsh said, with a smile. To Caslin, he carried the confidence and assuredness of a successful man but also managed a quiet affability that made him come across as an instantly likeable figure. Which Caslin felt was odd, for he rarely liked anyone on their first meeting. "My work takes me all over the developed world. Sometimes I lose track of exactly where I am."

"And ensures you keep odd hours."

"Quite true, Nathaniel," Walsh said grinning. "Do you mind if I call you, Nathaniel?"

Caslin shrugged to indicate he didn't mind, "What is it I can do for you?"

"Am I to understand you are leading an investigation into the murder that occurred the other day. The one at the flat, Farzaad... I'm sorry, his name escapes me."

"Farzaad Amin," Caslin offered. It wasn't being withheld and had been splashed across the media over the previous few days. "What of it? Did you know him?"

Walsh shook his head, "No, I'd never met the man. However," he said, shaking an index finger pointedly, "I am led to believe that you are following this up as a racially-motivated crime. Would this be correct?"

Caslin grimaced, exaggerating his expression, "I'm sorry. There's no way I can discuss an ongoing case with a civilian. I'm sure you understand. A couple of questions of my own spring to mind, though. How do you know that, hypothetically speaking and... why do you care enough to come to my door in the middle of the night? I have to tell you, *pretty creepy*, if you weren't such a well-mannered guy."

Walsh smiled, "Let me just say, I move in influential circles. Sometimes, I come across information that's not widely disseminated."

"That doesn't make me feel any more comfortable, I have to say," Caslin offered. "So, why are you here?"

"I think you're approaching this from the wrong angle," Walsh said, fixing his gaze on Caslin.

"Is that so? Tell me why?" Caslin asked, intrigued. Walsh smiled. Reaching into an inner pocket of his overcoat, he retrieved a small notebook and pen. Placing the book on the table, he opened it up to a blank page and scribbled something. Tearing the page out and folding it in half, he returned both notebook and pen to the confines of his coat and stood up. Picking the paper up from the dining table, he crossed the room to stand before Caslin.

Holding out the slip of paper, Caslin reached over and took a hold but Walsh didn't release his own grip. Caslin met his eye.

"If I were to tell you what I think I know, Inspector. You would probably have me sectioned," he said, releasing his hold on the paper. Caslin took it but kept his gaze on the man standing over him. "I often find it better for someone to choose their own path with which to reach their destination. That way, the journey is far more rewarding. Perhaps then, we can speak again. Please don't get up. I'll see myself out."

Caslin broke eye contact as Walsh left the living room, turning his attention to the piece of paper. He casually opened it as the sound of the latch to his front door, clicking into place, came to his ear.

There was a name written upon the paper, alongside a mobile phone number. The name was Alexander Nairn. Placing the paper on the side table next to him, Caslin stood and crossed the room. Coming to stand before one of the windows overlooking the street, he glanced down as Walsh and his minder exited Kleiser's Court and set off along Stonegate. He watched them until they disappeared from view a few seconds later.

There was something about that name that chimed in Caslin's memory but for the life of him, he couldn't remember why. Absolutely certain that he had never met the man nor come across him in an inquiry, Caslin left the window and returning to his seat, scooping up his phone. Accessing the internet, he typed in the name and hit return. Within moments a list of web links came up and then he realised. Alexander Nairn had been killed the previous year in York.

Caslin vaguely remembered the incident but knew it was covered by colleagues based out of the Acomb Road Station. Refreshing his memory with detail from a local newspaper, Caslin read how the property financier had committed suicide by throwing himself in front of a train. It had been broad daylight on a hot summer's day, witnessed by dozens of commuters. Nairn had died instantly. Scanning through several entries on the returned list, Caslin was none the wiser as to how the unequivocal suicide fitted into this case. Blowing out his cheeks, he brought his palms up to his face and rubbed at his eyes with the heel of his palms. Suddenly, he felt tired.

Scrolling through his contacts on his phone, Caslin reached the CID telephone number for the Acomb Road Police Station. He waited patiently for the call to be answered. It wasn't long.

"CID," an abrupt voice answered.

"DI Caslin, Fulford Road," he said.

"Hello, sir. It's Mark Sampson. Trouble sleeping? What can I do for you?"

"Hi Mark. I know it's going back a bit but do you recollect the Nairn suicide from last year? The guy threw himself—"

"In front of a train," Detective Sergeant Sampson finished for him. "Aye, I do. What of it?"

"Who was the investigating officer?"

"Oh… you've got me there. I'd have to look it up. Why do you ask… at four-thirty in the morning?"

Caslin laughed, "You know me, Mark. I couldn't sleep. Any chance you could fish out the file for me? I'll be over to yours first thing to have a look."

"Yes, of course. It's been a quiet one tonight. Only the little matter of the fire-bombing over your way that's put everyone on edge. It's mental. Did you hear about that?"

"Yeah, yeah, I heard something about it," Caslin said.

"Leave it with me and I'll dig out what I can. I'm not sure how much there will be, though. It was a pretty clean suicide, investigation wise anyway."

"Thanks, Mark. I'll see you," Caslin said, hanging up.

Rising from his seat, Caslin tossed his phone aside and headed into the bedroom. Not bothering to get undressed, he sank onto the bed and closed his eyes. However, sleep would not come.

THE SOUND of the car horn caught his attention. Checking for a break in the traffic, Caslin trotted between two cars and crossed to the other side of the road. Hunter leant across and opened the passenger door for him. Caslin levered it further open with his foot and slid into the seat. Passing Hunter, one of the coffees he had just purchased while waiting for her, he placed his own precariously onto the dashboard as he attached his seatbelt.

"How are you, after last night?" Hunter said.

"I'll be grand, don't worry," he replied, retrieving his coffee cup before Hunter pulled back out into the commuter traffic. The car behind flashed their lights, Caslin caught a glimpse in the side mirror unsure of whether it was an act of aggression or not. Hunter didn't comment so nor did he. Hunter negotiated the traffic of the ring road like a professional. A professional racing driver anyway. She never used to drive in such a manner, always being measured and methodical. Much like her approach to life in general.

"So, are you going to tell me why we're heading to Acomb Road?" she asked, tapping her steering wheel and sounding the horn to encourage a car in front to edge forward and allow her to take the next left turn. The car did so and she accelerated through the gap, the nearside front tyre sliding along the kerb.

"The station isn't going anywhere you know?" Caslin said. Hunter flicked a glance in his direction but said nothing. "Do you remember a suicide from last year? A guy killed himself by jumping in front of a train?"

"Vaguely," Hunter said. "What of it?"

"That's exactly what I intend for us to find out," Caslin replied, looking over at her. He considered taking the lid off his coffee cup, preferring not to drink through the slot but, as Hunter took another turn and he braced one arm against the door to steady himself, he thought better of it.

They pulled into the car park of the station ten minutes later. Far smaller than Fulford Road, largely due to the size of the area they policed, the officers based at Acomb Road were responsible for covering the western side of the city. Getting out of the car, Caslin finished what remained of his coffee while Hunter brought hers inside with them. They signed in at the front desk and were buzzed through into the back offices. They had both been here many times, Hunter in particular was greeted warmly by every face they came across. Having been stationed there in her first role within CID, as a detective constable, six years previously, she was a popular member of the team and most hadn't seen her since her enforced absence from the job.

On the way up the stairs they came across DS Sampson on the half-landing, presumably on his way home following the night shift.

"Sir," he said, shaking Caslin's hand. Hunter got a quick embrace bringing a big smile to her face. "It was DC Watkins who investigated your man, Nairn. He's upstairs," Sampson said, indicating over his shoulder, "I told him you were coming."

"Thanks, Mark," Caslin said. "Did you take a look yourself?"

"I did, aye," he replied. "I didn't see anything odd about it, though. Why, what's your interest?"

"Only a passing one," Caslin replied. Sampson acknowledged him, offered Hunter a wink and set off downstairs.

They resumed their course up to CID, entering the compact squad room moments later. DC Watkins noted their arrival and came over to greet them. He shook their hands in turn. Caslin hadn't come across the young man before. He guessed he was new to the team seeing as Hunter appeared to have no connection with him either.

"Tell me about Alexander Nairn," Caslin asked, as he was passed the case file and opened it to examine the contents.

"Relatively straightforward, sir," Watkins began. "A property financier, cum-developer. Left his office one afternoon and made his way to the railway line, clambered over a security fence and stepped in front of the next passing train."

"Witnesses?" Caslin asked, without looking up from the file.

"At least seven, sir," Watkins said. "Two people reported

seeing him standing behind the fence before scaling it to gain access to the line. The others watched as he casually walked onto the line as the train approached."

"Was there anyone nearby that he was communicating with or perhaps talking to on the phone?" Hunter asked.

Watkins shook his head, "No. He was alone on the track. Witnesses reported he appeared very calm. He was a well-dressed businessman who looked out of place there but no one saw a cause for alarm until the approach of the train."

"Were you able to ascertain his state of mind? Any history of mental illness, anxiety?" Caslin said, glancing up.

Again, Watkins shrugged in the negative, "Not at all. His colleagues stated he appeared quite normal. He had a stressful job but nothing that appeared to overburden him. I must say, his wife was shocked but, speaking with her later, she seemed to piece past behaviours together. Ultimately, she wasn't surprised by what he did."

"The coroner ruled it as a suicide," Caslin said, scanning the transcript of the coroner's summation.

"Yes. We couldn't see it any other way."

"And there was nothing unusual. Nothing that struck you as odd or out of place?" Caslin asked.

Watkins shook his head, "Not at all. It was my first case but, even refreshing it in my mind this morning I don't see I would have done anything differently. It was a slam dunk."

"Appears so," Caslin replied.

"Sir?" Watkins enquired. Caslin looked to him, raising his eyebrows. "Can I ask why you want to know? Did I miss something?" he asked, looking and sounding nervous. Caslin shook his head.

"Not as far as I'm aware. It looks pretty concrete," he reassured him and watched as a weight appeared to lift from the young man's shoulders.

"So, why are you looking into it?"

"I'm not. Not really," Caslin replied with a half-smile. "Nairn's name has come up in an unrelated matter and we have to follow it up. That's all. Can we borrow this?" he asked, indicating the file he held in his hands.

"You'll have to sign for it," Watkins replied before realising he was stating the obvious.

"Of course," Caslin replied. Watkins turned to find a pen and Caslin passed the file to Hunter. She looked him in the eye with an inquisitive gaze. She knew there was something here but had no idea what Caslin was looking for. She leafed through the paperwork while Caslin signed the appropriate documentation. "There you go," Caslin said, handing the sheet back to the detective constable.

"You'll let me know if I can help, won't you?" Watkins asked. Caslin nodded. "Or, if you come across anything… you know, that…?"

"We will, son. We will," Caslin said, clapping him on the upper arm. With that said, they bid farewell and left CID. Hunter tucked the file under her arm as they descended the stairs back to the ground floor.

"What's going on, sir?" she asked quietly, once she was confident they'd not be overheard.

"There's one thing missing from that file," Caslin said, lowering his own voice as they made their way along the corridor towards the front desk.

"What's that?"

"A reason."

"C'mon, sir. There isn't always a reason someone does this."

"True," he agreed. "But young Watkins up there didn't have much cause to look for one."

"And we do?" Hunter pressed, as they walked through the security door into the lobby and out into the car park.

"Oh, yes," Caslin replied in an upbeat tone. "We most certainly do."

"What are we going to do with it?"

"Let's start with his colleagues."

CHAPTER FIFTEEN

CASLIN FELT his phone vibrating within his coat pocket. Closing Nairn's case file in his lap, he took out the phone and briefly looked at the screen before putting it away without answering. Hunter glanced at him, her expression conveying an unasked question.

"Matheson," Caslin said.

"Do I take it she has no idea where we are?" Hunter asked, turning off the engine and withdrawing the key. Caslin shook his head.

"She'd only worry," he replied, smiling. Opening his door, he got out. Hunter did likewise. Caslin glanced around. Their destination was a modest two-storey office building, nestled in between several similar, making up a small commercial development just beyond the city limits. Caslin judged they were close enough to take advantage of the public transport system but equally well positioned to exploit the road links in and out of York. The site was modern and not short of tenants for the office space.

They made their way to the entrance, Caslin noting the names attached to the allocated parking spaces set out in front. Two regular discolourations in the brickwork indicated plaques had been removed fairly recently, from spaces adjacent to one another. Hunter reached the door first, opening it and indicating for Caslin to go ahead. Walking through, Caslin observed the interior. There were four desks. Two were clearly unoccupied, judging by their level of tidiness, with a third that had several piles of paperwork strewn across it in an apparently haphazard manner. They were welcomed with a warm smile from the only person present, a lady, seated behind the remaining desk. She rose and came around to greet them.

"Good morning," she said. "My name is Lisa. How can I help you?"

"Good morning. We're looking to speak with Thomas Grey," Caslin said, eyeing her. She was in her forties, power dressed and approached with a confidence that Caslin found momentarily unsettling. He didn't know why, seeing as he had never held any issue with women as authority figures. Grey was Alexander Nairn's business partner, named in the file that Caslin had been reading through on their journey back into the city from Acomb Road.

"I'm afraid Mr Grey's schedule is already full today. Would you like to make an appointment?"

Caslin brandished his warrant card, "We don't need one." Lisa eyed his credentials, glancing in Hunter's direction who smiled in return.

"Oh, I see. May I ask what it is regarding?"

"Certainly. It's regarding the death of one of your colleagues, Alexander Nairn." She tensed at the mention of the name, almost imperceptibly, but her professional persona slipped for the briefest of moments. Caslin picked it up nonetheless.

"Please bear with me, if you wouldn't mind?" she said, taking a step back before turning and walking the short distance to her desk. Picking up the phone, she dialled an extension. The call was answered quickly and she turned her back on them, speaking at an almost inaudible level. Hanging up, Lisa turned to face them. The mask of business-like demeanour had returned.

"He'll be with you shortly. Please take a seat, if you wish," she said, indicating an L-shape sofa arrangement in the corner behind them. Both of them chose to remain standing. Lisa returned to sit behind her desk while Caslin scanned the walls of the office.

There was a list of companies framed on the wall. Seemingly, this office housed the business activities of several others who were also registered at the same address. Elsewhere, there were copies of articles from professional publications citing awards attained by the company as well as photographs taken of successful developments, both at home and abroad. Caslin found his attention drawn to a commercial high-rise building in a skyline, he thought looked vaguely familiar.

"Where is this?" he asked Lisa who in turn, glanced up from her desk and looked over at the picture.

"Singapore."

"Oh," Caslin said, realising he was mistaken. "Do a lot of business there?"

"Not as much as we used to."

"Any particular reason for that?" No answer was forthcoming, though, as a door opened further along the only corridor into the building and a figure emerged. He almost glided down the corridor towards them. Caslin could tell he was eyeing them up as he approached. Acknowledging them with a nod, Caslin spotted an earpiece.

"Mr Grey will see you now," Lisa said.

The man sent to accompany them stepped aside, allowing Hunter and Caslin to go ahead with the gesture of an open palm. He fell into step behind them, keeping a respectful distance until they reached Grey's office. Their escort came past and opened it, indicating for them to enter. They were greeted by a suited man, in his fifties, who eagerly came across the office to shake their hands. He was stocky in frame, balding, with a well-lined face and tanned complexion. Evidently, he wintered in sunnier climes.

"Thomas Grey," he said, taking Caslin's hand.

"DI Caslin and DS Hunter, from Fulford Road CID," Caslin said.

"This is about Alex's suicide, I understand?"

"Of sorts."

"Please, sit down," Grey said, offering them a chair as he went to sit down behind his desk. "Would you like a coffee or something?"

"No, thank you," Caslin said, pulling out a chair and sitting down, Hunter alongside him. Glancing over his shoulder, Caslin saw Grey's minder, for he had no doubt that was what he was, take a position behind them to his left. He stood with his back to the wall, arms crossed behind his back but remained attentive.

"How then, may I help? I understood the inquest was closed last year," Grey asked, sitting forward, elbows on his desk.

"It was," Caslin began. "We're following up on another angle that has subsequently come to the fore. What can you tell us about Mr Nairn's state of mind at the time of his death? Why would he have taken the decision that he did that day?"

Grey blew out his cheeks, sitting back in his chair, "Hard to say, if I'm honest. I wasn't around much at the time as I'd been working away, on site."

"You deal in property?" Caslin asked.

Grey nodded. "It's a little more complicated than that. Acquisitions, developments, off-plan trading and the like."

"I see. Where is your largest market, would you say?"

"We are global, as are our investors," Grey announced, "and it's a globalised economy, no matter what some people may seem to think these days."

"So, were you aware of any difficulties that Mr Nairn was experiencing, financial, domestic or otherwise?"

"I thought this had all been covered?" Grey replied.

"Humour me," Caslin countered.

"Nothing specific." Grey shrugged. "But he was always someone who felt the pressure. They say divorce and buying a house are the most stressful things you can ever experience and he did the former. The latter, well, that's what we do, magnified by a factor of a hundred."

"Seems an odd profession to take up, in that case," Caslin said.

"I don't think either of us ever planned it, back in the day but we worked hard and you get out what you put in, don't you?"

"You knew him well?" Hunter asked. "I mean, you go back a long way?"

"Absolutely. We met in our twenties, got on well and it snowballed from there."

"Mr Nairn didn't have any business worries other than the general stress you mentioned?" Caslin asked.

Again, Grey shook his head, "No. Business has never been better. Susan, his ex, wasn't surprised about his suicide, though. She said he'd been struggling for a while but I didn't have a clue. I was just too busy to notice, I guess. To be honest, I really miss him both as a friend and as a business partner. It's been a tough six months. Why are you investigating Alex again?" Grey asked, sitting forward once more.

"We're not," Caslin said. "His name came up in an unrelated matter and we're following up."

"What matter?" Grey pressed, meeting Caslin's eye.

"We'll leave it there for now, Mr Grey," Caslin said, standing.

"Oh, really," Grey said, sounding surprised which piqued Caslin's interest.

"We're not sure how Mr Nairn fits into it but don't worry, we'll get to the bottom of it soon enough," Caslin said, smiling and trying to convey a determined attitude. Hunter cast him a fleeting glance but said nothing.

Grey took a deep breath, "Right you are. Well, if there is anything else you need, please get in touch and I'll see what I can do."

"Thank you for your time," Caslin said, offering his hand. Grey took it, shaking vigorously. Hunter smiled and inclined her head as she stood and the two of them made for the door. The minder opened it and they passed through, into the corridor. They were left to make their own way out.

Reaching the reception, Caslin stopped at Lisa's desk. She was just finishing a call and hung up as Caslin spoke.

"Lisa, can I ask you a couple of questions?" he asked. She nodded. "Did you know Mr Nairn well?"

"Yes, he was a wonderful man and a great boss. It was such a shame what happened."

"Were you here that day?" Hunter asked.

"Oh, yes. The office was full. We were much busier back then."

"Busier than now?" Hunter asked.

"Very much so," Lisa said, lowering her voice and nervously glancing behind her, back down the corridor. "There used to be four of us out here but now it's only me."

"They keep you busy?"

"Not recently," she replied.

"What can you tell us about that day, when Mr Nairn took his life?" Caslin asked.

"It started much as any other," Lisa began, "with a scheduled progress meeting between Mr Nairn and Mr Grey but it went a little sour."

"Mr Grey was also here that day? I mean, he wasn't away?"

"Yes, of course he was here. They only ever went away together. We used to call them the Krays. You know, after Ronnie and Reggie? They were like inseparable twins. Not that they are gangsters or anything," Lisa quickly stated. Caslin indicated for her to continue. "Part way through the meeting some men arrived, wanting to speak with both Mr Grey and Mr Nairn. It got a little nasty."

"Who were they?" Hunter asked.

She shook her head. "I don't know. Mr Grey said they were investors but I'd never met them before, but... they weren't the usual type of clients that we see here in the office."

"How so?" Caslin asked, intrigued.

"They were... I don't know how to put it. A little bit on the rough side. I mean, don't get me wrong, they had money, that was clear but they were... intimidating. I've never seen Mr Grey as animated as he was that day."

"What can you tell us about them?" Hunter asked.

"Not much, really. Foreign."

"Foreign?" Caslin noted. "Where from?"

"I don't know but they spoke English with an accent. Eastern Europeans, I would say."

"What was the issue?"

"They wanted payment. Apparently, they felt they were owed money and it was late in coming. There was a lot of shouting before they eventually left. I never found out the full details. I've no idea which development they were involved in, mind you. Mr Grey dealt with it personally. It was all very strange, though."

"What was?" Hunter asked.

Again, Lisa looked over her shoulder as if fearful of being overheard before leaning closer towards them, "Mr Nairn had expensive tastes. To be fair, they both share a love of material things but Mr Nairn kept an antique watch collection here, in the safe, in his office. He handed it over to those men before they left."

Caslin glanced at Hunter who met his eye and flicked her eyebrows as if to signal she was equally intrigued, "Tell me, what did Mr Grey's security do while all this was going down?"

"He didn't have them then. They appeared shortly after this incident. He always has one with him in the office and never goes anywhere without the others."

"Shortly after Mr Nairn committed suicide?"

"Yes," Lisa said, her brow furrowing as she spoke. "He'd never mentioned the need for any security up until that day."

"What happened after they left, the investors?" Caslin said.

"Mr Nairn came out of his office. He was pale... visibly shaken up. Frightened, even."

"And then?" Caslin asked.

Lisa shrugged, "He left the office without another word. That was the last time I saw him. Mr Grey told us the next day that he had been found on the railway line."

"Had you noticed any change in Mr Nairn in the period running up to his suicide?" Hunter asked.

"He was worried… preoccupied," Lisa replied. "Particularly, so soon after his friend's passing."

"His friend?"

"Martin Pocock," Lisa said. "He was a lawyer friend of both Mr Grey and Mr Nairn but I believe he was closer to Mr Nairn. He was a lovely man."

"And he died?"

"Yes, it shook them both up. The week before Mr Nairn's death, his helicopter crashed on its approach to Burleigh Park, on the weekend of the Horse Trials."

"How awful," Hunter said. "What did Mr Nairn say about it?"

"Nothing directly. He was clearly upset and had me cancel an order for his own helicopter the following day."

"He was buying one?"

Lisa nodded, "Yes. The exact same model."

"Did you give a statement about any of this to the police?" Caslin asked.

"No, I wasn't asked to," she replied. "Why, should I have? Is something wrong?"

Caslin shook his head, "No, no. We're just following up on a separate matter, don't worry. Here, take this," he said, passing her one of his contact cards from within his wallet, "and if you think of anything else, please give me a call. No matter how insignificant you think it might be. Okay?"

They excused themselves and left the building. Neither spoke until they were in the confines of Hunter's car. She started the engine.

"What do you make of all that?" she asked, looking over to him. Caslin thought about it for a moment before responding.

"I reckon there's far more to Mr Grey than he is willing to share with us. If business is booming why has he shed employees?

Plus, how many property developers have you ever come across who feel the need for a personal protection team?"

"None. Makes you wonder where his investors come from?" Hunter said. "And the others, Nairn and Pocock? The former was a definite suicide."

"Without a doubt," Caslin agreed. "Too many witnesses. What drove him to it, though, is still very much open for debate. When we get back to Fulford Road get a run down on Pocock and try to find out what brought the helicopter down. It could just be an unfortunate coincidence but you know how I feel about them. Likewise, let's take a closer look at Thomas Grey. Do me a favour," he said, glancing over his shoulder behind them, "and pull up around the corner, would you?"

"Sure. Why?" Hunter asked, engaging the car in gear and reversing out of their parking space.

"Just a hunch," he replied. Hunter set off as if they were leaving the car park only to turn in and pull up outside the building across from Grey's office. They were close enough to keep the entrance in view but far enough away to be confident they wouldn't be noticed. Caslin sat back in his seat and sought to get comfortable.

"Where are we going with all of this?" Hunter asked, putting her head against the rest behind her. Caslin sighed. He knew he didn't have a proper answer, not yet anyway.

"We've been steered in this direction for a reason," he said. "Although at this point, the reasoning escapes me."

"Who's pointing the finger?" Hunter asked but Caslin didn't reply, choosing to keep it to himself. At least for the time being.

They didn't have long to wait. The door to Grey's business opened and out stepped the man himself, mobile phone pressed to his ear with his bodyguard one step behind. He was clearly agitated and saying something that Caslin couldn't make out from such a distance. He was certainly unhappy.

Grey reached his vehicle, a black Land Rover Discovery and unlocked it. Turning to his minder, with his back to Caslin and

Hunter, he gesticulated with a raised hand, appearing dismissive. Whatever was said, he ended the call, tossed the phone into the car and climbed into the driver's seat slamming the door shut behind him. The bodyguard stood on the path alongside the car and watched as the Discovery was fired into life. The reversing lights came on and the vehicle moved.

"Right. This is us," Caslin said and Hunter sat upright, turning the key in the ignition. The car started and Hunter waited until Grey had reached the main road and was making the turn out, heading west. Only then did she engage first gear and set off to follow.

"Where do you think he's going?" Hunter asked.

"I don't know but he's rattled," Caslin said as Hunter slid into the line of traffic. They were four car lengths behind and heading towards the city centre.

Approaching the medieval walls, traffic slowed to such an extent that they would have no problem keeping up with him unless they got stuck at one of the traffic lights. Grey remained on the circular road, navigating around the city rather than entering the centre itself. "Oh, how much would I give to know what he's thinking right now?" Caslin said aloud.

Following the road, they crossed the Ouse, via Skeldergate Bridge, in sight of Clifford's Tower and watched as Grey took the next right followed by an immediate left onto Cromwell Road. Here, he pulled the car into a row of empty parking bays in the shadow of an established line of Beech trees. Hunter continued on up the hill and only pulled in herself once they were a relatively safe distance ahead, so as not to be observed. Caslin shifted in his seat, looking back down the road at the Discovery. Grey remained inside and Caslin thought he was making another phone call.

"Keep it running," Caslin said quietly. Hunter was watching proceedings in the rear-view mirror.

"Do you think he's waiting for someone?" she asked. Caslin didn't respond. He was curious and couldn't help but think they were onto something. His only wish was to know what. A few minutes passed and Grey put his phone away, resting both hands on the steering wheel. Staring straight ahead, he couldn't seem to keep his hands still for more than a few moments.

Soon after, another car came down the hill, passing them and slowing as it approached Grey's, before pulling in, in front of it. It was a silver Mercedes with tinted privacy-glass so they were unable to ascertain who or how many people were inside. Hunter noted down the registration number and picked up her radio, requesting the control room carry out a check on the vehicle with the national database. Having read out the index plate, she put the radio down and waited.

The daytime running lights switched off as Grey stepped out from his car and approached the Mercedes. A man opened the door to the front passenger seat and climbed out. He was heavily built, with a shaved head. He glanced around, surveying the immediate area before opening the rear door. Grey waited on the path, looking nervous, shifting his weight from one foot to the other and looking around furtively. A woman got out of the Mercedes. She cut a stylish figure, white-blonde hair, cut in a bob and sporting a cashmere overcoat, carrying past the knee.

Caslin knew her. The trademark oversized, cat-eye sunglasses were present, as was the pale, ivory skin of her complexion. Hunter's radio crackled as the results of the PNC check came back on the Mercedes. She picked up the unit only to pause as she registered what she was seeing.

"Well, I'll be damned," Caslin muttered, under his breath.

"What the hell is she doing here?" Hunter added, equally surprised.

"I have no idea but I'm going to enjoy finding out," Caslin replied as he watched Thomas Grey shake hands with Danika Durakovic.

CHAPTER SIXTEEN

THEY WATCHED as the conversation between Durakovic and Thomas Grey continued for several minutes. Grey became increasingly flustered as he drove home whatever point he was making. For her part, Danika remained calm with an impassive expression that Caslin knew only too well. From experience, he found it virtually impossible to interpret. Danika shook her head at several of the points Grey was conveying. This only seemed to further agitate him. Then it was Grey's turn to listen and despite several attempts to interrupt her, he did so with a pained expression on his face.

By now, Hunter had taken her camera from its case, tucked behind the driver's seat and was busy taking shots of the impromptu exchange.

"What do you think they're talking about?" she asked, just as Grey raised his hands, dramatically emphasising his point.

"When we get back to Fulford let's run a search through the Companies House Portal and see if any of Grey's business interests tie in with Danika's. I very much doubt these two were old school friends."

"Grey's name has never come up in relation to Durakovic before?" Hunter asked.

Caslin shook his head. "Not that I recall. The only property interests I remember she's involved in were multiple small to medium-sized enterprises that she uses to wash her money," he said, thinking about it while Hunter snapped away. Grey stood, crestfallen, as Danika turned away from him, sliding into the backseat of the Mercedes and the door was closed for her. He shook his head slowly, turning his face skywards.

"Sounds like he didn't get the response he was looking for," Hunter offered, taking a last photo of the encounter.

"It doesn't, does it?" Caslin replied. Grey watched the car pull out and set off in the direction that they themselves had come from. Rubbing his face with a palm, Grey's appearance was drained of the brash confidence that he'd exuded back in his office. The moment passed and anger flared within the businessman. Stalking back to the Discovery, he got in and slammed the door shut. Sparking the engine into life, the wheels squealed as he set off at speed. Pulling a U-turn in the road despite an oncoming vehicle, whose driver sounded his displeasure, Grey accelerated away in the direction of his office. Caslin and Hunter were left to consider what they'd witnessed.

"Shall we go?" Hunter asked.

"Aye," Caslin agreed. "Let's keep Durakovic's involvement to ourselves for the time being. Yes?"

Hunter looked over to him, attempting to read his expression, "Why?"

"Our recent brush with her has ruffled a few feathers upstairs," Caslin explained. "I don't want any suggestion the result of that case is clouding my approach to this one. At least, let's keep it under wraps until we know how this comes together."

"Forgive me, sir," Hunter said, Caslin met her eye, "but how does Nairn fit into our current case load? I mean, have we not got enough on already?" Caslin blew out his cheeks, weighing up a response. "After all, if you're asking me to keep quiet, I deserve to know what's going on. Right?"

Caslin nodded, "Someone, who I believe is close to Farzaad Amin has indicated we should look closer at Nairn's suicide."

"How is this person connected to Amin and what's their motivation?" Hunter said. Caslin turned his gaze forward and away from her.

"I don't know."

"Might he be... don't take this the wrong way... but, might he be playing you?"

Caslin let out a deep sigh, "There's always that possibility but I don't see it."

"How can you know?"

"You're right. I can't," Caslin conceded. "But it's fair to say that there is something going on here we're not aware of and I expect to find out exactly what it is. If I happen to get another crack at Danika along the way, then that's an unexpected windfall I'll happily accept. Can you go along with that?"

Hunter met his gaze and smiled, "Of course, I can."

THE SHORT JOURNEY back to Fulford Road was made in silence. Caslin kept replaying everything he knew about Danika's business operations in his head, trying to link her with Thomas Grey but none were forthcoming from memory. Furthermore, any connection to Farzaad Amin eluded him completely. Entering the station, they were buzzed through the outer security door. Making their way along the corridor, they took the left onto the stairs and up towards CID. A call came from below as they reached the landing of the first floor.

"Mr Caslin!"

Caslin glanced over the balustrade, down to the ground floor. It was one of the civilian desk clerks calling him, but ashamedly, he didn't know his name. Leaning back, out of view, he silently mouthed the question to Hunter who rolled her eyes.

"Simon," she whispered. "Don't worry, he's only worked here for a year or so."

"I've been busy," Caslin said, leaning over and calling down. "What is it, Simon?" he asked, shooting a wink in Hunter's direction.

"There's someone waiting to see you," he called. Caslin thought about asking more questions but instead, turned to head back down, lingering on the first step.

"You crack on with pulling the details on Pocock and the helicopter crash. Also, have Terry Holt gather any available intel on Thomas Grey. I'll see you in CID in a minute," he said, resuming his course down to the waiting clerk.

"Leave it with me."

"What do you have for me?" Caslin said as he reached the ground floor.

"I have a Mr Mitchell, Geoffrey Mitchell, waiting to see you in the visitor's room," Simon offered, guiding Caslin in the right direction. Now, Caslin remembered who Simon was. A former engineer, retired from his career and now having taken up residence on the front desk at Fulford Road as part of the civilian administration team. A new job to keep him busy. A slightly pompous man who believed no one knew the station better than he did. Not that his approach was borne out of arrogance, merely a lack of self-awareness regarding his impact on those around him. Harmless enough and probably a very decent man but not one that many wanted to find themselves alone with during the working day.

"What does he want, do you know?" Caslin asked, immediately regretting doing so.

Simon shook his head, "No. He would only speak with you. Reminds me of a cartoon I saw in the paper a few days ago. There was this man, sitting in an office and—"

"Another time, Simon," Caslin said as they reached the security door to the station lobby. Caslin opened it, passed through and turned immediately left to access the visitor's room. Never had he been so relieved to be walking blindly into a room as he was at that very moment. Entering, he swiftly closed the door behind him. If Simon took offence it wasn't evident. The man waiting for him rose from his seat before Caslin had a chance to introduce himself.

"Nathaniel Caslin?" the man asked. Caslin nodded, taking in his measure as he offered his hand. Geoffrey Mitchell took it. The grasp was far from firm and rapidly dropped. Caslin guessed he was in his early fifties, of slim build and smartly dressed in a high-end suit. He appeared to be nervous, his eyes flitting to Caslin and then quickly away.

"How can I help you, Mr Mitchell?" Caslin asked, indicating for them to take a seat. Mitchell shook his head.

"No, thank you," he declined. "This won't take long."

"Okay," Caslin replied. "What can I do for you?"

"I'm here to ask you to stay away from Karen," he said flatly. Caslin was thrown.

"I'm sorry. What?"

"Karen, your *ex-wife*," Mitchell reiterated. "I want you to leave her alone."

Caslin felt a pulse of anger course through him, "*Leave her alone?*"

"Yes," Mitchell said, fixing him with a hard stare. "Look... I know the two of you have a long history and... the bonds between husband and wife are strong, particularly when there are children involved but... it's time that you moved on."

"Who the hell do you think—"

"I'm Karen's future," Mitchell cut in. "You are very much her past."

"Well, maybe that's for her to decide?"

Mitchell walked around from behind the table where initially he'd been seated, coming alongside Caslin and looking at him sideways. His demeanour was not threatening nor intimidating but calm and measured.

"Karen told me... she told me what happened between the

two of you the other night," he said, his voice cracking momentarily as Caslin cast his eyes to the floor, inclining his head slightly. "It's understandable under the circumstances but you should be aware that it will not be happening again." Mitchell continued on and only stopped when he grasped the door handle. He waited there, both men with their backs to each other. "Please ensure I don't have to come here again, Nathaniel. It's embarrassing for me and I have no doubt that it's humiliating for you."

Caslin heard the creaking of the door hinges, coupled with the draught of air drawn in from the lobby beyond, as Mitchell left the room. The flash of anger subsided to be replaced by a curious mixture of guilt and sadness, akin to the realisation that a worst fear was now a brutal reality.

He took a deep breath and held it, attempting to overcome the swirling emotions within that were trying to assert themselves. Reaching up, he probed his temples in a circular motion with his fingertips before pressing them firmly against fiercely shut eyes. Standing in silence, he heard his phone beep inside his pocket. Taking it out, he saw he'd received a text message. It was from Karen and simply read – *I'm sorry*.

There was a knock and Caslin turned, replacing his phone in his pocket as he did so. Simon was standing there. His expression was one of concern.

"Are you okay, Mr Caslin?" he said. Knowing he wasn't standing before the most observant or intuitive member of the team, Caslin felt the need to gather himself.

"I'm fine, Simon. Thank you for your concern," he replied, forcing a smile. This seemed to satisfy him.

"They're looking for you upstairs," Simon offered.

"Thanks." Caslin stepped out from the room and increased his pace to ensure he walked alone.

Entering CID, Hunter clocked Caslin and made a beeline in his direction. She held a wedge of paper in her hands as she approached him. Reading the expression on his face, her own changed.

"Are you all right, sir?"

"Yes, why?"

She shook her head to indicate it was irrelevant, "Anything interesting going on downstairs?"

"No," Caslin replied bluntly, probably with a sharper edge to his tone than intended. Hunter appeared not to notice. "What did you find out?"

"The Air Accidents Investigation Branch sent me over a copy of their report. I'm just going through it."

"And?"

"The helicopter came down in good weather on its approach to Burleigh House. The ensuing fireball that followed upon impact killed both the pilot and passenger, Martin Pocock. The AAIB carried out an exhaustive inquiry that only finished last month. They found the machine had a well-documented maintenance record with no history of material failures or breakdowns."

"And the cause of the accident itself?" Caslin asked, mulling it over.

"They couldn't determine a compelling reason for it to come down in the manner that it did. Ultimately, they concluded it was *most likely* due to pilot error," Hunter stated, glancing at the document in hand.

"The traditional get-out clauses are still favoured then?" Caslin asked with no attempt to hide the sarcasm. "What of the pilot? What do we know about him?"

"Sam Abrahams," Hunter said, flicking back a page. "A former captain in the Army Air Corps. Served tours in both Gulf conflicts and the Balkans. Spotless record. He was cited as an above average pilot with three decades of experience and also worked, for a time, as an instructor. He had no known medical condition to indicate he was unfit to fly."

"And what of the machine itself? Any history of design flaws or similar accidents affecting that particular model of aircraft?" Caslin asked.

Hunter shook her head in the negative, "Not at all. It has one of the best performing safety averages in the industry."

"Pocock?" Caslin asked, just as Terry Holt joined them.

"I've got that here, sir," Holt said, brandishing his notes. "He was a successful lawyer having had a career that saw him work for several of the more prestigious city firms. He developed a reputation for being a specialist in contract negotiations, specifically surrounding the structuring of property investment finance. Having left his last appointment, he set up a company of his own that proved successful and catapulted him even further up the food chain. Not a rags-to-riches story but certainly upwardly mobile. No priors. Not even a parking ticket."

"Tell me, was his current situation investigated at the time of his death? Anything that was considered suspicious?"

Hunter shook her head, "No. The AAIB carried out their investigation and the jury at the inquest concluded it was a case of accidental death."

"His firm. Who's running it now?" Caslin asked.

"It collapsed shortly following his death," Holt stated. "Companies House records show it was racked with debt and from what I could find out there was no one to take the helm after the accident. A winding-up order was served by Revenue and Customs three months ago."

Caslin caught Hunter casting him an advisory flick of the eyebrows and he turned to see DCI Matheson entering CID. He acknowledged her approach and indicated for the junior officers to leave. Holt swiftly departed whereas Hunter managed to greet their superior before returning to her own desk. For his part, Caslin fell into step alongside Matheson and they headed for his office.

"I missed the morning briefing today," she said, as he closed the door behind them. Caslin offered her a seat but she remained standing.

"That's okay, I can bring you up to speed," Caslin said.

"That would be nice but first," Matheson said, "perhaps you could tell me why *you* missed the morning briefing?" Caslin sank into the chair behind his desk, casting a glance through the window into the squad room. He caught Terry Holt's eye; who was attempting to observe the goings on without appearing to be doing so. Caslin rolled his tongue across the inside of his lower lip. Matheson followed his gaze. "Don't blame Terry. You put him in that position."

Caslin shook his head slightly, "I had to follow up on a lead. It was important and the team here know their tasks."

"What took you to Acomb Road?" Matheson said, folding her arms before her. Word certainly spread fast.

"The suicide of Alexander Nairn last year, could well be related to the Amin killing," Caslin offered, judging Matheson knew more than she was letting on. He had to assume his leg was already in the bear trap and sought not to make the situation worse.

"How so?" Matheson replied without skipping a beat, confirming Caslin's suspicions.

"That's exactly what I'm trying to find out, Ma'am."

"And how have you come by this information?"

"A tip off," Caslin lied. "Anonymous."

The DCI unfolded her arms, softening her stance, "Do you think you can trust it?"

Caslin nodded solemnly, "There are legs in it for sure. How exactly it comes together, I'll be honest, I don't know... yet. But, I will."

Matheson stood in silence, almost as if she was assessing him. Most likely, he figured she was weighing up how forthcoming he was currently being. In truth, that was only as far as he felt he had to be whilst appearing convincing.

"What intelligence have you turned up regarding who was in

town on the day of the murder?" Matheson asked, switching tack. Caslin figured he'd passed the test, at least for now.

"Those names on the alt-right?"

She nodded.

Caslin shook his head, "Despite their best efforts to throw us off by splitting into smaller groups, most of those with form were tracked by our intelligence teams. At this time, we can't be certain of their whereabouts at the time of the murder, so there is still the possibility that one or more of them were involved."

"And how are you following up that line of inquiry?"

"We've gathered up as much of the CCTV, available across the weekend, as we could and we're running it through facial recognition software to track them and their whereabouts but—"

"But?"

"It's a painstakingly slow process with the available resources," Caslin said.

"Then perhaps… and please feel free to take this suggestion on board, you might want to focus on the more likely scenario rather than chasing the ghosts of last year?" she said with a cutting edge to her tone.

"It's worth following up, I assure you and until it's clearly to the contrary, I'll keep all available lines of inquiry open," Caslin countered, sitting forward in his seat and resting his elbows on the desk.

Matheson fixed him with a stare, "I want an update before the close of play, Nathaniel. I'm expecting to speak with the chief superintendent this evening before he delivers his press conference and it would be good for me to have something useful to say."

"I'll do my best, Ma'am," Caslin said respectfully. With that said, his senior officer turned and left his office.

Sitting back in his chair, he watched as she crossed the squad room, pausing as she came alongside Hunter's desk. Words were exchanged but as to what was said by either of them, he had no clue. Shortly after, Matheson made to leave CID and Hunter shot him a concerned look in passing. The DCI was certainly trying to keep him on a short leash and he was well aware that she'd still be both willing and able to hang him with it should the need arise.

Taking out his mobile, Caslin fished a slip of paper out of his wallet and unfolded it. Tapping the number into his phone, he spun his chair to the left enabling him to look out of the window. The sun was shining through the branches of the barren trees, belying the bitterness of the wind. The call connected and he waited patiently as the phone rang at the other end. Just when he was expecting the voicemail to cut in, the call was answered.

"Inspector Caslin, I wasn't expecting to hear from you so soon," Cory Walsh said, in greeting.

"Well, what can I say, you make a compelling argument," Caslin replied, turning back to observe his CID team, hard at work. "I think we need to talk."

"I'll message you when I get a moment," Walsh said and the line went dead. Caslin was surprised, removing the handset from his ear and checking the screen to see if the call really had been disconnected. It had. Standing up, he put the phone down and walked to the window, putting his hands in his pockets. His phone vibrated, followed by the accompanying sound of the beep to signify he'd received an SMS. Reaching back, he picked up the phone. Opening the message, he found it to be brief – *King's Staith, 10pm*.

Caslin deleted the text and put the phone in his pocket. He knew the street well. It was at the edge of the city centre on the quayside of the River Ouse and opposite the warehouses of the old merchant's quarter. The latter were now mostly luxury apartments with a historic view. Hunter appeared in the doorway to his office. He beckoned her in.

"What do you want me to do regarding Thomas Grey, sir?"

"Turn over his business affairs. Try to find any link to Danika Durakovic. If nothing shows there, search for anything that stands out as odd, particularly in relation to financing. These guys are wealthy but they're not funding their projects with their own capital. See if you can find out whose money they have access to? Make sure you do it quietly, though," he said, casting a sideways glance at Terry Holt.

Hunter followed the direction of his gaze and nodded, before turning to leave, "Will do, sir."

"Sarah?" Caslin called after her. She looked back at him, over her shoulder. "What did Matheson want?"

Hunter glanced away before answering, "Nothing much. She just said…"

"Said what?" Caslin asked, sensing reticence.

"She said to be careful."

Caslin nodded, chewing his bottom lip and raising his eyebrows.

"Sage advice," he said, waving her away. Hunter was only too pleased to.

CHAPTER SEVENTEEN

CASLIN DREW his coat about him, increasing his pace in an effort to shake the cold from his body. The bitter wind, channelled by the buildings cut through the narrow city streets in a fierce reminder that winter was far from over. The crisp sunshine of earlier in the day was now replaced by a dark, brooding expanse of cloud cover, threatening to burst into freezing rain at any given moment. Departing Spurrier Gate, Caslin took the right turn onto Bridge Street in the direction of the River Ouse. Upon reaching the bridge instead of crossing, he accessed the steep steps down towards King's Staith and left the hum of the traffic to pass above him.

Descending to the quayside, the sound of music and laughter carried to him from the nearby pub. For most of the year this area was well served by patrons sitting at tables along the riverside, making it one of the popular places to enjoy an evening out. However, for the next few months at least the cobbles would be accompanied by silence with only the water, lapping against the quay, one of the few sounds to be heard when the traffic died down.

Looking around, Caslin was alone. Thrusting his hands into his pockets, he chastised himself for forgetting to bring his gloves. In the lee of the bridge, he'd felt the benefit of shelter from the wind but once clear of it the icy breeze struck him. Turning his back, he sought to give his face some respite. Walking forward a few yards, he was able to get a clearer view along the river. In the distance, with the aid of the street lighting, he could see a man walking his dog on the edge of the Tower Gardens but he was heading in the opposite direction of him. Checking the time, it was a little after ten and Caslin shifted his feet. They were numb.

The sound of footfalls behind caused Caslin to turn as another descended the stone steps from above. The man was in his thirties, well dressed for the conditions in a blue all-weather coat and a woollen hat. He bore Caslin no heed as he walked past, taking the second turn onto Cumberland Street and heading up towards the city centre. Caslin eyed him for a brief moment before checking his watch again.

Without knowing where the meeting would take place, Caslin decided to get some circulation through his body and set off in the direction of the Tower Gardens. Passing Lower Friargate, he glanced up the street to see if a car was parked up, potentially waiting for him. A man stood a little way off with a mobile phone pressed to his ear, laughing and joking in conversation with someone but he was paying no attention to his surroundings. Caslin walked on.

A line of terraced, Georgian Townhouses ran to his left for the next hundred yards. Where he walked, at the quayside level, were the arched accesses to the basements. Now being used as garages or general storage areas, they were prone to flooding as and when the river burst its banks which it was liable to do with more regularity than Caslin remembered from his youth. Glancing up at the terrace, lights were on but curtains were drawn. The end of King's Staith brought him to the Boat Dock, where tourist trips along the river began and ended with the architecturally stunning, Skeldergate Bridge in the background.

Exhaling heavily, Caslin turned and looked back from where he'd come. The street was deserted. Reaching into his pocket, he took out his mobile phone and scrolled through the contacts until he found Walsh's phone number. Leaning against one of the many bollards lining the quay, Caslin waited patiently for the call to connect. It did so but failed to be answered. The call rang out after thirty seconds without cutting to voicemail. Checking the screen, he saw the connection had been terminated. He redialled, only to be diverted to voicemail as soon as a connection was made.

Putting the phone away, he looked around. A sense of irritation came to him. No doubt, Walsh would have a reason for being late or unreachable. Caslin didn't feel as if he was being played for a fool. After all, Walsh had approached him and not the other way around. With it now pushing half-past ten, Caslin figured he'd call it a day. Walking back the way he'd come, he reached the steps but on the spur of the moment, rather than head up, he ducked into the King's Arms for a swift nightcap. A wall of heat struck him as he opened the outer door. Business was far from brisk with only the regulars apparently in situ and Caslin was able to approach the bar with ease.

Ordering a pint of beer and a whisky chaser, he handed over a twenty and waited for his change, acknowledging the barman with a nod when he returned. A fire crackled in the hearth, comforting on a dark winter night. Caslin took a table at the front of the building with a window overlooking the river. Tossing his coat and scarf onto a free chair, he sank down. It'd been a long day. Rubbing at his face with his palms, he took a deep breath and then reached for the scotch, downing it in one fluid motion. The sting barely registered as he put the empty glass down and picked up his beer.

Running the events through his head, Caslin sought to make sense of the investigation. Without Walsh's intervention, he'd be far deeper into the workings of the neo-Nazi groups currently flooding the city rather than toying with Thomas Grey and the demise of his two associates. Keeping that information from DCI Matheson, among others, was both necessary and telling. He had nothing concrete with which to base these inquiries on and they wouldn't stand up to any form of scrutiny.

The door behind him opened as more latecomers entered. Caslin sipped at his pint. The two arrivals walked to the bar and signalled the barman for his attention. Caslin's thoughts drifted to Kuznetsov's apparent suicide.

He was still bothered by that case, not so much because of any evidence of foul play because there wasn't much of that, more his own reaction to the death. Had the fallen billionaire been an unemployed bricklayer found hanged in his garage, would Caslin be as sceptical about the suicide? He hoped he would approach them equally but the nagging voice in his head wondered whether he was guilty of somewhat overplaying the significance of one man's breakdown. *Why was that?* Self-analysis was useful, up to a point but beyond that merely caused analytical paralysis. Caslin cast his doubts aside and returned to his drink. A handful of patrons made to leave, clearly having had a cracking evening, and stumbled out of the door, behind him.

Caslin smiled and cast an eye around the pub. The two late-comers were propped up at the bar, one seated on a stool, the other standing alongside. Something caught his attention. The two weren't talking although the one standing had his back to him. Caslin stifled a yawn and then flexed the muscles in his shoulders, rolling them backwards in a circular motion to try and release the tension. Glancing at the clock on the wall, he knew he should head back rather than order another drink.

Standing up, he drained the remaining half of his pint and picked up his coat and scarf. Returning the empty glasses to the bar, the staff were out of sight when he looked to acknowledge the service and so, left without a word. Stepping out into the cold night air saw him shudder, such was the contrast from within the pub. Pulling his elbows tight to his sides, he rubbed his hands together before putting them in his coat pockets.

Heading to the right, Caslin mounted the steps up to Bridge Street and the most direct route home across the city centre to his flat, in Kleiser's Court.

A bus passed by on the road above, the rumbling sound replaced by the sound of the pub doors opening behind him. A brief glance over his shoulder saw a figure leave the King's Arms. The man braced against the cold, pulling a hat over his head and he too, began the steep climb to the street above. Caslin continued on. Cresting the top of the stairs, he angled right and eyeing a break in the late-night traffic, trotted across the road to the other side.

Reaching the old church on the corner, Caslin passed the entrance to Feasegate and crossed onto High Ousegate. The street narrowed and with its mix of three and four-storey shop units, it felt more enclosed. For some reason he felt on edge as if the hairs on the back of neck were upright.

Very few people were around at this time of night and Caslin became aware of someone walking a short distance behind him but on the other side of the road, over his right shoulder. Pausing at a shop window, Caslin made as if he was checking out one of the interior product displays, lingering over the detail whilst keeping half an eye on the reflection in the glass. As the figure honed into view, it was indeed the man who had left the pub at the same time. He paid no attention to Caslin and walked on, head down and earphones in.

Caslin shifted his eyes and watched as the figure disappeared from view in the reflection from the shop window. Stepping back, he looked to his right as the man reached the end of the street and took a left. Shaking his head, Caslin smiled at his own paranoia and set off.

Part way along High Ousegate was Peter's Lane, a narrow cut-through between the buildings – used largely by employees of the various businesses. The lane, little more than an alley, eventually opened out onto Market Street. Caslin passed down it. Only one source lit the route, an overhanging lamp near to a kink further up the passage. Barely a shoulder's width at its narrowest, the lane would be almost unnavigable if not for the seeping light pollution from the streets at each end. His footsteps echoed on the stone flags beneath his feet, reverberating off of the brick walls to either side of him.

Approaching the turn, where he expected the passage to widen to a more comfortable norm, allowing vehicular access, Caslin sensed someone else had entered behind him. Following the path to the left, Caslin chanced a glance back the way he'd come before disappearing from view. With scant seconds to make a judgement in the dark, he couldn't make out any details of who was coming towards him. A few metres ahead and the path turned once again, this time sharply to the right. Increasing his pace, Caslin made it around the corner and scanned the scene. There were multiple doorways, recessed rear-entrances to shops and their associated flats above as well as various gated routes into other buildings.

There were multiple options for where he could choose to conceal himself. A wooden door that offered access to a small yard was ajar and Caslin brushed aside some collapsed cardboard packaging with his foot in order to open it further and allow him in. He then pulled the door closed just enough to shroud his presence but still leaving him a view of the passage. He retreated into the shadows and waited.

Moments later, a man came into view, walking briskly. The same man Caslin had eyed in the reflection of the shop window. No longer was he the casual stranger making his way home from the pub. Now, he gave the impression of a focussed individual, alert and determined. Caslin recognised him. Not only had he been drinking with the other man back at the pub, but he had also appeared on King's Staith earlier, passing by Caslin and heading into town. Caslin waited, absolutely certain that he was being followed.

From his own experience, Caslin knew that surveillance teams seldom worked alone and this man certainly had at least one colleague. Confident he'd allowed enough time for his pursuer to round the next bend before he came out from his hiding place, Caslin edged forward. Reaching the next bend, he risked a glance around the corner. Having reached the junction with Market Street, the man was pacing with a phone clamped to his ear. Such was the emptiness of the city at this time of night, Caslin could make out every word.

"No. I think I've lost him... yeah, Market Street... probably heading home," he said, responding to questioning from the other end of the line. "I don't know... I didn't see anyone... okay, I will."

The man put the phone in his pocket and looked in both directions, unsure of which way to go. Caslin followed, a dozen paces behind. Quickening his own pace, he sought to make up the ground between them with the brighter lights and noise of the busier street to mask and detract from his approach. Setting himself, Caslin was buoyed at how his makeshift plan had played out. Confident he could comfortably challenge the man in a more public area, he stepped it up.

Late-night revellers passed by, granting further cover and Caslin increased the speed of his approach. Barely two steps behind, he braced to take down his target only to see him turn at the final moment with impossibly quick speed, dropping his shoulder as Caslin reached out. An iron grip took a hold of Caslin's forearm and without the time to process what happened, he found himself upended, seeing the streetlights above pass by in a whirlwind of blurred, orange light.

Striking the flag stones at an alarming rate, Caslin felt the air burst from his lungs. He rolled and came upright, lunging at his opponent who, in turn, advanced on him. Throwing himself forward into the man's midriff, Caslin clasped his arms around him and drove his head into his stomach. His opponent groaned as he was forced back and against a shop window, flexing under the pressure. The advantage was short-lived as Caslin felt a knee rise into his stomach, striking him forcefully. The pain shot up through his chest and again, the wind was knocked from him.

Losing his grip, Caslin slumped to his knees and was thrown backwards as the man pushed off. Trying to stand, a fist struck him across the left cheek and he was sent sprawling to the ground, arms flailing.

Panic flared within as he made to stand. Having lost both the element of surprise and the upper hand, Caslin knew he was in trouble. A crushing blow struck his ribs and he doubled over. The kick saw him collapse into a heap. Some excited shouts came from distance and Caslin sensed hesitation in his opponent because no further blows were forthcoming. Rolling onto his side, fearing the next onslaught, he was surprised to see a figure sprinting away along Market Street. Looking around, he was alone, once again.

Stumbling to his feet, clutching his side and using a wall to brace himself, Caslin winced as he stood. The shouts had come from intoxicated passers-by, eyeing the combat and seeking yet more entertainment. They slowed their approach as the realisation dawned on them that it was all over. Still, they mocked and jeered at the man who'd come off second best.

For his part, Caslin mouthed an expletive in their direction, which only encouraged them more and set off for home. Little more than a two-minute walk, the remainder of the journey back to his flat felt like it took far longer. Being no stranger to taking a kicking it had, however, been a while since his last and every step saw him wince with pain.

Reaching the entrance to Kleiser's Court, Caslin ensured he was alone when he unlocked the door to the communal passage and passed through. Locking it behind him, he leant against the wall and took a moment to catch his breath, appreciating the feeling of security. Thoughts rushed through his mind. Questions he had no answers to. There was no doubt that someone was taking a keen interest in his investigation but who and to what end, he had no clue.

Taking a deep breath caused him to grimace, such was the pain in his side. The stairs were taken slowly, each step sending a shot of pain throughout his body. Entering his flat, he pushed the door closed with the back of his heel, hearing the reassuring click of the latch as he walked into the living room. Letting out a groan as he dropped his shoulder and slipped off his coat.

Caslin passed over to the sideboard and overturned a glass. He took the stopper out of a bottle of Macallan with his teeth and poured himself a large scotch. Picking up the glass, he turned and went back to the hall and on into the bathroom, one hand supporting his left side at all times. First taking a mouthful of scotch, he put the glass down alongside the basin and, flicking on the vanity light, assessed himself in the mirror.

Turning his face sideways, the area around his left eye was reddening and already closing as a result of the swelling. It stung as he reached up, probing gently with his fingertips. Another mouthful of scotch followed before he felt prepared enough to remove both his jumper and shirt. Inspecting his ribcage, he found it was incredibly tender to the touch and he knew the bruising would be substantial. There was also a strong likelihood that he'd cracked several ribs but he hoped not. The notion that he should go to the hospital to get checked out came and went in an instant. If he had indeed cracked any ribs, they'd do little with them. He'd spend most of the night waiting to be seen and then be sent home and told to take it easy.

Running the cold-water tap, Caslin cupped his hands beneath the stream. With difficulty, he bent over and doused his face. The sensation was refreshing although punctuated by intense shots of pain. Picking up a flannel, he soaked it in the cold water and gently touched it to the side of his face before doing the same to his abdomen. It caused him to wince once again and he let out a deep sigh.

Finishing his scotch, he turned off the tap and left the bathroom with every intention of revisiting the bottle of Macallan. Something caught his attention. Standing in the hallway, he reached up and flicked on the light.

On the mat, in front of the entrance door, lay a brown C4 envelope. Not absolutely certain that it wasn't there when he'd arrived, Caslin crossed over to it. With difficulty, he crouched down and picked it up. The weight was significant. There was no addressee on the front, stamp or identifying mark to indicate where it had come from. Caslin tucked it under his arm and listened intently for any movement beyond the door. There wasn't any. Unlocking the door, he eased it open and glanced out onto the landing. Nothing moved and the security light, running off a two-minute timer, was no longer lit. Whoever left the envelope had long since departed.

Closing the door, Caslin locked it and made his way back through to the living room. Tearing open the envelope, he tipped the contents, a wedge of paper documents, out onto the coffee table and then retrieved the bottle of Macallan. Gently lowering himself into his chair, he placed the glass on the table next to the paperwork and poured himself another drink. Reaching up, he clicked on the lamp, bathing him in a soft light.

"Let me have a look at you," Caslin said to himself, picking up the first clutch of paper.

CHAPTER EIGHTEEN

THE ENVELOPE CONTAINED photocopies of official government documentation. Putting aside his immediate scepticism, a brief scan through the batch of papers revealed letters, reports and memos, all written on headed paper from their respective arm of the civil service. Caslin found himself looking at communiques from the Foreign and Commonwealth Office, the UK Treasury and the Home Office to name but a few. In every piece, he saw redacted sections, often heavily, concealing names, addresses or in many cases entire paragraphs. All of which, Caslin found to be frustrating as understanding what was being discussed would be tiresomely difficult.

A casual inspection revealed a lack of commonality to bring them all together. Sifting through, he put aside those that were heavy on figures and short on detail, turning his attention to a transparent sleeve holding papers stamped 'Eyes Only'. Sipping at his scotch, Caslin unhooked the string that bound the folder shut and opened it, withdrawing the contents. The first he laid eyes on was a one-page summary of a man, by the name of Valery Fedorin. Casting an eye over the photograph at the top of the page, he noted a serious-looking man, angular of face with a dark complexion, particularly around his eyes. Across the image was an official stamp to signify Fedorin was deceased.

Flicking through the remaining pages, Caslin counted six in total and all were similar dossiers on individuals with each recorded as having passed away. A sense of unease swept over him. The papers appeared authentic but never trusting what was fed to him was one of the first things he'd ever learnt in this job.

Returning to the first of the six, Caslin read through Valery Fedorin's recorded history. He had been a local official in *Troitsk* when he died as a result of a heart attack. It was a place Caslin had never heard of, so he looked it up, finding it to be a small district roughly forty kilometres south-west of Moscow. Fedorin's demise struck him as untimely and a little surprising bearing in mind he was only thirty-six at the time of his death. He was married and had two children, a son and a daughter. His birthplace, Rostov-on-Don, was listed as was his entire educational and employment history. The latter appeared largely related to local government, albeit at a low level. Nothing stood out to signify he should be of interest to UK law enforcement, let alone the Secret Service.

Turning to the next, Caslin found this one to be closer to home. He was a UK national, fifty-four years old, by the name of Dean Strauss. Strauss worked as a planning consultant, specialising in commercial infrastructure according to his summary. Having been born and raised in Chorley, Lancashire, he grew up and attended Balliol College, Oxford. No mean feat in itself, let alone for a working-class boy from the north of England.

Scanning to the bottom, Caslin sought out his cause of death. Strauss had died in what was recorded as a botched mugging in Berlin, four years previously. No one was listed as having been arrested, let alone convicted of the assault. Cross referencing Fedorin's details, Caslin sought to link the two but nothing obvious was forthcoming. Putting them aside, he moved quickly to the next with an expectation that clarity would come about soon enough.

The third detailed the life of a French solicitor who died in a car accident in Marseille barely six months ago. By all accounts, it was a hit-and-run in an unpopulated area on a rural road. No witnesses were recorded as having been present at the scene. Moving to the next, Caslin found a suicide of an Israeli financier who had thrown himself to his death from the roof of an apartment block in Tel Aviv.

The next dossier had apparently been forwarded to the UK agencies from the FBI. Another businessman, a naturalised UK citizen of Ukrainian descent, who had been found dead in his Floridian holiday home. The cause of death was recorded as an overdose of barbiturates. Immediately, Caslin found that interesting. He hadn't seen a death from barbiturates in a long time and this incident had been recent, only two years prior.

No stranger to sedatives, anti-depressants and illegal highs, Caslin knew the market for these synthetic drugs, used to slow the central nervous system, had been more or less eradicated. Their prescription use was almost entirely superseded by benzo-diazepines, with far fewer side effects and a much lower risk of accidental overdose. There were no details as to why or who had passed the file on to UK intelligence.

The remaining summary was that of a German man who had succumbed to complications following a stroke. He was listed as an employee of the BMF, the German Federal Ministry of Finance, although on secondment to the EU's Fiscalis 2020 programme at the time of his death. Caslin took out his phone and did an internet search as he had no idea what it was. Within minutes, he found it to be a six-year programme facilitating the exchange of expertise and information between European Tax administrations. Returning to the dossier, there were seemingly no suspicions raised regarding the death either at the time nor subsequently at home in Germany.

Re-examining each death, he double-checked for any links that might tie all, or any, of them together. Drawing air through clenched teeth in frustration, Caslin tossed the summaries aside.

On the face of it there were no geographical, professional or causes of death that suggested the cases were related. Somehow though, they were closely associated enough to draw the attention of the Intelligence Agencies of both the UK and the United States. If these files were genuine, they'd also found their way into the public domain. That did not happen without significant effort on someone's part.

Turning his attention to the other paperwork, Caslin first poured himself another scotch. His attention was drawn to an export licence, issued from the DTI, the Department for Trade and Industry. The licence was granted late August, the year before last and issued to a company by the name of *Henderson Holdings Limited*. The terms and conditions along with what the licence sought to facilitate the export of, as well as the associated values, were redacted as was the name of the person receiving the warrant. The reference at the top of the letter however, was not. The licence referred to *Project Obmen*.

Caslin sat back, sipping at his drink and wondered what the title referred to. Picking up his phone, he reconnected to the internet and typed the name into the search box. Initially, the search engine queried whether he had typed the name in error but below that were multiple hits against websites.

The first two related to German-Russian exchanges of academic expertise within the fields of culture and education. The next, highlighted regional educational-exchange programmes between Norway and Bulgaria. Beyond that, the hits proved to be ever more unlikely, linking to a low budget made-for-television film of a similar name.

Caslin closed down the search, acknowledging the decreasing relevance the further down the page he read. Following the brief inquiry, he was left none the wiser as to what Project Obmen could be referring to.

Finding a clutch of email transcripts, Caslin began to read through them. Many of the names, both senders and recipients, were redacted but their sources were not. They were internal emails sent across the UK government's servers. He found threads originating in the Foreign Office passing through the House of Commons and even the occasional link to the governing party's central headquarters. Frustratingly, almost the entire content of each thread had been redacted. Often, the surviving text were merely the conjunctions or transitional words. There was no way Caslin could even begin to understand the context or subject matter being discussed, only that they had been passed back and forth over a period of weeks and, in some cases, months.

Many of the threads originated from the Foreign and Commonwealth Office. It was one of the emails from this department where Caslin found a name, *F. Michaelson*. Scanning through the remaining emails, he found only one more reference to Michaelson. Within the thread, he appeared to be querying an inconsistency regarding a *register*. Although, any ability to further scrutinise the matter was severely hampered by an overuse of thick, black lines.

Caslin drew breath. The only register he knew of that might be of interest to a civil servant would be the Register of Members' Interests. This related to the personal affairs of parliamentarians in their wider lives. Every sitting member of the Commons had to respect a code of conduct with declarations of any financial interests that could potentially influence them. This ranged from financial reimbursements to company directorships, investments or familial connections.

Exhaling deeply, Caslin pondered whether Michaelson's query was significant or not.

Glancing at the time, it was well into the early hours. Sitting forward in his seat, Caslin placed his glass down and drummed his index and forefinger against the table, piecing it together. Picking up his phone, he scrolled down the contacts list, hovering over the name when he found it. Hesitation was not something he was ever accused of and he dialled the number, closing his eyes as the call connected. It rang for an inordinately long time before a male voice answered. It was a gruff acknowledgement. Caslin had certainly woken him.

"You do know what time it is, don't you, Nathaniel?"

"I'm sorry, sir. I didn't feel it could wait."

"What do you need?" Kyle Broadfoot asked. Caslin's former boss, now Assistant Chief Constable and head of the North Yorkshire Crime Directorate, didn't seem fazed by the lateness of the call. He knew his former charge only too well.

"Your connections, sir," Caslin replied, sweeping his eyes across the papers in front of him, "your connections."

LEANING against one of the four giant Doric columns of the Neo-Classical Yorkshire Museum, Caslin waited. Sipping at the coffee he'd purchased on the short walk from his flat in Kleiser's Court, his other hand was firmly planted in his coat pocket. With very little wind, the clear skies overnight had left a silver sheen across the manicured grounds sweeping out in front of him. The tree line, a little over a hundred yards away, masked his proximity to the city centre. In the distance to his left was the Minster, towering above the old town. Beyond the trees, the museum gardens continued on down to the banks of the River Ouse with York's central train station on the far side. The hum of the traffic, as commuters set about their day, carried to him on the breeze.

His thoughts drifted to Karen. Having not spoken to her since being warned off by her partner, Caslin felt a pang of guilt. Undoubtedly, he was certain she would want him to keep his distance. After all, she chose to share what happened between them and must have been aware of the potential consequences in doing so. It would have been easy to keep it concealed. At least, as easy as it ever is to keep a dark secret from those with the closest emotional ties. A matter of conscience perhaps?

His guilt arose from the situation with Sean. As parents, they needed to come together to support him and ease the boy through the damaged place he'd wandered into. As things stood, Caslin couldn't see how they'd be able to achieve that under the circumstances. Movement to his left caught his eye and Caslin turned to see the approach of Kyle Broadfoot. His face was pale and he bore a pained expression as he took Caslin's offered hand.

"Good morning, sir," Caslin said. Broadfoot nodded, in a return greeting inclining his head slightly.

"What on earth have you been up to?" Broadfoot asked, pointing at the side of Caslin's face.

"Oh… that… I fell down the stairs."

"They can be slippery, can't they?" he replied, obviously unconvinced. "Shall we?" he said, with an open palm, indicating for them to take a walk. "I don't fancy standing still for too long. Not on a morning like this."

Caslin agreed and they took the path that wound alongside the ruins of the medieval St Mary's Abbey and headed deeper into the gardens. Glancing over his shoulder, Caslin noted someone hovering in the colonnade at the entrance to the museum. He was unashamedly watching them.

Broadfoot noticed, "My driver. He'll wait there." Caslin thought no more about it.

"What did you find out?" Caslin asked, cutting to the chase.

"Direct as always, Nathaniel," Broadfoot said, with a smile.

"Well, you know me, sir. I'm not one for the formalities."

"True enough. I'm surprised you came to me with this. Tell me first why you're not using your own resources? I know you have them and, in the past, they've often proved far more useful than mine."

Caslin thought on that for a moment. It was true, he had connections of his own but they were strained these days.

"It's difficult to explain," Caslin said truthfully. "To do so would be a little… I don't know… rude? For want of a better word."

Broadfoot laughed, shaking his head, "Nate Caslin is worried about causing offence? I'd better make a note in my diary. A day to remember for the memoirs." Caslin smiled, glancing away and squinting in the bright morning sunshine. "Anyway. You served me quite a task to be delivered in such a short time."

"I have the feeling time is of the essence with this case," Caslin countered. "Besides, you have access to significant resources. Enough to get me a result, anyway."

"You seem very confident of that."

"You're here, aren't you?" Caslin said with an almost imperceptible shrug of the shoulders, finishing the last of his coffee and depositing the cup in a waste bin as they passed.

"The name you are after is *Finlay Michaelson*. He was a member of the civil service working in the Foreign and Commonwealth Office," Broadfoot offered.

"You said *was*. Where is he now?"

"He no longer works for the FCO, having left his post earlier this year," Broadfoot replied. "In fact, he left the government entirely."

"Where is he now?"

Broadfoot shook his head, "I don't know. Do bear in mind you only tossed this in my direction a little over seven hours ago."

"What did he do? At the FCO, I mean," Caslin asked, ignoring the senior officer's mild dig at him.

"Michaelson was a Grade 2 Senior, working in investment and business relations with UK trade and industry. He took the lead in supporting relationships between UK business and foreign enterprise."

"Do we know why he left?" Caslin asked. Having taken the left fork in the path they now arrived at the York Observatory. It was a small hexagonal structure, crafted from stone and encircled by well-established trees. Broadfoot stopped, turning to face Caslin.

"Now that's where it got a little interesting. In short, no. I haven't got the reason he left the civil service nor any specifics on what he was working on when he did so. Not through lack of asking, I might add but I'm waiting on people coming back to me.

Nathaniel," he said pointedly, "I never have to wait for people to get back to me. Not when requesting such basic information and, let us not forget, Michaelson was a senior official but not a permanent undersecretary nor sitting at director level."

"What does that tell you?" Caslin asked as Broadfoot resumed walking, Caslin falling into step alongside.

"That inquiries relating to Michaelson or his portfolio are flagged somehow."

"Flagged? By who?"

Broadfoot shrugged, "Could be any number of departments. I don't know but... it's certainly intriguing."

"What about *Project Obmen*? Anything?"

"No. Sorry. I've nothing on that. Had Michaelson made any direct references to it?" Broadfoot queried.

This time Caslin shook his head, "No, he didn't but with everything I received, it seemed significant. What with Michaelson being concerned with business affairs, I hoped he was linked to it and that would fill in some of the blanks."

"Can't help you there," Broadfoot said. "Speaking of sources. You asked after Cory Walsh?"

"I did. What can you tell me?"

"As much as you have probably found out under your own steam, I imagine," Broadfoot said. "A successful businessman. A billionaire, largely self-made. He's been making waves in recent years. Not only here in the UK but it's fair to say in much of the developed world."

"Why? What's he up to?"

"Lobbying anyone who will listen."

"To what end?"

"Tightening of financial controls in global markets," Broadfoot stated. "He's been trying to toughen up the regulation put upon foreign investments and money flows. It's almost a one-man crusade against financial corruption."

Caslin blew out his cheeks, "Good luck with that."

Broadfoot agreed, "If anyone ever wanted to move a mountain, it's him. Walsh hasn't been without success, mind you. He's been instrumental in legislative changes in over a dozen jurisdictions in the last five years. Some powerful names have had assets frozen or been blacklisted in the financial markets as a direct result of his campaigning."

"So, he wasn't lying when he suggested he has enemies?" Caslin said rhetorically.

"It's a stance that's won him as many enemies as it has friends. There have been repeated attempts to have him extradited on international arrest warrants. They've become almost an annual event for him. Not that any government has sought to enforce them."

"Who filed the warrants?"

"Russia. All of them," Broadfoot replied. Caslin didn't respond but he felt Broadfoot's gaze fall upon him. "Are you tying Walsh's crusade to the Kuznetsov suicide?"

Caslin looked away, his eyes drawn to the cenotaph in the memorial gardens on the opposing riverbank, directly opposite them. "No. To be honest, Kuznetsov has never been mentioned in this context. Unless, you know something I don't?" he said, stopping and meeting Broadfoot's eye.

Broadfoot chewed on his lower lip momentarily prior to answering.

"There has been some chatter," he replied.

"Regarding Kuznetsov's death?" Caslin clarified. Broadfoot nodded.

"GCHQ has reported a noticeable rise in high-level communication in the run up to, as well as the aftermath of, last week's events. Following on from Kuznetsov's death things dropped back."

"Do you think they're related?" Caslin asked.

Broadfoot locked eyes with him for a brief moment before breaking it off. His shoulders dropped at the same time. "It's your case, Nathaniel."

"One that I'm being pushed to sign off, sooner rather than later."

Broadfoot sighed, "Unsurprising. Under the circumstances."

"What circumstances?"

"Big picture, Nathaniel," Broadfoot said, setting off once more and gazing at some unidentifiable point in the distance. "The UK government has only recently come out of a decade of frosty relations with the Kremlin. The strength of that relationship has been tested again recently. Whether Kuznetsov's death was a suicide or something more sinister doesn't really matter."

"I think it matters to his family," Caslin stated, cutting a sharp edge to his tone.

"Not when it comes down to international relations. When the interests of the Crown are threatened everything else becomes secondary," Broadfoot replied. "Even an unfounded hint of impropriety could do untold damage."

"That's not my problem," Caslin said.

"Make sure it doesn't become so," Broadfoot replied. "I understand things haven't been great for you recently back at Fulford Road." Caslin flicked his eyes at Broadfoot and away again. The grape vine was evidently still intact.

"Really? I get on all right with Matheson. She's a decent enough DCI," he said as convincingly as possible.

"And Sutherland?" Broadfoot asked, referring to his successor as Caslin's detective chief superintendent.

He shrugged, "I've had worse."

Broadfoot grinned, "As an aside, I was disappointed you didn't take up my offer."

"I know," Caslin replied, not wishing to discuss the subject any further. "It wasn't the right time" was all he was willing to say. Wishing to change the subject, Caslin took out his phone. "Can you have a look at something, for me?" he asked, opening up his gallery folder and flicking through the photographs. Scrolling to the bottom, he found what he was looking for and passed the handset across. Broadfoot took it, holding it at arm's length to try and make out the detail.

"I don't have my glasses," he said, apologetically.

"Zoom in," Caslin suggested. "I just want to know who that is beyond Matheson, standing with Sutherland and ACC Sinclair?" Broadfoot used his thumb and forefinger to enlarge the image. The picture was the one Caslin had taken through the glass from his vantage point at the top of the stairwell, following the meeting he had been summoned to where he'd been practically ordered to tie off the Kuznetsov case. Broadfoot handed the phone back. His expression was impassive. "Well?"

"Commander Niall Montgomerie," Broadfoot said flatly. "He heads up SO15."

"SO15? That's the Counter Terrorism Unit."

"Yes. I work with them regularly," Broadfoot said. "I should imagine, he was present in York because of the tensions surrounding the protests."

"You imagine?" Caslin said, raising an eyebrow. "In your position, shouldn't you know?" Broadfoot nodded, his expression hadn't changed, remaining unreadable but Caslin knew him well enough to know that Montgomerie's presence was news to him. "Speaking of that intelligence chatter, you mentioned."

"Go on," Broadfoot said.

"Any increase relating to activities among the far-right groups? A suggestion that they had something special planned, a new campaign maybe?"

Broadfoot shook his head, "Nothing of note that would necessarily raise a threat level. We knew they were coming to York but that's been common knowledge for some time. As to carrying out a statement of intent, violent or otherwise, no, I'm not aware. That's not to say it's inconceivable, mind you."

"They're getting more organised, aren't they?"

Broadfoot agreed with regret in his tone, "Gone are the days where you find a bunch of skin-heads getting smashed and trashing a few Asian-owned newsagents. Your modern fascists, the skilled manipulators, are educated, well-financed, dress like Hipsters and are well aware of what we do to curtail their activities. Three-quarters of referrals to the government's deradicalization scheme are for those indoctrinated in right-wing ideology."

"Three-quarters..." Caslin replied, dumbstruck.

"I fear there's an ideological war coming, Nathaniel," Broadfoot said solemnly, offering Caslin his hand by way of saying goodbye. Caslin took it. "Just not the one most people in this country expected to see. Should anything else come my way I think you'll be interested to hear, I'll be in touch. In the meantime, should you need me you know where I am."

"Thank you for your time, sir."

Broadfoot set off, leaving Caslin standing alone in the grounds of the museum. He watched the senior officer depart, his driver coming to meet him and the two headed for the car park. Caslin remained where he was, mulling over what he had learned. Perhaps, the key point he found most enlightening was the unintentional offering. With everything Broadfoot said, the leap from Walsh to Kuznetsov was the most telling. Farzaad Amin's name never came up, not even in passing. To Caslin's knowledge, Nestor Kuznetsov had no bearing on Cory Walsh nor Amin's death and yet, Broadfoot drew the link. Intentional or otherwise it set Caslin's mind racing. Taking out his phone, he called DS Hunter.

"Sarah, it's Caslin. Drop everything you're doing and find Finlay Michaelson."

"Finlay Michaelson. Got it," Hunter said. "Who is he?"

"The key," Caslin replied and hung up.

CHAPTER NINETEEN

HUNTER NEGOTIATED the overtaking manoeuvre with ease. For once, Caslin felt certain she'd demonstrated enough caution. Leaving the tractor and its trailer behind, the car accelerated. Making the next turn in the road, Caslin reached up and tilted the sun visor. They were heading west, away from York towards Long Marston, a small village barely seven miles from the city. Slowing as they approached the outer limits of the village, leaving the open farmland behind them, Caslin focusing his attention on the road ahead.

"There should be a left turn coming up, signposted for the Village Hall," he said peering into the distance. As expected, they came to the intersection and Hunter took the turn onto Angram Road. There were houses to either side of them. A mixture of modern homes designed to blend seamlessly in although failing to do so, nestled in between aging brick buildings constructed over the past few centuries. Many were easily identifiable as converted agricultural buildings, juxtaposed alongside traditional farmhouses, often striking an odd-looking contrast with one another.

The houses to their left were replaced by a perimeter wall, running adjacent to the road and stretching forward for several hundred yards. Caslin knew this wall, with its mature trees beyond, shrouded their destination from the roadside. Ahead, the village church could be seen towering over an upcoming line of three or four houses at the edge of the settlement boundary.

"This one?" Hunter asked, slowing further and annoying the vehicle that had sped up behind them.

"Yes, the entrance should be just up here on the left," he replied, pointing with his forefinger. No sooner had he spoken, the turn onto the driveway came into view as the wall curved in and away from the highway. Hunter flicked on the indicator. The brickwork of the boundary wall must have been set prior to the advent of modern vehicles, such was the limited space on either side of them. The car following them accelerated aggressively once they were clear. Evidently, the driver was in a hurry.

The driveway was gravel lined and cut immediately back in the direction they had come before winding off to the right and up towards a large, detached Georgian farmhouse. Caslin cast an eye over it as they pulled up, coming to a stop. The brick building, with its stone detailing, clay pantile roof and elegant twelve-pane, sash and case windows struck an imposing figure in the mature gardens that surrounded it. Many of the curtains were still drawn, despite the setting sun now being at the rear of the house. Hunter glanced around. A detached, double garage lay ahead of them. It was closed with the fallen leaves of the established garden banked up against the doors, driven there by the wind.

"No car outside. It doesn't look like anyone's home," she said.

Caslin unclipped his seatbelt and opened his door. "We're expected. She'll be home," he replied, getting out. Hunter followed suit.

They approached the entrance. The door was oversized and original, judging by the thickness along with the detailing. Modern reproductions were easy to spot. There was no need to knock as the door opened before they reached it. The woman who stood before them cracked a weak smile. She was in her sixties, Caslin guessed, of slim build with a heavily-lined face. Her eyes were sunken and the welcoming expression appeared forced. Caslin recognised only too well the physical manifestations that coincided with mental torment.

"Mrs Michaelson?" he asked, already sure of the answer.

She nodded. "Inspector Caslin?"

He took out his wallet, showing her his warrant card. She barely glanced at it, merely stepping aside and beckoning them to enter. "Please, come in."

"This is Detective Sergeant Sarah Hunter," Caslin offered, as he stepped forward. Hunter smiled, in greeting, with another returned in her direction by their host. Mrs Michaelson led them along the hallway into the interior of the house, ushering them into what Caslin figured to be the drawing room.

An open fire crackled in the hearth. The room was traditionally decorated with wood-panelling to waist height on all four walls. Two large sofas were set facing each other to either side of the fireplace. It was here that they were guided to and offered a seat. A wall clock ticked and wood crackled in the hearth.

"Would you care for some tea or perhaps coffee?" they were asked graciously. Both Caslin and Hunter declined. Mrs Michaelson sat down opposite them, looking uncomfortable. Judging by her demeanour since their arrival, Caslin figured she wasn't a sedentary person and sitting still was not in her general make-up.

"Thank you for agreeing to meet with us, Mrs Michaelson," Caslin began, she smiled.

"Please, do call me Miranda."

"Once again, I am very sorry for your loss."

"Thank you, Inspector," she replied. Miranda Michaelson bore the stark pain of losing her husband. "Please, how can I help you?"

"As I said on the telephone, we're investigating a case in which your late husband's name has come up. Within his role in the civil service, he may well have been aware of details we're yet to uncover or may have come across some names of those who are involved," Caslin said softly. "I certainly don't wish to cause you any undue distress. Did he ever mention his work to you?"

Miranda shook her head, "I am terribly sorry, Inspector. Finlay didn't speak to me about his work. He rarely ever did. Perhaps earlier in his career, when he was confident he was in line for a promotion but even then, never in any great detail. Regarding anything within the last few years I'm afraid I can be of little help to you."

"Could we ask about why he retired when he did?" Hunter asked.

"Of course, yes," Miranda said, turning to her. "Everything was getting rather fraught domestically. I returned to nurse my mother… oh, it must be… four years ago now. She was finding the house to be far too much for her to cope with. Finlay remained in London, obviously, but he would travel up as and when he could manage to."

"And this caused…" Caslin struggled to find the correct word, "friction, between the two of you?"

"After a while living apart begins to cause problems. The pressure was certainly mounting," Miranda replied, her voice tailed off as she glanced out of the nearest window at nothing in particular.

"So, your husband took early retirement?" Hunter asked.

"Mother was ailing and I needed the support."

"And he moved here to help you," Caslin said.

"To be closer to me, yes," Miranda confirmed. "Or, at least, that was what he *said*."

Caslin sat forward, interested, "You have your doubts?" Miranda stiffened slightly. Had he not been looking directly at her, Caslin may have missed it.

"He would still spend hours in his study," she said, an edge to her tone. "Even though he was supposedly retired. I never got the impression that he ever really wanted to give it up. To be fair, he'd worked hard to get where he had and if the truth be known, I think he found it galling to step away because of the needs of my family."

"The relationship was difficult?" Hunter pressed but took care to be gentle.

Miranda chuckled, "Finlay referred to my mother as an *Ogre*. They never took kindly to each other. My father, on the other hand, was altogether different. Finlay was like the son he'd never had. They got on famously."

"Can you tell us about your husband's state of mind around the time of his death?" Caslin asked. "Did he convey any feelings to you or appear stressed, agitated, about anything?" She thought on it for a moment before answering.

"He was certainly withdrawn," she said. "More so than I'd ever experienced with him prior to that. However, he found our separation equally challenging and after four years of virtually living apart, I'm not entirely sure how recent that change in his manner may have been. I had no idea that he was... having the thoughts that he was."

"I am sorry you are having to revisit all of this," Caslin said.

"That's quite all right, Inspector. I think on it every day." The statement only led him to feel even worse.

"How is your mother?" Hunter asked. Miranda met her eye.

"She also passed away, two months ago," she said. "I have laid her to rest alongside my father just as she would have wanted."

"I am sorry," Hunter said, wishing she'd never asked. To lose her husband through suicide along with her remaining parent in such quick succession must have been extremely difficult to process.

"Don't worry, Dear. You weren't to know," Miranda said, warmly.

"Your husband's study, may we see it?" Caslin asked.

Miranda nodded. "Certainly," she said, rising. Caslin and Hunter also stood. "Please, come this way."

They were led from the drawing room, back into the hallway. Heading down the hall and to the left, Miranda showed them to a room at the rear of the building. Coming to stand before the door, she stepped to the side and turned to face them. "I must admit, I haven't been in there since... since I found, Finlay," she said, in halting speech.

"That's okay. There's no need for you to come in," Caslin said, placing a reassuring hand on her forearm. Miranda appeared grateful. "Tell me, has much been touched or moved from in there?"

She shook her head, "No. No one's been in there. Just the paramedics... oh, and the constable who came along after. I haven't felt ready to tackle it, not yet. You see, it was my father's study before Finlay took it over and, well... he passed away from a heart attack in the same room. They were so alike, those two. It is somewhat fitting, I suppose."

"Thank you," Caslin said, grasping the handle. Miranda excused herself.

"I will wait for you in the drawing room," she said before leaving them alone. Caslin cast Hunter a sideways glance and opened the door.

Caslin led the way. The room was almost a perfect square, with dual-aspect windows. The southern-facing pane allowed the room to flood with light as the winter-sun dropped low on the horizon. A traditional, hardwood desk was on one side of the room, set in from the wall, with the east-facing window behind the chair. Caslin indicated for Hunter to inspect the shelving units, stacked to shoulder height with lever-arch folders, while he approached the desk.

Coming around to the other side, Caslin pulled out the chair and sat down. There was a banker's desk-lamp in situ, antique brass fitting with an emerald-green shade. He pulled the switch and it bathed the surface of the desk in artificial light. Nothing much adorned the desk apart from a solitary wedding photograph, its dark brown hue giving away its age, and a little stationery so Caslin turned his focus to the drawers.

Glancing down, he noted the two pedestals, one to either side of him. Both had four drawers with one large double-width drawer interconnecting both units. He opened this one first and inspected the contents. Aside from some blank sheets of headed paper, a letter opener and some assorted envelopes of various sizes, he found nothing to pique his interest. As he was pushing it closed, he spied a ring of keys. Picking them up, he counted three, guessing they were for the locks to the desk. They were small, brass, with intricately cast patterns on the bow. Closing the drawer, he inserted one of the keys into the lock. It slid in effortlessly and the mechanism turned with ease.

Switching his attention back to the pedestals, he tried the drawers one by one. Checking all eight, Caslin found none of them to be locked. Then he set about going through them again although this time he spent more time on each as he analysed the contents. More than half of the drawers were empty and of the remaining ones, Caslin found nothing of note. There were old utility bills, some correspondence relating to a function being arranged in the local village and a scattering of receipts but nothing relevant. Having optimistically expected to find a diary, some handwritten notes or copied files that might generate a new lead, Caslin was left disappointed. Sitting back in the chair, he exhaled deeply. Hunter looked over from where she was scanning through a folder.

"Nothing?"

Caslin shook his head.

"No. If Michaelson brought his work home with him on the weekend, he didn't leave it here," Caslin said, dejected. "What about you?"

"Same here," she replied. "Most of this stuff relates to the farm and its holdings. Maybe he didn't keep anything after he retired or his files were down in London. He would've had his own digs down there after all."

Caslin blew out his cheeks, "Then what was he doing holed up in his study?" A thought struck him. Picking up the keys once more, he tried one in the lock of the first drawer in the pedestal to his right. The key turned smoothly. Pulling out the drawer, he then pushed it closed and then did the same again, only slower. Repeating the process with each drawer, Caslin found none of the locks to be stiff and the drawers were smooth in transition from closed to open. Pursing his lips, he sank back in the chair. Hunter crossed the room to join him, giving up on her search.

"A penny for them?"

"The drawers," he said, indicating them with a general sweep of his hand before scooping up the keys. She looked at them and then back at him.

"What of them?"

"They all work," he replied, as if that answered everything.

"I don't understand."

"This is an old desk. An antique, not a reproduction."

"So?"

"If you don't use them, things like these locks..." he pointed to the first drawer, down to his right, "the mechanisms are liable to seize up or at the very least, the wood swells, warps, stiffens, whatever, making keys harder to turn. Not here. Every lock works like a charm. The same with pulling out the drawers. There are no runners, no bearings to make it smooth. If you don't open them regularly, they'll get stiff or screech."

"So, the desk was well used?" Hunter asked, not quite following his line of thought.

"Very much so," Caslin confirmed. "And yet, half the drawers are empty and none of them were locked."

"And... if they were frequently locked..." Hunter followed the logic.

"That's right," Caslin said. "There must have been something to secure more valuable than headed paper and a few old electricity bills."

"But there's nothing," Hunter stated, glancing around the office. Caslin followed her lead and scanned the room for anything that might catch his attention. There were two canvas paintings, hanging on the walls. One to the left of the south-facing window, depicting a landscape, along with another above the fire-place. The latter was an inset, cast-iron Victorian addition with intricate detailing. A work of art in itself.

Coming out from behind the desk, Caslin crossed to the fire-place and examined the canvas hanging above. It was a portrait, seemingly of one of Miranda's ancestors. A portly man, with an angular jaw and red-faced complexion. Judging from the clothing he wore, Caslin assumed he may have been the first to own the family residence at some point in the eighteenth century.

"Look at these," Hunter said, over her shoulder. Caslin came to stand alongside her. She was casting an eye over some photographs, framed and hanging on the wall behind the desk. "This must be Finlay and Miranda, fairly recently," she said, pointing to a photograph apparently taken on a warm, sunny day. Miranda appeared much as she did now albeit with a far more relaxed demeanour and brighter eyes. The man next to her, with an arm around her shoulder was smiling and Caslin knew it to be Finlay Michaelson having come across his picture in the coroner's case file prior to making the drive out to Long Marston.

They were either photographs of family holidays from over the years or what looked to be special occasions, perhaps in far-flung locations but in many cases it was impossible to tell. Caslin hovered over one of the couple sitting astride horses with moun-tains in the background.

"I'd say that was Argentina, if I had to guess," Hunter offered, seeing Caslin ocusing on it.

"Really? You sound sure."

"Stephen and I travelled to Patagonia shortly after we got engaged. The light and the landscape are memorable. Those moun-tains behind them look like the Austral Andes," Hunter said. There was something in her tone that struck a chord with him. A note of melancholy perhaps? He wasn't sure and chose not to mention it.

"I've never been," Caslin said, moving along and scanning the next picture. Taking a step back, he focused on the arrangement.

There was something odd about it but he couldn't quite put his finger on what had sharpened his focus. Hunter noticed.

"What's up?" she asked.

Caslin shook his head, "I'm not sure. Can you put the main light on please?"

The sun had dropped below the horizon and the gloom of a winter afternoon was now sapping the light from around them. Hunter crossed the room and flicked the switch. The five-way, wrought-iron chandelier counteracted the growing darkness. At first glance, the arrangement of the framed pictures looked haphazard at best. They were not all of a uniform size, some were set in landscape while others were in traditional portrait style. Even so, something didn't look right to his eye.

Coming to stand before the desk, Caslin sought to tease out the thought currently lodged in the back of his mind. From this vantage point, he could see a slight discolouration in the wall between two pictures. Hunter caught sight of his lingering gaze and followed his eye.

"What is it?"

Caslin didn't answer but walked around the desk and approached the point he was focusing on. Reaching up with his right hand, he ran his fingers lightly across the wall. They stopped at a point and he tapped it with his index finger.

"The paper," he said, turning his body side-on and moving closer. "The paper has been bleached by the sun and here," he tapped the wall again, for emphasis, "there's a hole."

"There was another picture hanging there?" Hunter asked, scanning the remaining images. "What about over there?" she said, pointing to another anomalous gap between two frames and bearing a similar contrast. Caslin crossed to it and located a nail-hole for a picture hook.

"Good spot," he said, confirming the find. "We need to know when they were taken down."

"And why?" Hunter said quietly.

Caslin nodded his agreement. "I think Miranda is going to have to come in here after all. I'll go and get her."

"Take your time," Caslin said. Miranda Michaelson stood in the centre of her late husband's study, staring at the desk in front of her. Clearly, she was struggling to maintain her composure. The last time she was in that position was when she'd found her husband of forty-two years slumped at his desk, having ingested an overdose of painkillers.

"I don't know what I'm looking for," she said, her voice threatening to crack at any moment.

"Anything unusual or out of place, no matter how small or insignificant you might think it," Hunter offered by way of encouragement. Miranda closed her eyes, looking to the floor and took a deep breath. Lifting her head, she reopened her eyes appearing focused on what she had to do. Both Caslin and Hunter waited patiently. Miranda started with the desk, drawing her gaze across the surface before shifting her attention away.

"What about the contents?" Caslin suggested, indicating the drawers.

She shook her head, "I never went into them. Finlay was quite insistent that I should stay out of his work affairs and besides, he always kept them locked. The Official Secrets Act and all of that." Caslin nodded, briefly flicking his eyes to Hunter who indicated she'd noted the significance of the comment. Miranda turned and looked around the room, pausing at the portrait over the fireplace.

"A relative?" Caslin asked. Her eyes lit up momentarily and a brief smile crossed her lips.

"My great-great-grandfather, yes," she confirmed, with pride. "He bought this house with proceeds from investments made overseas." Miranda continued on, concentrating hard on the task set for her. Caslin did a little calculation in his head, giving a fleeting consideration to whether the profits needed to purchase a house such as this would have been garnered through means considered, these days at least, to be of an amoral origin. His thoughts were punctuated by an exclamation. "There!"

"What is it?" Caslin asked.

"A photograph is missing right there," Miranda said, pointing. "And another," she added, crossing to where Hunter had noted the second space.

"Do you know when they came down?" Caslin asked, endeavouring to contain his enthusiasm. It was soon dashed.

"No, I'm sorry," Miranda said. "I don't come in here very often."

"Do you remember what the pictures were of?" Hunter asked. Miranda thought on it for a while, her expression a mask of concentration.

"One was of a fishing trip, I think. Finlay went on it a few years ago. It was in the Mediterranean with some colleagues. He was quite excited as I recall. The photo was taken on board the yacht. Finlay appeared terribly dashing in that one."

"Who was he with?"

She shook her head, "It was some freebie excursion sponsored by companies through the DTI, I believe."

"Was it an official Department of Trade and Industry junket?" Caslin asked.

"I've no idea," Miranda scoffed. "It was several years ago and like I said, Finlay didn't discuss his work."

"And the other one?" Hunter asked but Miranda was noncommittal.

"I don't recall. I'm sorry."

"Did your husband have a computer here, at home?" Caslin asked.

Miranda nodded. "Yes, he had a laptop. He kept it there, in his desk." Caslin glanced over to Hunter, whose impassive expression belied the same feeling he was suppressing. They were on the right path. He knew it.

"WHAT DO YOU THINK?" Hunter asked. "Someone else has been in there, haven't they?" Caslin looked back at the house as she turned the car around and set off along the driveway. The tyres crunched on the gravel and Hunter remembered to turn on her headlights before they reached the highway.

"Miranda swears blind only herself, the ambulance crew and the police officer who attended, entered the study. Then it was the undertaker and a detective constable who we know signed it off as a suicide on the same day. Other than that, no one has been in there."

Hunter shot him a sideways glance, "So, that's that?"

"Is it hell," Caslin retorted. "You're right. Someone's been in there and cleaned it out."

"Do you think she knows who?"

"Some people are natural actors but not her," Caslin said, shaking his head. "I'll bet they did it under her nose and without her knowledge or consent. I want to know who and why? Michaelson was neck deep into, or up to, something. I'm absolutely certain of it. What I would give to know who was with him in those photographs."

"Someone made an effort to ensure no one would," Hunter replied.

"Or what he was involved in."

"Whatever it was it drove him to take his own life," Hunter said.

"That's what they say."

"Where do we go from here?"

"I want you to set up surveillance on Thomas Grey. For one, he's stressing about something and, more importantly…" he let the thought tail off.

"More importantly?"

"Well, first and foremost, he's still alive."

CHAPTER TWENTY

NURSING HIS PINT, Caslin's gaze drifted beyond the vaulted, brick ceiling and up into the next tier of Lendal Cellars. A man was propped up, one elbow resting against the bar, complaining about his day to anyone who'd listen. By all accounts, his friends were just as tired of listening to it as he was. The pub was quiet tonight. On any given day, the clamour of the crowd would merge into a general hubbub, replacing an overheard conversation with anonymity. This evening though, the freezing temperatures and driving rain were keeping people away.

For Caslin, the short walk across the centre to his favourite haunt was neither a distraction nor an escape. He did his best thinking alone and over the years had realised he could be alone even in a crowd. It was a state of mind. From his seat in a booth, situated in the lower section, Caslin could see right across the pub. Immediately clocking the figures as they entered from above, he watched them descend the steps. The first casually scanned the few people present whereas the other two, only a step behind, moved with the grace and agility of predators, furtively glancing around, assessing patrons as a hunter would their targets. Caslin had wondered how long it would be before he'd see them again.

One of the accompanying men dropped off, remaining in the

upper bar, near to the main entrance and set himself with his back to the wall and a clear line of sight in Caslin's direction. The other continued on, with Cory Walsh, towards him. The latter offering a partial wave as they approached. Caslin flicked him a greeting with a bob of his head.

"I figured you'd be stopping by at some point," Caslin said.

Walsh smiled warmly, splaying his hands wide, "Please accept my apologies for missing our appointment the other night. I was called away at short notice." Walsh removed his coat, followed by a scarf, and carefully folded the coat before laying both across the back of the padded seat to the booth. Sliding in opposite Caslin, he nodded another greeting before glancing towards his associate. "I'll have a scotch," he said, looking to Caslin who nodded. "Make that two," Walsh instructed and the man departed.

"Did you go anywhere nice?" Caslin asked.

Walsh exhaled heavily, "Copenhagen."

"Beautiful."

"It is," Walsh agreed, "but I flew in and out. I was only there for a couple of hours."

"Your phone didn't work?" Caslin said, mildly hostile. Despite accepting there could be justifiable reasons for his failure to show, Caslin still didn't appreciate being stood up. Walsh grinned. Caslin figured it was forced.

"I am genuinely sorry," Walsh said. He eyed the side of Caslin's face, taking in the bruising that was now a deeper shade of purple. "It would appear your time, since we last met, has been... eventful?"

Caslin finished his pint, placing the empty glass on the table. "Someone followed me the other night. When we were supposed to meet," he said, seeing no reason to keep it a secret, figuring Walsh knew more than he was letting on. He always seemed to be at least one step ahead. "But that's not news to you is it?"

"I'm not surprised to hear that, Nathaniel. If you weren't already under some form of surveillance, covert or otherwise, I'm certain you would've been soon enough," Walsh stated, with a brief shake of the head.

"Were they following me or looking for you?"

Walsh inclined his head slightly, appreciating the logic, "That, I couldn't say."

"Is that why you bailed on our meeting?" Caslin challenged. Walsh met his eye.

"I was in Copenhagen. Like I said," he replied, adopting a defensive posture. Walsh's associate arrived with two scotches, placing them on the table. He then stepped aside to Caslin's left, keeping his back to the wall and facing the open bar. His eyes never ceased scanning the room.

"Who is following me?" Caslin asked.

"It could be any number of people or agencies..." Walsh said with a brief shrug of his shoulders, picking up his glass. "Good health," he said, before sipping at the contents.

"Even yours?" Caslin asked, leaving his own drink where it had been placed. Walsh laughed. Caslin was sure it was genuine on this occasion.

"You think I would have you followed to our own meeting and then fail to show?" he said with a smile, shaking his head in a dismissive gesture. "And people accuse *me* of being paranoid." Caslin flicked his eyebrows at the absurdity of his own suggestion, sweeping up his glass and tilting it in Walsh's direction.

"Cheers," he said, tasting the scotch. "If someone is following me in order to get to you, you're taking a risk in coming here tonight."

"I take precautions, Nathaniel. It has become something of a habit... a very necessary one, in fact. I trust you received my little package?"

Caslin nodded, "Yes, thank you. I guessed it came from you. Well, you've certainly got my attention. Care to fill in the blanks?"

"What would you like to know?"

"Your connection to Farzaad Amin. How about starting there and we'll see how we go," Caslin said, sitting back and stretching one arm out, resting it on the back of the seat. "You said you didn't know him but that's not true."

"We go back a way," Walsh said, sucking air through his teeth, "and that's not an easy question to answer."

"I have time," Caslin said, revisiting his scotch.

"I'm sure you've done your homework on me by now?" Walsh asked, peering over the rim of his glass as he raised it. Caslin inclined his head.

"Naturally."

"And what did you find out?"

"You're a businessman. A very successful one by anyone's measure," Caslin added, "who's turned his hand to political lobbying."

"Is that what they say now? For a time, I was considered more of a revolutionary... an activist. Then I was downgraded to the more vanilla term of a *campaigner*. It loses some of its edge, don't you think?"

"I've also heard of *a one-man crusade*. How about that?"

"I do like that. It has a certain ring to it," Walsh said, grinning. He finished his scotch. Turning to his minder, he requested a refill. Caslin followed suit, finishing his scotch in one fluid motion. Walsh indicated another for him as well.

"Amin?" Caslin pressed.

"Amin was one of you," Walsh said, but before Caslin could respond, he continued, "in law enforcement, at least. Do you know how I made my fortune, the first time around?"

"No, I didn't get that far."

"You remember the Cold War and how we know now what life was like behind the Iron Curtain?" Caslin indicated he did. "Well, when that period came to an abrupt, undignified end and the former Soviet States began to open up politically, for a time at least, so did the world of commerce. Out of the ruins of a failed system new markets arose like a phoenix from the flames. Prime opportunities for those who had the capital, along with the courage, to embrace them. The likes of me were welcomed with open arms. We had the expertise. We had the knowledge."

"A lot of people got rich," Caslin said.

"Very," Walsh agreed, "almost overnight in many cases. I was one of those who started wealthy and enriched myself even further. Celebrated in Forbes, lauded by investment analysts the world over. I must admit, I thought I was a king."

"It didn't last?"

"On the contrary, the returns lasted for well over a decade... and then things began to change. A little at first, incremental changes below the surface that slipped by largely unnoticed."

"What kind of changes? What are we talking about here?" Caslin asked, interested.

"The wealth began to coalesce around the few, perhaps two to three hundred individuals, give or take. I mean personal wealth on a scale that most people just can't comprehend. Obviously, there were many others sitting below at different levels of the food chain and still are. But these few, in particular, began to soak up not only most of the money but all of the power. So much so that they began looking beyond the confines of their relatively young business empires and seeking out new challenges. New ways to exert their influence on the world. Money, in of itself, just wasn't enough anymore."

"For some people there will never be enough."

"True."

"Are you talking about politics?"

"Very astute, Nathaniel. These men knew how they'd come across their fortunes. They were often former members of the Politburo, high-ranking officers of the KGB or its successor, the FSB. They had the contacts, the training, as well as the skills to manipulate and succeed, particularly with a weakened government operating largely in chaos. It's no great secret that after the fall of the Communist system organised crime within Russia and her satellite states exploded into life with rapid expansion into the same areas I've been talking about."

"Russian gangs have operated for years, some for centuries."

"Of course, you are right. But now, they were doing so with the aid of those who once sought to stunt them. The foxes were taking charge of the hen house, so to speak. They were awash with cash."

"Are you saying all of the money was dirty?"

"After a fashion. Assets were open to access like never before. Infrastructure, gas and oil reserves – state assets owned and operated by a failing system. Without a strong government, businessmen could purchase these assets at knockdown prices, as little as a few dollars in some cases. Overnight, their true value was listed on the markets and you have billionaires made from absolutely nothing!" He snapped his fingers as if to dramatise the point.

"How was that even legal?" Caslin asked, incredulous.

"Technically, it wasn't but it was a new world for these guys. Greasing the right wheels allowed these deals to go through with precious little oversight."

"They paid off the authorities?"

"Absolutely. You have to remember the state of these places at the time. The governments were largely bankrupt. Many of these officials hadn't been paid in months. An approach, offering what equated to several years' worth of pay for what, signing over something that meant nothing to you personally? That was a no brainer."

"And this is how you were making your money?" Caslin said, as their second round of drinks arrived. Walsh sat back, the enthusiasm for his story visually draining from him, momentarily.

"There were no losers," he argued, although Caslin sensed he said so with little conviction. "At least, for a while."

"Go on," Caslin said.

"As I said, the power began to centre on a few and they, in turn, were jockeying for position. Whoever held the strongest list of contacts in their phonebook tended to win out. On occasion, the same people were being paid off by competing groups. Anyway, I digress," he waved his hands in a circular motion, "as the governments reorganised and reasserted some control, so the questions began to be asked. That is where Amin comes into it. Although, that's not his real name."

"What is his real name?"

"Kadyrov. Marat Kadyrov is how I knew him," Walsh said, his tone shifting from one of confident explanation to sadness, remembering a lost friend. "He was ideological. Perhaps naïve in his views of how things should be, but a very decent man. When I came across him we were on opposing sides. He was tasked with investigating organised crime and ascertaining how far their operations had penetrated the state apparatus.

Substantially, I would say but that's another story. Well before I ever met him, he'd been deployed by the intelligence services to infiltrate a Muscovite criminal organisation with links to other gangs throughout the Caucasus. His ethnic Kazakh background gave him the credibility that many of the other agencies just didn't possess. That experience made him an outstanding candidate for this new role."

"Hence why he could be passed off as an Afghan asylum seeker here in the UK?"

"It would appear so."

Caslin raised his glass, "Did he investigate you?"

Walsh inclined his head, "In a way, yes. He was following the money trail and I chanced across his radar."

"How did Kay... Kad...?"

"Kadyrov," Walsh confirmed.

"How did he wind up here in the UK, living under a false name?" Caslin asked, leaving out the more obvious question of *why he couldn't find any record of it?*

"He was a tenacious investigator, Nathaniel. You would have liked him. The two of you have much in common. To my knowledge, he'd uncovered a scandal involving the sale of construction contracts across several Moscow Oblasts."

"Oblasts?"

"I'm sorry. They are administrative centres or zones," Walsh explained. Caslin bid him to continue. "Marat's belief was that these contracts were granted off the back of multiple bribes, paid to various levels of government officials. The last I spoke with him, he was due to take his findings to his superiors with an expectation they would sanction more funds to enable him to widen his investigation."

"I guess it didn't go down that way?"

"I'm afraid that what followed I am not a party to," Walsh said. "However, suffice it to say, I didn't hear from Marat again. It was as if he disappeared. Apparently, it looks very much like he did so with the aid of your intelligence services."

"He turned to us?"

"My belief is that he offered up everything he had on his investigation to your agencies in exchange for safe passage to the UK."

"But you don't know?" Caslin asked, leaning forward.

Walsh shook his head. "When Marat vanished, he was helping me."

"How?"

"There's a way of doing things in Russia, Nathaniel. What you have you may not necessarily get to keep. Do you understand? Why do you think your country is awash with wealthy oligarchs, buying up houses, football clubs, expensive cars and any other material goods that catch their eye? Here, they can keep what they have."

"Someone explained that to me once. They came after you, didn't they? Or at least, your money."

"As I said, you are very astute, Nathaniel." Walsh's tone tinged with regret. For the first time, Caslin noted a real change in demeanour of the man sitting opposite him. Up until now, his confidence appeared unshakeable. A self-belief, no doubt garnered from his success in the business world appeared to be creaking under the weight of reality. "I found money was missing from my investments in Russia. Somewhere along the line funds were being syphoned off at an alarming rate. I couldn't trust my internal staff to recover it. I had no idea where the seals had been breached."

"So, you approached Kadyrov?"

Walsh nodded, "I figured that he was already moving in the right circles. He was different to others I'd come across over there – honest, perhaps? A man of integrity, certainly."

"And?"

"Shortly after was when he vanished," Walsh said, deflated. "I tried to contact him but he didn't return my calls. A little time passed and I approached members of his circle only to find that they too had been lifted from the street. I went to his family and it was only then that it dawned on me."

"What happened?"

"They were detained. I never found out why."

"What did you do?"

"I took the only sensible course of action. I left, as quickly as possible," Walsh said, picking up his glass and seeing off the contents.

"The country?"

"My home, the country, my business. Everything," Walsh stated evenly. "Once I was clear I set about liquidating my hold- ings. I did so as quickly and as quietly as I could. I figured that if they knew what Marat knew, all that I had told him, then they'd be coming for me and everything that I had. My fears proved to be extremely accurate as it turned out."

"How much did you lose?"

"Initially, a little over $200 million was unaccounted for," Walsh said, without skipping a beat. "I transferred out the remaining funds in the course of the following weeks and months. That isn't easy by the way. There are tight controls on moving that kind of money. Shifting it without triggering any alarms was no mean feat."

"And Kadyrov, how did you find him in the UK?"

"I didn't," Walsh said. "He contacted me several days before his death. He caught me completely off guard."

"Why?"

"I thought he was dead," Walsh stated, "or rotting in a Siberian labour camp."

"What did he want?"

"To meet," Walsh said, glancing around nervously. No one was within earshot apart from his minder.

"And?"

Walsh shook his head, "I was abroad with commitments I couldn't shake. By the time I was able to get back to the UK – it was the day he died, Nathaniel. The meeting never took place."

Caslin thought about it for a moment, "And his murder... who are you putting that down to?"

Walsh looked him square in the eye, "I'm a numbers man, Nathaniel. An analyst. I approach everything through the prism of the percentages. If I had to judge I would suggest someone is covering their tracks. Everyone knows what I am about these days. Marat certainly did. Why else would he contact me? Find out who had the most to lose from Marat's voice being heard and you will have your answer. I wouldn't rule out an agenda closer to home, though."

"Rather than one Russian-based?"

"It must be considered," Walsh said with a shrug. "If he was here at the convenience of your authorities, they might not appreciate my presence either."

"You have a high opinion of yourself," Caslin said, only partly in jest.

"If you have a strong belief in coincidence you may discount the suggestion, by all means."

"You steered me towards Alexander Nairn and his suicide," Caslin said, shifting the subject. "What do you know of him?"

"I know he racked up significant frequent-flyer miles between the UK and Moscow. Marat had him down as aiding the flow of money in and out of the city."

"Whose money?"

"Only a dead man could tell you that, Nathaniel. Not me."

"Thomas Grey. Nairn's business partner. What do you know about him?"

Walsh shrugged, "Not a name I'm familiar with. I'm sorry."

"Have you heard of a civil servant by the name of Finlay Michaelson or Project Obmen? Those names also appear in the files you sent me."

"If I had all the answers, Nathaniel, I wouldn't need you, would I?" Walsh said as he stood up. He picked up his scarf and wrapped it loosely around his neck before pulling on his overcoat.

"Is there somewhere you need to be?" Caslin asked, silently considering what had provoked the all-to-sudden departure.

"We're both searching for answers to the same questions."

"But is it for the same reasons?" Caslin fixed Walsh with a stern gaze.

"Only time will tell," he replied, with a smile. Glancing to his minder who signalled they were good to go, he set off towards the upper bar and the exit. Pausing as he placed his foot on the first step, he turned to Caslin, looking over his shoulder. "Thank you for your company, Nathaniel. I'm sure you'll be in touch."

Caslin replied with a brief nod of the head, raising his glass and tilting it in Walsh's direction. Digesting the new information, Caslin couldn't help but wonder if the developing case was a little above the level of a detective inspector from North Yorkshire Police. He felt his phone vibrate. Reaching for it, he found the call had disconnected before he could answer. The signal had been lost. Being underground in a brick cellar, he was impressed he'd managed to obtain a signal at all.

Sliding out from his seat in the booth, he picked up his coat and climbed the steps. Casually acknowledging the bar staff with a wave, he crossed the lower bar and mounted the next flight of stairs whilst reading the missed call alert. No sooner had he reacquired service upon reaching the street outside, the phone rang. It was Hunter.

"Sir, I put that surveillance detail on Thomas Grey but it's not good news," she said, sounding crestfallen.

"Why, what's going on?"

"We tried to pick him up at his office, then at home but he wasn't at either."

"Okay, keep looking—"

"No, sir, you don't understand, Uniform found his Discovery abandoned on an industrial estate out towards Clifton Moor. I'm on my way over there now."

"And Grey?"

"No idea, sir. I've put out his description but nothing yet."

"Send me the address and I'll meet you there."

CHAPTER TWENTY-ONE

THE KEYLESS FOB was resting on the central console and the lights of the dashboard display were on. The gearstick was set to the drive position and the logical assumption was the engine had either stalled or switched itself into an idle-mode. Caslin stepped back from the driver's door, open wide, with the corner wedged into the damp mud of the verge running to the side of the road. Arguably, the door had been opened in a hurry.

Scanning the road, he saw no rubber residue on the tarmac. Although the falling rain would have ensured there would have been none. Eyeing the length of the car from wing to rear, the paintwork was immaculate without scuff or scrape. In fact, there was no evidence nearby to suggest the car had left the highway involuntarily. Turning his attention back to the Discovery's interior, Caslin turned his collar up against the elements. The rain was now coming down in a steady drizzle with the light breeze making it feel even colder than earlier in the day.

"Was the door open when you got here?" Caslin asked over his shoulder, seeing the approaching Hunter.

"Yes. The traffic officers found it exactly as you see it," she confirmed, coming to stand behind him.

Caslin donned a pair of latex gloves and leant inside, casting an eye around the cabin. He looked for the obvious, blood stains or tears to the upholstery, anything that could imply a confrontation violent or otherwise. There were none. The leather, stitched into both the seats and doors, was as pristine as you might expect from such a prestigious marque of vehicle appearing as if it was fresh off the forecourt. A jacket lay casually across the rear seats but aside from a couple of fuel receipts, dated earlier in the week, and a fountain pen left in the pocket of the door, Caslin could see nothing of note.

"Did you find anything?" he asked Hunter, retreating from the car.

"A mobile phone. A set of keys, presumably for home and office," Hunter said. "That's it."

"Anything in the boot?"

"Nothing. It's empty."

"Any sign of Grey's security detail?"

Hunter shook her head, "No. I had the same thought, so I contacted Lisa. You remember, from his office?"

"Yes, of course. And?"

"She said Grey turned up to work alone this morning. She didn't know why and he went straight through to his office without a word."

"Interesting," Caslin said, considering the possibilities.

"She also told me he remained there alone, all day, flatly refusing to take calls and left unexpectedly around two o'clock this afternoon."

"Did she know where he was heading?"

"No. He didn't say."

"Anything happen of note, today?"

"Apparently not, no."

"And when did Uniform locate the car?"

"Shortly after nine, sir. A member of the public was finishing a back shift and called it in on their way home after finding it apparently abandoned. They thought it odd."

"Did they report seeing Thomas Grey or anyone else hanging around? Another car perhaps?"

Hunter shook her head, "There's not a lot of through-traffic around here this late in the day." Caslin surveyed the area. They were standing on the outskirts of an industrial estate with warehouse units in one direction and open farmland in the other. Within a half mile were large out-of-town retail units set alongside a bowling alley and chain restaurants, whereas here, once the businesses shut down for the day, there was nothing. Whatever motivated Thomas Grey to come to this location of an evening totally escaped him.

"Did you take anything useful off the phone?" Caslin asked hopefully.

"It was locked," Hunter said, confirming what Caslin already figured to be the case. "Although forensics have green lighted me bagging it and I've sent a runner over to Iain Robertson to see what he can do. He's pretty confident."

Caslin nodded approvingly, "Get a warrant for the records. Disturb someone's evening or wake them up if it comes to it. We need to know who he was talking to and where he's been in those seven hours. People don't drop off the face of the earth unless they want to or—"

"Someone forces them," Hunter finished for him. There was movement behind them as members of the CSI team arrived to run the forensic rule over the car.

Caslin addressed the lead officer, "Be thorough. I need help to fill in the blanks and I'll take whatever you can give me."

"Yes, sir," the lead figure said.

Caslin turned to see a uniformed constable standing a short distance away trying to get his attention. He looked to Hunter and inclined his head to indicate she should join him. They made their way across the road bracing against the increasing intensity of both the wind and the rain.

"What do you have?" Caslin asked as they approached her.

"I've found a briefcase up against the perimeter fence over

there," the constable said, indicating behind her towards the edge of an industrial compound.

She led the way and they stepped up onto the verge which, due to the combination of rain and uncut grass, was rapidly becoming treacherous under foot. Illuminated by the constable's torch, Caslin and Hunter spied the briefcase. It was open with what appeared to be the contents strewn nearby. Loose sheets of paper, trapped in the sprawling vegetation, were wet-through and proved largely illegible whilst others were being carried on the wind, distributed to a far wider area.

Kneeling, Caslin inspected the briefcase itself. Without touching it, he eyed the locking mechanism and found neither of the catches had been forced. Whoever had opened it did so with knowledge of the code or the owner hadn't shifted the numbers in order to secure it. Still wearing his gloves, Caslin lightly checked the remaining contents. The internal sleeves contained several folders and Caslin partially pulled one out, casually thumbing through the papers and clocking the letterheads for Grey's company. Reluctant to risk their ruin, he quickly put them back where he'd found them. Glancing at Hunter, he said, "Make sure forensics detail this and then get it back to Fulford Road and go through it."

"Will do," Hunter replied.

"Good spot, Constable," Caslin said, standing.

"Thank you, sir."

Caslin pointed at the briefcase, "It's a pain in the backside but I want you to walk this stretch of road and retrieve everything that looks remotely like it may have come from that briefcase and pass it to DS Hunter."

"Yes, sir."

"What do you think?" Hunter asked him, falling into step alongside as Caslin reached the highway. He contemplated his answer before speaking. Stopping, he glanced back towards the uniformed constable before looking in the direction of the Discovery, with three CSI officers crawling all over it.

"Despite his best attempt to appear calm to us, Thomas Grey is hiding something. His behaviour seems somewhat erratic at best since we paid him a visit."

"Because of us do you reckon?"

Caslin flicked his eyebrows up accompanied by a slight shake of the head, "He didn't surround himself with private security because of us but we rattled him. Of that I'm certain. It's just that I can't quite figure out why."

"And why did he ditch the bodyguards?"

"Perhaps he came out here to meet someone."

"Without his protection?"

"He met Danika Durakovic without them," Caslin said, meeting Hunter's eye.

"You think she has a hand in this?"

He shrugged, "And therein lies one of the mysteries here. We were all over Danika's operation for what, the better part of eight months?"

"At least."

"And Grey didn't pop up on our radar once," Caslin said. "Considering how well they seemed to know each other, don't you find that a little odd?"

Hunter nodded, "We need access to Grey's phone to see who he spends time talking to."

"That's where I'm headed," Caslin said. "You get the scene squared away and I'll meet you back at the station."

"The warrant could take a while," Hunter said, "particularly at this time of night."

"I have faith in you, Sarah," Caslin said with a wink and a smile. He turned and headed back to his car. Increasing his pace, Caslin reached the car and clambered in, happy for the respite from the rain. Such was the volume of water in his hair the moment he leant forward to put his key in the ignition, water ran down his forehead. Shaking his head, he wiped his brow with the palm of his hand before starting the car. The windscreen was already steaming up and he set the blowers to maximum.

Reaching for his mobile, he found Iain Robertson's number and dialled it.

"I know what you're going to ask and no, I haven't accessed the phone yet," Robertson replied from his laboratory, without the courtesy of even a basic greeting.

"Please tell me you're not waiting for a warrant?" Caslin replied, also happy to dispense with the pleasantries. Robertson laughed.

"The last time the authorities tried to get the encryption of one of these handsets cracked by the manufacturer they fought it tooth and nail. It took months... and they won, too."

"Yeah, I could do without that," Caslin said, turning on the wipers to clear the screen in front of him.

"I figured you wouldn't have the time for that—"

"Nor the patience," Caslin cut in.

"Indeed. So, I've been designing an ingenious hack. Off the record, obviously," Robertson said with a reassurance that came involuntarily with his Scottish accent.

"You can crack it yourself?" Caslin asked without meaning to sound sceptical but the tone did so involuntarily.

"You don't keep me around for my charming demeanour," Robertson replied.

"Your brilliance never ceases to amaze me. I'm on my way. I'll see you in fifteen to twenty minutes," Caslin said, hanging up.

Caslin put his mobile down and engaged first gear but as he did so the handset beeped. Taking the car out of gear, he glanced at the screen and saw he'd received a text. The number was unfamiliar to him. Opening it, there was only one sentence. It read: *Your new friend is in danger.* Caslin sat back, touching the handset to his lips. The message wasn't signed. Intrigued, he typed out a short response – *Which friend... and who are you?* – there was a pause that lasted long enough for Caslin to figure he wasn't going to get a response but just as he was about to set off again, the mobile beeped. He read the reply – *Trust me.*

No stranger to the occasional threat over the years, Caslin had to admit this struck him as a little different for he had never received a warning via his mobile before. There was one obvious candidate, the mysterious texter could be referring to but if it was him, Cory Walsh, then this wasn't new information. After all, the man was a walking advert for paranoia. Caslin pushed for some clarity – *And you are…?* – he waited for a reply but none was forthcoming. Having let a few minutes pass, he put the mobile down and allowed his mind to wander as to who might be offering him the heads-up as well as why.

CASLIN FOUND Iain Robertson hunched over a table in his lab paying close attention to something in front of him. He'd expected to find him peering into a computer screen in an attempt to hack the passcode to Thomas Grey's mobile using some kind of self-designed algorithm.

Instead, Robertson glanced up and met his arrival with a scalpel blade in hand with slivers of what looked like jelly on the table before him, alongside Grey's handset and pieces of rolled out Plasticine. Robertson met Caslin's quizzical look with a broad smile.

"It's more twenty-first century than you probably think."

"It'd have to be," Caslin replied, approaching the table. "Any joy?"

"You timed it about right. I'm not far off finding out," he replied, turning back to what he was doing. Caslin watched as Robertson peeled out a thumb-sized blob of what looked under closer inspection to be a transparent silicon from a knob of the Plasticine. Laying it before him, he then took the scalpel and began slicing a thin portion across the domed lump, taking great care not to break the surface. For some reason, Caslin held his breath, reluctant to speak and risk breaking the obvious concentration. Once Robertson was through, he sat up, the sliver of gelatinous material on the edge of his forefinger and exhaled deeply. "That ought to do it."

"Do what? What is that anyway?"

"That, young man," Robertson began, despite him being only three years senior to Caslin, "is how I'm going to get you into this mobile."

"Okay, I'll bite," Caslin said. "How?"

"First, one of my techs lifted a decent fingerprint from Grey's Discovery. The engine start button provided a rather detailed one. Once I had that, I applied a little magic dust to the print..." Caslin eyed him suspiciously. "Okay, I scanned it into my computer at a 300dpi resolution. Then, I mirrored it, shrank it back to normal size and printed it out onto a glossy, transparent slide. Using silver conductive ink alongside standard black, I could produce a fingerprint to fool the sensor."

"Ahh... right. That's more of what I was expecting," Caslin said with approval. "So, what's with all the play dough, jelly and stuff? Although, I see you're missing the glitter glue and farmyard shapes."

Robertson laughed, "Problem was, it didn't work. I've seen it done with some brands but this is top of the range and I think the software recognised the fact it was a copy."

"How so?"

"Your biometric sensors pretty much work the same way across the manufacturers. You record your print and it registers your pattern. The handset need only recognise three points of your pattern to unlock the phone, sometimes more but the premise is always the same."

"But that didn't work?"

Robertson shook his head. "The poorer systems can be fooled by a photocopy, believe it or not. Whereas the more secure ones are a little smarter. They might require ridge definition on the pad, a raised print for example. However, this model," he said, indicating Grey's handset, "goes a step further."

"Go on," Caslin said, genuinely interested whilst suddenly concerned about the security of his own mobile.

"I'll show you," Robertson said, smiling and turning back to his handiwork. He lifted the sliver of jelly and, reversing the handset on the table before him, laid it carefully over the finger-print sensor. "This system was developed a couple of years ago but is still being applied to the manufacturer's ridiculously expensive current model as if it's new tech. The software not only detects the presence of the ridges but also whether there is any heat behind the print."

"So, the owner has to be alive?"

Robertson frowned, "Do you ever think you've worked too many murders, Nate? I was going for 'present' and not necessarily still alive. The idea is this will bypass anyone faking a print. I suppose, to follow your train of thought, the actual finger must be used and in theory, would still need to be attached to the owner. Or then again, still warm as a minimum."

"Now who's worked too many crime scenes?" Caslin said playfully.

"Possibly," Robertson agreed. "To get around this problem, I took the print and spayed it with a fine mist of glue. Then, I pressed it into a mould fashioned from the Plasticine, ridges and all. I mixed a fast-setting epoxy-resin or crazy-glue, if that helps you to understand," Robertson said in a condescending, paternalistic tone which caused Caslin to crack a smile, "and poured it in. I've allowed it to set, then sliced out the print and here we are."

"Is it going to work?" Caslin asked, turning his gaze to the mobile.

"Let's find out," Robertson stated. Reaching forward, he lightly placed a forefinger onto the print he'd so carefully created and pressed down. A split-second later, the phone vibrated and lifting the handset revealed an unlocked screen. Robertson's face split a broad grin. "Never trust the advertising," he said with a nod, passing the handset to Caslin.

"You truly are a magician, Iain."

"I know," Robertson replied. "Just not fully appreciated within my lifetime."

Caslin took the offered handset and set off for CID, already tapping through to the stored text messages and recently dialled lists. In both, he found multiple entries dated for that very day. Already the excitement was building. Reaching the door out of the lab, Caslin paused and turned back to Robertson, already beginning to clear up the mess he'd made.

"Iain, out of interest. How do I secure my phone?" he asked. Robertson looked skyward for a moment, considering the question.

"I would argue that if someone is duplicating your fingerprint using 3D printers, epoxy-resin or latex copies... then you have bigger problems in your life than securing your mobile phone."

Caslin nodded, "Good point."

CHAPTER TWENTY-TWO

Hunter entered CID just as Terry Holt connected the mobile to his laptop. Now, what was visible on the handset was displayed on a projector screen. Caslin acknowledged her arrival and filled her in as she took off her overcoat, shaking off the excess water before hanging it up.

"We're in," Caslin explained. "Grey had a text conversation during the day."

"Who with?" Hunter asked, pulling up a chair and rubbing her cheeks to freshen her face. The clock ticked past midnight but there was no sign of anyone looking to go home.

"It's an unknown number," Holt said, "but they know each other. That much is clear."

"Put it up," Caslin said, pointing to the large screen. Holt did so, bringing up the conversation with a couple of clicks. "The first one was received by Grey before eight this morning." Hunter turned her attention to the thread.

07:52
> *We need to talk.*
07:57

I know… it's been a while. Things been manic.
08:00
Arriving today. I expect to see you.
08:20
York? When?
08:22
Will call. I want an answer.
08:43
Not easy. Working on it.

"The number's unknown but where does it originate?" Hunter asked. Meeting Holt's questioning glance, she continued, "The international code?"

Holt looked at the number, "It's +7. Where's that?"

"Russia," Caslin stated, even further intrigued by the revelation. "Run the number through the system and see if we can track where it's been and where it is now. If the carrier's passed through an airport today, it might help us pin down a name to go with it or at least, narrow the list.

"Interesting that Grey knew who it was despite not having the number saved," Hunter added. "When do they communicate further?"

Holt scrolled down, "Around lunchtime."
13:30
Checking in. You'd better be worth my time. They're pushing.
13:34
I'm on my way. I'm trying.
13:36
No excuses. No time.

"Is there any more?" Caslin asked.

Holt shook his head, "Not in this thread. They haven't communicated before either."

"Not on this number," Hunter said. Holt shot her a dark look. She ignored him.

"What would we give to have been a fly-on-the-wall in that

meeting? What are they talking about do you think?" Caslin said aloud.

"Money," Holt said. "Got to be. Grey's into property and that's all.about money at the end of the day."

"Go through the emails and other text threads to see if you can grant us a steer," Caslin said to Holt. Turning to Hunter, he continued, "Track the number. Find out where it is and where it's been."

"You think this person has a hand in Grey's disappearance?"

"I think it's related but too early to say in what way. He left his office shortly after two, I recall. It's reasonable to suggest he was on his way to that meeting. Track Grey's phone at the same time and see if the two intersect. Then we'll have a location. You never know, we may find Grey himself."

"I'll get on it," Hunter said, rising from her seat. Caslin returned his gaze to the text thread up on the screen. Whoever the newcomer was, reading between the lines, Thomas Grey was giving them the run-around to such an extent that they'd travelled to York to confront him. Whether Grey had an appropriate answer could well determine the condition in which they would him. That is, *if* they could find him.

"Sir," Hunter called from across the squad room. Caslin turned to see her with a phone pressed to her ear and an excited expression upon her face. "We've got him." Caslin jumped up, grabbed his coat and hurried across the room, shouting over his shoulder to Holt.

"Terry, take over from Sarah and map their paths. I'll give you a call later."

"Will do, sir," Holt replied. If he was annoyed at being passed Hunter's tasks as well as his own, he didn't show it. A reaction that didn't go unnoticed by his senior officer. Such was the team's determination to get a result.

"Where is he?" Caslin asked as Hunter left the room alongside him.

"Here, in York. He's at Bootham Park."

Caslin stopped and turned to her. "The psychiatric hospital?"

he asked, looking puzzled. "I thought that'd been declared unfit and closed down."

"It was. Then they realised there was nowhere else to take people and reopened it."

"Bootham borders Clifton. Grey's car was abandoned... what... a quarter of a mile away?"

"If that."

"Come on. Let's get over there."

———

BOOTHAM PARK HOSPITAL was sited adjacent to York's main hospital on the northern edge of the city centre. In order to reach it, Caslin had to cross the River Ouse twice when navigating the city centre but fortunately, in the early hours, their journey took less than fifteen minutes.

Turning off Clarence Street they took another couple of left turns in quick succession before pulling into the car park of the imposing three-storey Victorian building. The car park was nigh on deserted and Caslin was grateful the rain had ceased. The breeze was ever present and he braced against the cold. The clouds had momentarily cleared revealing a crisp night, bathing the open grounds in front of them in a silver light.

Hunter got out of the passenger side and closed the door. Caslin locked the car and they headed down the path towards the entrance. Off to the right was the hospital's chapel, cutting an eerie figure set within the surroundings of the barren trees. They reached the front door, a double door of heavy wooden construction set front and centre in the neo-classical frontage. Pressing the buzzer, they waited, illuminated only by the moonlight as the sound carried through the interior of the building.

The intercom crackled into life and they were greeted by a female voice.

"Hello, how can I help?"

"DI Caslin and DS Hunter from Fulford CID. We called

ahead," Caslin said, glancing up at the camera above and to the right of the door.

"Please come in," the voice said and the accompanying click indicated the door was open. Hunter pushed the door inwards and they stepped through. Barely had they closed the door behind them, they were met in the lobby. Caslin watched her approach. She was in her forties, dressed in black trousers, a blouse and a pink cardigan. The photo, clipped to the cardigan, was the only indication that she was staff. "Hello, I'm Grace Anderson."

"DI Caslin," he said once again, showing her his warrant card. Grace eyed it briefly and then acknowledged Hunter, beckoning them to follow her. The lights in the communal area appeared to be on a timer with minimal illumination.

"You're here to see Mr Grey, I understand?" Grace asked. "I'm sorry, I didn't take your call."

"That's right," Caslin replied. "What is his condition?"

"I'll leave the discussion of diagnosis to the attending specialist, if you don't mind," she said, leading them up a staircase and onto the first floor.

"You're not a doctor?" Hunter asked.

Grace shook her head, "No. I'm a facilitator. Dr Ashman will meet with you."

"Thomas Grey was admitted earlier tonight," Caslin said.

"Yes. Shortly after 8 p.m." They reached a half-landing between floors and she led them to the rear and into a two-storey wing tacked on at some point in the past. "He was admitted to our acute inpatient ward for assessment."

"Is that complete?" Hunter said.

"I believe so, yes," Grace replied, approaching a locked door. She swiped a pass key and the lock disengaged. Stepping aside, she allowed them to enter first. The corridor was brightly lit in stark contrast to where they'd been. It was clear they were standing in the lobby of a secure unit. A small nurse's station was set in front of them with three doors beyond, each with the same locking system as the one behind them. From behind the desk a young man rose to greet them. Caslin was mildly surprised to find this was Dr Ashman and he was at least ten years Caslin's junior. Although, that seemed to happen more frequently than it used to.

"Dr Ashman?" Caslin asked, offering his hand. The young man took it.

"Inspector Caslin. Pleased to meet you," Ashman said, smiling. He then shook hands with Hunter. "Please, come through to the office."

He led them into what was a shared office, little more than a four-metre square rectangle with a solitary desk, multiple filing cabinets and shelves. Almost everywhere they looked was stuffed full of loose paperwork, files and folders. Dr Ashman seemed to notice.

"You'll have to forgive our apparent untidiness. We were closing, then reopened for emergency cases and now we take on outpatients as well."

"It takes time to ramp everything back up?" Hunter asked.

Ashman shook his head, "Most of the hospital is still mothballed and the latest swing of the pendulum will see us shut down pretty soon. A new unit has been given the go ahead by the planners."

"Couldn't make up their mind?" Caslin asked casually.

"I think we were a knee-jerk response to the lack of mental-health provision currently available in the system," Ashman stated, offering them both a seat. Caslin declined. For his part, Ashman leaned against the desk, folding his arms before him.

"Thomas Grey?" Caslin asked.

"Admitted last night," Dr Ashman confirmed, reaching for a folder on the desk. Opening it, he scanned the first page. "You'll understand I must respect patient confidentiality?"

"Of course," Caslin said. "However, this is a murder investigation and Mr Grey is a figure in our investigation."

"He came to us exhibiting both physical and mental trauma."

"To what extent, physical?" Hunter said.

"He has superficial cuts to both wrists. Early toxicological tests have returned evidence of amphetamine ingestion," the doctor said. "Accident and Emergency performed a gastric lavage to remove the contents of his stomach, just in case, and then shipped him over here after their initial assessment."

"How do you view the cuts? Are they defensive wounds?" Caslin asked. The doctor shook his head.

"Not in my opinion, no. They are more likely to be self-inflicted."

"Is Grey suicidal?"

"That shifts me into an uncomfortable position of supposition," Ashman said.

"Uncomfortable... how?" Caslin pressed. Ashman sucked air through his teeth before setting his expression in a frown.

"I wouldn't suggest his heart was in it."

"He's faking?" Hunter asked.

"The levels of amphetamine in his blood stream would suggest otherwise," Ashman said, "and without doubt he has been expressing levels of mania that are entirely consistent with a paranoid complex."

"Driven by what? Recreational drugs?"

Ashman shook his head whilst scanning the file before him, "This is his third stay with us and he's exhibited the same behaviour on each previous occasion but this is the only time drugs have come back positive in his samples."

"Can we speak with him?" Caslin asked.

"Certainly, but you might find him somewhat erratic. I'm reluctant to prescribe any anti-psychotic medicine until I'm sure of what is currently in his system. That won't be until mid-morning at the earliest."

A piercing alarm sounded throughout the ward, everyone in the room jumped in shock. Dr Ashman was first to react and hotfooted it out of the office, Caslin and Hunter only a step behind. Grace Anderson met them in the lobby and responded to the doctor's unanswered question.

"One of the patients has attacked a nurse," she said. Caslin found her matter-of-fact tone slightly alarming. He figured it was a reasonably common occurrence.

"Which patient?" Ashman asked.

"Mr Grey," she replied. Caslin and Hunter exchanged glances. A male nurse joined them and together they passed through the furthermost door into the ward. The small party broke into a run and the noise level increased as they approached the scene of the disturbance.

The corridor opened out into what Caslin assumed to be a patient's activity room. Chairs and tables were upended in every direction. Two nurses were attempting to restrain Thomas Grey on the far side of the room. For his part, Grey was resisting to such an extent that his face was a shade of deep crimson as he hurled abuse at both men. The three staggered slightly to the left and Grey managed to free an arm, striking the man to his right a downward blow with the point of his elbow.

Caslin was shocked to see such a change in the businessman. A third nurse crossed the room under instruction from Dr Ashman to try and subdue Grey. Caslin tried to follow but felt the doctor's arm come across his chest to deter him.

"Please allow my team to do its job, Inspector," Ashman said firmly. Regrettably, Caslin did as requested. At that moment, Grey broke free and grabbed hold of the first person he could, sinking his teeth into the man's ear. The nurse screamed. Grey released him, spitting out a mixture of blood and saliva, gleefully screaming at the injured man.

"You bastards won't take me!" he shouted, blood staining his teeth and lips as he was forced backwards, staring wild-eyed at those trying to subdue him. "I'll fucking die first!" Losing his footing, or having his stability forcibly taken away, saw Grey fall to the floor. All three nurses, now with the upper hand attempted to pin Grey to the ground. Caslin's thoughts passed to the multiple occasions where he and his colleagues had come across drunks who needed to be arrested. On some occasions, such was the ferocity and determination of their quarry, it could take six grown men to manage the situation and take the man down.

Almost as quickly as the drama had arisen it subsided. Grey was placed into restraints, including the deployment of a spit-hood and despite his best efforts, he could no longer wreak damage on the staff. He was unceremoniously carted away, presumably to a secure private room. An eerie silence descended. Caslin felt his heart race. A quick glance at Hunter saw her confirm similar. Grace excused herself, leaving the three of them alone.

"I'm sorry, Inspector Caslin. Your conversation with Mr Grey will have to wait," Ashman said, tension in his voice. Caslin nodded his understanding.

"Tell me. Has Grey behaved like this on the other occasions that he's been here?"

Ashman shook his head, "Never violently, no. He has been known to kiss other patients and there were a couple of incidents where he... how should I put it... he has wandering hands, with certain members of staff."

"Charming," Hunter said, raising her eyebrows.

"Not only with the women," Ashman offered, "and I don't see that as overtly sexual behaviour. Speaking from a purely clinical standpoint anyway."

"Do the women see it that way?" Hunter asked.

"Not always," Ashman replied, with a brief shake of the head, before adding, "nor do the men, by the way." Hunter exhaled heavily, smiling, as much from the release of tension as from the doctor's light-hearted additional comment.

"When will you let us speak with him?" Caslin asked.

"First thing in the morning. You won't get a lot of sense from him now.

"When he was admitted, did he have anything on him at all?" Caslin asked.

Dr Ashman shrugged, "Nothing, apart from the clothes he was wearing."

"Any of these drugs you were talking about?"

"No, sorry. What is all this about?"

"That's just what we're trying to find out, Doctor," Caslin said, his eyes drifting away in the direction where they had taken Grey.

Caslin's mobile rang and he excused himself from the conversation, stepping away to the other side of the room. It was Holt, back at Fulford Road.

"Sir, I've had some joy with the mobile networks," he said excitedly.

"Go on."

"I tried to find out who the mystery number is registered to but what with it being a Russian company and it being the middle of the night, I've had no luck. However, I tracked the signals back to see which of the local transmitters the two have connected with and looked for a link. They cross paths in only one place."

"Give me some good news, Terry," Caslin asked, drawing Hunter's attention to the conversation. He beckoned her over.

"South-west of York, sir," Holt said with enthusiasm. "And seeing as our mystery caller was travelling in to the area, I thought it likely he would be staying at a hotel. There are only two that are within range of that particular repeater station."

"Good work, Terry," Caslin said. "Have you called them yet?"

"No, sir," Holt replied. "I figured it'd be better to turn up unannounced."

"Agreed. Which hotels?"

"The Windsor Garden Lodge and The Centennial. If it were me, I'd start at the latter."

"Why?"

"Judging by the circles these guys tend to move in I'd expect five-star all the way. The Windsor would be slumming it at only four."

"Text me the address and we'll meet you there," Caslin replied. Hanging up, he turned to the waiting Hunter. "Looks like it's going to be a long night, Sarah."

CHAPTER TWENTY-THREE

THE LOBBY of The Centennial Hotel was of a noticeably higher standard than most others Caslin had frequented. His initial perception of the double-height atrium was that five stars didn't do the building justice. The lobby opened up to reveal marble panelling to the walls, ornately decorated archways to the interior and stunning frescos that drew the eye upwards.

An open fire crackled away to his left, despite the lateness of the hour, with leather seating of the finest craftsmanship set out before it. The ambient lighting was calming and soft music played. Caslin recognised the artist, a modern classical piece by Elskavon but he couldn't recollect the title. The concierge appeared at reception from a back room, Terry Holt a step behind. He saw Caslin and Hunter, acknowledging them with a brief wave. He came from behind the desk as they approached.

"What do we have, Terry?" Caslin asked.

"Only one man fitting the bill checked in earlier today, sir," Holt said, barely concealing his excitement. "A Russian national by the name of Alexander Koliokov. The system tells us his key card hasn't been active since lunchtime."

"So, he's here?" Hunter asked. Holt nodded.

"Room number?" Caslin asked.

"311. This way," Holt stated, setting off and indicating the direction of the lifts. "Third floor."

The concierge followed on, appearing rather interested. Caslin guessed this wasn't his usual night shift. The interior of the lift matched the plush surroundings, polished steel walls that shone with a golden tint. The doors slid open and they stepped out onto the third floor. They all looked for the numbering to guide them but a voice spoke from behind.

"To the right," Caslin glanced back and thanked the young man who was accompanying them. The small party made their way along the corridor until they reached Room 311. A 'do not disturb' sign hung on the door handle. Holt met Caslin's eye and he nodded. The constable rapped his knuckles on the door three times. They waited but there was no sign of movement within. That was unsurprising bearing in mind they were approaching one o'clock in the morning. Holt tried again only this time with more force. Still, there was no reply. Caslin turned to the concierge standing a few steps behind them, watching expectantly.

"Open it," he said flatly. The young man didn't hesitate and came forward producing his master card. He placed it into the slot and the LED changed from red to green. Caslin indicated for him to step away to a respectable distance. Taking a firm grip of the handle, he eased it down and cracked the door open. Collectively, the three took a deep breath. Terry Holt was first through with Caslin and Hunter a half-step behind.

"Police!" Holt barked in an authoritarian tone. It wasn't a raid but they wanted to be sure the resident knew who was coming. No one responded as they entered. The lights were out, the suite in darkness. Hunter located the nearest light switch and illuminated the entrance hall. Koliokov had booked into a suite consisting of two bedrooms, a lounge, the bathroom as well as access to a private roof terrace. The group spread out and searched for the Russian, flicking on lights as they went.

"Nothing in either bedroom apart from a suitcase," Hunter called out.

"Bathroom's clear," Holt shouted. Caslin stood in the lounge hands on hips.

The room was dressed to perfection. It barely looked as if anyone had been present since the hotel staff had last serviced it. A gust of cold wind drifted over him and Caslin turned to see the curtains swaying gently. He was joined by the other two. He indicated towards the doors where the breeze originated. The access to the roof terrace.

The three moved over and Hunter threw back the curtains. Outside, despite the darkness, they could make out the figure of a man sitting alone in a recliner. Caslin saw a switch to his right and assumed it was for the outside. He pressed it and the figure was bathed in a pool of off-white light, strung out around the terrace. The mix of soft light amid the now falling rain cast an eerie picture particularly as the water had aided the spreading pool of red beneath him.

"Explains why he didn't answer," Hunter said under her breath. Caslin gently pushed the door open with his elbow ensuring he didn't touch the handle and potentially damage any forensic evidence. Drawing his coat about him, he turned to Holt.

"Go back downstairs with the concierge and take a look at their CCTV. I want to know if this is Koliokov and whether anyone else turned up who cannot be accounted for today. Was he alone, did Grey show up and if so, who was he with? And while you're at it, give Iain Robertson a call and get his team out here."

"I'm on it," Holt said, turning to leave.

Caslin followed Hunter out onto the terrace. Both were careful where they put their feet. The falling rain was pooling on the stone tiles of the terrace, washing the man's lifeblood out from beneath him. They got as close as they dared. He was obviously dead and had been for some time, his pale features drained of all colour. He wore suit trousers and a pink and white striped shirt, unbuttoned at both collar and cuff. A cursory examination revealed his wrists had been cut but vertically rather than horizontally as the majority of suicide victims tended to do. Doing so ensures a faster rate of bleeding and in turn brings on an expedient death.

Further to those wounds, Caslin counted at least four, but possibly five, slashes to the throat three to four inches long. Two of which appeared relatively shallow but others were evidently deeper.

"I don't see any defensive injuries," Hunter said, raising her voice above the howl of the wind and the driving rain. "And I can't see any weapon," she added, casting an eye around them.

Caslin shook his head, "Nor me."

"Looks like an elaborate suicide," Hunter said but sounded less than convinced. "With a vanishing blade, too."

"Travel all the way to York from Russia to top yourself on the roof of a poncey hotel," Caslin said appearing dismissive.

"It doesn't make any sense," Hunter agreed. "Maybe he didn't like what Grey had to say?"

"Or maybe Grey didn't appreciate the visit?" Caslin said before glancing skyward. The rain was increasing in intensity. He looked around, noting the terrace wasn't overlooked by any other hotel window. Surrounding them was open land. A small estate with a well-designed and cultivated landscape of trees and foliage. The nearest building adjacent to this one was well over three hundred metres away, without a clear sightline. "Let's go and see what this guy brought with him and then catch up with Terry and the hotel cameras."

The two of them returned to the lounge grateful to be out of the rain. This time they were more thorough but the detailed search provided nothing fruitful. Koliokov had unpacked upon his arrival but all he brought with him was an overnight bag containing two changes of clothing and essential toiletries. Inside the bag, Caslin found the man's passport and opening it to the photograph page, he was quite certain this was the man sitting outside in the rain. He brandished the passport towards Hunter who leaned over and nodded her agreement. Hunter opened a drawer beside the bed and took out a black, leather wallet. Opening it, she thumbed through the contents.

"Anything interesting?" Caslin asked.

"A few thousand Roubles. A couple of hundred in Sterling. Credit cards and…"

"What is it?"

"… a picture of a girl young enough to be his daughter by the look of it."

"Maybe it is his daughter?" Caslin said. Hunter exaggerated her expression turning the corners of her mouth down.

"Not dressed like this," she said, removing the picture, turning it and presenting it to him. Caslin scanned the image of the young woman, barely eighteen in his opinion and scantily clad in erotic lingerie in a provocative pose. He blew out his cheeks.

"Well, you'd bloody well hope not," he concluded. Hunter replaced the photograph back into the wallet.

"Any sign of his phone?" she asked.

"No," Caslin replied, heading back into the lounge. Hunter followed. Crossing the room to the bar, Caslin spied an open bottle of scotch. Approaching, he found there were two glasses on the counter and he sniffed at them. Both had contained scotch but were now empty. There was an ice box open alongside them. Koliokov had either drunk two glasses himself or shared a drink with another. Caslin hazarded a guess it was Grey. He pointed them out to Hunter, "Make sure CSI lift the prints off of these. I'd put money on it one of these has Grey's prints all over it."

"You think he's at the centre of all of this don't you?"

"Perhaps not the centre but he's involved and could be the key to unlocking what's going on."

"You sound quite sure of that."

"There are a lot of people moving in and around his circle who are turning up dead at the moment and there's one thing for certain," Caslin said, leaving the thought hanging in the air.

"What's that?"

"He's the one who is still alive," Caslin said flatly.

"For now."

"Sure, he's probably in the safest place right now."

A uniformed officer arrived at the entrance to the suite and Caslin told him to secure the scene until forensics arrived. Together, Caslin and Hunter made their way back downstairs to the lobby and found Holt sitting in the concierge's office analysing the security footage.

"What do you have for us, Terry?" Caslin asked. Holt sat back in the office chair and spun it around to face them.

"We have Thomas Grey arriving shortly before two thirty this afternoon," Holt said, indicating to the monitor beside him. The concierge hit play and they rolled the camera footage on. They watched as Grey entered the hotel lobby and purposefully made his way to the reception desk. A short conversation followed and the clerk made a telephone call whilst Grey waited. He stood before the counter one hand in his pocket.

"Looks pretty relaxed, I'd say," Hunter said.

"He does but it's shielding his anxiety. Look how he's drumming the fingers of his free hand on the counter and shifting his feet. He's trying hard to appear casual but I'd say he's anything but."

"Good shout," Holt said. "I'd missed that."

"Is he alone?" Caslin said.

"Yes," Holt said. They watched as the clerk replaced the receiver and the two shared a few more words before Grey set off in the direction of the lifts. "Presumably he's just been given Koliokov's room number. No one follows him. There's another angle showing Grey enter and exit the lift alone on the third floor. We don't have him entering Room 311 but he reappears in the lobby barely fifteen minutes later."

"That's quick," Hunter said, surprised.

"Doesn't give him much time for that scotch," Caslin said, Holt looked up quizzically but didn't pursue the question. "Can you bring it up?"

"Of course," Holt said and moments later they were watching

Grey re-entering the reception from the lifts. However, on this occasion, he appeared agitated. Every movement was in haste as he glanced about the reception changing direction several times before heading for the entrance doors and out into the car park.

"Was he looking for something or someone?" Hunter asked.

"Almost as if he was expecting someone," Caslin said. "Terry, can you roll that back so we can see it again please?" Holt did so and they watched the footage again. "Can you see any indication he's been in a confrontation? Damage to his suit, dark patches that could be blood perhaps?"

They all viewed the footage intently seeking the telltale sign that Grey had a hand in Koliokov's death. Holt slowed the footage down in places and replayed it in others but the images were just too small to give that level of detail.

"Do you think he *is* looking for someone or not?" Holt asked.

"What are you thinking, Terry?"

"I was just wondering if he might have been trying to avoid being seen. Look here," Holt pointed to the screen with the pen in his hand, "he changes direction twice and both times are when either a member of staff or another guest comes close. What's he hiding?"

"Blood?" Hunter asked. "Although that's pure conjecture at this point."

"Terry's right, though," Caslin agreed. "Maybe he doesn't want to be tied to the scene."

"Didn't notice the cameras," Holt added sarcastically.

"Maybe not thinking straight?" Hunter said.

"All right," Caslin said, "let's walk through it. Grey arrives for an impromptu meeting with someone he's been avoiding. What that's about we can only guess at but most likely it's to do with—"

"Money," Holt interrupted. "Most likely big money at that."

"Yep," Caslin agreed. "I would suggest Grey either owes Koliokov or they have a joint commitment and Grey hasn't come through with his end of the deal. Koliokov wants answers because he's feeling the pressure at his end."

"And Grey doesn't have them or, at least, not the answers he wants to hear," Hunter said.

"Which leaves us with the question – was Koliokov dead or alive when Grey arrived?" Caslin asked.

"Or when he left?" Holt added.

"To follow it through," Hunter continued, "Grey leaves having instigated, or come across, a suicide or committed a murder and staged it as a suicide. Does he then have a mental collapse due to the pressure of the situation and winds up at Bootham Park?"

"What are you suggesting?" Caslin asked.

"It's convenient is all I'm saying. What if Grey could have had himself committed for his own safety? As you said earlier, he's in the safest place possible right now."

"That would suggest he walked in on something and he's… what… hiding in Bootham Park?" Caslin asked. "And people say I'm cynical," he mused openly.

"No," Hunter countered, "real cynicism would be to suggest that if he had a hand in Koliokov's death, being detained under the Mental Health Act gives him an out if it ever comes to trial? After all, what did Dr Ashman say regarding his apparent suicide attempt – his heart wasn't in it?"

Caslin sighed. Hunter was right in both scenarios. They needed to talk to Thomas Grey and get his view of the day's events but that wasn't going to happen until the morning. He rubbed at his temples with the tips of his fingers, suddenly feeling the fatigue wash over him.

"All right, let's call it a day now and go home, get some rest. Grey isn't going anywhere and let's face it nor is Koliokov. Tomorrow morning, we should be able to get Iain's initial thoughts on what went on here tonight. Likewise, we'll be able to get some sense out of Grey and figure out just what is going on. Terry, first thing tomorrow I want you to run a check on this number," Caslin said, passing a slip of paper with the mobile number where the mysterious texts were being sent from.

"Okay. Who does it belong to?"

"That's what I'm hoping you can tell me. If not, tell me where it's been would you?"

"Yes, sir," Holt said, taking the paper and reading the number as if trying to glean some information to get ahead of the game.

"Shall I pick you up in the morning and we can head straight over to Bootham Park?" Hunter asked.

"I'll meet you there. I've got an errand to run first."

"Sounds intriguing."

"I figured I'd stop by and have a word with Danika."

Hunter exchanged a worried glance with Terry Holt before looking back to Caslin, "Durakovic? Do you think that's wise, under the circumstances?"

"Why? Because I've been warned to stay away from her?"

"The thought occurred, yes," Hunter replied. Caslin grinned.

"Sometimes you take all the fun out of this job, Sarah, you really do," he said with a wink. Hunter raised her eyes to the ceiling accompanied by an almost imperceptible shake of the head. Holt looked to the floor masking a nervous smile.

CHAPTER TWENTY-FOUR

CASLIN PRESSED THE INTERCOM BUTTON. There was a brief delay until a gruff voice answered.

"I'm here to see Miss Durakovic," he said.

"Do you have an appointment?" the male voice responded, in heavily-accented English. Caslin cocked his head slightly and sighed looking up at the camera to his right.

"You know who I am. Just open the bloody door."

A few seconds passed and Caslin heard the locking mechanism retract before the oversized entrance door opened. He was met by two men, nondescript henchman of Danika's retinue. He recognised neither. The first beckoned him inside with the second closing the door behind them and falling into step as they made their way through the house.

Caslin was surprised to find once the door closed the outside noise of central York dissipated quickly, despite their proximity to the train station and the press of the daily commute. Danika Durakovic lived in a Georgian townhouse, part of a redevelopment in the city centre only attainable for the rich or shameless. Danika fitted comfortably into both categories. Approaching a set of full-height double doors, Caslin was told to wait as his escort passed through them and into the room beyond. He looked to the other chaperone.

"Nice place you have here. Immoral earnings paying well this year?" he asked with a casual flick of the eyebrows. The man said nothing but he smirked. Caslin found it smug and unsurprising. The wait was momentary as the doors before him parted and he was ushered in.

Danika sat behind a large ornate desk crafted from hardwood and traditionally adorned with a green leather finish, watching his approach intently. Immaculately presented as always, in her white suit, blonde bob and fastidiously applied make up. Her hands were set out before her forming a tent with her fingers, elbows to the desk. The tips of her fingers touched her lower lip and Caslin assessed her as curious, if not amused, by his presence.

"To what do I owe this honour, Mr Caslin?" she asked, her lyrical tone purring as it came to him.

"Are you sure you don't want to pat me down?" Caslin asked with a hint of sarcasm, eyeing the two extra bodyguards present to his left and right, with both his former escorts standing behind him. Danika laughed. It was genuine.

"Really, there is no need," she said, casting a glance at the associate closest to her right. "I have it from highly-placed sources that you have been instructed to steer clear of me."

"Is that right?" Caslin said, inclining his head slightly. She was correct.

"And yet, here you are."

"In the flesh," Caslin stated, smiling.

"I'll spare you some time, Inspector but please be brief. I have a business to run."

"Yes, running an empire of prostitution, drugs and general racketeering can be time consuming can't it?"

The smile faded, "My solicitors have your chief constable's office on speed dial, Inspector. What do you want?"

"Information."

"From me? The last person you drew information from within my organisation proved far from reliable."

"I can make it worth your while."

"How so?" Danika replied, sitting back in her chair. The curiosity piqued once again.

"You and I both know I've been warned to stay away from you," Caslin began. Danika nodded her affirmation. "And you and I both know that's unlikely to happen."

"You are persistent, I'll give you that," she said. "What is it you are offering?"

"How about a period of grace?" Caslin said.

"Temporary?" Caslin nodded. "So appealing, Inspector but not much of an offer. If I'm to be honest."

"Anything more than that would be a lie," Caslin stated. "You know I think you're a low life. One day I'll take you down and anyone standing alongside," he said, casting a glance to her right and meeting the gaze of who he perceived was her most trusted lieutenant. They stood, locked in a steely gaze until Danika broke it.

"You offer little by way of favour, Inspector. I trust what you want is worth similar?"

"Very astute," Caslin said. "I want to know your connection with Thomas Grey?"

"Ahh… I see, Thomas," Danika stated, her face splitting a broad grin. "It is a fleeting one. He worked with my late husband on occasion rather than with me." Caslin figured that to be truthful bearing in mind Grey had failed to materialise in his previous investigation of her affairs.

"So why did he come to you?"

Danika's grin remained in place although the corners of her lips gave away the slightest tell that he had caught her off guard, if only a little. "Thomas always had the capacity to be sloppy. Most of the time he is prudent but when the pressure comes about, he has the capacity to make rash moves and that leaves him vulnerable."

"Likewise, anyone who he does business with?"

"Quite so, Inspector. Hence why I do not."

"He is in trouble?"

"Is that a question or a statement?"

"That's what I want you to tell me. What did he want when he came to you?"

Danika took a deep breath looking sideways to her associate who met her eye with an unreadable gaze. Caslin waited. She returned her focus to him.

"Thomas wanted to know if I could help him."

"With what?"

"I have connections. I know people," she said as if that answered his question. Caslin indicated he wanted more. "It would appear, Thomas has fallen foul of those who you really want to stay on the right side of."

"Which people?"

"The scary kind," Danika said flatly. "The type you never want to meet."

"Even you?"

"For some it's an occupational hazard," Danika said. "Thomas wanted my help to head them off."

"He wanted your protection?"

Danika laughed, "You have a very high opinion of my levels of influence, Inspector. As it happens, so did Thomas. No, he sought my intervention on his behalf."

"And what did you tell him?"

"That… unfortunately… plans were already in motion," she replied coldly. "There was nothing I could do for him."

"What plans?"

"Of that, I cannot say."

"Or won't?"

Danika didn't respond but Caslin had his answer. "Grey's business has been struggling for a while now. Do you know why?"

"I'm afraid you have exhausted my knowledge of Thomas

Grey's affairs, Inspector," Danika said, "as well as my patience. No doubt we shall speak again but I trust it won't be in the near future?"

Caslin met her stare and held it. He was not going to get any more information than he already had, despite a cast-iron certainty she knew far more than she was letting on. Without doubt, Grey was in trouble. If Danika was frightened for him, and bearing in mind what was happening to his associates, then he was on borrowed time.

The meeting was over and Caslin was escorted from the office without a farewell and back out to the street. The door closed behind him and Caslin set off to his car. The thought occurred that perhaps the mysterious texts he was receiving were unrelated to Cory Walsh and directed towards Grey. His relationship with Walsh was low profile and he had kept it largely to himself.

Despite the relationship Caslin endured with Kyle Broadfoot being somewhat fractious on occasion, his superior held his confidence and he had no reason to doubt him. Maybe he was reading more into the messages than he should have. Thomas Grey was in real jeopardy and his money troubles were the logical root cause. But who did he owe and where was the money? Caslin was looking forward to putting these questions to the man himself.

Turning away from the main traffic route, the background noise level dropped and Caslin took out his mobile. He called Terry Holt at Fulford Road.

"How are you getting on with that phone number I gave you last night?"

"I have as much as I can for now," Holt said apologetically. "It's an unregistered burn phone purchased here in the UK."

Caslin wasn't shocked, "What else can you tell me?"

"With the help of the manufacturer and network provider I was able to track it through the supply chain back to where it was distributed and sold. It was purchased in London. Incidentally, that is where much of the network activity takes place. Other than that, it's frequently used here in York. Sometimes both locations in the same week," Holt explained.

"Any particular location, here in York, I mean?"

"It's weird."

"How so?"

"The only records I have place it in the city centre where there are multiple hits but nowhere else."

"What does that tell us?"

Holt thought about it, "Either the owner lives in the city and never ventures out, always arriving by train…"

"Plausible," Caslin agreed. "Or?"

"Or they switch the phone off whenever they leave the centre," Holt concluded, "which is weird, if you ask me?"

Caslin reflected for a moment, "Tell me, where is it now?"

"It's not currently active on the network, sir. But I've flagged it and should it be turned on, I'll get a notification."

"Good work, Terry."

"Hunter's here and wants a word," Holt said as Caslin was about to hang up.

"We've had a package delivered, sir," she said, excitement edging into her tone.

"What is it?"

"Miranda Michaelson. You remember Finlay's widow?"

"Yes of course. What about her?"

"She turned up a copy of one of the photographs that were missing from the wall of her husband's office. You remember? She really liked one of them and Finlay got her a copy but she'd forgotten all about it. We jogged her memory," Hunter said. "I've scanned it and I'm emailing you a copy. You should get it any second." Caslin flipped through to his email account on his phone.

"Yes, I have it," he said before downloading the attached file. "What about the other one that was missing?"

"No such luck but she added that she thought it was a shot

taken in the inner sanctum of Westminster but she still couldn't recollect who Finlay was with."

Slowly, the picture revealed itself to him. It was as Miranda had originally described. A shot taken on a fishing trip somewhere in the Mediterranean.

Five men, appearing as close friends, huddled together at the stern of the yacht brandishing their catches and grinning to the camera. On the right was Michaelson and next to him was a face Caslin didn't recognise who had an arm around the shoulder of none other than Thomas Grey. The two remaining men, Caslin knew very well. On the far left stood the larger-than-life figure of Nestor Kuznetsov, grinning broadly. Alongside him was the familiar face of Cory Walsh.

"Son of a bitch," Caslin muttered.

"What's that, sir?" he heard Hunter say almost inaudibly. He brought the handset back to his ear, feeling a wave of embarrassment wash over him. Not through his choice of language but more because he felt like an idiot. The realisation that he may have been played somewhere along the line.

"Nothing. Don't worry," he replied, multiple scenarios cascading through his mind as he tried to bring everything together. He exhaled deeply. What the hell was going on?

"We have some leads to follow up on. I'm going to try and find out who these guys are," Hunter said, "along with where Grey, Michaelson and Kuznetsov tie in."

"Okay, great," Caslin said, reluctant to offer his own take until he had something coherent to say. "Actually, I want you to pass that on to Terry Holt so you can meet me at Bootham Park. I'm on my way over there now. Tell him to focus on the old guy with his arm around Grey, would you?"

"Why him, in particular?" Hunter asked.

"Because I know who the other one is already," Caslin said before hanging up.

As he walked, Caslin pieced together a timeline of events as he saw them. Michaelson, in his role at the Foreign Office, worked within business and trade relations. This brought him into contact with the likes of Walsh and Kuznetsov. Grey's presence suggested investments in property deals. The logical follow through would be to assume they were possibly shady in origin or at least financed unconventionally. Michaelson, however, from Caslin's understanding, had made some inroads into something that he considered potentially unethical. What Caslin figured to be a reference to the Register of Members' Interests. Furthermore, Walsh had been a vocal campaigner for transparency and good conduct in international business in recent years.

The two scenarios were poles apart and yet somehow, they were enmeshed together. One thing was for certain, Kuznetsov had severe financial woes, being declared bankrupt and subsequently those within his sphere were finding similar events befalling them. Not least, several winding up dead in questionable circumstances. Apparently, while Kuznetsov was riding high, so were those around him and similarly when he fell, the others went down like a domino effect. Caslin's phone vibrated in his pocket.

Taking it out, he saw a text message alert. It was from his unknown advisor. The message read – *They know where he is. Protect him.* Moments later, Holt was calling. Caslin answered.

"Where is it, Terry?" Caslin asked. Holt was immediately thrown at the psychic abilities of his DI but gathered himself quickly.

"Central London, sir," Holt confirmed.

"Can you be more specific?"

"No, it's already been switched off. The handset was active for less than a minute and sent a text—"

"To me," Caslin cut in. "It's a warning. I think someone knows where Grey is and they're looking to put him down... permanently. I think we need to take Thomas Grey into protective custody. Speak to Matheson and get some bodies over to Bootham Park and we can take it from there."

Caslin hung up and then scrolled through his contacts picking out a number and dialling it. He increased his pace. The phone rang at the other end and just as he was about to give up the call was answered.

"I'm a little busy, Nathaniel. Can this wait?"

"You lied to me!" Caslin said, his tone one of controlled anger. "More than once."

"I guess it can't," Cory Walsh replied.

CHAPTER TWENTY-FIVE

"You TOLD me you had no connection with Nestor Kuznetsov," Caslin said, "and yet here I am, looking at a shot of the two of you holidaying together. You look pretty tight from where I'm standing."

"I was protecting myself... and you, for that matter," Walsh countered.

"Is that so?" Caslin said. "How does this fly for you? A business associate of yours, heavily into illegal money laundering and bribery turns up dead in suspicious circumstances. That doesn't look good for the poster boy of international financial ethics does it?"

"You're getting carried away, Nathaniel," Walsh said calmly.

"Convince me. Give me a good reason not to have you arrested on suspicion of Kuznetsov's murder."

"To my knowledge, Nestor's death was a suicide."

"There are far too many Russian-backed money-men killing themselves at the moment and all of them tied either to you or Nestor Kuznetsov," Caslin said.

"You're quite right, Nathaniel. There are. I've tried my level best to keep my contacts safe and preferably out of sight until it was time to blow it wide open."

"Blow what wide open?"

"Listen, this goes beyond simple money laundering, although that's a major part of it. We're talking billions of dollars in cash and assets. That's what Nestor was. He enabled money to be funnelled out of Russia. Moscow imposed strict procedures to restrict the flow of capital out of the country. An exodus of money leaves the system vulnerable. People need to get creative in order to do that."

"Why do they have to?" Caslin asked.

"Modern Russia doesn't work like the United Kingdom, Nathaniel. Just because you have possession of money or assets it doesn't mean you get to keep it. The rule of law is dictated by whoever holds the power. No, the only way you can keep what you have is hold it where they can't touch it."

"You mean abroad?"

"Exactly. Particularly in a country such as yours where the judicial system is *almost* incorruptible," Walsh explained. Caslin reached his car, unlocked it and got in.

"And Kuznetsov facilitated this?"

"Yes. He was one of many who made a fortune off the back of state assets and used that to his benefit."

"So, you're saying the Russian State are trying to get their money back?" Caslin asked, eliciting a chuckle from the other end of the line. That annoyed him.

"It's not their money. It's the citizen's money. The taxpayers. Look, see the Russian Oligarchy as something of a game of thrones. The power shifts and coalesces behind different figures who each have a stake in the game. They are all after the same outcome: to obtain as much wealth and power as they can. To do so, they need to be on the right upward curve to do well. If you make a mistake, then your world can collapse around you."

"Like it did for Kuznetsov?"

"Correct. He cultivated his own network but overplayed his hand. The upshot was he had to leave the country but he didn't stop."

"He lost out politically but his location in the UK meant he was in a perfect position to help others funnel money out of the country," Caslin said. The clouds were clearing if only a little.

"That's right."

"His enemies want what he and his circle have and also to cut off his route for others."

"Yes."

"So why not just take out Kuznetsov? Why are they going after the others?" Caslin asked, feeling stupid.

"Because Kuznetsov is one of many. How many wealthy Russians do you know who live in London, let alone elsewhere in the world? They all need access to those with the skills to shift money around using a variety of methods. They take advantage of multiple shell companies, trust funds, hedge funds and the like. Not to mention investing heavily in real estate and infrastructure projects.

You need a small army of people to pull this off. They have the skills. If you cut down the top man another will step in and utilise the network. No, they need to kill it dead and send a message to anyone else who thinks they might like a piece of that action. If you have the right skill set then you can join in. You may well draw fantastic wealth to you but it's a high-stakes business and ultimately the reciprocity for all that money is your blood… and maybe that of your family."

"Who are these enemies you speak of back in Russia?" Caslin asked. There was a pause at the other end and Caslin had to check that the line hadn't been disconnected. It hadn't. "Cory?"

"In Russia, when you break it down there is ultimately only one man who wields that much power."

"You're talking about the president?" Caslin said softly, not quite believing the words coming out of his mouth.

"The richest man in the world bar none," Walsh confirmed. "With his own worldwide network of people laundering money in plain sight.

"Get out," Caslin said, wanting to disbelieve him but knowing in his heart it was true.

"Aided and abetted by non-Russian nationals the world over," Walsh said. "They don't just use their fellow citizens to do this but also utilise those more sympathetic to their goals."

"How do you mean?"

"How much Russian money is there invested in the banking system or in the London property market? What do you think would happen if that was withdrawn? This isn't hidden, Nathaniel. This is in plain sight as I keep telling you. That is why I kept you in the dark. It was as much for your protection as for that of me and my sources."

Caslin drew breath, "What of Thomas Grey?"

Walsh sighed, "He's a fixer. A damn good one."

"A fixer?"

"Adept at moving money without setting off alarm bells. He is very skilled when it comes to property investments."

"Tell me about Project Obmen? I believe it got Finlay Michaelson killed."

"You're not wrong," Walsh said. "*Obmen* means interchange in Russian. It's a large infrastructure project south of Moscow, part of the city's expansion. Effectively building new districts projected to house upwards of two million people over the course of the next fifteen to twenty years.

You're talking all utilities, public roads and railways, subway trains, leisure facilities. It's one of the largest and most ambitious construction projects going on right now anywhere in the world."

"How did this get Michaelson killed?"

"The details… I don't know… and that's the god's honest truth, Nathaniel. Nestor was heavily invested against my advice. There was certainly a lot of money to be made but pulling it off in the Kremlin's backyard was a big ask. Had they managed it, then that would have been one in the eye for the powerful and one hell of an embarrassment for the president. Nestor always had to push it that extra yard, you know? He overexposed himself and those around him."

"And now they're paying the price," Caslin said.

"I wasn't trying to fob you off, Nathaniel. I really am busy. I'm on my way to a meeting but we can talk more later if you want."

"Okay. I'll give you a call if I have time later today," Caslin said. "Where are you anyway?"

"I'm giving a deposition around lunchtime. I'm travelling there now," Walsh said. "Part of that whole *blowing it open* thing, I was telling you about."

"Okay, take care of yourself and I'll speak to you later."

"I always do, Nathaniel. You know that." Walsh hung up.

Caslin put his mobile in his pocket and started the car. The scale of the investigation threatened to overwhelm him and now he understood why the case had been allocated for a swift closure.

Frosty international relations would take a turn decidedly for the worse if it became public knowledge that effectively, the Russian State was executing their enemies on British soil. From a political point of view, the loss of life to a few low-level criminals paled into insignificance in comparison to an international incident with a global power.

However, it wasn't only criminals who were paying the price. Marat Kadyrov was a diligent investigator examining the theft of public assets and in his mind, until he found out otherwise. Finlay Michaelson was a civil servant doing his job. It didn't matter how high the pyramid went, Caslin was damn sure no one would get a free pass if he had anything to do with it. Maybe those at the very top were out of his reach but there would be plenty in between who were not.

Taking the turn into Bootham Park, Caslin pulled up alongside Hunter's car. It was empty, so he figured she was inside. Stepping out, he braced against the cold. The rain of the night before had passed to be replaced by an overcast day with a light wind. The temperature was low but at least the weather had lost some of its bite. He set off towards the entrance only to see Hunter emerge and walk in his direction with an expression like thunder.

"What's going on?" Caslin asked as she got within hearing distance.

"They've only gone and bloody discharged him."

"Since when?"

"Eight, this morning," Hunter said barely concealing her anger.

"Can they do that?"

"Apparently, he wasn't sectioned. He self-presented and was therefore a voluntary inpatient. They carried out an assessment this morning and judged him not to be a danger to himself or others and let him out."

"You have got to be bloody kidding me?" Caslin said. "He looked pretty dangerous last night when he took apart those nurses."

"No one has filed a complaint and until they do, Grey is free to go," Hunter said.

"Who picked him up?"

"He got a taxi," Hunter said. "I don't know where to but I've got the company name and I've given them a call to find out where he was dropped off. I'm waiting on them coming back to me. There was a shift change and the day staff don't know."

"I'll bet it's one of two places, either his apartment or the office. Put a call into ops and get Grey's description out there. He is to be detained on sight for his own safety."

"Sir?"

"I think his life is under threat. You head over to the office and I'll go to his place. If the taxi firm get back to you let me know or meet me there, yeah?"

"Got it," Hunter said and both of them got into their respective vehicles and set off.

Caslin remembered that Thomas Grey had a penthouse apartment in the city. He managed to keep it in the settlement following an acrimonious divorce from his wife during which he had spent three months in prison for failing to grant the court access to his finances. Knowing what he now knew, Caslin figured the reason for Grey's refusal was obvious. The apartment was in the shadow of York Minster, in the heart of the city's old town, not far from where Caslin lived in Kleiser's Court.

Leaving his car in a side street, the remainder of the journey was spent negotiating the narrow streets impassable by car. Even in the grip of winter, tourists were beginning to congregate around the Minster for guided tours. Caslin brushed past them without apology, such was his haste to get where he was going.

Grey's residence was located in a converted brewery building, now a bespoke refurbishment of luxury apartments. Turning the corner, Caslin heard a muffled shout and looked up to see a body falling from above, arms flailing as he came down. Within seconds he hit the railings on the edge of the street with barely a sound.

Caslin broke into a sprint, covering the ground in a matter of seconds. Thomas Grey was stretched out before him, impaled with the points of three metal railings protruding from his abdomen. One passed through his right shoulder. The second pierced his left lung, back and front, with the third having punched through the thigh of his left leg. Caslin stepped forward, putting his arms under Grey's body in a vain attempt to take the weight of the body and ease the draw of gravity. Grey convulsed, his body in spasm as he involuntarily spat blood from his mouth.

Realising the impossibility of his chosen course of action, Caslin tried his best to support him with one hand and call for help on his phone with the other. Blood was pouring from multiple wounds and seeping into Caslin's clothes as well as onto his hands. The latter were slippery and he swore as his handset slipped out of his grasp.

"Hang in there, Thomas," Caslin said under his breath.

"Bloody hell!" Hunter's voice came from behind him. He was pleased to see her. The taxi firm must have confirmed the drop off to her and her arrival couldn't have been better timed. "What can I do?"

"Get us some back-up and call an ambulance," Caslin barked, "and the Fire Brigade. They'll need to cut him off these bloody spikes!" The weight of the businessman was not insignificant and supporting him was not a task Caslin was finding easy. A few passers-by came to see what the commotion was about and without being instructed ran over to assist Caslin. Between the three of them, they took Grey's weight but what Grey knew of it was debatable. His body was going into shock.

Casting his eyes upwards, Caslin spied an open window on the top floor. That was where Grey had fallen from. Jumped or pushed, Caslin was unsure? He was itching to get upstairs and find out. Hunter got off the phone.

"They're on their way. ETA five minutes," she said before following Caslin's gaze. "Did you see anyone?"

"Nope," Caslin replied, his voice straining due to the physical exertion. Grey's breathing was ragged and coming in gasps which in turn, were spacing further and further apart. Caslin already knew their efforts would be in vain. He looked up at the window again. "We need to get in there."

"We need to wait for back-up," Hunter said, meeting his eye. Caslin knew that was what the rulebook said but hesitation only gave a would-be assailant those extra, precious seconds to make good their escape.

"I know. I would go…" he said, imploring her with his eyes. It was an order he couldn't give. Hunter took a couple of steps towards the entrance only to stall a moment later. Looking back at him, he could see the fear in her face. She couldn't hide it even if she wanted to.

"I… I'm sorry… I can't," she stammered. Caslin cursed under his breath and looked away. Sirens could be heard approaching from the south and a patrol car arrived alongside an appliance from the nearby Kent Street Fire Station. Caslin instructed the two police officers to assist the members of the public in supporting

Grey and once he was sure the appliance crew were aware of their responsibilities, he detached himself and ran towards the entrance. Hunter followed.

Residents had come from within their apartments once they heard the sirens, giving Caslin and Hunter access to the communal parts of the building. They located the stairwell and took the stairs two at a time. Caslin outpaced his detective sergeant and reached the threshold of the top floor nearly a full minute ahead of Hunter.

He approached the door to Grey's flat and found it secure. Hunter arrived behind him and Caslin pointed to the locked door. She moved aside and he stepped back. A short two-step run up and Caslin drove the base of his foot at the lock. The first attempt was unsuccessful but with a second, the door began to give but wouldn't break. A third attempt saw Caslin give in. It was a fire door and was unlikely to give way.

"I'll be back," Hunter said and took off down the stairs. Caslin tried to catch his breath. The exertion of the run and the efforts to break down the door were catching up with him. A few minutes later, Hunter reappeared with one of the firemen in tow. He carried with him a hydraulic ram. Hunter directed him to the door and he applied the cylinder to the lock. The pneumatic system was deployed and seconds later the door burst open as the locking mechanism gave way. Caslin pushed open the door and ran in, Hunter only a step behind.

Inside, the lounge area was a scene of devastation. The coffee table was overturned, whatever had been on it was now scattered across the floor. Two chairs were upended and there was broken glass sprayed out in a radius of roughly a metre. Hunter looked at Caslin.

"Fight?"

He shrugged, "Possibly. Careful what you touch." He made his way over to the open window and looked out. The paramedics had arrived and were clearly trying to stabilise Grey while the appliance crew set up their cutting gear. It looked as if Grey was still alive. At least, for now. Caslin found his attention drawn to the exterior window ledge. It was crafted from stone and was original to the building, garnering the build-up of debris one might expect. There were eight distinct lines that he could make out, almost as if they were gouged out of the natural accumulation on the stone.

"What do you see?" Hunter asked, coming to join him. He pointed out the marks. "What do you make of that?"

"I heard a shout or a muffled scream, I'm not sure which just as I rounded the corner to see Grey falling."

"My god, that's awful. Do you think he may have jumped?" Hunter asked. Caslin pointed to the marks again.

"I don't know of many suicides where the victim shouts or screams before the fall and fewer still who cling onto the window ledge to preserve their life that bit longer. Do you?"

"No," Hunter said. "And you didn't see anyone?"

"No." Pressing his fingers against his eyes, Caslin cursed.

"Where do we go from here?" Hunter asked. Caslin shook his head. His phone beeped and he saw another text. Feeling thoroughly deflated, he opened it – *You must protect hm. Why aren't you acting?* Caslin shook his head and typed out a reply – *It's too late. They've already got to Grey.* The response came back immediately and it was angry – *They were always going to get to Grey. He was dead months ago, he just didn't know it. Why aren't you in London??? I told you they know where he will be…*

Caslin looked out of the window at the scene below. The frenetic activity had ceased. Grey was still impaled on the railings and it was clear that he had passed away. Caslin was crestfallen. Turning his thoughts back to the spate of texts, he called Terry Holt back at Fulford Road.

"Yes, sir. What can I do for you?"

"You tracked this mobile for me. You said it was in York and London but never left the city centre?"

"Right."

"Where does it report most frequently in London?"

"Wait one and I'll check," Holt said. Caslin cast Hunter a glance and she was curious as to where he was going with the inquiry. "The area the phone connects to the network towers is triangulated in central London, between the Embankment, Leicester Square and... Holborn. I'm sorry, sir, my knowledge of London's geography is sketchy. I don't know where that is."

"That's where you spend your time if you have a bit of money," Caslin offered. "Tourist central at the weekends but..."

"What are you thinking?" Hunter asked.

"Where does Raisa study?" Caslin asked.

"Kuznetsova?" Hunter clarified. Caslin nodded. "At the London School of Economics, I think. Why?"

"That's on the edge of Covent Garden."

"So?"

"If you were studying at the LSE, and you had a bit of money behind you, you might choose to live in Covent Garden which is slap bang in the middle of the area Terry just gave me. I would live there if it were me and I had Raisa's background."

"You think she's what... the source?"

"The other guy in the photograph, Cory Walsh," Caslin explained, "campaigns against financial fraud. He was a friend of Nestor Kuznetsov's and I believe he was feeding him information as was Marat Kadyrov and possibly, Finlay Michaelson. It may be what got them killed."

"And this Walsh... they're taking out his sources? He must have some powerful enemies."

"Trust me, you wouldn't believe me if I told you the half of it but yes, it's a distinct possibility. Terry," Caslin turned his attention back to his phone, "are you still there?"

"I'm still here."

"Is the handset active?"

"Erm... yes. It is," Holt confirmed. "Heading south along the Victoria Embankment."

"Terry, get me a helicopter."

"I beg your pardon?" Holt said with obvious surprise.

"Get onto the National Police Air Service and get me a chopper, now. And tell them to make sure it's fuelled. Don't take no for an answer. Then I want you to route me a call through to Niall Montgomerie. He's the commander of the MET's Counter Terrorism Unit."

"Leave it with me," Holt said and hung up. He didn't know what was going on but he knew better than to question him once a course of action was set.

Turning to Hunter, Caslin said, "Come on. They can pick us up from Dean's Park. That's the closest place they can safely land a helicopter."

"Where the hell are we going?" Hunter asked.

"We're off to London…" Caslin said before adding, "to see the queen." He said it with such a straight face, so Hunter would no idea whether he was serious or not but she fell into step, regardless.

CHAPTER TWENTY-SIX

CASLIN'S PHONE rang as the distinctive sound of rotor blades could be heard approaching from the west.

"Caslin," he said. It was Terry Holt.

"I have Commander Montgomerie for you, sir. I'll patch you through." The line beeped and Caslin knew they were connected.

"Commander, I don't have a lot of time so I'll need to keep this brief," he began.

"Go ahead, Inspector."

"I have a real and present threat against the life of Cory Walsh, obtained from a credible source," Caslin explained. "Walsh is due in Parliament today to deliver a deposition. I understand from my source that an attack is highly likely."

"That's one of the most protected complexes in the country. How will they manage that?"

"I don't have the details, sir, but my guess is that Walsh's campaign relies upon a degree of media coverage to keep it in the mainstream. He is unlikely to enter Parliament by way of the back door. This is one occasion where he will want to be high profile and visible," Caslin said, raising his voice to counter the incredible noise coming from the twin engines of the descending helicopter.

"Who is your source?" Montgomerie asked.

"I would prefer not to say at this stage, sir. I believe she is under duress and with what she knows I imagine the hit team are keeping her very close by. That's why my contact with her has been sporadic and limited. She is already in the area and if she is, then so are they. DC Holt can provide you with jackets on the suspects and DS Hunter and I are en route to London. Walsh is due to appear at lunchtime."

"Perhaps we should contact him and postpone his appearance?"

"I'll guarantee he won't go for that, sir," Caslin practically shouted as he made his way to the waiting helicopter, stooping to avoid the downdraft of the spinning blades. "Besides, if we postpone, so will they. At least on this occasion we'll have the drop on them."

"Call me when you land," Montgomerie stated. Caslin cancelled the call and made up the short distance remaining to the helicopter. The officer seated in the rear opened the door looking first to Hunter and then Caslin.

"No one's told us where we're going," he said, looking confused.

"Well, you and your co-pilot friend are staying here," Caslin stated, pointing to the front and indicating one of the pilots to disembark.

"You can't leave us here," the man said.

"Yes, I think you'll find I can... out," he said firmly. Hunter glanced at him.

"I've never been in a helicopter," she said with a half-smile.

"Don't worry," he said, offering her a hand as she climbed up into the rear, "it's just like taking a ride in your Giulietta."

Minutes later, the rotors were at maximum speed and they were lifting off. With only space for three passengers, the two crew members who remained behind watched with a degree of bemusement as their ride ascended into the sky without them.

"What's the flight time to London?" Caslin asked once he'd figured out the internal communication system.

"I'd say it's around two hundred miles and usually we would be looking at around ninety-minutes' flight time," the pilot advised. "Although with a favourable wind I can probably shave ten to fifteen off that. Are we heading for the London Helipad at Battersea?" Caslin shook his head, a movement unnoticed by the pilot, concentrating on gaining them elevation out of the city.

"No, I want you to set down on the roof of Scotland Yard," Caslin stated. In the rear, Hunter grinned but no one saw.

"I'll need clearance for that," the pilot said.

"You'll have it," Caslin said with confidence whilst secretly hoping he could deliver on the promise.

THE PILOT PROVED to be incredibly accurate with his estimation as they found themselves entering London airspace within an hour. In order to accommodate their approach without a scheduled flight plan, Air Traffic Control directed them to approach via the east and come into London along the path of the Thames at a height of five hundred feet. They were given clearance to descend once they had passed Blackfriars Bridge and then Waterloo Bridge, bringing them into visual sight of Scotland Yard.

"Are you feeling like you're coming home?" Hunter asked from the rear.

Caslin smiled, "Hardly. They moved from Broadway a couple of years ago and put it here. They brought the name with them but I've never set foot in this building."

"Shame," Hunter said. "Still, maybe you'll get to see some of your old friends." Caslin didn't respond. He hadn't considered that possibility and the thought filled him with anxiety. He buried it.

They touched down on the roof-top helipad and both Hunter and

Caslin clambered out. Caslin threw the pilot a brief wave in appreciation and they were stepped away from the chopper. Both of them felt unsteady on their feet and Caslin's hearing was affected by the changes in noise and pressure they'd been subjected to. They were met as they reached the steps down from the pad. A young officer, shielded his eyes from the dust disturbed from the rotating blades.

"I'm DS Collins. Commander Montgomerie has asked me to assist you, sir," Collins shouted in order to be heard above the roar of the engines.

"Get us to the House of Commons as quickly as you can," Caslin shouted, leaning in.

"That's a three-minute walk, sir. Once we're out of the building. This way," Collins said, guiding them along a walkway and towards the roof-top access door. Passing through, Caslin was momentarily thrown. A grinning face greeted him as the bearer came striding towards them. It took a moment for him to recognise her. She had grown her hair and altered the colour, at least he thought so but was often the last to notice such things.

"Nate Caslin," she said approaching and throwing her arms around him. He tensed but was warmed by the gesture. Hunter raised an eyebrow but said nothing as the woman ended the embrace. "Someone told me you were coming but I couldn't quite believe it."

"It's great to see you," Caslin said, his own face splitting a broad and genuine grin. "You're looking well. I'd like to catch up but it'll have to wait."

"I know. I'll catch you later," she said as the group moved on.

"What's the state of play with Walsh's protection?" Hunter asked, casting a curious glance in the direction of the woman as they went.

"Under orders from Commander Montgomerie we've not communicated with Mr Walsh. However, we've deployed spotters on the adjacent buildings and we have roaming plain-clothes teams outside. The pictures of the suspects provided by your DC Holt have been circulated to every member but as yet they haven't been seen. We are looking to intercept before they can make a move on the target."

"Excellent," Caslin said, glancing across at Hunter and reassured that SO15 were at the top of their game. They took the lift straight down to the lobby with no stops at any other floor. They left the building, stepping out onto the embankment and Caslin took an immediate right heading for the Houses of Parliament.

"Do you really think they'll try and carry out a hit outside such a high-profile location?" DS Collins asked, almost as if he thought it a near impossibility.

"Walsh rarely stays in the same place for any length of time. I think he spends his life travelling the globe and keeps his inner circle incredibly small. That way, his organisation is tight and trustworthy. They might not get a better shot at him than they will today."

Midday in central London, around the Houses of Parliament was never a quiet occasion. People were milling, grabbing an early lunch or dashing to the next meeting. Parliament was sitting following the Christmas break which brought out the journalists, commentators and lobbyists who routinely filled the Commons.

Caslin eyed the surrounding buildings on both sides of the Thames but he couldn't make out the spotters that Collins assured him were present. He felt his apprehension rising. There was something of a media scrum threatening to develop as print journalists jockeyed for position with television crews aiming to get the best shot. Cory Walsh was today's draw. Caslin felt he had played down his deposition appearance today.

DS Collins advised him Walsh was scheduled to present evidence to the Treasury Select Committee regarding the role played by money laundering in the UK banking system. His appearance was expected to be the lead story on all major news networks in the country with Walsh promising an explosive revelation. This scenario only managed to heighten the trepidation that Caslin fostered. In Walsh's own words, this was a high-stakes business and Caslin wanted to ensure that at least one man didn't forfeit his life in pursuit of a code of decency like so many others already had.

Caslin's phone rang and he answered it without looking at the screen such was the attention he was paying to the gathering crowd.

"Sir, it's Terry Holt. I thought you'd want to know the phone is active. Are you on site?"

"We're outside Parliament, Terry. Where is she?"

"I have her just crossing at Lambeth Bridge and taking a right through the Victoria—"

"Tower Gardens," Caslin finished for him. He drew the attention of DS Collins, "Tower Gardens. Heading this way."

Collins took up his radio and relayed the information to the undercover team as well as the spotters. Everyone responded they had no eyes on the target. They were close and Walsh was due at any moment. Caslin looked to his left, down Abingdon Street and Millbank beyond. To the right was Parliament Street with the Square in the foreground. From a close personal protection point of view this was a nightmare scenario despite the high level of police presence. There were any number of buildings where a sniper could operate without fear of discovery and the volume of people made spotting individuals a nightmare. They waited. Holt was still on the line and Caslin asked him, "Where are they now?"

"The signal's dropped. I don't know. When is Walsh due?"

"Any moment," Caslin confirmed hearing the tension in his own voice. He looked to Collins who shook his head. The crowd appeared to surge towards the road and Caslin figured the star of the show had arrived. Flash bulbs went off at an astonishing rate as Cory Walsh stepped out onto the pavement. His ever-present bodyguards were by his side and uniformed police officers sought to keep the crowd at bay but it was nigh on impossible. Caslin scanned the crowd.

"Talk to me, Terry," he asked, stress creeping into his tone.

"I don't know. It's probably down to the surrounding buildings disrupting the signal," Holt stated, staring at his screen.

Caslin searched the crowd before him for recognisable faces. And then there was one if not two.

"There!" he said, pointing them out to Hunter and before anyone else could react, he set off. Caslin was certain one of them was Grigory Vitsin and the other, one of Kuznetsov's security team.

They were within two metres of each other and closing in on Cory Walsh's entourage. Caslin tried to shout to Walsh's body-guards or the officers accompanying him to the entrance of Parliament but with the media barrage of shouted questions and calls for photographs there was little chance of him being heard. The targets were on the other side of the crowd and Caslin burst into the melee pushing and shoving without recourse to try and get to intercept Vitsin or to reach Walsh's side.

Protests were thrown in his direction but he ignored them as he unceremoniously battled his way through. All of a sudden, the crowd parted before him and Caslin saw the second target and hurled himself forward. His approach was noted at the last moment and he took a blow to the side of his head for good measure but Caslin pressed on taking as firm a hold as he could.

Using his momentum, he put the man off balance, placing his own leg behind the target's and flipping him backwards. They both ended up striking the pavement with Caslin atop his quarry. The advantage of surprise was quickly lost however and despite having the initial upper hand, Caslin found himself heaved side-ways and away. His opponent was younger, stronger and clearly more adept at street fighting. Caslin rolled and came to his feet just in time to block an incoming strike. He failed to block the second or the third and felt a swift kick to his stomach and he crumpled.

Looking up through the corner of his eye, he expected the knockout blow only to see a blur pass before him, swiftly followed by his opponent hitting the ground face first. The fog in his mind cleared and he saw Hunter standing before him, extend-able baton in hand.

Rising, Caslin had no time to convey his gratitude as Vitsin came into view, barely steps from Walsh. Caslin screamed and charged forward. Walsh's security reacted at the same time and advanced to intercept the Russian. The first took a glancing blow from a cosh as Vitsin wielded it from side to side. His expression, one of maniacal fury.

The second grasped Vitsin's wrist and they became locked together in a battle of wills as much as one of physical combat. Caslin raced forward and dived head first into Vitsin's midriff, knocking the wind out of him. The Russian staggered but managed to maintain his position until DS Collins arrived in the fray and between the three of them, they managed to overpower and wrestle him to the ground. Despite their superiority, Vitsin continued to fight like a man possessed of an inner strength that Caslin couldn't comprehend.

"You've failed, Grigory," Caslin barked as they disarmed him. "It's over."

A scream went up from behind and Caslin felt the crowd surge once again, only this time away from them. Vitsin was on the floor with both Walsh's security and DS Collins pinning him to the ground. Caslin knelt and turned to see Cory Walsh staring at him, a look of astonishment upon his face. He took a step forward, then staggered for two more before collapsing to the ground. Caslin looked around and then he saw her. Her hair was cropped short and recently dyed. She cut a figure in stark contrast to the one he remembered but it was undeniably her.

"Nyet, Raisa!" Vitsin shouted from his position on the floor before letting out a guttural, primal scream that carried despite the commotion encompassing them. Caslin saw the blade in her hand. It was four inches long and glistened with fresh blood. Cory Walsh's blood.

Hunter stepped forward striking Raisa's wrist with her baton and the blade dropped to the floor, as did the young woman with a corresponding yelp of pain. Hunter was on to her in a flash, pinning her down and securing her with handcuffs. Caslin scrambled over to where Walsh lay, immediately seeing the darkness spreading beneath his neatly pressed white shirt.

"Call for an ambulance!" Caslin shouted to no one in particular as he reached forward, tearing open the shirt and looking for the entry wound. He found it in the chest and he applied pressure with both hands to try and stem the flow of blood. There was only the one wound but the blood was reddish-brown.

Caslin knew that was serious. The darker the shade of blood, the more vital the organ was that had been punctured. He was in no doubt that Walsh's heart had ruptured. Caslin sought to comfort him as Walsh reached out, gripping his hand. Their eyes met and Walsh appeared to be pleading with him, fear etched into his face but no words were forthcoming. Caslin watched as the light faded from his eyes and within moments, Cory Walsh was dead.

Caslin tore his eyes away from the man lying before him, fighting back the tears. He looked to Hunter who stood a few feet away appearing somewhat shell-shocked. Raisa Kuznetsova hung her head refusing to meet anyone's gaze. Grigory Vitsin wept unashamedly. Caslin scanned the crowd, watching on intently in a stony silence. An eerie calm descended before The Palace of Westminster, the likes of which was unseen with the possible exception of Remembrance Sunday. Caslin's gaze fell on one figure in particular. He seemed to notice the scrutiny and turned to walk away. Caslin stood. His hands as well as his forearms were covered in Walsh's blood but he didn't care.

Stepping away, he saw Hunter looking at him, her mouth moving but he didn't register the words. Walking past her, Caslin followed the retreating figure towards the main entrance picking up his pace as the man glanced back over his shoulder and noted the interest. He in turn, increased his own speed passing through the security gate having revealed his identification to the officer on duty. Caslin approached but the uniformed constable held up his hand.

"I'm sorry, sir, but the Palace is in lockdown," he said. Caslin took out his warrant card and raised it whilst identifying himself.

"I'm DI Caslin from North Yorkshire Police."

"I'm sorry, sir, but you're not cleared," the officer stated.

"Then tell me who that was." Caslin indicated towards the man who had been allowed through only moments earlier. "You can do that, surely?"

"That was Lord Payne, sir." Caslin looked beyond the officer and stared towards the entrance as if willing the man back into view.

"Should I know him?"

"I wouldn't know, sir."

"He looks familiar but I can't place him," Caslin muttered, flicking a dismissive gesture towards the constable signifying it didn't matter and turning away. Hunter came to join him.

"Are you okay?" she asked. Caslin cast one furtive glance towards the building behind them and gave a casual shake of the head.

"Ah... forget it. It's probably nothing."

CHAPTER TWENTY-SEVEN

Entering the custody suite, Caslin and Hunter were guided towards the cells. DS Collins led the way. The booking-in area was rammed. There was hardly ever a quiet day for the MET. A whistle drew his attention and Caslin turned and to his surprise it was aimed at him. Hunter clearly recognised the woman they'd briefly encountered earlier as they came down from the helipad. Caslin warmly welcomed her approach.

"Isabel," he said in greeting. There was no embrace on this occasion. "You're looking great."

"I can't say the same for you," she replied, "but the black suits you… and it's flattering." Caslin glanced down at his shirt and laughed nervously. Someone had been kind enough to raid the stores and find him some clean clothes. He now wore the jet-black undershirt of the MET's standard issue uniform. Hunter exaggerated the clearing of her throat. Caslin glanced across.

"Oh, sorry. DS Hunter meet DI Isabel Covey."

"Sarah," Hunter added. "Pleased to meet you."

"Likewise," Covey said taking Hunter's offered hand.

"Isabel was my DI when I was based here," Caslin added, remembering their time fondly.

"DCI now, Nate," Covey added, with a wink.

Caslin inclined his head, "Congratulations. Thoroughly deserved, I expect."

"Yes, it was," she said smiling. "Listen, I have to go but check in with me before you shoot off, will you?"

"I promise," Caslin said.

"You promised three years ago, too," Covey said, moving away before looking over her shoulder and adding, "but you broke that one." Caslin waved with a mock grimace.

"Shall we?" DS Collins asked, inclining his head towards the cell block. "I don't know how much time we will have." Caslin agreed.

A uniformed constable came with them, holding a set of keys. He led them into the block and took the second left turn. The corridor was short with doors to eight cells, four on each wall, facing one another. Approaching the second one on Caslin's left, the constable slid in a key and unlocked it pulling the metal door wide. He stepped aside.

"Give him five minutes," DS Collins told the officer who nodded. Caslin entered but the others remained outside and the door was closed. Raisa Kuznetsova sat with her legs brought up before her, hugging her knees on the vinyl-coated mattress, the only source of comfort in the eight-by-four-foot room. Her head was pressed forward and she rocked gently to and fro. She didn't acknowledge his arrival.

"Raisa." Caslin sought her attention. After a few moments she took a deep breath, sniffed, drew her wrist across the base of her nose and raised her head. Her eyes were puffy, bloodshot and lined red. She had been crying. Her right hand and wrist were bandaged, no doubt down to the force of Hunter's strike with her baton.

"What do you want, Mr Caslin?" she asked softly, her voice almost cracking with emotion. She was clearly trying to process the enormity of what she had done this day. It wasn't going well.

"I just want to know why?" Raisa snorted a laugh in response but it wasn't genuine humour, then the tears fell once more.

"You couldn't possibly understand," she said dismissing him.

"Probably not," Caslin said. "He was a friend of your father's."

"Who got him killed," Raisa bit back.

"And your father walked a dangerous road. One largely of his own choosing. Cory Walsh didn't deserve for his life to end like that." Raisa looked up and met his eye, quietly replying with a slight shake of the head.

"No, he didn't."

"Then why?"

Raisa remained silent for a few moments. Caslin waited patiently. She stared at a nondescript place on the wall appearing thoughtful as she wiped the tear streaks from her face.

"Have you ever heard of *Maskirovka*?" she asked, her gaze returning to him.

"No," Caslin replied, shaking his head.

"My father explained it to me when I was a little girl," she said with a warm smile. "*Maskirovka*. The age-old Russian art of deception. It is ingrained in our culture or at least, within the military. They still teach it to the officers – have done for centuries."

"Go on," Caslin encouraged, moving closer and asking if he could sit. She nodded and he sat down alongside her.

"It is quite simple really," she explained, her expression taking on another faraway look. "*Deny, frustrate and obfuscate* was how my father used to put it. Apply those terms to any act of Russian foreign policy and you will see Maskirovka in action – Crimea, Ukraine... assassinations..." she said the last, rolling her head in Caslin's direction and meeting his eye with a fleeting look. "Just when you think you know what is going on... everything changes... and by the time you catch up it is usually too late." Caslin sat back, resting his shoulders and the back of his head against the tiled wall of the cell.

"What are you telling me, Raisa?"

"That it's too late for you, Inspector Caslin," she said with regret edging her tone. "You want to understand?"

"I do, yes."

"My mother still lives in Moscow," Raisa said, before adding almost inaudibly, "and I have a half-sister, Roxanna. She is only seven. So much confidence. Roxanna can light up a room just by entering it. She's adorable and I would do anything for her, Inspector. Anything." Caslin realised he'd been holding his breath and exhaled deeply.

"They could have come here, to the UK. There is always a way. We could have protected them," he said, thinking aloud.

"And tell me who is going to protect them from you?" Caslin found that to be an odd question and his expression conveyed the feeling. Raisa turned to face him, sitting cross-legged and raised her chin, taking in a deep breath. Caslin met her gaze. "Oh... Mr Caslin. I think you are a decent man but..." she said softly, reaching across and gently placing the palm of her hand on the back of his and pressing down ever-so-lightly, "you still don't understand these things and I'm not sure you ever will."

There was a double knock on the door. Caslin held their eye contact for a few seconds longer. He figured there was more that Raisa could say to enlighten him but at the same time, he had the sense that she would say nothing further.

"It is time," he said. Raisa turned away, dropping her feet to the floor and stood up. As did Caslin.

"What happens now?" she asked fearfully.

"Did they not say?"

"I don't think I took it all in."

"You've been charged with Cory's murder. You'll be taken from here to a magistrates' court where, no doubt, they will refer you to Crown Court for trial. In the meantime, the magistrate will give their permission for you to be held on remand in prison until the date of your trial is set."

Raisa smiled nervously, "Piece of cake, right?" Caslin nodded, reaching across and gripping her upper arm in a gesture of support. Despite what she had done, he still felt protective over her. The cell door opened and Caslin felt her physically beginning to shake as two officers stepped through to collect her. He was unsure whether this was a result of an adrenalin surge or the dawning realisation of the magnitude of her predicament. She was handcuffed and led from the cell, casting a last glance back at him over her shoulder. He stared forward, expressionless. DS Collins appeared once the three were out of the cell.

"Next one?" he asked. Caslin nodded.

GRIGORY VITSIN WAS SITTING on the floor at the far end of his cell. He glanced up as Caslin entered but said nothing. He cut the look of a broken man, far from the brash arrogance that Caslin had attributed to him in the past. The cell door was closed behind him and Caslin leant against the wall, his hands in his pockets. Neither man spoke for a full minute before Caslin broke the ice.

"All of this could have been avoided if you had just come to me rather than sending those cryptic texts."

Vitsin snorted a derisory response, "And you would have believed me?"

"I may have." Vitsin laughed.

"You…" he said, much more like the man Caslin expected to see, "would have trusted… me? I don't think so." Caslin often kept an open mind but on this occasion, the Russian had a valid point.

"Probably not," he said, with a shrug.

"Honesty," Vitsin said, nodding. "For that, I salute you."

"How long have you and Raisa been an item?" Caslin asked. Vitsin shot him a dark look. "It's pretty obvious. Remember I am a detective."

"For almost a year now," he replied, confirming Caslin's suspicions. That was why Holt's tracking of the mobile records showed it so frequently in both London and York. "How did you know?"

"I didn't. Not until this afternoon anyway. I presume her father didn't know?" Caslin asked. Vitsin shook his head in reply.

"I guessed not. That's why you always switched the phone off when you got back to York, so you never ran the risk of her calling you once you were back by Kuznetsov's side on his estate."

"He would have gone mad. His daughter taking up with scum like me," Vitsin said. "And he would have been right. She deserves better than me. What will happen to her: Raisa? She will be going to prison for a long time, yes?"

Caslin nodded, "Yes. A long time."

"How long?"

Caslin thought about it, "It's premeditated murder. If she pleads guilty, then she'll get a reduced sentence but we're still looking at life with a minimum term of eighteen to twenty years. If she has a decent legal team around her, they may be able to successfully argue some mitigating factors and bring that down a bit."

"That is a very long time," Vitsin said, looking up at Caslin with a forlorn expression.

"Yes, I'm afraid there's no way around it."

"And me?"

"The bodyguard you thumped has no interest in pressing charges but they're looking to have you deported for causing a public disturbance and affray," Caslin said flatly. "The decision hasn't been rubber-stamped yet but it's looking likely."

"It gets me out of the way, doesn't it," Vitsin said with a smile.

"You could be home by midnight."

"You know that deportation order may as well be my death warrant?" Vitsin said, his expression one of resignation. "I won't even make it out of the airport before they pick me up."

"You could help me to help you," Caslin suggested.

"How so?"

"You could tell me why you killed Nestor Kuznetsov?" Caslin asked casually. The question brought another laugh from the Russian, this one boomed out as he shook his head in disbelief. "There's no need to deny it. I know Kuznetsov was unable to set his own noose in the way it was secured. The pathologist believes it's nigh on a medical impossibility. Did he ask you... or beg you to help him?" Vitsin looked up and met Caslin's eye and at that point, he knew his theory was correct irrespective of whatever response was forthcoming.

"I underestimated you, Inspector," Vitsin said. "Back home many of the detectives are either incompetent or corrupt. Some are both... that, I assure you is a tragic combination."

"He wanted your help to die and you agreed."

"Yes. He was about to lose everything. His business, his money... property... along with his reputation."

"His reputation?" Caslin scoffed. "You say that as if he had a decent one!"

"He knew what he was," Vitsin argued, his eyes narrowing at Caslin's sneering response. "But he still had his dignity. They were about to strip him of even that. Nestor couldn't face the humiliation. He asked, pleaded... and then he begged me to help him."

"He could have gone out a different way. Gone solo with some pills and a bottle of vodka."

Vitsin chuckled, "You don't know him. Despite all his bluster and arrogance, he needed someone by his side that he could trust. He wanted it clean and yes, I helped him. I do not regret it."

"Go on the record," Caslin said. Vitsin shook his head. "If you go on the record you'll be arrested and face a manslaughter charge. At worst, you'll do seven to ten years and then you'll be out."

"And what then? I will still be deported."

Caslin had to concede the point, "Yes, in all likelihood."

"Then what is the point?"

"Things may have changed back home. It is a long time." Vitsin processed the idea. Caslin could see the thoughts churning through his mind.

"And what of Raisa? She will still be in prison."

"She will get out eventually."

"I will be an old man by then, Inspector whereas Raisa will

still have time for a proper life. Perhaps, even a family," he said with regret, "but it will not be with me."

"You could give her the choice. She may surprise you."

Vitsin smiled but it was without genuine humour, "And you think she will still love the man who confesses to killing her father? She blamed Walsh. It didn't matter what I said. Had I told her, she would have blamed me. I didn't want to lose her, Inspector."

There was a knock at the door and it opened outwards. DS Collins stepped forward clutching some paperwork.

"This has come through from the Home Office, sir," he said. "Mr Vitsin is set to be deported today."

Caslin turned to Vitsin, "You have the legal right to challenge the—"

"I won't be challenging anything," Vitsin said, interrupting him and standing up. "It is time for me to go home," he said, offering his hand. Caslin took it and they made eye contact in a show of mutual respect. Both men set out to achieve one goal that day… and both failed.

CHAPTER TWENTY-EIGHT

CASLIN LEFT the cell without another word acknowledging DS Collins with a brief nod as he passed. Hunter was waiting for him in the corridor.

"What do we do now?" she asked.

"Head home, I guess. There's nothing for us here."

"For a moment I thought you were home," Hunter said playfully. Caslin laughed.

"I don't suppose the helicopter is still on the roof is it?" Caslin asked. Hunter shook her head.

"I can arrange a lift over to King's Cross for you," a voice said from behind. They turned to see DCI Covey approaching. She stepped aside, allowing free passage for Vitsin to be escorted from the cell block. He walked with his head high and Caslin noted him silently mouth the words 'I love you' to Raisa as they crossed paths in the custody suite.

"Much appreciated," Hunter replied.

"You'll be in time to catch the last train," Covey said. "Unless you fancy a night in the city. It'd be like old times."

Caslin smiled, "Another time, I promise."

"There's that word again," Covey said, grinning.

"Are you looking for us?" Caslin asked.

"Commander Montgomerie asked that I convey his gratitude to the two of you. He was impressed with how you carried yourselves today."

"I'm not," Caslin grunted. "We had one goal and completely screwed it up. I don't suppose he mentioned anything about Walsh's deposition?"

"The dossier he was due to present was brought in, if that's what you mean?"

Caslin nodded, "And what is to be done with it?"

"It will be assessed and passed on to the relevant authorities."

"Assessed by who? Which authorities?"

Covey shrugged, "I don't know, sorry. Come on, let's get you guys squared away. We'll have time to grab a bite to eat if you fancy it?"

"Not for me," Caslin said, heading back towards the custody suite. "I've lost my appetite."

Covey passed Hunter a questioning look, "I guess some things never change. Any idea what's got into him this time?"

"None," Hunter replied, setting off after Caslin, "but I guess we're passing on the meal."

She caught up with Caslin as he was leaving the custody suite, the double doors nearly catching her in the face as he released them, such was his turn of pace.

"Nate!" she called, trying to get his attention. He slowed and looked back at her.

"Sorry, I didn't know you were there."

"What's gotten into you?" she asked. Caslin shook his head and set off again, purposefully striding along the corridor. "Where are you even going?" He stopped. She had a point. He had no idea where he was going.

"There's something wrong. I can feel it."

"You and your instincts again," Hunter said, smiling. Caslin didn't return her good nature. Taking out his mobile, he called Terry Holt back at Fulford Road.

"Terry, do you have any news for me?"

"Nothing major," he said. "Oh, hang on, I did have some joy with that photograph the old widow brought in… Miranda Richardson."

"Michaelson," Caslin corrected.

"Yeah, her. Anyway, I've identified the other guy in the photo. It came up on Google image, can you believe that? You'll never guess who it is, though. He's a member of the House of Lords."

"Payne," Caslin said firmly. Holt was surprised.

"Yeah! Lord Payne. How the hell did you know that?"

"Did you check him out?"

"Only the headlines of his bio. I mean, what with Walsh being killed today, I figured there wasn't a great rush to go into detail."

"What did you find out?" Caslin asked, guiding Hunter into an empty room off the corridor. She flicked on the lights and he switched the call onto loudspeaker as she closed the door. Holt's voice sounded disembodied and there was an echo on the line. They ignored it.

"Lord Payne of Whittingdale," Holt began. "Seventy-four years of age, he was made a life-peer in 1996 by the then Conservative Prime Minister. Attended Eton before going on to Oxbridge—"

"Anything more recent?"

"Erm… let me see," Holt said, clearly scanning through his notes. "Has had a successful business career on the boards of several multi-nationals and still sits on the board of one or two. He's currently Deputy-Chair on the Treasury Select Committee… should I go on? I mean, I pulled his associations from the Register of Lords' Interests."

"Michaelson wrote about the register. What businesses is he still actively involved in?" Caslin asked. Hunter's interest was piqued. She leaned in closer.

"TTF… where he's a non-executive director, they are tied to big pharma… YP Global Holdings… again non-exec…" Holt sucked air through his teeth as he scanned his notes. "Henderson Holdings Ltd."

"That one!" Caslin said. "What's the interest there?"

"He's the current chairman of the board," Holt stated. "Why?" Caslin hung up. Hunter stared at him. Caslin closed his eyes.

"What's going on?" Hunter asked him. "Who are Henderson Holdings?"

"They were involved in Project Obmen. Michaelson was querying export licences granted to them a couple of years ago."

"And Michaelson knew Payne," Hunter said.

"And Michaelson is very much dead having raised concerns about a conflict of interest."

"You don't think..." Hunter began but didn't finish the question. Caslin furiously rubbed at his temples with the palms of his hands releasing a controlled howl as realisation dawned.

"Cory Walsh said he was going to blow it wide open today. They were his exact words when he spoke to me earlier," Caslin said, locking eyes with her. "Lord Payne is the deputy-chair of the committee that Walsh was scheduled to come before."

"You do know what you're saying don't you?" Hunter said, lowering her voice as if fearful someone would overhear. Caslin didn't have an opportunity to respond as DCI Covey appeared at the doorway.

"There you are!" she said. "I'll give you that lift to the King's Cross now if you like?"

"I'd like to speak with Commander Montgomerie beforehand, if you could see to that?" Caslin asked. Covey shook her head.

"He anticipated you would. He told me he would be in meetings for the remainder of the day so he'd be unavailable. But, if you wanted to leave your details with his office, then he'll set up a telephone call later in the week." Caslin looked at Hunter. She was thinking the same as him.

"Later in the week?" Covey nodded. "Bastard. We'll see about that." Caslin brushed past her and stalked into the corridor beyond. "Which way is his office?"

"Is there a problem?" Covey asked, following.

"I want a word."

"You're wasting your time," Covey said, catching up to him. Caslin turned to face her.

"It's my time to waste."

"He won't see you," Covey hissed, lowering her voice.

Caslin shook his head. "What do you know about this?"

"About *what*?" Covey countered. "I know Montgomerie. I've worked for him for the last couple of years. If he sets a position then it takes an awful lot to shift him. He's like an oil tanker. Forget it, Nathaniel. You're not going to get anywhere with this and..."

"And what?"

Covey shook her head. It was a telling gesture.

"For your own sake... just let it go," she implored him. Caslin knew then without another word being said, Covey was looking out for him.

"I'll not need the lift. I'd prefer the walk," he said, meeting her eye. "It was good to see you, Isabel. Congratulations on the promotion but forgive me, I need some air."

"Nate... I'm sorry," Covey said as he departed. Hunter came alongside, appearing awkward. "Some people don't change. He's still bloody impossible." Hunter gently chewed her lower lip before tilting her head slightly to one side.

"You'll get no argument from me," she said, offering a weak smile before following her DI.

"Something I said?" Covey asked.

"Don't worry. I'll see you," Hunter said over her shoulder and took a right turn, roughly in the direction Caslin had gone and also where she remembered the main entrance to Scotland Yard would be found.

HUNTER WALKED out into the late afternoon sunshine. The wind was up bringing a much-needed change in the weather. The long shadows cast by the trees lining the road stretched across to the edge of the River Thames. Hunter walked for ten minutes along the Victoria Embankment before she found Caslin. He was seated on a bench adjacent to the stone wall, separating the path from the water below. She hesitated about approaching him. He appeared lost in thought, staring across the river in the direction of Westminster Bridge with the London Eye in the background.

Summoning some courage, Hunter walked up to him and sat down alongside but said nothing. After a few seconds, he glanced towards her and away again.

"Beautiful scene," she said. Caslin looked around, nodding his agreement.

"Yes, it is," he said. Hunter noted he was toying with the black leather wallet she knew contained his warrant card, turning it over and over in his hands.

"What are you thinking?"

He blew air out of his nose and smiled, "Whether it's all worth it." He added no further detail.

"Walsh's evidence will never see the light of day, will it?"

Caslin shook his head, "I very much doubt it. All this time we were looking to the east when the demon was in our own back yard."

"Payne?" Hunter asked. Caslin shrugged.

"Or someone else with a vested interest. We'll never know, will we? Walsh told me these shady characters have established networks spanning both countries and nationalities. Where there's money you'll find plenty willing to sacrifice their morality in exchange for a few quid."

"You think it stretches to the likes of Montgomerie?"

Caslin shrugged, "Kyle Broadfoot once suggested that when it came to the greater interest of the Crown any others may well become subordinate. Is the commander involved? Probably not but we all have our paymasters, don't we?"

"I don't doubt you. Do you think we've had two teams operating at the same time and working to keep the secrets? One international and another domestic?"

"That would be my guess," Caslin said with a sigh. "Independent of one another and answering to different masters but each with similar goals. Michaelson made waves, asked questions... made himself a threat."

"Farzaad Amin, Kadyrov, whichever – a domestic hit?"

"He made enemies in the one place he thought he was safe," Caslin concluded. "Is it beyond Russian intelligence to find a defector in the UK? Probably not – but when have the Russians ever cared enough about what we think to try and misdirect us?"

"The race angle, you mean?"

Caslin nodded, "Kadyrov was an inside job. I'm certain."

"How can you be so sure?"

"Too much theatre. They wanted to have us chasing the hard-right extremists. The Russians wouldn't bother their arse with all that."

"Their approach is subtler. They go for the extravagant only when they want to make a statement," Hunter said. Caslin agreed.

"You know, Raisa told me at length how her father described the Russian art of deception. She called it *Maskirovka*."

"Right."

"I think we have a few of our own quite skilled in that department. Far better skilled than you and me anyway," he said quietly. "No offence," he added, glancing over to her.

"None taken," Hunter said. Caslin fell silent, slipping back into himself. They sat in silence, staring across the Thames for a few minutes.

"Can I tell you something my father once told me?" Hunter asked.

"Sure. Go ahead."

"It's one of the fondest memories I have from my childhood. It might even be how I ended up joining the police force," Hunter said, remembering the day many years previously. "He told me about a famous quote, I can't remember it exactly, so forgive me for paraphrasing. He said that all it takes for evil to flourish is for a good man to do nothing. Have you heard that before?"

"Yes," Caslin said, smiling. "I think it was Edmund Burke who said it… or something very similar. What's your point?" he asked, looking at her. She met his eye and placed a reassuring hand on his forearm.

"Don't do nothing, Nathaniel. Please," she replied, glancing at the wallet in his hand. They locked eyes and Hunter held his gaze for a moment longer. She shuddered against the cold. The sun was deceptive and sitting still only made the cold penetrate that much deeper. She stood up. "I'm going to make my way over to Kings Cross. I'll get us the tickets and you can meet me there. I'll be grabbing a coffee and something to eat nearby. Okay?"

Caslin nodded, "Okay."

"Call me when you're ready," Hunter said, walking away.

Caslin was left alone. He watched as two small vessels passed by on the river, considering what Hunter had said. He glanced in the direction she had walked but she'd already disappeared from view. Opening his wallet, he eyed both his warrant card and the adjacent constabulary crest. Closing it, he stood up and crossed the pavement to the wall, turning his gaze to the water. Sunlight glinted off of the surface leaving a silver sheen flickering in the ebb and flow. Taking a deep breath, he reached into his pocket and withdrew his mobile. Scrolling down through the contacts, he found what he was looking for and dialled the number. The call was quickly answered.

"Nathaniel, this is unexpected. What can I do for you?"

"The vacancy we discussed. Is it still open?"

Kyle Broadfoot drew breath, "It can be. Do you want it?"

"One condition."

"And that is?"

"I get to choose my own team."

"That… might not be possible."

"I'm afraid it's non-negotiable," Caslin said firmly. There followed a period of silence as Broadfoot mulled it over.

"I'm sure we can work something out," he replied finally.

"Done," Caslin said and he hung up. Touching the top of the handset to his lips, he stared back across the water at a couple walking along the opposing riverbank. "I will do something," he told himself quietly.

FREE BOOK GIVEAWAY

Visit the author's website at **www.jmdalgliesh.com** and sign up to the VIP Club and be first to receive news and previews of forthcoming works.

Here you can download a FREE eBook novella exclusive to club members;

Life & Death - A Hidden Norfolk novella

Never miss a new release.

No spam, ever, guaranteed. You can unsubscribe at any time.

FEAR THE PAST - PREVIEW
DARK YORKSHIRE - BOOK 5

THE OTHERS LOOKED LIKE they were settling in for the night so he stood, turned and lifted his coat from the back of the chair. Slipping his right arm into the sleeve to howls of protest mixed with the laughter, spewing over from the anecdote being recounted. He shook his head.

"It's getting late and you guys aren't going anywhere."

"It's not late," came the joint protest from several around the table.

"I'm driving and I've had too much already," he countered.

"Aww... Jody, just get a cab. The evening's only just getting started."

"I've got a lot on tomorrow," Jody stated by way of an apology.

"That's the joy of being the boss. You get to make your own hours."

"And I still need to pay the bills," Jody replied, shaking his head whilst zipping up his jacket. Glancing through the window to the car park beyond, he tried to assess whether the rain had stopped or not. The darkness enveloped almost everything in view and what little he could see was masked by the steam from the warmth of the pub condensing on the panes. "I'll see you guys in the morning," he said, heading off. Glancing back at the small group, revelling in their impromptu gathering, he blew out his cheeks and muttered under his breath, "Those of you who make it in anyway."

The pub was popular, even midweek, and he had to pick his way through the bar avoiding elbows, chairs and stools as he went before reaching the side exit, leading to the car park. The toilets were adjacent to the route out and he hesitated. Did he need to go? No. He'd be home in less than ten minutes and he could hold it. Pushing open the door, it swung away from him easily. The wooden door had seen better days, a length of gaffer tape secured a large crack in the pane alongside chipped paint and multiple dents and scrapes - most likely down to the enthusiasm of the patrons coming and going over the years. The nights here could get pretty rowdy. He had to admit to being involved upon occasion.

Stepping outside, he was struck by the stark contrast to the interior and he shuddered against the cold. Descending the steps to the car park on unsteady feet, he walked towards where he'd parked the car. Calling a cab in order to get home would be sensible but he dismissed the thought. It wasn't far. Light rain was falling and he looked up, into the nearby streetlight in order to better judge the intensity. It was much the same as when he'd arrived two hours earlier. Had he known the plan, if indeed it was a plan, was to have a session at the pub he probably would've declined the offer. However, it was sold as a catch-up meeting. One they would often have and to be fair, usually in a pub. More often than not this one. It had been a while, and his absence was leading to friction, he could feel it even if nothing was being said. He couldn't afford to allow that to continue and feared it was already too late but, in any event, he'd made the effort.

Jody looked back over his shoulder in the direction of the pub as he approached his car. He could make out the team - his business partner along with their small entourage of administrators - still inside, their movements indicating the party was going in full swing. Turning back, he eyed his BMW and crossed towards it, fishing out the key fob. He smiled to himself but it was tinged with both elements of relief and regret. The relief came from the knowledge that he'd managed the evening without having to be too vocal. Expecting a grilling for not pulling his weight in recent weeks, he found the absence of business talk to be refreshing. The regret was born out of keeping secrets. Necessary secrets. After all, that was the nature of the beast but somehow, on this occasion at least, it felt disloyal. *Who was he to talk about loyalty?* A virtue that was by all accounts diminishing in importance within the world he moved in. Once, it was arguably the primary requirement but not anymore. The sense that someone had his back was a distant memory and paranoia, his closest friend.

Perhaps it had always been this way and he hankered for the nostalgic past that never existed. Certainly, his father always told him people lived in the memories of days gone by and, as a result, missed what was unfolding before their very eyes. Having never understood what that statement meant, it was easy to dismiss but now, many years too late, his father's words made perfect sense to him.

Shrugging off the melancholy that threatened to take root, he opened the door. Not wishing to get rainwater running onto the driver's seat, he took off his coat and threw it into the rear. A sound nearby made him look in the direction that he thought it came from. There were a couple of charity recycling points at the edge of the pub's boundary, large metal deposit bins for clothes by the look of them. Taking a couple of steps forward, he waited for his eyes to adjust to the surroundings. Illuminated only by the streetlights, the surrounding trees and bushes were shrouded in darkness and their gentle sway in the breeze was barely visible. Jody stood still, the hairs on his neck were raised as he stared into the gloom. What had he heard? The rain was forgotten, his hair was now soaked and the water was beginning to run down his face and yet still, he peered into the shadows.

"Is anyone there?" he called, narrowing his gaze. No reply.

Realising he had been holding his breath, he retreated towards his car. Noting the rain driving in through his open door and onto the leather interior, he cursed himself. Irritated at allowing his imagination to run riot, he reached the car and took hold of the frame of the door. With one last look back towards the trees he shook his head, smiling and feeling foolish. "Get a grip, man," he said under his breath.

Jody didn't hear the movement behind him, nor see the reflection of the amber streetlights glinting off of the metal hammer as it came down on the back of his skull. He fell, unconscious before striking the ground. Multiple blows followed with the only accompaniment being the sound of his assailant's exertions whilst wielding the weapon. There was no resistance.

Soon, all that could be heard was the sound of the intensifying rain, coming down in sheets and striking the tarmac all around him.

ALSO BY J M DALGLIESH

The Dark Yorkshire Series

Divided House

Blacklight

The Dogs in the Street

Blood Money

Fear the Past

The Sixth Precept

The Hidden Norfolk Series

One Lost Soul

Bury Your Past

Kill Our Sins

Tell No Tales

Hear No Evil

The Dead Call

Life and Death*

*FREE eBook - A Hidden Norfolk novella

Visit jmdalgliesh.com

Audiobooks

The entire Dark Yorkshire series is available in audio format, read by the award-winning Greg Patmore.

Dark Yorkshire

Divided House

Blacklight

The Dogs in the street

Blood Money

Fear the Past

The Sixth Precept

Audiobook Box Sets

Dark Yorkshire Books 1-3

Dark Yorkshire Books 4-6

Hidden Norfolk

One Lost Soul

CPSIA information can be obtained
at www.ICGtesting.com
Printed in the USA
BVHW041752080522
636476BV00012B/84